A Most Desirable Marriage

Hilary Boyd

W F HOWES LTD

This large print edition published in 2015 by
W F Howes Ltd
Unit 4, Rearsby Business Park, Gaddesby Lane,
Rearsby, Leicester LE7 4YH

1 3 5 7 9 10 8 6 4 2

First published in the United Kingdom in 2014
by Quercus Editions Ltd

A CIP catalogue record for this book is available
from the British Library

ISBN 978 1 47127 490 9

Typeset by Palimpsest Book Production Limited,
Falkirk, Stirlingshire

Printed and bound in Great Britain
by TJ International Ltd, Padstow, Cornwall

MIX
Paper from
responsible sources
FSC
www.fsc.org   FSC® C013056

To Joni, with love.

CHAPTER 1

11 June 2013

'Are you looking forward to tonight?'

Lawrence sat opposite her at the café table, his head bent as he tore off the end of his croissant and began to smear it with apricot jam. When he looked up he seemed to Jo to be miles away, the expression in his light blue eyes almost pained.

Then his face brightened and he smiled. 'You know me, I love a good party.'

'But this isn't *just* a party.' Whatever he said, he must be bothered about retirement, even if he wouldn't admit it. He'd been strangely distant for weeks now.

'It'll be a laugh, everyone pitying me on one level for being so decrepit, and envying the hell out of me on the other.'

'"With one bound he was free", you mean. But you're hardly "decrepit".' Despite being nearly sixty-three, Lawrence's hair – wavy and almost on his collar – was unfairly thick and a clean, bright white (no pepper and salt, no yellow). His tall figure was lean from the daily journeys across London to college on his bike and his clothes were universal GAP cottons, embellished by an antique silk scarf, a second-hand tweed jacket, a pair of Blundstone boots; everything was worn with an almost theatrical flair. Lawrence wasn't a show-off exactly. But he enjoyed being noticed.

'*You* don't think so because you're as decrepit as I am.' His expression was teasing. 'Face it, Jo, we're just a couple of old codgers now.'

Jo laughed. 'Ha! You be an old codger if you like, but don't bloody include me in your codgerdom.'

For a second his eyes met hers, but there was no answering laughter. What she saw was a flash resembling panic before he bent to his croissant again. She waited, but he didn't speak.

'This retirement thing has really got to you, hasn't it? Obviously it'll be strange at first . . . twenty-nine years at the same place is a long time,' she said into the strained silence. Although she remembered his first day with absolute clarity. They had been living in a tiny flat in Acton at the time. Cassie was three, Nicky a tiny baby and Jo still on maternity leave from the BBC. She'd made Lawrence a packed lunch in a Tupperware box: ham and mustard sandwiches, a bag of salt and vinegar crisps, an apple. He'd laughed, touched that she'd bothered. This job at a prominent London university was significant, a real step up from the college in Reading he'd been teaching at

2

for four years, with the added bonus of no commute and much better pay.

Lawrence grinned, gave a shrug. There was no trace of fright on his face now. She wondered if she'd imagined it.

'It will be great . . . not being tied to a schedule,' he said.

Jo reminded herself that even after thirty-seven years of marriage, her husband was still bafflingly unable to talk about what was going on in his head. He was such an intelligent, articulate man – something of a star lecturer at the university and hugely popular with his students – and on the surface very open and sociable. But as far as his emotions were concerned, he was a closed book, even to her. 'And we can get on with organizing the China trip.'

'Yes . . .'

'You do still want to go?' Jo had tried a number of times in previous weeks to pin her husband down to dates. Lawrence had been to the Great Wall of China twice before – he specialized in Chinese Studies – but they'd always wanted to go together. When Lawrence had suddenly announced the previous Christmas that he planned to retire and write books, they had both agreed it would be the ideal time to go. But since then he had persistently dragged his heels whenever the trip was mentioned. Jo kept seeing deals online and was desperate to grab them.

'You know I do. I just can't think about anything

3

until this party's over and I'm properly shot of the place.' His tone was almost sharp.

'Sorry . . . I didn't mean to nag.' She had thought it might provide a distraction to get him over leaving the college, a place that had been such a massive part of his life.

Lawrence sighed. 'You weren't . . . *I'm* sorry. I suppose I am a bit wound up about tonight.'

Lawrence's party – organized completely by his friends – was being held in the basement of a Vietnamese restaurant in Old Street, a favourite haunt of the university staff. Twenty-five people were crammed into the airless low-ceilinged room – baking on such a hot June night – tables set up on three sides of a square, with Lawrence in the middle of the top table. It looked more like a wedding than a retirement party to Jo.

'Good to see you, Joanna,' Martin Pryor, an overweight, shambling philosophy lecturer in his late sixties – nose hair sprouting like summer wheat and more famous for his drinking than his teaching – grabbed her hand. 'Come to reclaim your old man, eh?'

'You make him sound like a suitcase, Martin.' She tried not to cringe as he pressed his sweaty, bearded cheek to her own.

'Aren't we all no more than empty vessels on the carousel of life?' He waved his glass at her. 'Get you another?'

She nodded and drained what was left of her

4

red wine. Getting drunk seemed the way forward. Despite Lawrence's long tenure, she knew only a handful of his colleagues, the few that had been asked home for dinner or those she'd bumped into at parties over the years. She dreaded the long evening ahead. Jo was very much the outsider and, contrary to her expectation, there was never any riveting discussion about, for instance, philosophy or world politics at these get-togethers. Just college gossip and endless complaints about pea-brained students, bossy administrators and the utterly lamentable pay. She was sure she wouldn't be allowed to sit next to Lawrence.

'So how's the writing going?' As Jo had predicted, she was nowhere near her husband, but sandwiched between Shenagh – Lawrence's alarmingly glamorous head of department – and a morose research student called Nigel who gave only monosyllabic replies to Jo's attempts at conversation. The seat opposite was still empty.

'Fine . . . yes,' she answered Shenagh. In fact her latest book for the Young Adult market – as teenagers were called these days in publisher-speak – had sold barely two thousand copies, and her publisher was havering about commissioning another. They wanted vampires, wolves and the supernatural apparently, and Jo wrote about family breakdown. Her first five books, especially the third one, *Bumble and Me*, had attracted an enthusiastic following, but even these fans seemed to have deserted her now for fangs and blood.

5

'I'm afraid I haven't read any of them,' Shenagh was saying – somewhat smugly Jo thought. 'Do they follow the same characters?'

'No . . . different people each time. Although it'd probably have been more commercial to stick with a single family . . . follow them through.'

'I imagine readers get attached to fictional role models. Especially teens, no?'

Jo nodded, irritated that this woman seemed to be telling her how to write books. She was boiling, flushed in the face, sweat trickling down her spine. The blue dress she had on was only cotton jersey, but it felt like a strait-jacket in the heat – the wine probably hadn't helped. Shenagh, on the other hand, looked like the original ice-maiden, her fair hair falling shiny and straight to her shoulders, her pale skin, pale eyes, pale rose shift dress the antithesis of warmth. If I stare at her for long enough, perhaps I'll turn to stone; Jo suppressed a smile at the thought.

A latecomer suddenly clattered down the narrow basement stairs to whoops of welcome from his colleagues. Jo's heart lifted. The seat opposite must be his; she was saved. Arkadius Vasilevsky, Lawrence's Russian colleague and now friend – they had also become regular chess partners in recent months – had been to the house on a number of occasions since he joined the college three years ago. He was lively and funny and both Lawrence and Jo enjoyed his company. She watched as he slid round the back of the tables to hug her husband, then made his way to the empty seat, leaning over to kiss her before sitting down. In his forties, Arkadius was dark and very handsome in a chiselled, polished way. But his real attraction was a smile of the utmost charm, which lit up his blue eyes and perfect teeth, radiating a genuine and irresistible warmth.

'It's ridiculous. He is not old enough for this,' he pouted, waving his hand at Lawrence.

Shenagh, clearly as pleased as Jo that Arkadius had put an end to their dreary dialogue, nodded enthusiastically, 'He'll go on to greater things, I'm sure. Maybe a television slot about China. Such a star, we'll miss him terribly.' Her voice held an almost love-struck note, which Jo noticed with some irritation.

'The students are not happy, I read their tweets. They vote his course the best of all of us,' Arkadius said, generously.

'Are you looking forward to having him to yourself all day?'

Shenagh's question sounded patronizing to Jo, although she knew she tended to see insult where there probably was none when it came to her husband's colleague. Jo hadn't taken to her from the start, and it wasn't helped by Lawrence's endless praise for her and her brilliant running of the department since she became its head six months ago.

'I don't know,' she mumbled, genuinely not sure. It was enough of a shock to have just turned sixty herself, let alone have a husband who was retired. It seemed impossible that they had both got to this stage in their lives. She was suddenly aware of Arkadius staring at her, searching her face, really searching, as if he wanted to uncover something fundamental.

Embarrassed, not understanding why he was staring, she turned away.

'For better, for worse, just don't end up making his lunch,' Shenagh joked, and Jo heard the tinny echo as she joined in the laughter.

Arkadius's next words were interrupted by the sound of spoon tinkling on glass, and everyone became silent for the speech, a rambling but nonetheless witty tribute delivered by Martin Pryor, as the person who had known Lawrence the longest.

'God, it was suffocating in there . . . but you did it!'

They were slumped in the back of an Addison Lee taxi, on the way home to Shepherd's Bush.

Lawrence sat with his eyes closed. 'Mmm . . . just glad it's over.' He yawned.

'It went well, don't you think? They all talk about you as if you're a complete superstar.'

'Do they?'

'It must be good to know you did such a great job.'

Her husband just nodded, looking out of the window at the shuttered shop fronts of Clerkenwell.

'I was lucky, I had Arkadius. He helped dilute scary Shenagh. Nigel hardly said one word.'

'Never does.'

She turned sideways to look at him. It wasn't like Lawrence to be so quiet. Normally after a party they would gossip nineteen to the dozen.

'You OK?' she asked, reaching across to take his hand. Obviously he wasn't, but she knew he wouldn't articulate his distress, not least because he'd been so insistent about retiring early – a decision she'd questioned at the time and still didn't really understand.

He glanced over briefly, squeezing her hand hard. 'Yes, fine. Just really tired.'

The rest of the journey was spent in silence.

When they got home they both wandered through the sitting room to the kitchen, Lawrence running the tap to get some cool water, getting two glasses from the cupboard above the dishwasher. Jo pushed open the long glass door that ran the width of the kitchen and concertinaed against the wall at one end – they'd had it put in the previous year to give the room more light. She walked out on to the stone patio and breathed the close night air with relief. She had been dreading tonight, but it was over and now they could begin the next phase of their life together. Yes, she was nervous – she'd always been a very private person, and couldn't imagine how she would cope with her husband around all day. But part of her was excited. She and Lawrence had first and foremost always been friends, and they still had so much to say to each other, so much in common, so much they both wanted to achieve. Retirement – if you didn't call it that – could be a stimulating time of their life.

'Will you bring the chocolate?' she called through, and sat down in one of the battered wooden garden chairs, kicking off her black pumps and feeling the cool stone under her bare feet. Lawrence's tall figure wandered out, placing the water in Jo's hand and laying the chocolate bar – half-finished and wrapped in foil – on the rusty wrought-iron table next to her. Clutching his own drink, he stood at the edge of the stone terrace and looked off into the night.

Jo held the glass against her hot cheek. 'Say something.'

Her husband didn't move for a moment and didn't reply. Then he turned. His face was lit by the glow from the kitchen and she saw him blinking furiously, his hands wrapped tightly round his glass.

'Are you all right?'

He seemed frozen, a pillar, hardly breathing. 'That beef was very salty, wasn't it?'

'Was it? I stuck to the fish.'

'Sensible.' He turned away again.

'So how does it feel then? To be free?' Jo's tone was light, but looking at his rigid back she decided he must be in some sort of shock. The reality hitting him: that he was actually retired, was without a job for the first time in his adult life,

had said goodbye to his colleagues and friends . . .
'You'll miss everyone.'

He didn't reply and she decided to stop trying
to cajole him into telling her how he felt. It never
worked with Lawrence. The background hum of
London was the only sound in the garden as they
both fell silent. She broke off a square of chocolate
and bit into it. Still brittle from the fridge, it tasted
pleasantly sharp on her tongue – eighty-five per
cent cocoa the packet boasted.

Her husband walked past her and laid the
tumbler on the table. Crossing his arms tight
across his blue cotton shirt, he stared down at her.

'I need to tell you something.' His voice was
almost inaudible, but the tone was enough to send
a chill through her body. 'I don't even know how
to say this . . . but I've got to tell you.'

Jo waited, her heart pounding, her mouth dry.
She had no idea what the matter was, but she had
a sudden, urgent desire to stop him speaking, to
block her ears and refuse to listen to what he was
about to say. He seemed to be waiting for her
permission to go on, but she wouldn't look at him.

'I've fallen in love.'

She heard the words, but they seemed ludicrous,
beyond understanding.

'I've fallen in love,' he repeated, as if he knew
she hadn't taken it in, 'with someone at college.
That's why I took early retirement. I just couldn't
handle it any more . . . the deception.'

'Fallen in love?'

He frowned at her, as if she were being dim. She knew who it was, of course. Pretty, blonde, ice-maiden Shenagh, all youth and hero-worship. So bloody obvious. No wonder she was smug with her tonight. She waited for him to say her name.

'This isn't something I planned, Jo. I promise not. I don't know . . . I don't really understand it at all. But I feel so strongly, it's like an illness. I honestly don't know what else to do.' He looked as if he might cry, his face, bathed in the light, tortured. She was glad her own was in shadow.

'Who is it?' She prompted quietly, disbelief preventing her from taking anything he was saying seriously. Say it, she urged, silently. Get on with it: say the bloody woman's name.

'You won't understand, Jo. How could you? I don't either.' There was a long pause.

'Lawrence.' The word was like a pistol shot.

'OK . . . it's Arkadius.'

Joanna stood, cold and shaking, leaning for support against the high stool in her friend and next-door-neighbour Donna's garden hut. It was just after six the following morning. The hut was more of a studio than a shed, taking up the whole width of the garden and half its length – Donna made pots and was usually at work by five-thirty. She and Jo had been friends since they became neighbours, both working from home, both in need of multiple cups of coffee during the day. The stool was a familiar perch for Jo. She dropped her hand

12

to stroke Max, Donna's Border Terrier, who was looking up at her with his dark, pansy eyes as if he knew she was in trouble. His rough coat felt warm and reassuring.

Donna was small and pretty, her short dark hair chaotic and spiky around her face, her bright blue eyes – always alive with mischief – vivid against the soft white of her skin. She shook her head, rubbing her damp hands, dusty pale from the clay, on the butcher's apron swathed round her thin body.

'I can't get my head around it. Lawrence? Gay?'

'Not gay, he says. Bi.'

Donna shrugged. 'Splitting hairs. He's still having sex with a man.'

The words hit Joanna like a truck. She almost retched.

'Darling, sorry . . . sorry, that was a bit . . . look, sit down, I'll make some coffee.' Donna gently pushed her friend down on to the filthy, clay-spattered stool and wrapped her arms around her. Joanna was taller and broader than Donna, but the hug was strong and close. Jo resisted at first, her body stiff from shock, then she sighed deeply and rested into the embrace. It seemed like the first time she had breathed since the previous night.

Donna went to the back of the hut and unscrewed the aluminium espresso maker, knocking the old grounds into a plastic bag hanging from a hook, spooning fresh coffee from a battered tin into the metal basket, filling the bottom with water from a plastic bottle, then setting the coffee pot on the single-ring electric stove that sat on the wooden ledge beneath the window. Jo had seen her do this so many hundreds of times over the years, and the ritual was infinitely soothing.

Neither she nor Lawrence had slept.

'I never meant this to happen,' he had kept repeating, clearly distraught. 'But I'm in love . . . I love him.'

She found herself responding as if it were a friend telling her a story. 'How . . . how did it happen?'

'God . . . it was like a lightning bolt. You know, a proper *coup de foudre*. We've been friends for a while of course, as you know. But just friends, I promise. I was very fond of him, but I hadn't ever thought of him in that way . . .' He'd broken off, checked her face. But she must have looked reasonably sane, so he'd ploughed on, 'Then one evening we were having one of our chess games. We play quickly, it's challenging and a lot of fun. You know he's way better than me, but I'm catching up. Anyway . . . our eyes met, and I just . . . well, I just started shaking . . . like he'd cast a spell over me.'

'When?'

'When?' he asked, as if it were a bewildering question.

'When did your eyes meet, Lawrence?'

He told her it was a year ago, 'about'. He couldn't

14

remember exactly. And they hadn't had sex imme-diately, in fact not for a long time, he said, with an odd show of pride. But that seemed to be the only thing he couldn't remember. On and on he went, no longer even seeing her apparently, just chronicling every emotion, every look that had passed between him and Arkadius. Talking to himself. Maybe trying to explain it to himself. And she didn't have the energy to stop him. They had stayed outside for what seemed like an eternity to Jo – the sky was getting lighter and she was shaking with cold – but still he wouldn't stop. Finally she dragged her frozen body inside and wrapped herself in a woollen shawl that was lying over the back of the sofa, then huddled in a ball against the cushions, still no closer to understanding what he was talking about.

'It's best if I leave, I think,' he'd said, following her to the sitting room. She thought he was like a performer coming down from a show, all buzzy and loud.

'Leave?' she asked, dazed. 'You mean you're going to live with him?'

Lawrence shook his head, his expression surprised. 'Lord no. Arkadius wasn't even expecting me to tell you. It wouldn't work anyway, me living with him.'

'So where will you go?'

Her husband sat down on the chair opposite. 'Well, Martin's going to Greece for the summer . . . you know he's got a shack there where he

15

channels Socrates or something. He said I could borrow his flat till October.'

'So it's all planned.'

'Don't Jo . . . please. I didn't plan any of this. I still can't believe I'm even thinking it.'

'But you are.'

He nodded slowly, gave a long drawn-out sigh. 'Yes . . . yes, I suppose I am.'

'He seemed so detached. As if I meant nothing to him . . . almost as if I was someone else, as if he was telling a friend.' Joanna took the mug her friend offered, one Donna had made herself – a small, slab-built cup decorated with a delicate leaf pattern etched on a stone-white glaze. The coffee, as usual, was teeth-achingly bitter and hot, but this morning Jo didn't complain.

'Is he on something?' Donna sipped from her own mug.

Max gave a short bark and Donna opened the door of the hut and let him out into the garden.

'You mean drugs?' Jo snorted.

'Well you might think it's a dumb idea, but all this sounds totally daft, Jo. Just ridiculous. Maybe he's in the early stages of dementia and it's affecting his cognitive processes. I heard of someone once who—'

'Lawrence has never even smoked a cigarette.' She closed her eyes, opened them again. 'But you're right . . . he is on something. Love. Way more powerful than any actual substance.'

16

'Oh, darling. I'm so sorry. What are you going to do?'

'Do? I haven't the faintest idea. What can I do?'

Donna twisted her face, frowned. 'Fight for him? Tell him how stupid this is, how he's throwing his life away.' She paused. 'I don't know, but *something* . . .' She took her friend's hand. 'Because you know he's going to regret it, don't you?'

'Maybe not,' Jo said. 'Maybe this is what he's always wanted.'

There was absolute silence in the cluttered studio. Joanna loved it here. She loved the smell of the cool clay mingling with Italian coffee; the soft squeak of the wheel; the tins filled with upside-down brushes, knives, modelling tools; the slips and glazes and rows of finished ceramics with their vibrant colours; clay spatter on every surface. 'Maybe this is who he is.'

'Oh please!' Donna groaned. 'I know you're in shock, sweetheart, but you can't just roll over and accept this. You know who Lawrence is, for heaven's sake, you've been married to him for a million years. He's never shown any sign of fancying a man before last night . . . or anyone else for that matter. I've been flirting with him for decades and he's never responded.' She stopped and stared at Jo, her eyes wide with significance. It was a standing joke between them; Donna's light-hearted but nonetheless shameless flirtation with any and every member of the opposite sex.

'Not flirting with you doesn't make him gay. It

17

just means he has principles.' Jo realized she was defending him still. And in fact, contrary to what Donna said, her husband did have a propensity to flirt. But not in a way she found threatening. Jo had always taken it as his natural exuberance, his love of bonding with people – the very characteristic that made him such a successful teacher. 'Anyway, he's not likely to have told me, is he . . . if he did. Or if he had.'

Donna frowned. 'You think he's done this before? With other men?'

'No . . . well, no, I'm sure he hasn't. But then up until last night I was sure he loved me and we were walking hand in hand into a blissful retirement.' She stared blankly out of the window, where Max was sniffing something fascinating under one of the rose bushes along the fence. 'Is it possible, at the age of sixty-two, suddenly to start fancying men . . . out of the blue? And actually have sex with one, without having had the least inclination to do so before?'

'Doesn't sound very likely.'

'Exactly.'

'I mean we all know that lots of happily married men "cottage" on the way to or from work with guys in public loos. They probably think of themselves as essentially "straight" . . . and their wives never find out.' The look Donna gave her was apologetic, but Jo couldn't associate the men Donna was talking about with her husband.

Another silence was broken by the wail of a police siren on Shepherd's Bush Road.

'So you're saying you think he might have done it before?' Jo asked, in too much turmoil to make any sense of her own thoughts.

Her friend shrugged. 'I suppose it's possible. So how long . . . has the thing with Arkadius been going on?'

'He said he couldn't remember exactly. But further down the line he got carried away and mentioned August . . . nearly a year ago. A *year*, Donna! That's certainly when he started meeting him after work for their "chess games". But why should I believe a word he says?'

'What, you think it's longer?'

'I don't know.'

They sat, heads bowed, thoughts whirling.

'Is it worse that it's a man?'

'You mean would I rather he'd run off with Shenagh Miles, for instance? I thought that's who he was going to say it was, when he told me he was in love.'

Donna came and put her arm around her friend's shoulder again.

'And honestly?' Jo raised her red-rimmed eyes. 'The answer is Yes. *Yes*, I would a million times rather he'd run off with Shenagh. At least that would have been explainable, within the range of possibilities.'

'Maybe a different sort of hell. But hell whoever it is, poor darling.'

19

Donna put her coffee cup down on the window ledge, reached for the pot. 'I always liked Arkadius,' she mused.

'So did I,' Jo said, remembering the way his smile lit up his handsome face. The thought of his gross betrayal of friendship should have made her angry, but she didn't feel anything at all.

CHAPTER 2

13 June 2013

Nicky sat draped over the kitchen table, his head resting dramatically on his folded arms. Jo wanted to reach over and brush her hand over his dark-blond curls, but knew better than to pet her twenty-nine-year-old son. When he finally raised his blue eyes to her – his father's to a T – she saw how shock had blanked his expression.

'Did you know?' Nicky asked, rubbing his hands over his face as if to erase the conversation.

'About Arkadius? Not till two days ago.'

'No, I mean did you know he found men attractive?'

'No.'

'He never gave any hint?'

Jo shook her head. Lawrence had already gone when she got back from Donna's the previous morning. He'd taken just one bag of his things. She had wanted him to be there so badly, even after all he'd revealed. It hurt her that he had left without saying goodbye. She went searching the rooms like a lost child, the pain of his absence unbearable.

Please let me tell the children, a note on the kitchen table requested, along with the assurance that he was willing to talk about anything at any time and ending with love sent, 'as always'. Which had elicited the first flash of anger from her. As if anything could ever be 'as always' again.

But Nicky had dropped by unannounced, and Joanna wasn't able or willing to dissemble.

'Will you ring him?' she asked her son.

He looked at her blankly, shook his head. 'No. *No*, Mum. And if he calls I won't pick up. I mean what the fuck would I say to him? "Oh, hi, Dad. Mum tells me you've left her and shacked up with that nice Russian guy you brought round for barbecues. No probs."' He threw his hands in the air, bringing them down hard on the table. 'What does Cassie say?'

'I haven't spoken to her. Dad wanted to tell you both.'

'Yeah, he texted earlier . . . must have been why.' He gave her a puzzled frown. 'Aren't you angry?'

She didn't answer at once, because she didn't know. At least she was sure she must be, but mostly she just felt as if she was a passive bystander in her own drama.

'Not yet.'

'I don't understand,' Nicky seemed to be talking to himself. 'You and Dad have the perfect marriage. How can he leave . . . and after all this time? Was

22

something wrong between you? Were you arguing or something?'

'No. Nothing. Nothing that I was aware of anyway.' And however much she looked back over the past year, she couldn't find any turbulence at all in her marriage, only the recent tension that she'd mistaken for anxiety about retirement . . . and the regular chess evenings that Lawrence seemed very keen not to miss.

'God . . . listen, do you want me to stay for a bit?'

She shook her head firmly, touched that he had offered. 'I'll be OK.'

'Mum! Dad's run off with a man and you're *"OK"*? How can you be?'

She couldn't help laughing. It must have been a laugh touched with insanity, because Nicky didn't join in. But it did sound funny. Then a moment later the laughter turned to sobs. Horrified – Jo never cried in front of her children, or anyone else except Donna, who seemed to expect it of her – she quickly brushed the tears away and tried to take a steadying breath. But she was so weak, so utterly exhausted, that she found she couldn't control herself. Nicky seemed unfazed by her tears. He came round the table and pulled her to her feet, turning her until he could wrap her in his arms. He was tall like his father, and broad from all the working out he did – aspiring actors were required to have the body of a god these days – and she welcomed his strength.

'I'll make you my spag bol,' Nicky insisted. And although she had no appetite at all, the process of him cooking calmed her down. Her son was not an instinctive cook – unlike Cassie, who could throw together a sumptuous, last-minute meal from stuff she dug out of the fridge. He still followed a recipe to the letter, spending hours chopping the onion fine, precisely measuring ingredients, setting the timer, checking and stirring relentlessly.

There are things that can be relied upon, she thought, as she watched her son: Nicky cooking up spaghetti bolognese; Donna brewing her Italian coffee; constructing a sentence until it pinged like an un-cracked glass; pressing a bulb into the dark soft earth; digging my fingers into Max's coat. Actions that would last and be repeated in some form or another for ever. Emotions were another thing. Bought up on a seesaw of emotional in-stability, Jo had never trusted emotions, never really understood their mechanism.

On one side of the seesaw was her beautiful, unhinged, utterly fascinating mother – unreliable to a fault – who sprayed her emotions about like the sprinkler system on the lawn, until everyone was soaked. And on the other, her father, the exact opposite; a man who exhibited barely any feel-ings – not even love . . . especially not love – just a dogged sense of duty to his wife and daughter and the solid Gloucestershire community where they lived. She explored feelings relentlessly in her

24

writing, but it was as a blind person trying to describe a visual landscape.

Some part of her, she realized now, had been waiting for Lawrence to behave like this since the day they met. The weight of the years made little difference; the fear had always been there. She'd fallen in love with his confidence, his ability to talk to anyone, to take charge of things, to know how the world worked. But the flip side of this worldliness, in Jo's eyes, had always been that she might lose him to one of the many with whom he so regularly bonded.

'Dad'll come back. He's bound to,' Nicky was saying. 'He's just having a mortality drama.' He stopped stirring to peer at her. 'You know the thing. God-am-I-that-old-is-life-really-over sort of panic.'

'With a man?'

Nicky shrugged. 'Yeah . . . that's too weird.'

Jo sighed. 'I'd say.'

'We should call Cass. She's got to know what's happening.' Nicky put the wooden spoon down carefully on the draining board and dug in his jeans pocket.

Jo stood up. 'No, please darling. I can't cope with talking to her yet.'

'I'll tell her then.'

'Don't, not now. We can do it later, after supper.'

Cassie, she was sure, would be hysterical. Her passionate daughter would scream and shriek and demand answers. She'd rail against her father

25

and expect Jo to join in. Ever since she was a small child, the family had been in thrall to Cassie's moods. And just as her bad moods were dire, her good moods were a life-force that could light up the room, charm them all into forgiving her. She currently lived in Devon with her eco-obsessed husband, Matt, but Jo knew she would want to be on the first train to London as soon as she heard.

Nicky looked dubious. 'OK . . . but . . .'

'Dad promised he'd call her. Let him explain.'

Lawrence Meadows rang the bell – to his own house. It hurt Jo more than she could explain. She wondered why she'd agreed to his request to come round and 'talk things through'. But the truth was that she wanted desperately to see him, even if it hurt like rubbing salt into an open wound.

'Hello.' He waited like a guest for her to stand aside and let him in. He stood tall, with his customary elegance, but his face had the decency to look drawn and pale. They both walked through to the kitchen, Jo put the kettle on, brought out the tea. The glass door to the terrace was open; it was another hot June afternoon like the night of the party. But not like the night of the party.

'I don't know why you're here.'

'I didn't say goodbye properly . . . and I thought . . . well, that you deserve an explanation,' he said, hovering on the edge of the terrace.

She didn't reply. No one, not even her clever

husband, could explain love. And no way was she going to listen again to how his eyes had met Arkadius's over a row of pawns and he'd lost his mind. So she just completed her task: brewing the tea, pouring it into two mugs, putting them on the flower-pattern plastic tray, adding milk to his cup, honey to her own, placing two spoons alongside the mugs, carrying it outside. Her recent endorsement of mindless, repetitive action was working for her so far. They sat next to each other in the two wooden garden chairs, she handed him his tea.

'You must want to ask me stuff,' he suggested.

Jo didn't look at him. 'Not really.'

'Jo.' He laid his hand on her bare arm. 'Please. I can't make this any easier for you, but at least I can listen to how you're feeling . . . you must be angry, upset.'

Don't *you* dare tell me how I 'must' feel, she thought as she snatched her arm away, her stomach knotting with outrage at his calm, almost patronizing delivery.

'If you think I'm going to scream and sob and beg you to come home, you can think again.'

'I don't expect you to.'

'Well, what do you want to hear then? That I'm fine, that I understand? That it's perfectly normal sixty-two-year-old behaviour to leave your wife and family for a Russian history professor in his forties?'

'No . . .'

'So what is there to talk about? Seems like a *fait accompli* to me. You have somewhere to live, someone to love, an exciting new life.'

'Jo . . . please . . . it's not like that.'

'In what way is it "not like that" exactly?' She had been determined not to cry, and she didn't, but she almost frightened herself with her sangfroid.

'I told you the other night . . . I didn't plan this. I love you so much, you know I do. I'd never intentionally hurt you. But this thing with Arkadius has just sent me wild. I didn't know what else to do, except stay here and lie to you. Would you rather I'd done that?'

She shook her head. 'Don't make me responsible for what you do, Lawrence.'

'You know I didn't mean it like that.'

'The children think you've been at it all your life.'

Lawrence bowed his head for a moment. 'I know, and I understand why they do.' He turned to her, his light eyes pleading. 'But I swear on their lives I haven't. Not ever. Not with anyone, woman or man.'

For a second her mind skittered back to a moment decades ago. They had been having a cheap supper in a Thai café in Acton – Lawrence loved finding new places to eat. The tables were side by side in a row, and a very pretty girl had sat down next to Jo, opposite Lawrence. Jo had got more and more jealous as her husband's eye

28

constantly wandered in the girl's direction. She'd become sulky and refused to speak to him. But once outside, Lawrence had grabbed her, laughing, kissed her hard on the mouth as they stood in the dark on the pavement outside the café.

'Don't be like that. I'm sorry, I'm really sorry if you think I fancied her. She had a sort of fascinating face, that's all. You've seen those people . . .' And when she still refused to be mollified, the jealousy winding a tight knot in her guts, like a stabbing cramp, he had just gazed at her. 'I love you, Jo, you know I do. More than anyone else on the face of the earth.' As he spoke he had pushed her against the cold wall, kissing her urgently, clasping her face in his hands, his gaze intense with desire, until jealousy had been totally replaced by her own arousal.

Now, as she looked up at her husband, the memory laid a trail across his features, like a cruel mirage that seemed to compound his betrayal.

'They also think you're having a senior moment . . . that you'll come to your senses and be back.'

Lawrence didn't answer immediately, and Jo found herself counting the seconds, holding her breath as she waited for him to confirm that this was, indeed, a possibility.

'I . . . I feel too crazy to . . .'

'I don't think you'll be back. I'm just telling you what the children say.' She interrupted his stammering reply, unable to bear another reiteration of the truth.

29

Cassie had been on the phone for hours the previous night. Lawrence had told her before Nicky had the chance, so perhaps she'd vented her rage on him, because she was calm and very supportive with her mother. Jo, always loath to ask for help, had felt for the first time that Cassie was the adult, herself the damaged child. Cassie had offered to come to London, or as an alternative, suggested Jo stay with them in Devon for a while. But Jo had refused both options. She loved her children for their concern, but at the moment she needed to be alone. People wanted answers; they wanted to know what the plan was. But there was no plan.

Her husband got up, put his mug back on the tray. He had tears in his eyes. 'I'm so sorry, Jo.'

She felt her throat constricting and looked quickly away as he hovered, his shadow over her face as he blocked out the sun.

'I'll call you,' he muttered.

'Don't,' she replied.

'The children—'

'Cassie and Nicky are adults, Lawrence. They make their own decisions.'

He nodded and turned to go.

Joanna sat in front of her computer in her upstairs study, her sanctuary. The room was piled with books – her own and other people's – both on the shelves and off them, stacked on the floor, the filing cabinet, the windowsill, leaving space only

30

for her large beech computer desk and ergonomic chair. Looking over the garden, it was hot with the afternoon sun. Normally she would be working in there every day, but she hadn't been into her study or checked her emails since the night of the party; she'd been existing in a numb cocoon. Now she found nearly forty messages from her friends, colleagues, her agent, all relating to that other time, her normal life, before Lawrence's baffling announcement. How would she tell them? The Meadows had an enviable marriage, everyone knew that. Would they laugh now, enjoy the fall from grace? She was ashamed to think they might, but had she and Lawrence been a bit smug? Donna's twenty-odd years with Walter had ended in separation four years ago – the only argument between them by then being who should keep Max – as had many of her other friends' long relationships. But the Meadows had seemed immune to the threat of boredom and sexual in-fidelity, even surviving their children's departure from home without a glitch.

She decided she wouldn't answer any but the most pressing email. The news would filter out anyway, it always did. And until then she could pretend.

CHAPTER 3

30 July 2013

'I'm worried about you.' Donna had her concerned frown on, one she wore a lot these days with Jo.

'Yeah, so you keep saying. I'm just not sure what you expect me to do that would stop you worrying.'

Donna lay on the grass outside the hut, her head on an ancient patchwork cushion, steadying a glass of red wine with her right hand. Jo sat on a folded tartan rug, leaning against the wooden wall of the hut. It was late, after nine and still not quite dark, warm enough for them not to move inside.

Donna pulled herself up, crossed her legs in the navy crumpled-linen trousers, making Max – snuggled next to her – stir in his sleep and open one eye. 'Not sure either. But you seem so calm. As if Lawrence has just gone on an extended trip to China or somewhere, not actually left you . . . perhaps for ever.' Donna held up her hand as Jo was about to protest. 'I'm saying it how it is – or at least how it might be – darling, because you don't seem to get it. Sorry to sound cruel, but

32

you do understand that Lawrence . . . well he might not come back.'

Jo didn't answer, just rubbed her eyes, as if she was having trouble seeing clearly in the half light.

'You've got to face it one day. Otherwise you'll just stay in this limbo for God knows how long . . . waiting.'

'And this facing it? How exactly does that work? Sounds like you won't be satisfied until I've had a nervous breakdown and been carted off to the bin.'

'Don't get upset. Of course I don't want you to have a breakdown. It's just your life seems to be going along as usual. I can't see that anything's changed.'

Which was true. It was six weeks since he'd left, and the time had plodded past in a determined effort on Jo's part to Keep Occupied. She'd got into a rhythm each day: reading, gardening, walking and the gym, even making bread – which she hadn't done for years, though the loaf turned out leaden and sour – dropping in for coffee or wine with Donna. Her husband called every few days but she didn't answer the phone, and she hadn't told a single person about the separation. Lawrence had occasionally taught a Human Rights course at Columbia University's summer school. He would be away in New York for nearly three weeks in August. Now felt like then to her, Donna was right.

'You should get back on the horse,' her friend

was saying, 'before it's too late. It'll help you move past Lawrence.'

Jo stared at her in amazement. 'You mean . . . men?'

Donna giggled. 'Well, women if you like . . . on the principle that if you can't beat 'em, join 'em.'

'You are joking.'

'Of course I am . . . sort of.' Donna leaned forward earnestly, her hands cradling her wine glass. 'OK, I'm going to be blunt—'

'That'd be a first.'

'Yeah, yeah. But seriously, darling. I reckon you're still hanging in there on the shaggable index. Sure, you're sixty, but you don't look it: tall, slim, legs up to your armpits, those stunning grey eyes . . . you've even got muscles in your arms. Your hair could do with some attention, but I'd fancy you if I was that way inclined.'

Joanna brought her hand up to her hair, self-consciously aware that the thick, layered, light-brown – tinged with grey – mop her friend referred to was long overdue for a cut and colour.

'But the horrible truth is that you're on the cusp. Another few years and your choices'll be limited to the drooping willies, paunches and bad teeth of the ageing British male. Not a pretty sight.'

'Thanks. So encouraging.' Jo held out her glass for a refill. 'Anyway, aren't you forgetting something? You didn't go out at all, not for months after you and Walter split.'

'That was different. I was in love with someone

who wasn't in love with me. That bastard Julian broke my heart. Walter's departure had nothing to do with any of it.'

'And my heart's not broken?' Jo heard the tremor in her voice.

Donna didn't reply, just got up and came to sit next to Jo, wedging herself on to the rug and clasping Jo's hand tightly. 'I know it must be, darling. But I think I'm glad to hear you say it.'

Jo got off the two-coach train at Barnstaple and looked around for her daughter. The platform was normally deserted, but today there was a crowd of over-fifties back-packers milling around the small station. Cassie's tall figure hurried towards her, long, golden hair flying behind her in the wind as it had when she was a child. Jo was always taken aback by her beauty. Cassie had her father's aquiline nose, her mother's large, grey eyes and thick, dark eyelashes, a clear complexion now enhanced by a light summer tan, the whole put together in a robust, charismatic beauty that drew the eye of every man she passed, despite the plain T-shirt, jeans and sandals she wore.

Cassie squeezed her mother tight. 'So glad you came, Mum.'

'Me too,' Jo replied, although she had her usual reservations about the visit. It wasn't Cassie – she loved being with her daughter, and missed her terribly since she'd moved to Devon. Even earnest, humourless Matt (such an odd choice for her extrovert daughter) was bearable for short periods. The challenge was their eco-house.

Matt had built it himself entirely from recycled materials. It had taken him years of painstaking work – he lived in a prehistoric canvas army tent on site throughout – and it was still unfinished when he'd met Cassie. She'd helped him out, driven him on, mainly out of self-preservation, and it was now habitable – to Cassie and Matt at least. Sitting on the edge of Muddiford Wood, north of Barnstaple, no other house in sight, a stream running alongside the extensive vegetable patch, it looked like a large woodsman's cottage from a fairytale, except for the solar panels taking up most of the south side of the pitched roof. And although two ecomagazines had dubbed it 'idyllic', Jo preferred 'primitive'.

It was freezing in winter (despite the state-of-the-art Swedish wood-burning stove), boiling in summer, full of spiders, recycling bins and coir matting that skinned your feet if you were stupid enough to go barefoot. And if that weren't enough, it was also noisy with the endless clucking of the chickens and grunting of Moby, the pig, in the run outside. But she could just about put up with all that. It was the composting loo that proved the last straw. Not only did it stink in all seasons, attract flies in summer and wobble alarmingly when she sat on it, but she was constantly aware of sitting above the collected poo of weeks. That it was covered in a thin layer of sawdust and aerated by some mysterious method that Matt had unsuccessfully explained about fifty times, was no consolation.

Jo could tell that Cassie was nervous about seeing her for the first time since Lawrence's news.

'Do you and Dad talk?' her daughter asked in a low whisper, as soon as they were seated at the back of the Ilfracombe bus.

'Not for weeks. I asked him not to ring. Although he keeps leaving messages.'

'He's sent me loads. Texts *and* voicemail. But I haven't called him since he told me.'

'You should, darling.'

'Mum! Dad has left you – and us – so he can shag a bloke. Why should any of us speak to him again, *ever*?'

Jo wished everyone would stop pointing this out. Did they think the horrible fact had somehow escaped her?

Cassie's voice had risen, but the three other people on the bus didn't even twitch, they seemed to take no interest whatsoever. Perhaps it was standard practice in north Devon.

'Whatever he's done he's still your father. You don't want to lose touch.'

Cassie was silent for a moment. Jo knew how hurt she must be. She idolized Lawrence.

'That's what Matt keeps telling me, but I don't know how to talk to him . . . what to say. And the longer I leave it, the worse it gets.' Jo heard the stubborn note in her daughter's voice.

'Believe me, I understand, darling. But it's almost harder for you and Nicky than it is for me.'

Cassie shot her a bewildered glance. 'Uh, *no*, Mum. I don't think so. *Your* life has been turned upside down.' She sighed. 'I'm just embarrassed . . . for him as much as myself.'

'My life hasn't really changed.'

Now her daughter's look was astonished. 'How can you say that?'

She shrugged. 'Well it hasn't. The only difference is that your dad doesn't come home any more.'

'And that's not relevant?' Cassie grabbed Jo's bag. 'This is our stop.'

Joanna was up early the next morning. The day was cloudy and still. It wasn't the chickens or the thin futon that had kept her awake this time. Still dressed in pyjamas, she put on her daughter's wellington boots and wandered outside, taking long, deep breaths of the clean air, heavy with impending rain. She missed the country, but Lawrence had a horror of anywhere without people and a pavement and they'd rarely spent much time out of cities, except on a beach, which didn't seem to panic him in the same way as green rolling hills.

Jo went over to lean on the fence that supported Moby's pen. The pig was an Oxford Sandy and Black, a breed which even had its own pig society – set up, according to Matt, to get it recognized as a true rare breed. Moby was pretty, with his light sandy coat and black blotches, his lop ears almost covering his eyes. He snuffled over to Jo and stared up at her with his buried black eyes. 'They'll never eat you, will they?' she asked softly. But the pig was clearly unconcerned by her question and wandered off, riffling the mud with his snout as he went.

She looked round for Matt. She'd heard him get up and go out hours ago. Matt was always happier outside. After a short while in the house, he would just wander over to the hooks on the wall by the door and collect his anorak, pull on his battered striped beanie without a word, as if he'd been programmed. Cassie would ask 'Where are you going?' but his answer was always vague. Jo thought he'd probably gone for a ride now – bikes were his only hobby outside his eco-obsession – and she was glad she didn't have to face him yet.

There had been an argument the night before. Nothing serious, but they'd all had quite a lot to drink – Jo had brought a good supply of wine with her – and she knew she was doing it, pushing Matt's buttons. She found herself almost enjoying it. But it was Cassie, of course, who'd been upset and the guilt had stopped Jo sleeping. There was something about her situation at the moment – a sort of pity badge – that seemed to give her licence to behave badly. And with her son-in-law it was all too easy.

It had started with him retrieving the camomile

teabag Jo had dropped, after some thought, into the recycling bin labelled 'Paper and Card'. It was one of five, the others bearing the respective tags: Plastics; Glass; Aluminium Foil/Tins; Electronic (including things like printer cartridges, batteries). Matt had then pointedly placed it in the stainless steel compost bucket behind the sink.

'It's confusing. Can't you just have two bins? Biodegradable and non-biodegradable?' Jo asked.

Matt's look was careful, clearly controlled. 'It's not that simple. Have you seen the inside of a recycling plant?'

She confessed she hadn't. 'But honestly, does any of all this have an impact on Global Warming? Are you really saving the planet by putting the teabag in the compost and not in the bin?'

'I think we've had this conversation before, Joanna. I've told you why I do it,' Matt said, a trifle pompously. He was a small man, shorter by a couple of inches than Cassie, and wiry, lean, his dark hair floppy and long, his complexion permanently weathered. But his potential good looks – she reminded him of Neil Oliver, the Scottish historian – were marred, in Jo's opinion, by the almost fanatical light in his grey eyes, which seemed to bore into her, monitor her actions, find fault. He had been a banker in his previous life, a successful one by all accounts, and the single-minded, relentless pursuit of profits had now transferred itself to his current alarming eco-fervour.

'Look, I'm the first one to hate waste, I get why you want to recycle as much as possible; your dedication is commendable. But I don't see why you have to be so obsessed about it. Never buying anything, not having a TV, no car . . . not even a fridge.'

Fridges consumed more energy than any other household appliance according to Matt. So they kept milk and butter in a lidded bucket in the stream when the weather was hot, the rest in a larder built on the back of the house with cool, slate shelves. 'It just seems spartan . . . punishing. And it takes up so much time.' Jo could tell her daughter had become tense, but she pushed on. 'Or do you really enjoy it?'

Jo realized she'd been wanting to say all these things for the whole of the three years Cassie and Matt had been together. Until now she'd been careful, respectful of his lifestyle choices for Cassie's sake. And there were aspects of Matt she liked, not least his clear love for her daughter. But her son-in-law seemed to have got worse of late: more fanatical, more obsessive, as if he were trying to reduce their lives to something almost nineteenth century. And in the light of Lawrence's departure, she seemed to have lost the will to control herself.

Matt's face had gone solid. 'Of course we enjoy it, don't we, Cass? It's the perfect life. I mean, how lucky are we not to have to do a dreary, crowded commute and sit in front of a toxic computer screen for nine hours every day? Most people are jealous, Joanna. They say they wish they were brave enough to do the same.'

'It certainly takes bravery,' Jo commented. She turned to her daughter. 'But don't you sometimes wish you could buy a new pair of trainers, not wear shoes someone else's smelly foot's been sweating into? Or just open the fridge to take the milk out? Grind some fresh coffee? I mean how much energy does a grinder really use?'

Neither of them spoke, Cassie gave her husband a tightlipped smile which seemed to say 'Please humour her, she's in pain.'

'I am looking into the coffee thing,' Matt conceded. 'There might be a rationale for using a cafetière. It seems that because instant is brewed, then freeze-dried, then brewed again by us, it probably uses more energy than fresh.'

Jo threw her hands up in the air. 'Some sense at last.'

'But to grind it ourselves might not work,' Matt went on, ignoring her outburst. 'Coffee already ground is processed on an industrial scale. Not great, but probably better than hundreds of individual machines. It's hard to get accurate stats.'

'Oh, for Christ's sake, Matt. Is a ten-second burst once a day really going to bring the planet to its knees?'

Her son-in-law shook his head in patient exasperation.

'Maybe not. But if you apply that to everything . . . You have to understand, it's cumulative.'

'OK for you to say, you don't even drink coffee. But Cassie does.' Jo stubbornly persisted, although she knew she was being ungracious.

'Mum, please. Can you stop? This isn't your home. We don't tell you how to live.'

'I know, I know. But I look at you both, two highly intelligent people, and all you ever do these days is bang on about the energy consumption of a light bulb or a coffee grinder. Don't you get bored?'

Matt didn't reply. Although it was late and dark by now, he walked slowly over to the pegs, put on his anorak, dug his hat out of the pocket and opened the door. His back was rigid with umbrage.

'Thanks, Mum. Thanks for ruining a lovely evening.' Cassie got up and took her glass to the sink then turned to face her mother, her beautiful face bewildered. 'I know you're upset about Dad. But it's not fair to take it out on us.'

'This has nothing to do with Dad. I just think you're wasting your life.'

Cassie, normally so feisty and argumentative, had merely raised her eyebrows and started to wash her glass.

Now it had begun to drizzle. Jo shivered, drew her cardigan closer round her body. She realized she didn't feel very well, sort of headachy, her throat scratchy when she swallowed. She had another two nights with her daughter and she didn't know how she would get through them. She should never have come. Obviously she would apologize to them both this morning, but she despaired of finding a neutral subject they could all talk about. Topics fell between the devil and the deep blue sea: the destruction of the planet or Lawrence. She walked back towards the house, anxious to get warm and fend off what she thought might be an impending cold.

She and Cassie took the bikes to the local Pick-Your-Own farm after breakfast, to get some sweet corn, green beans and strawberries for supper. The rain had stopped, but it was muggy and Jo was sweating by the time they got there.

'Need to do more exercise, Mum,' Cassie teased, her own face bright and glowing with youthful vigour. 'It's only two miles.'

'I do lots I'll have you know. I do a Pilates class, walk, garden . . .' She got off the bike and felt her legs threaten to buckle beneath her. Clinging to the handlebars, she waited for it to pass.

'Mum? What's the matter?'

'It's OK . . . just felt a bit wobbly. Not used to the biking I suppose.'

'Do you want to sit down or something?'

'No, I'm fine.'

They walked the rows of strawberries, each with a cardboard trug that Cassie had carried suspended from the handlebars of her bike, bending to catch the best of the crop. Her daughter was eating as many as she put in the box.

'You always did that as a child, when we went to stay with Etty.' Jo's mother had refused to be called Granny or anything similar, so Cassie, and subsequently Nicky, just picked up and adapted her real name, Betty.

'I remember. But they were her strawberries, weren't they? We didn't go to a Pick-Your-Own.'

For a moment they stopped picking. 'That over-grown fruit cage was a nightmare. You always came out scratched from head to toe.'

Cassie laughed. 'And Etty took no notice.'

'Nothing new there, then.' Staying with her mother was always an ordeal for Jo. But oddly, since Betty had been such a useless mother, she'd taken great pains to be attentive to Cassie and Nicky. Unreliably, of course – she couldn't be left alone with them – but full of wild ideas which the children adored, such as playing what Betty called *cache cache dix* – a game that involved hauling furniture from the house into a circle on the lawn, draping it with towels, then getting the children to run around, hiding behind a table or a chair, without being seen by the person standing in the middle. Or teaching them, aged five and three, how to pluck a pheasant. Or taking armfuls of clothes out of the wardrobe and dressing up along with the children.

'She was fun,' Cassie said. Betty had died from

a stroke following a fall when Cassie was fifteen. 'Do you still miss her?'

'Not really.' But in truth Jo did miss the fact of her mother. And without the constant reminder of her inconsistencies, the edges of Jo's historical anger at the appalling way she'd behaved when she was growing up had faded somewhat.

'She probably wouldn't have turned a hair if you'd told her about Dad.'

Jo gave a short laugh. 'No . . . I expect not. I wonder if he's let Granny know.'

'Hope not. She'd die of embarrassment.'

Lawrence's mother was the exact opposite of her own. Conservative and particular, she and his father – two teachers – had led a constrained life in a suffocating close in a small Suffolk town, fretting constantly about their hedge, the neighbours putting rubbish out on the wrong day or playing loud music or building extensions or parking in someone else's space or letting their children shout or their dogs bark . . . or just breathing. Lawrence and his elder brother, Rick, had catapulted themselves out of there on the day they each turned eighteen and had barely gone back since. His father was now dead, his mother in a home in Ipswich, about which she never stopped complaining, mostly racist comments about the long-suffering nurses.

'I don't suppose I have to visit her now,' Jo said, experiencing an odd moment of relief.

*   *   *

46

By lunchtime, Jo knew she would have to lie down. She felt exhausted, light-headed.

'I think I'm fighting something off. A good snooze will sort me out.'

But she didn't wake till after five, and she was shivering, feverish, her body heavy and lethargic so that she wasn't sure she could stand upright.

'I'm going to call the doctor,' Cassie said, hovering anxiously over her mother.

'No! Please . . . it's just a bug. I'll be fine. I don't want a fuss. Anyway, there's nothing they can do.'

That was the last thing she remembered clearly. It was as if she'd retreated behind a barrier to the outside world. She could still hear what people were saying, see the worried faces that loomed close then receded, but she felt no ability, or indeed any obligation, to respond. There was something inordinately restful in this absence.

When she finally woke, all she could remember was a dream about Lawrence. The dream was based in a real event – Cassie's tenth birthday party when they'd taken three of her friends to a go-kart track in Kent for the day. Lawrence had been on fire to have a turn himself. In the end he'd sneaked off to the adult track where the girls and Jo eventually found him. They'd cheered him on: he was impressive – fearless and exuberant, and had been on a high all the way home in the car. But in the dream version Jo was alone – no Cassie or friends – and was terrified as she watched Lawrence ride the kart. He was going faster and faster, seemingly out of control, no regulation helmet on, and didn't hear her when she screamed her heart out for him to stop. She knew beyond a shadow of a doubt that he was about to die and that she was powerless to prevent it. The dream-fear haunted her as she woke, her heart fluttering anxiously in her chest, although she pushed the images away, not caring to examine the significance.

'God, Mum . . . you really scared us,' was the first sentence Jo properly understood, her daughter's words pulling her back to the normal world. 'It's nearly two days. Are you feeling better?'

Cassie perched beside her on the bed, holding her hand. Her face was pale and pinched with worry. Jo struggled to speak, clutching her daughter.

'I'm so sorry, darling.'

'Don't be sorry. You were ill. The doctor said you probably had a virus and just to keep an eye on you. But you seemed so far gone, Matt was on the verge of calling an ambulance last night.'

Jo attempted sitting up, but her body seemed to have lost substance, her limbs floppy and recalcitrant when she tried to instruct them. Eventually, with Cassie's help, she heaved herself into a sitting position, her head against the wall. Cassie grabbed another pillow from the chair and propped it behind her.

'Would you like some tea?'

Jo nodded. While Cassie was making it, Jo tried to make sense of what had happened, but her thoughts blurred. All she was aware of was a powerful desire to slide back into that other world where nothing touched her, nothing was expected of her.

The mug of chamomile tea was warm and present between her palms. She took a sip and the liquid seemed to blaze a path through her lethargy, bringing her cells to life.

'I've never experienced anything like that before,' she murmured.

'Mum . . . the doctor thought . . . she said it might be a virus, but it also might be the result of . . . well, a sort of delayed shock—'

'Shock?'

'I told her about Dad.'

Jo just stared at her daughter. The first she was aware of the tears was Cassie moving to embrace her, holding her close. Jo usually found crying hard, the tears squeezed reluctantly from her with effort, her face contorted. But now they flowed copiously and without help, reaching inwards in their stream to touch the hard, dry stone of grief she had shut away and barely acknowledged since the night Lawrence left.

'Oh, Mum,' Cassie muttered into her hair. 'You mustn't keep things bottled up. You always say Dad is bad at expressing himself, but you're just as crap.'

Jo pulled away, wiping away the tears as best she could. 'I didn't know what else to do. I mean what are the rules for dealing with these things?'

Cassie shook her head. 'None, I suppose. I'm not criticizing you. It's just, I think it's better to talk about it than not.'

'But then you only burden everyone else, and they don't know what to say.'

'It's not what *they* say, it's what you say . . . just getting it out in the open is the trick.'

Jo wasn't so sure, but she didn't have the will to debate the point.

It was another five days before Joanna sensed some vitality beginning to return. In the interim she felt like an old lady for the first time: weak and fractious, alarmed by her inability to take charge of her life.

'I don't know how to thank you both,' she told Cassie and her son-in-law the night before she was due to go home. They had all found a sort of peace together since she'd been ill, tacitly avoiding contentious issues, instead talking about books, politics, health, anything that wasn't too close to someone's heart. 'What a nightmare. Your mother comes for a three-day visit and stays ten, raving and incapacitated. You'll never ask me again.'

Matt chuckled. 'Just glad it wasn't permanent . . .' then obviously realizing his remark could be taken the wrong way, he quickly added, 'You being ill, I mean . . . not the staying here bit.'

'Well, either would have been grim,' Jo conceded with a smile.

'Are you sure you're OK to go home?' Cassie

asked. 'You can stay as long as you like, you know that.'

'Thanks, but I'm quite sure. I don't feel a hundred per cent, but that'll take a while I think. I need to get home, get on with my life.'

CHAPTER 4

14 August 2013

'OK, I've got this gorgeous man who's dying to meet you.' Donna's grin was deliberately bright and fixed, no doubt fully aware of the reception she'd receive.

'Very funny.'

They were walking along Shepherd's Bush Road towards the green, heading for Waitrose in Westfield. It was an indulgence, Tesco was much closer and cheaper, but Donna was bored with it and wanted something different. Max trotted along on his lead between them.

'No, seriously, darling. He's Swedish and in publishing . . . totally unattached. You'll love him.'

'And when exactly did you meet a Swedish publisher?'

Donna chuckled. 'Oh, you know. Out and about.'

Jo had lost track of her friend's social life since Walter had been given his marching orders. But Donna was eclectic; she seemed to know everybody from ambassadors to sculptors to property developers to film directors and journalists, having a particular penchant for older, successful males. She was discreet about her dalliances with these (frequently married) men, even with Jo, who had voted early on not to be too involved in the detail, knowing the liaisons were always fleeting and that at the first whiff of commitment, Donna would be running hard in the opposite direction.

'Just a drink, perhaps dinner. He's such a sweetie. It'd do you good to hang out with a man again. He's not after sex.'

'You asked him, did you?'

'Well . . . not exactly. And of course, never say never. But I meant he's a gentleman. He wouldn't leap on you if you didn't want it.'

Joanna sighed. 'I can't.' She hadn't been out since getting back from Cassie's. She cried a lot – seemed like the more she practised the more proficient she became – but it felt soothing, not despairing and she didn't hold back. And the outside world seemed to be a threatening place. She had no idea how she fitted in now she was on her own.

Lawrence had been to the house while she was away, and taken more of his things. His wardrobe was almost bare now, only a very old pair of trainers on the floor, a jacket he never liked and a couple of summer shirts swinging on the empty rail. One, a baggy, viciously bright aquamarine cotton, they had bought when Lawrence's case failed to materialize on what was supposed to be a romantic weekend in Barcelona. Jo remembered how excited she'd been to get away alone with Lawrence, the children left with his parents in Suffolk. But losing the case had cast a bit of a pall over their time together, Lawrence – cheapskate that he was – loath to spend money on a decent shirt he didn't need, but also hating people thinking he wore cheap ones from Carrefour. In the end, though, the shirt had made her laugh so much that his good mood had been restored.

Not knowing that he'd been back, the sight of the empty wardrobe had made Jo gasp. It felt like burglary, as if she'd been robbed. Which I have, she'd thought, gazing at the space where her husband's clothes had hung for more than thirty years – the scent of him, so comforting and familiar, gone too. She had wanted to ring him right then, the phone poised in her hand. Wanted to scream at him until her throat closed up. But she hadn't.

Donna stopped in the middle of the street and turned to face her.

'Look, darling, I'm not asking you to fall in love or even bonk the man. I'll be there too, so it won't seem like a date. I just think it'd be fun for you both, get you out of that house for a change. Go on, give it a try. He's only over here till Monday, so if it's a total disaster you never have to see him again.' She was peering up into Jo's face, her light eyes full of amused entreaty.

'Why is he on his own?' Jo asked, giving herself time to think about her friend's request.

'Divorced. Everyone in Sweden is divorced . . . well, slight exaggeration, but over fifty per cent according to Brian.'

'Brian? Who's Brian?'

'This Swedish guy I'm telling you about? Do keep up.'

'He can't be called *Brian*.'

'It's a perfectly normal Swedish name. They're not all called Lars or Sven you know.' Donna's tone was huffy in the face of Jo's mockery, and to appease her friend she bit the bullet and agreed to go. She could always change her mind.

'But only if you promise to come too,' Jo added.

Donna beamed. 'Good girl. We'll have a laugh, a few drinks, it'll be fun.'

'Tell me you don't fancy him yourself.'

'God no!'

'Why not? Is he awful?'

'No, he's gorgeous . . . just not my type.'

As they wandered round the supermarket, Jo tried to imagine being with another man, lying beside him, smelling him, touching his skin, kissing his mouth. It was impossible. She'd met Lawrence when she was twenty-one, in her last term at college. He was working a summer job at the graduate recruitment fair they had at her campus, a large blue-and-white banner tied across his body advertising the sponsors. She'd made a joke about sandwich men – of which there were many in the seventies, wandering up and down streets clamped between wooden boards displaying anything from marketing messages to dotty religious tracts – and they'd struck up a conversation. Before Lawrence there had been two fellow-students, just awkward drunk sex which Jo had taken more as a necessary rite of passage than something significant. Lawrence, as far as she was concerned, was her first. And, indeed, her last. But sex with him had been great from the start, fun and inventive. An image – one she fought off on a minute-by-minute basis these days – of her husband in a naked embrace with Arkadius, flashed behind her eyes.

'Is it just sex?' she asked Donna, when they were seated in an open café area upstairs in the stuffy shopping centre, two tall glass mugs of coffee in front of them on the table.

Donna looked at her blankly.

'With Lawrence. Is that what's driving him?'

'You said he claimed to be in love.'

'But what does that mean? Is he in love with Arkadius in the same way he was with me?'

'I suppose. There's only one way isn't there . . . where you feel sick and mad and delightful and can't bear to be away from each other for a second.' Her friend's face took on a wistful air.

Jo winced. 'So he looks at Arkadius and feels exactly what he felt for me?' she repeated.

'The details will be a tad different, obviously. But basically, yes.'

'I just can't imagine it.'

'You'd be able to if Arkadius was a woman though, wouldn't you? You'd just hate the bitch!'

'Hate them both.' Jo dragged some foam from the edges of her cup and stirred it into her coffee. 'Why don't I hate Arkadius?'

'Because you don't really believe it,' her friend replied gently. 'Have you spoken to Lawrence recently?'

'He leaves messages sometimes. "Are you all right?" "Just checking to see how you are", that sort of thing. But I don't see any point in telling him I'm not. He's hardly going to do anything about it, is he?'

'Probably not.'

'I just wish I could get the image of them in bed together out of my mind. How can I do that?'

'Not easy. When Julian ran off with the trollop, that's all I could see: them naked and all over each other. Torture. Only way is to get on with your own life.'

Jo sighed. 'Swedish Brian you mean.'

'Not necessarily Brian. Or any man. Just doing stuff that totally involves you.'

For a moment there was silence between them.

'How's the writing going?'

'Nowhere. Frances at Century says I've got to come up with something really strong if I want another commission from them. The whole family saga thing just isn't grabbing the YA market.'

'Great sense of loyalty these people have. You've been with them for what, ten years? And then they just dump you.'

'It's not about loyalty, it's about cash. And she

57

hasn't dumped me yet. But I can't write about vampires, they don't mean anything to me.'

'So write about something that does . . . like bisexuality. That's strong, and spot on for hormonal teenagers who don't know which way is up.'

Jo considered this. 'Hmm . . . not such a bad idea.' Then she threw her hands in the air. 'But that's the point. I don't understand it either!'

'Well, research it. Find out. You must admit it's a great idea.' Donna looked pleased with herself.

'Yeah . . . OK. I might look into it. I've got to do something to earn money, now that . . .' she tailed off, suddenly bored by her one-track mind always coming back to bloody Lawrence Meadows.

'You didn't tell me he was a *child*,' Jo hissed, when Swedish Brian left the table for the men's room.

They were in a Vietnamese restaurant off Holland Park, white table cloths, bamboo screens, flickering tea lights. Donna scrubbed up well, a far cry from her clay-splattered, apron-wrapped pottery persona. She had on a crimson embroidered silk jacket and black trousers, her short dark hair sculpted and shiny – unlike its usual spiky mess. Jo felt positively dowdy in her plain white T-shirt and jeans.

'He's not. He can't be a day under forty-eight.' Donna cocked her eyebrow. 'About Arkadius's age I'd say.'

'Yeah, OK. But that *is* a child, Donna. You can't

seriously have thought that he'd fancy me, especially dressed like *this*.'

The Swede was charming, good company, gently flirtatious . . . and young. Jo did think he was attractive, in an objective sort of way, but she was almost embarrassed that she did. It seemed sad and undignified.

'Don't be ridiculous, darling. Anyway, you look chic, not like me, the proverbial mutton dressed as lamb. But hey, I'm not quite ready to resort to a paper bag over my head.'

Jo smacked her friend's hand across the table and they both began to laugh.

'Have I missed something?' Brian spoke impeccable English with a slight awkwardness of inflection which made him sound more ponderous than he was.

Both women tried to control themselves, Donna unsuccessfully.

'Sorry . . . sorry, Brian,' she spluttered. 'Jo was just complaining that you were a bit on the young side for her.'

'Donna!' Jo blushed, unable to meet his eye. 'I didn't mean—'

'There is no such thing as too young or too old, I think, Joanna.' He was smiling as he reached for her hand and brought it up to his lips to kiss, which sent Donna into further paroxysms of mirth.

By the time they wheeled out on to the street, they were all drunk.

'Come back to mine,' Donna insisted, hailing a

passing taxi with authority and bundling Brian into the back before he had a chance to resist.

Donna's sitting room was Bohemian in style, with rust-coloured velvet sofas, button-backed armchairs, Turkish rugs, battered leather poufs from Morocco, and glass-globe standard lamps throwing a soft yellow light. But the art was modern and expensive. It was a comfortable, elegant room.

'Sit, sit! What'll it be? I've got almost everything. Whisky, gin, Armagnac, Cointreau, Grey Goose in the freezer, wine, both sorts . . . champagne even, although that'll be warm.' Donna hovered by the door that led to the kitchen. She had what Lawrence described as a 'refugee' attitude to alcohol. Her father, a doctor and a committed Quaker, never drank, so nobody else in the family was expected to either. 'I admit I stockpile the stuff,' she told anyone who saw the extensive drinks cupboard. The Meadows, by comparison, had a cupboard that contained the occasional bottle of wine and, pushed to the back of the shelf, an array of dusty bottles containing liqueurs in lurid, sickly colours, mistakenly collected on foreign holidays by an enthusiastic Lawrence, then never touched.

The Grey Goose, ice delicately clinking in the cut-glass tumbler, was delicious. Jo was drunk already, but she didn't care. She was cosy and safe, sunk into the cushions on her friend's soft velvet sofa, shoes off. Brian was next to her, the talk between the three of them fast and funny and totally inconsequential. Life could be good. Fuck Lawrence, she thought and held her glass out for another vodka.

'OK, you have to go now. I've hit a wall,' Donna announced suddenly, slumped in the armchair, her eyes fluttering closed.

Brian chuckled. 'We are all lucky we haven't hit walls.'

Jo wasn't sure what he meant, but she laughed anyway. Donna just batted her arm towards the hall. 'Go, go. Shut the door on the way out.'

'Don't go to sleep in the chair,' Jo cautioned, as she bent to kiss her friend's cheek.

'See her home!' Donna shouted to Brian as they both weaved through the furniture, and Brian raised his hand in acknowledgement.

'I live next door,' Jo giggled as they shut the front door and began to walk down the path to the gate. The night air was cool and refreshing on her hot cheeks and it was beginning to spit with rain.

'I know, you told me.'

'Did I?' She felt his hand steadying her arm as they reached the pavement.

'Which way?'

Jo indicated the house on the left. Brian followed her up the path.

'You don't have to come all the way.'

'I said I would see you home.' Brian's diction

61

had become more precise the drunker he became, as if he were holding on to his English with great care.

Jo put her key in the lock and pushed the dark blue door open. For a moment they hovered on the doorstep.

'Well, that was really fun. Thank you.'

'I enjoyed it too. I'm very happy to have met you,' the Swede said, then lurched drunkenly towards her and gave her a kiss, full on her lips, which seemed to last for ever. Jo was surprised – no one had kissed her on her mouth for years, except Lawrence of course – but she made no move to push him off. She found herself welcoming his kiss, testing it as you might the appropriate firmness of a new mattress.

Brian pulled away, seemingly unaware that he had done anything unusual. 'I hope I will see you soon?'

'That would be good.'

She watched him to the road, then gently shut the door.

The next thing she was aware of was the persistent ringing of her landline beside the bed. She automatically reached for it.

'Hello?'

'Jo, it's me.' Lawrence's voice shocked her upright in bed. The room looked chaotic, her clothes, which she'd obviously stepped out of as she staggered to bed, were strewn all over the oatmeal carpet, her bra still inside her T-shirt, the patchwork quilt lying in a twisted lump by the door. She was naked, the effort of putting on her nightclothes clearly a step too far. She didn't reply to Lawrence. Her head pounded and her mouth was sticky and dry, prompting the inevitable and immediate regret about the last two shots of vodka.

'I'm outside. Can I come in?'

'Now? Why?'

'I need to pick up some things.'

His voice wrenched at her gut. It had been weeks since she'd spoken to him and she didn't know how to react.

'I won't take long . . .' he was saying.

She began to drag herself out of bed, the phone still clutched in her hand.

'Yeah, OK. Just a minute, I'll come down.'

Pulling on her T-shirt and pyjama trousers, then her dressing gown, she glanced in the bedroom mirror. She looked like a recent arrival at rehab: her face was drawn, her eyes red, her hair squashed and tangled. Her dull, dehydrated skin was saved only by the edge of a tan. She groaned. Of all days, she thought as she quickly downed the glass of water she always kept by her bed – which was definitely the day before yesterday's – brushed her hair and slapped a dollop of moisturizer around her face.

Lawrence was standing on the path, texting on his phone when she eventually opened the door. He looked well; tanned and fit, his white shirt rolled to his elbows. She noticed his bike propped against the wooden fence and it was seeing this, the machine that had been for ever joined at the hip with her husband, his obsession, his uncomplaining companion, that made her want to cry.

'Hi.' He glanced at her and she could tell he was surprised. 'Sorry, I thought it'd be a good time . . . it's nearly ten.'

When they were together it was rare for them to stay in bed later than seven-thirty; they both naturally woke around that time. And ten o'clock was when Jo would have a break from writing, a cup of tea. She suddenly resented him knowing this about her.

'Late night,' was all she would say, but she took pleasure in the slight narrowing of his eyes as he took in her dishevelled state.

She held the door for him. He passed her, so close she could have touched him. They both, from habit fostered over decades, walked through to the kitchen, where her husband leaned against the work surface next to the kettle, his hands behind him, holding on to the edge of the wood as if for support.

'I just need to pick up a couple of maps and a few more books,' he said. Lawrence had a huge collection of maps from a lifetime of travelling, which stretched over three shelves in his study.

'You're going away?'

'Umm . . . yeah . . . last week in August.'

'Where?' She asked because she knew what his answer would be, and she knew it would hurt her, and she wanted it to. She particularly wanted him to see that she was hurt.

He looked suitably embarrassed. 'Sardinia.'

'So you, with your fertile brain and a zillion maps, couldn't find anywhere else to go on this vast planet? You had to choose *our* place, the place we've been to a thousand times . . . together?'

'I wanted . . .' Lawrence stopped, knowing, perhaps, that whatever he said he would be digging a deeper hole for himself.

'You wanted to what? Show Arkadius?'

He didn't reply, just shifted awkwardly against the work surface. Jo sat down on a kitchen chair. She was battling a third presence in the room. But it wasn't Arkadius so much as their decades-old and hitherto unquestioned love hovering between them like an impatient ghost, waiting to be acknowledged. She could tell that he was sensing it too. All they had together now was reduced to these stilted, angry sound-bites.

'I still haven't heard from Cassie.' Lawrence may mistakenly have thought this was safer ground.

'She's embarrassed. She doesn't know what to say to you.'

His lips pursed. 'What shall I do?'

Not my problem, Jo thought, enjoying a moment of Schadenfreude that her husband wasn't having it quite all his own way.

'Keep trying, I suppose.'

65

'If you speak to her—' He stopped, obviously seeing the look in her eye. 'No, OK. I won't ask.'

Jo was dying for a cup of tea – her head was emitting a regular dull, dehydrated thud – but she didn't want to offer him one, then have to sit with him, watch him across the table, remind herself of what was now clearly the past.

Lawrence drew himself up, away from the side. 'I'll just get what I need,' he said, still hovering, brushing his white hair back from his face, waiting for something, she wasn't sure what. 'Was it a fun night?' he finally asked.

'Yeah, great,' she said. 'A friend of Donna's, a Swedish guy . . . we got a bit wasted.' She tried to sound casual, as if this were something she did all the time, deliberately not mentioning Donna's presence. Let him think it was more than just a few Grey Geese.

'Oh . . . good. That's good.'

She thought he was doing the same thing in return, playing the same game of studied nonchalance. Or maybe he really didn't care that she'd been out with another man. Maybe he was relieved.

When he left soon after, his precious maps of Sardinia tucked discreetly between two books so as not to give offence, she made herself the tea she was longing for and sat down, mulling over this latest uncomfortable encounter with her husband. It was then that she suddenly realized it was Lawrence's birthday. She'd remembered it all week, of course, but the vodka had done its worst.

She sat up straighter. Had he intentionally chosen today to come round? Was he expecting a card or something? It seemed an odd day to choose if he wasn't. For a moment she felt bad that she hadn't even said Happy Birthday. He would think she was being deliberately mean. Jo wondered if either Cassie or Nicky would ring him. She doubted it, certainly in Cassie's case. But Lawrence took family birthdays very seriously. There would always be presents, a homemade cake, some sort of celebration to mark the passing years.

As she took her cup to the sink, she glanced up at the cork board, where Nicky's birthday photo from three or four years ago had pride of place among much more ancient holiday snaps. Faces glowing in the light from the chocolate cake candles, all smiling, Matt even looking happy, Lawrence waving to her as she took the picture. Tough, she thought, staring at her husband's features. You chose Arkadius.

CHAPTER 5

17 August 2013

'I t's not good news. I spoke to Frances and she really likes your new treatment. She said the bisexual theme was "very real", I think was how she put it. But . . .'

Jo groaned. 'But she's not going to publish it.'

She had spent quite a bit of time researching bisexuality online, not just for her book but in the vague hope of understanding Lawrence's behaviour better. It seemed to come down to the plain fact that some people are attracted to others, regardless of gender. And although the number of people who actually defined themselves as bisexual – now defined by some as 'pan-sexual' – was small, according to Stonewall, there were thought to be many more who simply had an 'aesthetic, romantic or sexual attraction' to more than one gender over a lifetime. This was a crumb of comfort to Jo. Clearly you didn't need to have actual sex with both to feel bisexual. So maybe Lawrence hadn't until now.

One man she emailed reminded her that most

people had preferences within a sex – blonde hair, small breasts, fat/thin etc – so why did everyone think it weird when the preferences included both genders? Jo saw his point, but still couldn't imagine herself having sex with a woman. It certainly, by all reports, was not an easy option to identify yourself as bi. 'No one understands,' another correspondent complained. 'People think we're greedy, helping ourselves to both sexes. And promiscuous. Although they can't prove it, because we aren't, not any more than any other group.'

She and her agent, Maggie, were seated on stools at the counter of a tapas bar in Soho, each with a glass of cold white wine. It was barely six and a Tuesday, the small bar still almost empty. By seven it would be crammed and noisy.

'Not exactly. She's prepared to give it a go . . . very kind of her I must say . . . but she's only offering two five, divided into the usual three chunks.'

Jo sighed. 'Two and a half grand? Bloody hell. I got three times as much last time. It's not worth doing for that.'

'Well, don't be too hasty. It's just the publishing industry is in dire straits at the moment. And if you get a smaller advance you'll make the money on royalties more quickly.'

Jo could hear Maggie struggling to put a positive spin on it.

The frenetic white-jacketed chef, cooking on a grill against the wall, reached over from behind the wooden counter, delivering a white dish of hot, salty green *pimientos de padrón*, placing it between them with a flourish, followed swiftly by a platter on which lay thin slices of Serrano ham overlapping each other at one end, while on the other was a heap of small crumbly nuggets of parmesan cheese. The room was hot and smoky from the cooking.

Maggie picked up one of the peppers by the stalk and popped it in her mouth. 'Ooh . . . hot!' she flapped her hand in front of her open mouth. 'But yummy. Love them, don't you?'

Jo nodded, but she found her agent's news had robbed her of her appetite. She was beginning to be really worried about money. Lawrence was helping her out at the moment, but she knew that couldn't last if her husband was going to set up on his own. She had no pension beyond the miserly offering from the state and it wouldn't be long before Lawrence would ask her to sell their beloved house. The thought made her feel sick.

'You know you can't rely on royalties,' she said.

'Yeah, look, it's not great. I can probably get her up a bit. But she keeps repeating the fantastical/supernatural spiel – for the hundredth time. The implication is you're being perverse not changing your style.'

'So I can churn out the same as everyone else? Seems pointless.'

'I know you like Frances, but I think we need

to consider looking for another publisher. One who sees you a bit differently.'

Maggie was silent as she made short work of the ham and cheese. She was in her early fifties, plump, pale, hardworking, usually dressed in serviceable black or navy and dealing with three teenaged boys who took up too much of her time.

'Would the others sing a different song?'

'You still have enough kudos from *Bumble and Me* to get their attention at least.'

Jo had written the book five years ago. A story about a neglected teen with a loyal cat who saves her from all kinds of dangers with his strange psychic powers. It had been a success, even optioned by a television company, although the adaptation had never seen the light of day.

'I'll give it some thought. I think Helen at Johns, Carr might get you.' Maggie glanced at her watch. 'Christ, got to go. Mark's in Berlin and I daren't leave the three musketeers alone too long, they'll get ideas.'

She grabbed her bag from the floor, looking hassled suddenly. Jo knew she had a long journey back to Hackney and would probably have to cook supper when she got there.

'You OK to get this?' Maggie asked as she reached to kiss her on the cheek.

'Of course,' Jo said, not wanting to think about the bill yet. 'I'll stay a bit and finish my drink.'

Maggie pulled a face. 'Wish I could stay with you.'

Watching her hurry off along the street, Jo felt suddenly bereft and had a ridiculous urge to cry. Instead, she ordered another glass of white which was deliciously cold and citrusy, and picked at the remains of the tapas, the sharp, nutty texture of the cheese sitting pleasurably on her tongue. Lawrence would like this place, she thought, unable to stop the tears filling her eyes.

'Is this seat taken?' A man in a well-cut blue suit, about her age, with slicked back grey hair, rimless spectacles and an incipient paunch was indicating the stool that Maggie had just vacated.

'Not any longer.'

He didn't appear to understand. 'So I can sit here?'

'Of course.'

'Sorry . . . I couldn't hear you.' He sank on to the stool gratefully, clutching his briefcase to his chest.

'Phew.'

Jo smiled. Normally she wouldn't have dreamed of responding to a strange man in a bar, but tonight she found she wanted company. He ordered a large glass of red and some spicy sausages, then turned to her.

'Can I get you another?'

'Thanks, but I've probably had enough.'

'One more can't hurt, can it?' His smile was charming, lifting his otherwise heavy jowls. 'What was it?'

She told him.

'So . . . what's upsetting you?'

'Me?' Jo was taken aback.

'When I came in . . . you looked as if you were crying?'

His accent was polished and confident.

She didn't know what to say.

'Don't tell me. Some bloody fellow's gone and broken your heart.'

She couldn't help laughing.

'We're a bunch of bounders and bastards,' he went on, warming to his theme, despite Jo not having said a word in reply. 'Apart from me, of course. I'm honest Joe, reliable as the day is long.' He took a large gulp of wine and gave a contented sigh. 'Needed that.'

'Bad day?'

'Terrible. Non-stop since eight-thirty this morning – except for a break for a dodgy prawn sandwich, which is probably killing me as I speak – and not a deal in sight.'

'What sort of deal?'

'I'm a mediator. I . . . well, I mediate. Company disputes. Conflict resolution. They argue; I sit with them till they stop.'

'Sounds interesting.'

'You're being polite.' He munched on one of his sausages with relish.

'I'm not. It must take some skill.'

His tired eyes lit up suddenly. 'I do love it. I just find it fascinating, waiting for the chink in the armour, playing back to them what they've actually said, not what they think they've said. Offering solutions. It's bloody satisfying when it works.'

'And bloody frustrating when it doesn't?'

They talked easily together, ordered more wine, more food. By eight-thirty the noise made conversation difficult and they were being jostled from behind by the crowd leaning over them to buy drinks.

'Come on, let's get out of here. My flat's only in the next street. This is my local.'

'Thanks, but I should get home.'

'Now? It's so early. I promise I have no ulterior motive except some cold wine in the fridge and no one to enjoy it with.' He was raising his eyebrows at her, the expression in his eyes amused and self-assured.

'I can't come to your flat. I don't even know your name.'

'Easily solved. Hugh Davenport.' He held out his hand and shook hers firmly as she introduced herself. Then he reached into his inside jacket pocket and removed a card, holding it up to her. 'These people can vouch for me, can't you, Jesus?' He pronounced it as a Spaniard would: Hey-zoos.

The man who had been doing most of the grilling of the tapas turned his sweaty face towards them and grinned at Hugh.

'You want me tell this lady you not a bad boy?'

'Something like that.'

Jesus shrugged, turned to Jo. 'I kill him tomorrow if he try anything. You just let me know.'

'See?' Hugh already had his hand in the small of her back, guiding her out into the Soho night.

Jo tossed a mental coin in her head: she liked him; she didn't fancy him; he really was a mediator, his card said so; he knew the chef at the tapas bar who obviously liked him too; she was too old to be a target for sex; it was early, she didn't feel like being alone; she was bored to death with her life.

His flat was up a narrow, steep flight of stairs, two floors above a sports shop. It was obviously his London pad rather than his home, as it was sparsely furnished with laminate wood flooring and basic John Lewis in conservative navy and beige. There was nothing in the fridge but six bottles of the same New Zealand Sauvignon and an opened packet of coffee tagged shut with a yellow plastic clip. He probably has a wife and four children in Hampshire, Jo thought, although there were no photographs to prove this.

'God, glad to be out of that mayhem. I usually get there earlier.'

'You go to the same place every night?'

'I'm only in town two at the most. My home's in Kent. But yes. It's easy and quick. I often have work to catch up on.'

'Don't let me stop you working.'

'Oh, not tonight. Sit down, I'll open a bottle.'

He also pulled a packet of cheese straws from the cupboard and splayed them in a bowl, then sat down beside her, there was no choice. Jo suddenly wished she hadn't come. Hugh had been relaxed in the bar, but now he seemed to have something on his mind which was making him tense, as if he too were regretting her presence.

'One glass and I'll go,' she said.

'Will you excuse me while I make one phone call?' He drew his mobile from his pocket. 'Won't be a sec.' He disappeared into the bedroom and was gone a long time. Jo was just on the point of tiptoeing out, when he reappeared, his tie and suit jacket off.

'Sorry, sorry . . . had to call my daughter. She's had a problem with a leak from the upstairs flat and the bloody man won't cough up for the damage. I talked to my solicitor today and I wanted to let her know what he said.'

'Please, I really should go.' Jo was already on her feet, the glasses of white almost untouched on the table in front of them.

'Don't . . . don't go yet, Joanna. I'm a hopeless sleeper and I loathe television. What can I do for the next few hours if you run out on me?' Again, the charming smile, the pleading eyes. 'Anyway, it's a terrible waste of good wine.'

She sat down again.

It took them a while before they finished the bottle. Hugh asked her about her work, her family, Lawrence – he was a good listener, obviously a prerequisite of his job – making her laugh with his boyish humour. She found out almost nothing about him. This is my life now, she thought. Sitting on strange sofas with men I don't know, hoping, I suppose, if I'm very lucky, to fall in love with one of them someday. But falling in love seemed a ridiculous idea. She loved Lawrence, and however much she told herself not to, her heart continued to yearn for just one look from her husband's blue eyes that said he loved her too.

When she got up to go, a little wobbly, Hugh got up too.

'Thanks for rescuing me,' she said, as they stood by the door. 'I was in need of company tonight.'

'The pleasure was all mine.'

He held her gaze, as if asking her the question. She said nothing, so he began to draw her towards him, lowering his head as if preparing to kiss her. Why not? she asked herself. But her heart wasn't in it, her body only remembered the way Lawrence's body fitted so well with her own, and she drew back from the strangeness of another mouth.

'No?' Hugh had a quizzical smile on his face.

'Sorry,' she replied.

He shrugged. 'It could have been nice. But maybe we're a bit old for one night stands.'

She laughed. 'Put like that . . .'

He held the door open for her at the head of the dark stairs, reaching to push the press-button timer switch. Jo couldn't see a thing in the dim light.

'Will you be all right getting home? I could call you a taxi . . .'

'I'll be fine.'

'Ring me if you feel like it. You know where I am of a Tuesday night.'

'I will,' she said, although she knew she wouldn't and she was sure he knew it too.

'I really don't think it's such a great idea to go to a strange man's flat alone, darling. You'd only known him for ten minutes.'

'I know, but he seemed OK. I did think about it.'

'Hmm . . . not exactly reassuring. You've got to be much more careful. You're a novice at all this. He could have been anybody.'

'Well, he was "anybody". But if I'd met him online, as you keep suggesting, would it have been any safer?'

'You're not supposed to go back to a strange man's flat *wherever* you meet him. Once you're alone with someone, anything can happen.' Her friend's tone was aunt-like and severe.

'Yeah, well it almost did. He sort of offered to kiss me.'

'NO!' Donna shrieked, pulling the pottery wheel, on which spun another fledgling pot, to an immediate halt. 'So all this shrinking violet behaviour is a front! You're a shameless flirt, Joanna Meadows. Two men trying to take possession of your lips in a week? That beats my recent batting average into a cocked hat!'

'Swedish Brian just slipped I think, too drunk

to stand up straight. The other one was being polite.'

'Men don't kiss women out of politeness.' She wiped her hands on her apron.

'I'm sure they do sometimes. Anyway, it was depressing.'

'Why? Didn't you fancy him?'

'I didn't, but it's not that. He was a decent man but . . . he wasn't Lawrence.' She felt tears in her eyes. 'How do I ever replace him, Donna?'

Her friend sighed. 'Wish I knew, darling.' She got up from the stool and opened the door for Max, who was outside snuffling to get in. The Border Terrier immediately came over to Jo, licking her hand and jumping up to be patted.

'Hey Maxy,' Jo took the little face in her hands and stared into his pansy eyes. 'Tell me the secret . . . go on, I'm sure you know.' The dog wriggled out of her grasp. She looked up at Donna. 'I just wonder how he can love me for so long, and then suddenly not love me at all. I've tried to do the same, but it's not working.'

'I'm sure he does still love you.'

'That's even more stupid then.'

'If you were in the grip of a sexual passion, you'd probably forget him . . . certainly in the short term.'

Jo growled with frustration. 'Yes, but how do you get in the grip? That's what I want to know. I mean I'm sure having it off with Hugh or Brian wouldn't be horrible exactly . . . but passion? One so huge it'll make me forget Lawrence? How likely is that?'

Donna shook her head from side to side, considering. 'You just never know. I had a friend once who—'

'Don't tell me . . . she was eighty and bonked the milkman every minute of every day until she died.'

Her friend chuckled. 'Close . . .'

'It's OK for you. You don't want commitment. You scarper at the first whiff of love. I'm not like that.'

Donna was silent for a moment. 'I suppose I am happier on my own. I mean Walter and I rubbed along fine, but even in the early years I had a wandering eye. Don't know what it is, but the thought of being like you and Lawrence – faithful for hundreds of years – makes me positively nervous.'

'That didn't work out so well though, did it . . . for me and Lawrence.'

'For nearly forty years it did.'

'And you're not scared, as you get older, that you'll run out of men to have affairs with and end up totally alone?'

'Losing my sexuality scares me stiff. But I don't see how having a permanent partner would solve that. I'd just be stuck with someone who only makes love to me because I'm there. *And* he'd probably expect me to cook his meals and wash his smalls.'

Donna picked up Jo's mug and her own and went over to the windowsill to make a fresh pot of coffee.

'I took him for granted,' Jo muttered, suddenly and painfully struck by the sheer comfort of being Lawrence's wife. Of going out with him to social events, of knowing he would be home in the evening and she could tell him, over a glass of wine, all the things – be they thoughts or actual events, either trivial or vitally important – that had happened during the day. Of knowing there was someone there who was always on her side, who would actually listen when she told him a boring story about delays on the Central Line. Of waking in the night, worrying, and being able to get a cuddle and some common sense. Of sex with a person who knew her body as if it were his own. And unlike Donna, she enjoyed cooking for Lawrence, didn't resent washing his socks, although she drew the line at ironing his shirts. She wasn't pretending it was perfect, but the comfort was intrinsic, aside from the usual ups and downs of married life. No passion she was ever likely to enjoy in the future would wipe this from her memory.

Her friend's expression was weary. 'Darling, listen. What's gone is gone. You have to try and move on. There are probably hundreds of men out there who think as you do, who want real commitment. You just have to look.'

But it was the thought of the looking that Jo found so depressing.

'Mum, I've got a job!' Nicky's voice was buzzing with excitement. 'I'm round the corner . . . can I come over?'

'Of course. What is it? What's the job?'

'I'll tell you when I get there. Be about ten. Bye.'

Jo was sitting at her computer looking unenthusiastically at the list of publishers Maggie was suggesting. She didn't want to move, she liked the publisher she was with; they'd done a good job for her. But could she afford to write the book for so little? Maybe I should find a proper job, something that pays me regularly, she thought. It had never been an issue before, with Lawrence basically supporting her writing, then money coming in from *Bumble and Me*. But what could she do? Trained at the BBC, she had written and directed *Play School* and other children's programmes until she was in her forties, when the commissions dried up. But she wouldn't be welcome at the BBC – or anywhere else – at her age. She was glad when Nicky interrupted her gloomy reflections.

'So . . .' Her handsome son stood in front of her, his hands held out expressively towards her. 'Jimmy just called. It's a play at the Bush, starting next week. Not a big part, but I'm the friend of the main character, who's an alien who makes close relationships with me and a girl, but we don't know he's an alien, and it all goes pear-shaped.'

Nicky paused for breath, his eyes bright with excitement. 'Jimmy says it's about how much you can really know someone. The writer is this poet guy who sounds a bit bonkers, Jimmy says, but I don't give a toss. It's the *Bush*, Mum! Like, everyone who's anyone in the theatre sees stuff at the Bush. It is *the* actors' theatre.'

'That's brilliant, darling.'

'And . . . and, wait for it. Guess who got the part of the alien?'

Jo barely had time to shake her head, when Nicky burst out, 'Travis . . . Travis Rey!'

Jo wracked her brain. She never got used to her children's assumption that she could recall every inch of their life with perfect clarity. And if she failed to, they would look dismayed, shocked that these people, events, schedules didn't hold equal significance for her and the rest of the world. Luckily she managed to recall who Travis was.

'Umm . . . American Travis from drama school?'

Nicky nodded approvingly. 'Didn't even know he was back in town. God, we had such a laugh at the audition. Neither of us thought we had a hope in hell. But he just did a New York fringe gig that got him standout reviews. And they made us do a scene together, so perhaps our chemistry clinched it.'

Jo did remember Travis from Nicky's days at LAMDA. Being in west London, Nicky had often brought his friends back for supper, the kitchen suddenly full of these charming, often beautiful, endearingly show-off drama students who took over the evening with their lively banter. Travis stood out among the butterfly crowd not only because he was American and mixed-race, but because he was always quieter, less talkative than the others.

'God, Mum . . . this could be a real chance. A couple of mentions, that's all it takes.' He grabbed her and twirled her round, his energy and excitement barely contained.

Jo made Nicky a sandwich and they sat on the terrace while he told her about the play. It was scheduled to run for six weeks, with a three-week rehearsal period.

'So have you seen Dad?' she asked when discussion about the play was exhausted.

'Nope. But I've talked to him a couple of times, OK?' Nicky sounded defensive.

'Cassie hasn't even done that . . . at least she hadn't when I rang last week.'

'Mum . . . not being rude, but you shouldn't get involved with us and Dad. He's made his decision.'

'I know. But—'

'But he's our dad and we should keep in touch. We'll regret it if we don't, blah, blah . . . we have heard you.'

Her son was biting his top lip, an age-old sign of irritation.

'I'm not doing it on his behalf,' Jo insisted, although this was not strictly true, 'I just know how easy it is to lose touch with people . . . let resentments build up till it's hard to go back.' And she did know; she'd done it with her own father. Unlike Lawrence, and admittedly without the ease of mobile phone communication, Gerald Hamilton had barely made the effort to keep in touch after he left them the day before Jo's fifteenth birthday. She understood better now how hard the terrible incident – and the gossip surrounding it – that drove him away must have been for a man of such rigid probity. But she was not to blame for any of it, although she was never sure that her father saw it that way. He had always lumped Jo and her mother together disdainfully as 'women'. Not people, not his daughter and his wife, just members of a sex for which he had little respect.

And when he made grudging contact with her in the ensuing years it was strained and unsatisfactory; Jo dreaded seeing him. They would invariably meet at the Hilton Hotel, Paddington – because Gerald's train to Gloucester went from that station – and sit opposite each other with tea in a white china pot on the table between them for exactly one excruciating hour, during which time he quizzed her about the mechanics of her life, never about how she actually was. Then as soon as the hour was up, he would look at his watch, tell her his train was about to leave, and bid a formal goodbye, the look on his face one of absolute relief that it was over.

He was still alive, as far as Jo knew – she hadn't

heard that he wasn't – still living in a seaside flat in Ramsgate, but she hadn't seen him since the last terrible visit four years ago. The thought that she should make the effort often pricked her conscience, but the powerful reluctance that followed the thought meant she never did anything about it. And despite what she advised the children, she didn't regret losing touch. But Lawrence had been a good father, hers had not.

'I know, but you just have to trust me and Cass on this one.'

She smiled. 'I do.'

'No you don't. You think we're both still five.'

Nicky was silent, pressing his index finger on to the crumbs from his sandwich and eating them until his plate was tidy. 'It'd just be gross to have to be polite to Arkadius.'

'You can tell Dad that.'

'It's not because he's a man . . .' Nicky went on, as if she hadn't spoken, 'I wouldn't want to meet *anyone* Dad was having sex with. It's different for Cass. You know she's totally not prejudiced in any way, but the man thing really freaks her out. And it freaks her out that it freaks her out. She can't get her head around it.'

Jo watched her son's troubled expression and cursed Lawrence. How dare he be so bloody, bloody selfish?

Her son raised his head. 'Tell me how *you're* doing, Mum.'

She smiled. 'OK . . . you know . . . I miss him,

I can't help it. But I'm trying to get on with my life.' She heard Donna's exhortation to 'move on' ringing in her ears. This was what everyone wanted her to do, because they couldn't help, couldn't do a single thing to change her sad, stuck, lonely situation. It was making them feel bad as well.

'That's good,' Nicky said, obviously wanting it to be true.

Jo felt the first drops of rain, which the overcast day had been threatening since dawn. They both got up.

'Uh, Mum? Just a thought . . . say if it's a bad idea . . . but Travis is looking for somewhere to stay while he's doing the play. He had a flat share set up but it's fallen through he says. I wondered . . . how would you feel about him staying here?'

'Here?' Jo echoed, alarmed.

'I haven't asked him or anything,' Nicky said quickly. 'He'd pay, obviously, and it'd be a good use of my room.'

Was her son trying to protect her from loneliness?

'I'm fine on my own,' she said.

'I know, Mum. This isn't a set up. No pressure if you hate the thought. As I said, I haven't mentioned it to him.'

As Nicky prepared to go, Jo considered the proposition. It would make sense financially, of course, but how would she feel having a virtual stranger in her home? Her isolation was a precious protection, a shield against reality. At some stage I'll have to meet the challenge of the rest of my life, she thought wearily, or sink into something a lot more scary.

'I could bring him round for supper . . . so you could meet him properly?' Nicky was suggesting.

She took a deep breath. 'OK . . . yes, why not? But don't say anything to him yet. Promise?'

As soon as her son had gone, she regretted her decision. I can still change my mind, she told herself.

CHAPTER 6

19 August 2013

Jo had insisted Lawrence meet her in a café on Holland Park if he needed to talk. She didn't want him in the house again because his real presence activated the ghost presence she was trying to dispel, and each time he turned up she had to start all over again.

She deliberately got there late. This wasn't easy for someone so neurotically punctual, but she hated the idea of him seeing her sitting alone at a table waiting for him.

Instead, she caught sight of him before he realized she was there, and viewed him almost as a stranger. He looked tense, hunched over his coffee, gazing at the screen of his phone. He jumped up as soon as he spotted her and held out a chair for her to sit down. They didn't embrace.

'How's it going?' he asked, as he might a friend over whose life he held no sway.

She couldn't work out how to answer, whether to take the banshee route: 'How do you bloody think it's going?' Or to appear cool and unfazed by her new life. Before she had made a decision, he was asking, 'Do you want a coffee?'

'Please . . . cappuccino.'

He looked surprised, as she had intended he should – small triumph. She'd drunk milky lattes for as long as there had been the choice in London cafés.

'Too much milk,' she explained and he nodded.

When they both had their drinks – his another large black coffee – she watched him take a deep breath. She knew exactly what he was going to say.

'Jo . . . we need to talk about finances.' He wriggled with discomfort. 'As you know, I have to move out of Martin's flat by the middle of September. And obviously I can rent somewhere in the short term . . . but . . . but I don't have the resources . . . not when I'm giving you money as well, to afford anywhere for long . . . not now I'm living off my pension.'

'So you've decided to jack in the affair and come home?' She adopted her most innocent expression, but she couldn't help smiling at the shock on his face. 'Joke,' she added softly.

'Please, this is hard enough without you taking the piss,' he snapped. Then he looked immediately contrite. 'Sorry . . . it's just I'm under a lot of pressure at the moment.'

'Are you?'

He looked at her suspiciously, but this time her query had been genuine.

'Why?' she prompted when he didn't answer. 'I thought now you'd retired you'd be shot of all the stress.'

'I can't really talk about it . . . it's not fair on you. But money is certainly a part. And the children.'

She was intrigued. Money and the children were "a part"? Did this mean Arkadius was playing up already?

'So you want to sell the house.'

He seemed caught off guard by her bluntness. 'Well, yes . . . I don't see we have a choice.'

Despite her bravado, Jo's gut churned as she faced the prospect. Her beloved house . . . *their* beloved house, witness to their love, their life, their children's childhood. The first time they'd seen it, they'd both known. It was a wreck, and the wrong end of town – Shepherd's Bush wasn't trendy back then. But Lawrence had looked at her, raised his eyebrows ever so slightly, and she had just smiled. The day they got the keys, they had perched side by side on the scabby kitchen work-surface – soon to be ripped out – swinging their legs like children as they gulped sparkling wine from two paper cups and toasted their future.

'It should sell well, especially if we catch the autumn market. We've paid off the mortgage, so there'll be plenty to divvy up . . . we'll both be able to get a decent place.' He paused in his clearly rehearsed spiel, his eyes meeting hers with reluctance. 'I mean we probably would have downsized in the next few years anyway. It's an expensive house to run and with the children gone we don't need all that space . . . we wouldn't have . . .'

'OK.'

'OK? So you're all right with it?'

'Yes.'

He stared at her, waiting, perhaps, for her to really understand what he was telling her. But she'd been expecting this. She had steeled herself. And she knew it was the only way for her to stop worrying about money too. Yes, she could make it really hard for him – which, insultingly, he seemed to expect – but right now she didn't have the stomach for a fight.

'I'll get on to a couple of estate agents, see what they value it at. Do you have a preference?'

He looked nonplussed. 'For what?'

'Estate agents, Lawrence. Do you want me to use anyone in particular?'

'I hadn't really thought—'

'No, well,' she interrupted him. 'I'll find some.'

'That's great,' he said, his voice leaden.

'If that's all you wanted to talk about?' She drank the last of the horrible cappuccino, which was far too strong and would probably keep her awake till she was ninety, and pulled her bag up from the floor.

'I suppose . . . yes.'

He seemed oddly reluctant to let her go. Did he honestly expect her to sit and shoot the breeze about the weather and the price of tea? More likely he wanted a self-pitying moan about the children, which she was not prepared to countenance.

'OK, well, I'd better get back.' She got up. 'I'll email you a list of agents.'

'Right. Thanks, Jo . . . and thanks for being so understanding.'

God, she thought, swallowing the bile that had suddenly risen in her throat. There he was, almost home free, and the idiot had to ruin it.

'"Understanding"?' Her voice rose a couple of octaves. 'You think I'm being *understanding?*'

Lawrence's eyes widened.

'The only thing I understand is that you're a selfish . . . pathetic . . . transgressive . . . moron.' She spoke quietly, very slowly, enunciating each word, which, despite her rage, she'd chosen with care. Then she turned on her heel and flounced out of the café.

'Matt's being a pain.' Cassie's voice sounded tired.

'Oh, dear. Can you talk?'

'Yes, he's gone . . . taken Moby to the abattoir.'

'No! You're really going to *eat* Moby?'

'Well, yeah Mum. As my dear husband keeps reminding me, that's the point of keeping pigs. You feed them up and then you eat them. And in our case, barter them. Amazing what you can get for a few free-range, rare breed pork chops.'

'He just seemed more like a pet to me,' Jo said,

93

remembering his black eyes peering up at her from the pen.

'That's what we've been fighting about for the past few days. Matt thinks I'm a wet townie for getting sentimental when I knew he would have to go one day. I tell you, there's no way on this earth I'll let one morsel of Moby's flesh pass my lips.'

'Nor me. We're hypocrites though. I, for one, am quite happy to eat someone else's Moby.'

She heard her daughter sigh. 'I suppose. But Moby *was* more of a pet to me. Matt's always out doing something. The pig was my only friend.' Cassie gave a soft laugh. 'He was such an escape artist, I spent most of the time chasing him in the woods.'

'Are you saying you're lonely, darling?'

'No . . . not really. But it's hard, Mum. I know we both make out everything's idyllic here, and in most respects it is . . . but just the daily slog of not being able to access normal things, like a packet of frozen peas for instance . . . can get fucking boring sometimes – you've said it a million times, I know. Especially when I can't say anything to Matt without him rolling his eyes like I'm a total loser for not appreciating his precious Eden.'

'It's not fair on you.'

'I think it would be OK if he'd just acknowledge that it *is* difficult sometimes. It's his obsession that everything has to be perfect all the time that drives me mad.'

'Could you get a job locally? Something to get you out of the house?'

'Doing what?'

'I don't know . . . maybe you could work for the local paper . . . environmental articles or something?'

'Yeah . . . not very likely.'

'Why not? You're a journalist. You have stuff you can show them. I'd have thought they'd be gagging for someone with your experience.'

'I did reviews and the odd article for *NME*, Mum. Not sure working for a trendy music rag'll cut the mustard with a rural weekly mostly concerned with pot holes in the road.'

'Worth a try?'

'I don't know . . . I'll speak to Matt.'

There was silence between them for a moment. Jo wanted to scream at her daughter that Matt didn't own her, that it wasn't up to him whether she worked or not. But she knew that would be incendiary talk. She just worried that her feisty daughter was losing her independence, being subsumed by her husband's wilful zeal.

'Take a break, come up for a few days,' Jo suggested. 'I'd love to see you.'

'I'd love to see you too. But I can't . . . there's so much to do at the moment, I can't leave Matt with it all. He's getting two more piglets . . . he says you've got to have more than one because pigs need company. We shouldn't have left Moby alone apparently. He's picking them up on the way

95

back from the abattoir so as to make the best use of the borrowed truck.'

'OK . . . well, you know you're always welcome.'

'Thanks, Mum. Love you.'

'Love you too, darling.'

Travis Rey seemed to have grown into himself since she'd last seen him. Jo realized he must be fortyish by now – he'd come late to drama school – and he had filled out. His six-foot frame, which he held with poise, was chunky and muscled. He wasn't regularly handsome, but his face had a quiet charisma, it drew the eye with its light gold skin and large, dark eyes, straight nose and engaging grin. Travis had dyed his hair blond recently – perhaps for some part – and it was growing out, the tips bleached white by the sun, giving him the strange look of a Renaissance saint, the ones with a halo attached to the back of their head.

'Beer?' Nicky asked his friend, reaching for the six-pack he'd brought along.

'Thanks, that'd be good.' Travis held the bottle by the neck, swinging it to and fro by his side.

Jo was putting the finishing touches to the supper, frying brown bread croutons in garlic olive oil for the Caesar salad.

'Anything I can do, Mum?'

'Umm . . . no, I think it's under control.' She tipped the croutons on to a paper towel to drain and began tossing the salad in the dressing, then sprinkled parmesan shavings and finally the croutons on top. 'If you could take this outside,' she handed Nicky the salad bowl, 'and I'll bring the chicken.' She hadn't known what to cook. It was so long since she had made a meal for more than just herself, she felt almost nervous presenting the food.

'These too?' Travis had picked up the salt and pepper mills and some blue-and-white cotton napkins from the worktop.

'Oh, yes, please.'

She realized it wasn't that warm once she'd sat down at the wrought iron table. But the men seemed fine, even though both were in T-shirts, so she didn't suggest they move. There was a pause as they all settled, and she detected a slight tension between them, perhaps based on Nicky telling his friend something along the lines of 'You don't know, I didn't say a *word*, remember? But I'm sure Mum'll go for it if she likes you.'

'Nicky said you plan to stay over here for a while . . . after the play?' Jo felt compelled to fill the awkward silence. 'By the way, congratulations on that.'

Travis grinned his lopsided smile. 'Yeah, uh, thanks . . . I kinda like it here.'

'I hear you had quite a success in New York with a play?'

The American glanced at his friend. 'It was an off-off-Broadway, so not the big time, but yeah, I got a bit of heat.'

'Great.' Jo wished her son would contribute a

bit more instead of sitting there hunched over his drink. It was going to be a long evening.

'But I'm back and forth across the pond,' Travis was saying. 'Like a tart I go where the money is.'

'Not true,' Nicky laughed. 'You go where the part is. If you were after money you'd camp out at the gates of Warner Bros and wait to be discovered.'

'Wouldn't take long,' Jo observed, almost to herself, then was embarrassed when Travis caught her glance.

'I love British theatre. Best in the world. If I could get stuff here . . .'

'But neither of us'd say no to a starring role in a film or a mini-series, right?'

Travis laughed. 'Right.'

Jo handed round the sliced roast chicken, the salad and poured herself a glass of white wine. Nicky had lit the two fat red candles on the table, which competed with the glow from the open kitchen door.

For a while they talked about theatre. Jo and Lawrence had been avid theatre goers, although she realized their trips had fallen off in the months before he left. The last play they'd seen had been a new one, a two-hander in the West End, months ago. They'd both hated it, despite all their friends saying it was a must-see. In the interval, she remembered, they had stood sipping their drinks in the crowded bar.

'Not sure I can take much more,' Jo whispered.

'Do you think something incredible happens in the second half?' Lawrence asked.

'Maybe, but do we care?'

'It's had such brilliant reviews . . .'

Jo pulled a face and for a moment they both hesitated. They very rarely walked out of a show, not least because the tickets cost so much.

'Sure?' he asked.

'I am. Are you?'

He nodded. Without another word they knocked back their wine, put their glasses down on the varnished wooden ledge against the wall, and swiftly made for the exit. By the time they reached the street they were giggling like guilty school kids bunking off.

Now she felt dull and inadequate as the conversation between the two men sparked back and forth, each with strong opinions about recent productions, although she noticed Travis took a more generous view of some of his peers – Nicky's appraisals could be excoriating.

'I've got to catch up,' she said. 'Make the effort.'

'Mom took a long time getting her life together after Dad passed. It must be hard for you right now.' She saw alarm flash across Nicky's face and assumed a surreptitious kick under the table.

'Thanks, Travis, but it's not the same. Lawrence isn't remotely dead.' Quite the reverse. He was very much alive – in love, damn him – even the burden of work removed from his shoulders. 'No point in pretending it hasn't happened,' she added, addressing her son's unease.

'Don't knock pretend, Mum. Everyone thinks I'm joking when I tell them.' He raised his eyebrows at her. 'How's it going, Nicky?' He adopted a higher, slightly affected voice. 'Oh, things could be better, you know . . . Dad's run off with a man.' 'Ha, ha . . . yeah, I always thought my mum had the hots for the school nurse back in the day.'

Jo and Travis couldn't help laughing.

'Funny in the telling maybe.'

For a moment they all avoided each other's eye.

'It's nobody else's business,' Jo commented eventually. She turned to her guest. 'Sorry you had to sit through the family cabaret when you just came round for a quiet supper.'

Travis shrugged. He didn't seem at all embarrassed.

Later, as the men got up to go, Jo came to a sudden decision.

'If you want to stay here while you're doing the play, Travis, you'd be very welcome.'

She saw Nicky and Travis exchange surprised glances.

'Yeah? Are you sure? I'll pay of course.'

Jo shrugged. 'We can talk about that another time. But if Nicky's happy for you to go in his room . . .'

'No problem.'

'It'd be great for me . . . if you're totally sure?'

The American's enthusiasm was infectious, and Jo found herself smiling back. It would be a bit of money and he wouldn't be here for more than a couple of months. He couldn't be, not if the house sold. She remembered, guiltily, that she hadn't told Nicky or Cassie about the fact that an estate agent was coming round in the morning to make a valuation, but decided now was not the time.

'I am sure. You can move in whenever you like.' Done deal. She liked Travis Rey.

'Tina Brechin spelled B-R-E-C-H-I-N,' said the estate agent from Foxtons, tagging this information on to her introduction – presumably because it was pronounced Breekin – as if it were one of those improbable multibarrelled names the upper classes are so fond of. She was a brunette, tall and rather plain, in her thirties, classically dressed in slim black trousers and a white silk T-shirt, pearls and pumps and a huge diamond engagement ring on her manicured hand. She looked like something from a bygone era.

'It's a *really* lovely house, Mrs Meadows,' she said, after she'd spent an hour peering into every room, gazing from the windows, opening cupboards, standing silently in the garden, perhaps checking for noise levels. She jotted down details as she went along in her brown leather notebook, sucking the end of her Mont Blanc biro as she contemplated the selling potential of the house that had been Jo and Lawrence's sanctuary for close to

101

thirty years. Now she packed her book and pen back into her large Mulberry bag and took the chair that Jo indicated on the other side of the kitchen table.

'I hope you don't mind my asking, but are you wanting to sell quickly? Do you already have somewhere else in mind?' Her accent was clipped and business-like. When Jo hesitated, trying to decide how to answer and only succeeding in panicking, Tina breezed on, 'Because obviously this will affect our decision about the asking price. I don't imagine we'll have any trouble selling – the market is buoyant in London at the moment, as I'm sure you know; all those foreign buyers. I'd say the only downside of the property is that there's no ensuite in the master bedroom. People expect one at this price. And the downstairs rooms could do with brightening up – nothing major – especially in here, if you want to sell at the top of the market.' She looked around the kitchen, her gaze settling on the garden. 'Lovely mature garden. That counts for a lot. And the glass doors . . . very stylish.'

'We had them done last year.'

Tina nodded, waiting for Jo to answer some of her questions.

'Are you saying we should paint the place before we put it on the market?'

'It's up to you, of course. But people have very little imagination, I'm afraid. First impressions count. If this room and the sitting room were smartened up a bit, fresh flowers, tidy away all the mess . . . well, not mess, but you know what I mean. You want maximum impact as soon as the buyer steps through the door.'

Jo tried to see her home as others might see it. 'It's quite a while since we had it painted,' she conceded.

'You'd get back the small outlay ten-fold in the asking price.'

'OK . . . I'll think about it.'

'The other thing is timescale. I don't think we should put it on the market before the second or third week of September. Let everyone get back from the Med and the children back to school. This is a family house.'

'No, that's fine. There's no hurry, we're just downsizing.' Which is essentially true, she told herself, slightly ashamed of the equivocation. But Tina-whatever-her-name-was didn't need to hear the sordid details. Part of her, she knew, was still hoping that something would happen – the horse might talk – and she wouldn't have to sell after all. It seemed impossible that she would no longer wake up in, come home to, this house.

Tina talked on, estate-agent speak about photographs, online presence, Foxtons percentage, most of which Jo tuned out, her mind on the past, not the future.

'Right, fine.' Tina seemed to have finished. 'So why don't you let me know when you've done the paint job, and I'll have Mike come over and do the photos. And if there are any other questions . . .' She handed Jo her card.

When Jo closed the door on Miss Brechin, she went and curled up on the sofa, drawing the soft tartan-wool rug close around her body, up to her chin, and wept silent tears of loss.

The following day, Travis moved in. He and Nicky arrived around five in the afternoon, with one small wheelie case. And Jo was surprisingly glad to see them.

'Is that it? Or is this the advanced guard?' Jo asked, indicating his luggage.

'Nope, this is it. I travel light.'

'I'll take him up,' Nicky said, grabbing the bag.

'Will you both stay for supper?' she asked, when the two men came down half an hour later. Nicky shook his head.

'Thanks, Mum, but I'm meeting someone at seven.'

Travis looked awkward suddenly. 'I . . . thought . . . if it's OK with you, that I'd stay in, sorta settle myself. But you don't need to do dinner for me, Mrs Meadows. I can pick up something round the corner.'

'Jo or Joanna, please. If you're going to stay here, you can't call me Mrs Meadows,' Jo said. 'House rule.' And it came to her that in truth she no longer *was* Mrs Meadows. She'd kept her maiden name for her books: Joanna Hamilton. Maybe she should call herself that in future.

Travis grinned. 'Jo . . . OK.'

'And I've got food, if you want to join me. It'd be a good time to discuss all the arrangements.'

The American nodded. 'Yeah, great, if it's not any trouble.'

'Right, guys. I'm off. I'll leave you to it,' Nicky declared, with the slightly smug air of having accomplished his goal.

In a way, despite Jo's sudden nervousness at being left alone with a virtual stranger who would not be going home, she was glad when Nicky left, forcing her to bite the bullet and get used to Travis one-to-one.

'Hot date.' Travis nodded his head towards Nicky's departing figure.

'Really? I'm just his mother. I know nothing.'

'Seems pretty intense about her. But he hasn't introduced us yet.'

'Hmm . . .' Nicky rarely brought his girlfriends home. Jo knew that when he did it would be serious. She handed Travis a beer. 'You can have wine if you'd prefer?'

'Yeah . . . wine'd be good . . . only if you're having some.'

Jo poured him some red and then they caught each other's eye and both laughed.

'We've got to stop being so polite to each other. It'll exhaust us.'

'Hey, I come from the have-a-nice-day culture . . . I can't do anything else.'

They carried their glasses to the table, where they sat opposite each other.

'Yes, but I like that American courteousness . . . for instance the way characters in films often say "Ma'am" or "Sir".'

Travis smiled. 'Sorta old fashioned, I guess.'

'It's respect. We seem to have completely lost it over here.' She suddenly heard what she'd said and shook herself. 'Christ, I sound like Disgusted of Tunbridge Wells.'

The allusion was lost on Travis, who just raised a puzzled eyebrow.

'It's the prim middle classes expressing moral outrage. I promise I'm not really that kind of person.'

'Oh those guys! We have them too . . . whole swathes of the Midwest. But I'm from the west coast. We're mostly laid back surfer-dudes. Nothing prim about a Californian.'

As supper went on, Jo realized she was enjoying herself. Travis was charming, well-read and interested in a wide range of subjects. He made her laugh too, a rare commodity in recent months. When they finally cleared the table and made their way up to bed, she realized it was after eleven.

'Oh . . . my . . . God. That boy is so super-cute. He sort of reminds me of that gorgeous actor . . . Chiwetel Ejitor. You know, the guy in that brilliant

106

slave movie.' Donna had dropped in for coffee and met Travis on his way out for a run. He'd shaken Donna's hand and said, with a totally straight face, 'Pleased to meet you, ma'am.' Then flashed an innocent grin at Joanna, who couldn't help laughing.

'Ejiofor. Chiwetel Ejiofor.'

'That's him.'

'You think Travis is cute?'

'Umm, yes.' Her friend eyed her for a moment. 'You mean you hadn't noticed?'

'He's Nicky's friend.'

'So?'

'So . . . well, you don't see your son's friends in that light.'

'Darling, I see all men in that light. Friends of whoever. Men are men, and they're either cute or not cute. And that boy is *cute*.'

Jo held her hands up. 'OK, I hear you. Can we drop the subject?'

'No need to be touchy. I was just making an observation.'

'I'm not being touchy . . . OK, well maybe I am a little. But he's a nice guy and it's helpful having him here . . . bringing in a bit of cash. I just don't want to complicate things with you hitting on him, that's all.'

Donna pouted. 'I'd never do that . . . without your permission that is.'

They both laughed. 'He's almost young enough to be your son,' Jo pointed out.

'And yours.'

'Yes, but *I* realize that. I'm not sure you do.'

Her friend gave an amused shrug. 'Age shall not wither us, nor the years condemn.'

'You're muddling up Cleopatra with Laurence Binyon. *Age shall not weary them, nor the years condemn.*'

'Whatever. But I refuse to be withered or wearied by age or anyone else for that matter. Not under any circumstances.'

Donna took a sip of the coffee Jo had made, pulling a face at the weediness of the brew as she always did.

'So how long's he staying?'

'Until the play's over I suppose. A couple of months?'

'Right. So . . .' Donna hesitated. 'Did the agent come round? I saw Foxtons-type totty hovering on the patio yesterday morning,'

'I wouldn't call her "totty" exactly, but yes. She says I've got to paint the kitchen and sitting room.'

Donna groaned. 'They always say that. Are you going to?'

'I want to get the most I can . . . not being greedy, but if we're both going to get a flat and have some left over to live on—'

'You can't be more than five minutes from me, remember?' Donna dropped her head in her hands. 'Christ, I can't believe you're not going to be next door any more. What will I *do*?'

'Don't.'

'Are you totally positive that you can't keep it? Just for the time being. I mean, isn't it poor diddums' problem if he can't afford to rent a flat?'

'It is . . . but I suppose it's mine too.'

'Yes, but you're not responsible for Lawrence's finances any more. Obviously he'll get half in the end, but not before he's filed for divorce and gone through the courts. That could take *years*. Why are you kow-towing to him like this? Hasn't he done enough to ruin your life without uprooting you from your beloved home as well?'

There was silence in the room. Jo winced at the word 'divorce', although she realized that was what it would come to eventually.

'I don't want to fight with him.'

'Doesn't have to be hostile. But if he wants half of the house, you should make him work for it. That'll take for ever, by which time things might have changed for you. You could have the hots for a millionaire toyboy with a yacht in Monte Carlo and not give a fig about the house by then.'

Jo laughed. 'I wish.' Although she didn't. The thought of some perma-tanned euro smoothie tossing his money about in a yachting blazer and pressed white jeans wasn't doing it for her. She wanted her husband back.

'Honestly, you should think about it. Don't make it so bloody easy for the bastard. How dare he walk out on you like that and then click his fingers and expect you to sell up the family home just because he doesn't want to spend his precious pension on rent? How bloody *dare* he?' Her friend's voice was at fever pitch, her blue eyes flashing.

Jo considered what she was saying.

'So you think I could delay it then? Just say it's not a good time and that I'll think about it later?'

'Of course. Why not?' Donna nodded approvingly. 'What can he do?'

'Well . . . he could refuse to pay me any more money.'

'Could he? But even if he did, I can lend you some for now if you're short. You can pay me back when you sell the house.'

Tears welled up at her friend's offer.

'No . . . no, I couldn't do that.'

Donna held up her hand. 'Please . . . don't be so ridiculous. Of course you can. You know I've got pots of the stuff and I never use it. It'd only be a loan.' She reached across and patted Jo's arm. 'Think about it at least, darling. You can't let that selfish husband of yours railroad you. It's too important.'

'OK, well Frances has come back with an improved offer. Basically another fifteen hundred. Not great, but perhaps better a bird in the hand.' Maggie told Jo over the phone. 'I mean it's up to you. But it'll take time to get another publisher on board, and then they may offer the same as Frances . . . plus we have the problem that Century won't bother to promote your old titles in the future—'

Jo sighed. 'You think I should accept it?'

Maggie was silent for a moment. 'Up to you of course, but it probably makes sense to stick with what we know, despite what I said the other day. Frances seems quite keen on the idea; they wouldn't be negotiating if she wasn't.'

'OK.' Jo knew she wasn't really in the right frame of mind to sell herself to anyone anyway. 'As you say, bird in the hand.'

'You think you can face writing about the subject, do you?'

'Since it's all I think about, I might as well. Could help get it out of my system.'

'Poor you.'

'Don't feel sorry for me, Maggie. Worse things happen at sea.'

'I suppose.' Her agent sounded doubtful.

'What, you think my life's worse than shipwrecks, drowning, sharks?' Jo challenged, laughing. 'Great.'

'No, I don't, I totally don't,' Maggie said quickly. 'I didn't mean that. But I've told you, just looking at the *photo* of a shark makes me puke.'

When Jo had put the phone down she realized that even if she took her husband's needs out of the equation, she would have no choice but to sell the house. There was no way she could live on the paltry advance – spread over eighteen months – from the publishers. And she couldn't imagine anyone giving her a proper job at her age.

CHAPTER 7

26 August 2013

'Come with me,' Travis said as he munched his toast at the kitchen table. 'It'll be fun.'
'Will it? I went years ago with the children: horrible screechy whistles, pounding music, sweaty people crammed together like sardines, screaming kids . . . and boiling hot, as I remember.'

'Says the paid-up member of the Disgusted of Wherever Gang.'

'Tunbridge Wells. Sorry.' Jo smiled. 'Carnival just isn't my thing. And why do they have to leave out the definite article? Shouldn't it be THE carnival? Isn't carnival just a noun, rather than a proper noun? It's annoying.'

Travis waved his half-eaten toast in the air. 'Whoa! You *really* don't like it.'

'I just remember hating the noise and being worried I'd lose the kids. But maybe I'd feel different now.'

'You should give it another go. Hey, why not? You can always quit. And it's cold out there today, no chance of "boiling", as you put it.'

Jo glanced at her lodger. She found, just in the few days he'd been in the house, that she was increasingly drawn to his company. His rehearsals didn't start till the day after Bank Holiday and Nicky seemed permanently glued to his new girl-friend, so Travis had spent a lot of time just hanging around, either reading or studying his iPad, listening to music with his headphones. She'd cooked him supper every night, despite his protes-tations that she shouldn't, and she'd looked forward to it. He was such easy company and it made her realize how lonely she'd been over the summer. Now she hesitated.

'I'll cramp your style.'

'Yeah . . . sure you will.' He flashed a smile. 'No way I want to go on my own.'

She knew he was being kind, but the holiday stretched empty ahead of her.

'If you're serious . . . OK . . . OK, I'll come.'

'Awesome!'

'But you don't have to look after me. If you want to go off on your own . . . I'll be fine getting back.'

Travis raised his eyebrows. 'Says my maiden aunt.'

'Oh, and one more thing. I won't dance.'

'Sure, Aunty. I hear you, Aunty.'

They walked up through Shepherd's Bush and down Holland Park, turning left into Ladbroke Grove. It was early in the day, cold for August, with grey, lowering clouds, but already crowds – including families with young children, reminding Jo of her panic when she'd brought Cassie and Nicky – were piling up from the Tube station, the tangled thump of music loud in the barbecue-scented air.

'OK so far?' Travis glanced sideways at her, a quizzical smile on his face.

'Yup. Don't seem to have come over all queer yet.'

They talked little as they made their way up the hill, both just absorbing the atmosphere, Jo enjoying the sense of anticipation as they approached the hub of the street festival. The head of the procession of floats had got as far as Westbourne Grove, and the pavements here were pressed tight with people contained behind the metal crash barriers. All along Portobello Road were food concessions – every conceivable type – but with a preponderance of West Indian jerk chicken and curried goat sending off mouth-watering aromas of meat and spices.

'Oh my god . . . we gotta get some.' Travis was standing close up to a large grill, peering down at the sizzling, golden-brown chicken pieces and sucking in the pungent smoke as if it were fresh air. 'My belly's gone into spasm.'

'You've only just had breakfast.'

Travis nodded. 'Yeah . . . OK, perhaps we should wait a bit.'

As they walked on, the infectious beat of the steel drums set the American dancing along the pavement. His movement was confident and sexy as he became absorbed in the rhythm and Jo found her own body twitching to join in. Travis saw her face and laughed breathlessly.

'Come on girl . . . move that booty.'

But Jo came over all self-conscious and just grinned, pretending she was absorbed in watching one of the floats going past with a gorgeously attired girl sporting a massive peacock-feather headdress. The mix of drums, the ear-splitting blasts from metal whistles on Rasta ribbons that many people sported, music, shouting, singing, cooking smells and smoke, rubbish underfoot, the press of people, was intoxicating. Jo took a long breath. Enjoy it, she told herself. Relax.

After a while, she and Travis bought some jerk chicken and rice and peas in two recyclable brown containers, two cans of Coke and retreated to a low wall on the far side of Ladbroke Grove.

'Jeeez, that . . . is . . . *hot*,' Travis said through a mouthful of chicken leg. His eyes widened.

'Too hot?'

'You like spicy?'

'Yes . . . well, not head-blowing spicy.' She took a bite from her own and the chilli hit the back of her throat, making her cough and bringing tears to her eyes. 'See what you mean. But it's good,' she added through tingling lips.

'My mom used to cook spicy curries a lot.'

'Was she from the West Indies?'

Travis laughed. 'No, Wisconsin. If you're referring to my colour, my grandmother on my father's side was from West Africa. Cote d'Ivoire. My grandfather was French. He met her when he was working for the government there after the First World War, and they emigrated to the US.'

'Interesting. But you grew up in California?'

'Yeah, San Francisco. Dad was an anthropologist at Stanford. Mom looked after me and my three crazy brothers. What about you?'

'Me?'

'You English?'

She nodded. 'Apart from a Danish great, great something on my father's side . . . boringly English, I'm afraid.'

'I thought you had a Scandinavian look about you.'

She looked at him askance. 'Really?'

'Yeah . . . tall, good bone-structure, those light eyes.' He was studying her now, his head on one side, and she felt a blush rise to her cheeks.

'I did go to Copenhagen once, with Lawrence,' she gabbled, 'and they all talked to me in Danish as if they expected me to understand, so perhaps you're right.'

Travis reached over to take her empty cardboard carton and looked around.

'Where should we put the trash?'

At that moment a band of six or seven men in their early twenties, Hawaiian shirts, hugging tall tinnies and clearly drunk, surged down the crowded pavement next to them, chanting something raw, repetitive and threatening – although they seemed in their own space, uninterested in the rest of the crowd. Most people cleared a path for them nonetheless, but another group standing about smoking on the corner, wearing baseball caps and huge white trainers, chose not to. Jo watched as they turned towards the drunks, silently fanning out across the pavement. None of them spoke, but they were intentionally blocking the way. The drunks came to a halt, the chanting stopped.

'Let's get out of here.' Travis was beside her. 'Someone's going to get their ass kicked in a second and it won't be pretty.' He grabbed Jo's hand and pulled her along, pushing through the carnival crowd. As the people thinned out he began to run, dragging Jo along with him, hands still clasped, both breathless as they sailed down the hill towards the Holland Park junction. They came to a halt outside the Tube station. Jo bent over, laughing and gasping in equal measure because she felt alive for the first time in a long while.

'What are you trying to do to me?'

Travis grinned. 'Nothing like getting the oxygen pumping.'

'Nothing like giving me a heart attack.'

Once they'd got their breath, they set off again at a normal pace. 'Do you suppose it was a planned meet?' he asked.

'What, like a gang thing?'

He nodded. 'Maybe. I'm certain they knew each other.'

'You think?'

'Sure . . . the ones on the corner looked like they were expecting them.'

'Glad we got out then. There's usually at least one stabbing at the carnival, although it's better than it used to be.'

'One sounds good by California standards. There's that about every hour in LA.'

'You don't have to come home with me, you know,' Jo said as they walked along. 'I can just about manage.'

Travis looked at her sideways. 'Hmm . . . you think?'

'Ha, ha.' She paused. 'But listen, thanks for making me come. I had a great time.'

'Yeah, me too.'

'It hots up later on. You should go back, you'll enjoy it.'

The American shook his head. 'Nope. I'm done. Those whistles fry my brain. Anyway, Nicky said he might be around later to hang out . . . *sans* the girlfriend.'

Travis went off to meet Nicky, and Jo was glad he had gone. Because as she sat alone on the sofa, a glass of red wine in her hand, thinking about the day, she had a horrible sense of understanding. Travis *was* cute, as Donna had told her. And she, Jo, found him uncomfortably attractive. That moment when he'd taken her hand, when they'd run together, laughing, down the hill . . . she had felt almost happy.

You're a pathetic old woman, she told herself firmly. He's at least fifteen years younger and can't have the faintest notion of finding you attractive. So pull yourself together.

She knew she was probably just reacting to losing Lawrence. All her life she'd had this man at her side; the two of them a unit. Even in the years when the children were small and they were both working, she doing the bulk of the childcare and the housework along with her job at the BBC, Lawrence off every morning to his precious college, never even asking if she could manage it all, just assuming she would. Trying times, but he had still been there, always. And today she had enjoyed being pulled along like a teenager on the arm of another man. That was all there was to it. That and a fact that she hated to admit: she was lonely. Travis could have been any man, she told herself, and I would find him attractive.

'Did you have a nice time?' Jo asked, regretting her question immediately – she had no desire to hear the answer.

'Yes, good,' Lawrence answered at the other end of the line, his reply understandably cagey.

Jo found herself imagining them, her husband and Arkadius – young and trim and tanned – swimming in the sea at dawn, the salty coolness of the Mediterranean a pleasing shock when they'd just got out of bed, the light soft on the water, which was often so still, early in the day. They would have been looking forward to breakfast on the terrace: fresh orange juice, coffee, crusty bread with ripe tomatoes and goat's cheese. She shook herself.

'I rang to find out if there'd been any movement on the house.'

'Umm . . . yeah . . . about that . . .'

'Did the agent come round?'

'I think we need to talk, Lawrence. Can we meet?'

'We could. What's this about, Jo?'

'Are you around later? Same place?'

She heard the puzzled silence as she refused to answer his question.

'Sure. Could be there about eleven-thirty.'

'See you then.'

Jo felt a quiet churning in her stomach as she contemplated telling her husband that she wasn't going to sell the house yet. She knew how much he worried about money. Always had, it was the one area of his life that his exuberance and flair failed to reach. Brought up in that careful, penny-pinching, hedge-trimming way of his parents, it was in the blood. She had always been more cavalier, more certain that something would come along. Of course now she was paying for that nonchalance with her lack of pension and publishing prospects. But she was adamant she wouldn't give in to his anxiety. Not yet.

He was sitting at a table outside when she arrived. The day was warm and she was sweating from the walk. This time he didn't get up or offer to get her a coffee, although he had his own, half drunk, in front of him.

'Hi.'

'Hi, you look well.' Which he did, his fair skin tanned as much as it ever did, his blue eyes bluer by contrast. He was wearing the grey-and-white-striped shirt with the button-down collar she had bought him about five years ago – one of his favourites.

'So what did you want to say that couldn't be said over the phone?'

Jo sat down, taking her time. On the way over she had been working out how she would tell him. Her instinct was to apologize, but she remembered Donna's rant, and deleted that bit – *she* had nothing to apologize for. In the end she decided there was no good way of delivering bad news, so she just came out with it.

'I don't want to sell the house just yet. I don't feel ready.'

Lawrence's expression darkened. He probably knows, she thought, that it won't help if he gets angry.

'OK . . .' the syllable was drawn out. 'And what made you change your mind?'

'Meeting the Foxton's girl; facing the reality of having prospective buyers snooping round the house; the thought of moving from our home.'

'But you must have realized all that before.' His voice was tight.

'I suppose, in theory.'

'Well, I can't afford to rent a place and sub your life, pay for all the stuff on the house. I just can't do it on my pension.' Jo watched him take a deep breath. 'You said you were OK with it. I've predicated my whole life on having that money in the next two months or so. The house is a goldmine. I know it'll be snapped up the second it goes on the market.'

Don't apologize, she repeated to herself.

'I mean when do you think you *will* be ready? Two months, six months? When, Jo?' His panic was palpable in the rapid blinking of his eyelids, the twisting of the empty sugar packet beside his cup. Not his, he didn't take sugar.

'I don't know,' she replied truthfully.

'So . . . what? I'm supposed to hang fire until you are? This is my house too, you know. I'm the one who's paid the mortgage all these years. I paid for the glass doors to be put in. I paid for the new boiler . . . Anyway, it's ridiculous, you living in that huge house on your own.'

Jo's heart was emitting a dull, angry thud in her chest.

'The whole thing's ridiculous,' she said quietly.

'What's that supposed to mean?'

'Well, you and Arkadius, us being apart . . .'

Lawrence took a long, bitter breath, raising himself up in his chair from his previously slumped position.

'Right. I see. This is all about revenge, is it? You

paying me back for leaving you. Everyone said it would come to this.'

She didn't answer immediately, wondering who 'everyone' was.

'No. It's about me not wanting to move from my home. I don't think I'm being unreasonable. You haven't been gone even three months, Lawrence.'

She saw the anger in his expression drain away, to be replaced by a pained bewilderment.

'What's going to happen?' he said, and it was almost a wail, a childlike cry for help, and seemed to Jo much larger, much wider than the issue about the house.

'I promise I'm not being difficult . . . it's not about taking revenge.' She gave him a wry smile. 'Although don't think that hasn't crossed my mind.'

He didn't smile back. 'I just can't afford it all, Jo. I really can't. I've found a flat, but it's an arm and a leg . . . what with that and the money I give you, I won't have anything left.'

'Where's the flat?'

Lawrence hesitated. 'Off Tottenham Court Road . . . it's only tiny.'

She raised her eyebrows. 'Hardly the cheapest end of town.'

'I knew you'd say that. But it's near Arkadius. OK, I could have got somewhere cheaper in the sticks, but then I'd spend my whole life travelling back and forth.'

Diddums, as Donna would say. 'It's your business where you get a flat,' she said, 'in fact all of this is your business, your choice, Lawrence. I don't see why I should be penalized . . . made to feel guilty for not facilitating *your* life.'

He sighed dramatically. 'So what do you expect me to do?'

She didn't know what to tell him, but his attitude rankled. A man in a leather jacket walked out of the café and stood on the pavement just feet from their table, his back to them, talking in what Jo took to be Russian on his mobile phone, loudly and angrily. Lawrence glared at him.

'Look, the agent said the downstairs needs tarting up. So I'll get that done, make the place look as good as it can. When that's finished, I'll see how I feel.'

'Right. Great.' The anger was back. 'Well if I can't bank on the house money, I'm going to have to reduce the amount I pay you every month.'

'So that you can afford your exorbitant rent?'

'I can't do both, Jo. And if you're going to be stubborn about the house, I don't see what alternative I have.'

'You won't blackmail me into doing what you want, Lawrence. If you have to reduce my money, then go ahead.'

He looked surprised. 'And what will you do?'

'Like you care.'

'Of course I care.' He dropped his head in his hands. 'Oh God, this is such a mess. I'm sorry . . .

I didn't mean to sound as if I was pressuring you, but I can't help it. I *am* worried about money. The pension'll only go so far.'

'So you keep saying. Listen, why don't I do my thing, you do yours. You are anyway. I'll let you know about the house.'

She got up.

'Jo . . .'

'Bye.'

She was shaking as she walked back. She'd intended to go to the supermarket, but she couldn't do anything but stagger home. As soon as she got through the door she burst into tears, only to be confronted by Travis, clearly on his way out for his daily run, dressed in his grey tracksuit bottoms, his headphones slung around his neck. He didn't say a word, didn't ask any questions as he noted her tearstained face and opened his arms. She didn't resist, just took the brief moment of respite his hug was offering before embarrassment overcame her.

'Sorry, sorry. This isn't part of the contract, mopping up your pathetic old landlady. I'm so sorry.'

'God, you Brits love to apologize. No need, I assure you. Crap day at the office, was it?'

She gave him a wan smile. 'I just told my husband, well, *ex*-husband I suppose he is now, that I'm not going to sell the house yet.'

'Right . . . and I'm guessing he didn't take it too well?'

125

'Something like that. Sorry, you'd better get off. Thanks for listening.'

'Will you be OK?'

'I'll be fine. I just . . . he made it so hard. Or I did. Whatever, it wasn't fun. I hate seeing him.'

That night it was Cassie's turn to cry – tempestuous sobs that made it difficult for her mother to understand a word she said – caused by another row with her husband, this time about the vegetable garden.

'Calm down a bit, darling, I can't hear what you're saying. Say it again? He did what?'

'He fucking accused me of sabotaging our whole lifestyle because the lettuces bolted,' Cassie repeated.

Jo had a sudden vision of a bunch of lettuces dragging themselves free of the soil and making a run for it over the chicken wire. 'Hurry up chaps, before those eco-nutters get us!'

'How can that be your fault?'

'It wasn't. But I wasn't upset enough apparently. And *I'm* the Veg Monitor. I'm the one who's supposed to make sure we eat the ripe stuff and don't waste any. But we planted too many of the damn things. If we'd eaten them all we'd have died of gut-rot or bloody boredom.'

Jo found she couldn't suppress a chuckle.

'IT'S NOT FUNNY, Mum.'

'No, I know, I'm sorry . . . it was just the thought of the lettuces.'

'I mean what the fuck's his problem?' her daughter went on as if Jo hadn't spoken. 'Does it *really* matter if a few lettuces go over and can't be eaten? The seeds cost nothing virtually and we didn't have to do anything except plant them. But it's the *waste*. Matt just can't abide *waste*.' She harrumphed. 'They can be composted, for God's sake, or fed to the pigs. We'll end up consuming the little buggers eventually.'

'Darling, is he all right? It's all becoming a bit weird, don't you think?'

'What's becoming "a bit weird"? What are you suggesting?'

'Well, it's fine to want to live a sustainable life-style. He just seems a bit extreme about it all.'

'Are you saying he's nuts?'

'No, not nuts exactly, but I mean, getting hysterical about a few lettuces . . .'

She heard her daughter sigh. 'It's not really the lettuces. He thinks I'm not committed, that's what all our rows are about. He claims I was as keen as him when we first met – I suppose I'm to blame for giving him that impression – but he's got more keen and I've got more pissed off. And when I tell him I didn't sign up for this level of planet-saving, he gets nasty and accuses me of being a spoiled brat and not supporting him.'

'And how do you feel when he says that? Is there any truth in it?'

There was another silence.

'I don't know, Mum. I love him so much. But he's changed. And I don't know what to do.'

She heard Cassie begin to cry again.

'Oh, sweetheart, you've got to talk to him. Find a time when you can have a proper discussion, and lay it out really calmly. Tell him exactly how you feel, point out how you think he's changed. Matt's a good man, and he loves you too.'

Cassie sighed heavily. 'Yeah, I know he does, and of course you're right.'

'Have the talk sooner rather than later. Otherwise it'll fester, you'll get resentful.'

'OK, OK, I'll find a time, I promise.'

Jo heard Cassie blowing her nose.

'I'm so sorry, Mum. I didn't want to burden you, especially when you're going through such a hard time. But he drives me mad when he's like this. He's so clever, and he turns everything round on me so that I don't know what I'm trying to say and I always end up being the bad guy.'

'Where is he now?'

'God knows. Weeping over the dead bodies of the lettuces for all I care. By the way, why are you whispering? Is someone there?' Her daughter's voice was suddenly sharp with suspicion.

'My new lodger . . . the American friend of Nicky's? He probably can't hear anything from your brother's room, but it is late.'

'Oh, yes, you said. How's that working out?'

'Good. I like having someone around.'

'Nicks said it was Travis someone, but I can't

place him from that bonkers lot he hung out with back then.' She gave a long sigh. 'Anyway, Mum. Thanks for listening. I'd better go.'

'Will you be all right?'

'Probably,' Cassie replied, her tone indicating the exact opposite.

CHAPTER 8

7 September 2013

'Tuck your toes under, hands flat on the mat and gradually straighten your legs, keeping your knees soft. Shake out your hands, let your head hang loose, then slowly begin to bring yourself upright. Pelvic floor up, tummy in, un-curling your spine bone by bone until you're standing straight.' The Pilates teacher – an astonishing woman in her seventies who had the body of a lucky forty-year-old – beamed approvingly at the class. 'Good work everyone,' she said, giving them a brief clap.

Jo rolled her eyes at Donna as they picked up their mats and returned them to the pile in the corner. She was exhausted; it was weeks since she'd attended a class. It had only been Donna's nagging that had dragged her out this Saturday morning. 'You can't let yourself go just because that dimwit's legged it. Come on, it'll make you feel better, you know it will,' Donna had insisted, not leaving the kitchen until Jo had agreed to accompany her.

They walked – or wobbled in Jo's case – downstairs to the changing room.

'You and actor boy seemed very cosy on the terrace the last few nights.'

'Cosy? What do you mean?'

Donna's wry smile made her uncomfortable. 'Hmm . . . I mean what I say: you looked very cosy together.' She raised her eyebrows. 'Am I wrong?'

The blush rose quickly and unexpectedly to Jo's cheeks. 'He gets in late from rehearsals and is all wired up, so we just sit with a glass of wine for a while and chat, that's all.'

Her friend continued to give her the eye. 'So you don't fancy him just a teensy weensy little bit? Nothing like that going on?'

'Shhh!' Jo looked around the changing room. There was one girl drying her hair, head upside down, over by the mirrors, totally oblivious to them or their conversation.

'Ooh, bit sensitive, aren't we?'

Jo gave her an irritated look. 'OK,' she dropped her voice as she pulled on her jeans. 'If you must know, I do find Travis attractive. But obviously I—'

'STOP *IT*!' Donna interrupted, a wicked grin lighting up her face. 'I knew it. I bloody knew it.' Her voice had risen again, and Jo glanced anxiously at the girl in the corner again.

'For God's sake, darling,' Donna hissed. 'She doesn't even know you're here. What the hell are you so worried about?' She paused. 'Unless—'

'There's no "unless" about it. Nothing's happened and nothing will, obviously. We just get on really well.'

Neither of them spoke again as they pulled on their clothes, packed away their exercise kit and combed their hair. Piped music, far too loud, was emanating from a speaker in the corner of the ceiling, a torch song that Jo had heard a million times – something about angels – but never properly identified.

'It's thrilling,' Donna commented, linking arms with her friend and giving her a squeeze when they were outside on the street again.

'Nothing thrilling about it,' Jo muttered. 'It's stupid and I wish I hadn't told you now.'

'Don't be like that. I think it's just what you need. A bit of flirting, a reminder that you're not dead yet.'

Jo laughed. 'I don't flirt. And he has no interest in me whatsoever. How could he? Anyway, as I've said before, he's a close friend of Nicky's.'

'Not sure how that's relevant.'

As they waited to cross the road, Jo turned to her. 'Travis is fifteen or more years younger than me, Donna. Or have you forgotten?'

Her friend sighed. 'How could I have forgotten? You tell me every time his name's mentioned. God, you're so obsessed with age, darling. From the way you bang on, anyone'd think you were a bent old bag in a cardie. Look at Helen and Alex: twenty-five plus years between them and they've

132

been married for yonks. Joan and Percy, Sam Taylor-Wood and Aaron. Why should it be different for you?'

'It just is.'

'Right, well that's a very intelligent response.'

Jo was silent, remembering the frisson between her and Travis the previous night. They had been out on the terrace again, as Donna had noted, and it was late. She was a bit drunk because she hadn't eaten since a crispbread and cream cheese around five – cooking seemed pointless for just herself. In fact she'd been about to go to bed when Travis came home.

'Fancy our nightly glass?' he'd asked, waving a bottle he'd brought with him. 'I'll never sleep, the stuff's just buzzing round my head.' He'd paused. 'And it's a wonderful night.'

'OK, why not?' It was Friday and she'd got nothing ahead of her over the weekend except the dreary task of deciding what she was going to do with the stuff in the kitchen so that she could begin to paint. And secretly she'd been hoping he would ask.

Travis had lit the candles on the table, and they'd sat as they had twice before that week, side by side in the wooden chairs, both with a glass of red, the night air balmy for September, as it had been for days now. For a while he'd regaled her with stories about the odd habits of the play's director. Apparently she would stare at him or one of the other actors really hard, then repeat a request over and over, like a mantra, almost to herself without apparently being aware of what she was doing, which caused both concern and a certain amount of concealed hilarity.

'Just makes you wonder if she's having a breakdown or something,' Travis had commented. 'Like, she's got this totally cool reputation, but maybe she's losing it.'

'Surely the producers see what's happening?'

'You'd have thought.' He'd shrugged. 'Listen, I think it's an awesome play – even if the writer and director are a bit nuts. So powerful, the thing about how much any of us can know each other.'

There was a short silence.

'Did you sense anything . . . about Lawrence? I mean before he told you.'

Till then, their conversations had not touched on the personal, despite ranging widely round many subjects. And mellow from the wine, Jo did not shut him down as she might have done sober.

'That he was in love?'

'Yeah . . . and that he liked men?'

Travis's questions had been matter-of-fact, and she'd found herself answering him in the same vein.

'No, neither. Stupid, isn't it? He was pretty tense in the run-up to retiring. But I thought it was about that, about leaving the college he'd spent twenty-plus years at. It never entered my head for a single second that he was having it off with his friend . . . *our* friend . . .'

'Christ, I can't imagine how you'd deal with that.'

She'd smiled at him. 'I still can't believe it's happened, to be honest.'

'What if his thing with the Russian fell apart. Could you take him back? After what he's done.'

The thought of Lawrence coming back was overwhelming. But she knew she was thinking of them being together as they had been before the betrayal, reinventing a time which was gone for ever now. And there was the sex thing. Could she erase the image of him naked, wrapped around Arkadius's lithe body? Could Lawrence? No, it was never going to happen.

'Don't know if I could,' she'd muttered, almost to herself.

Travis hadn't replied; just gazed at her appraisingly.

And as his dark brown eyes met hers, the moment seemed to stretch out, lasting way longer than it was supposed to. It was as if they were both held in the unmoving eye of a storm, Jo's pulse thumping like a drum.

'He's a fool,' Travis had said softly as she'd suddenly been overcome with embarrassment and started shifting in her chair, clearing her throat, unnecessarily brushing her hair back from her face. Anything to distract herself from the unnerving surge of desire his look had evoked.

Travis still seemed relaxed, however, and she'd immediately begun to wonder if she'd imagined it.

'I'd probably better get to bed,' she'd tried to sound casual.

'I might stay out for a bit,' he'd replied, and they'd bid each other a friendly good night.

'I'm being ridiculous,' she told Donna as they reached the end of their road and turned in. 'I'm sure it's completely in my head.'

'What is?' Donna was peering up at her.

'Oh, nothing really.'

'What sort of "nothing really"?'

Jo hesitated. 'Just a look, that's all. And I'm sure I misinterpreted it. I'm such an old saddo. A man gives me a pitying glance and I get hot under the collar.'

'Sounds like more than pity if you had that sort of reaction.'

'Well, it wasn't. So drop it, will you? I feel stupid enough without reliving it over again.'

'What are you doing, Mum?' Nicky was frowning as he saw the pile of things Jo had placed on the kitchen table: a dusty jelly mould that used to hang on the wall; the kitchen clock; the ancient rack that she and Lawrence had been given by a friend for their wedding, from which used to hang metal spoons, a spatula, a potato masher, a ladle and had never been taken down; the cork board with all the family snapshots.

'I'm going to paint in here.'

'OK, seems a bit radical.'

Jo still hadn't had the conversation with her

children about selling the house. She took a deep breath and put down the Phillips screwdriver she was using to undo the frosted-glass up-lighter beside the stove that hadn't worked for decades and was covered in a thick layer of grease.

'Coffee?' she asked her son.

'Thanks.'

They stood leaning against the work surface with their mugs.

'As you've probably realized . . . now that Dad's left . . . this house . . . umm, we've talked, and it looks like I'm going to have to sell up.'

Nicky's face was shocked. 'Sell the house? Why? You can't, that's not fair.' He put his mug down sharply on the side. 'This is our *home*, Mum. You can't sell it.'

'I don't have much choice, darling. Dad can't afford to rent somewhere on his pension, and as you know, I don't earn that much . . . he's always had to subsidize me since I left the BBC.'

'But that's *his* problem. No one asked him to behave like an arse.' The muscles in his cheek stood out as he clenched his teeth. 'You know I saw him the other day?'

Jo shook her head.

'Yeah, we met in town, had a drink at a pub in Soho. He never said a word about this.'

'No, well, he's pretty keen I get on with it. How did it go with Dad?'

'OK, I suppose. Just we couldn't talk about the one thing I wanted to talk about because he didn't bring it up and I didn't know how to. So I banged on about the play and sort of general stuff, and he never mentioned his own life once. It was dumb.'

'He was probably embarrassed. It'll be better next time,' Jo suggested.

'Will it?' Nicky looked despondent. 'But the house? Are you really going to put it on the market?'

'Not yet. I've told Dad I need some time.'

'Is there no way you can keep it, Mum?'

'I don't see how. And it doesn't make sense, me being alone in this big place.'

'You could take in lodgers, like you have Travis. If you had two, wouldn't that be enough to keep the place ticking over?'

'Not sure I want to do that, darling. Travis is great, but having strange people hanging about on a regular basis?' She paused. 'And then there's Dad. He needs to have somewhere to live. It's as much his house as it is mine.'

'Fuck him.'

'If he took me to court he'd get half.'

Nicky stared at her. 'Took you to court? Dad'd never do that.'

She didn't answer. The truth was she had no idea what her husband might or might not do any more.

'Anyway, I thought I'd spruce it up, so that in the event I have to sell, it'll get the best price.'

At that moment, Travis came downstairs.

'Hey.'

'Hey,' Nicky replied.

'Sorry, am I interrupting something?' Travis's glance shot between Jo and his friend.

'No. Mum was just telling me she's selling the house.'

'Oh, yeah.'

Nicky frowned. 'You knew?'

'Your mom mentioned it to me this morning,' Travis said. Jo had pretty much avoided the American since Friday night. She'd made sure she was in her bedroom when he came home from rehearsals on Saturday evening, embarrassed at what he might have thought *she*'d thought about the look that had passed between them.

'Does Cass know?'

Jo shook her head. 'I didn't want to tell you both until I'd made up my mind about it.'

'But what about us?' Nicky asked, his voice rising with indignation. 'Me and Cass? It's our home too. You and Dad can't just make decisions behind our back. Don't we have any say at all?'

'We should have talked to you about it, I know. But it's complicated for me, seeing your father. Obviously I know what the house means to you, darling. And believe me, I hate the idea as much as you do. But with neither of you living at home any more . . .'

'Cassie's got a proper place – not that I envy her that particular one – but I haven't. I still see here as home.' His voice had taken on a hurt tone, with which Jo completely sympathized.

'Hey, buddy, could be worse,' Travis gave Nicky an encouraging pat on the back. 'Remember, *Where your mother is, there your heart will be also.* Matthew 6:21.'

Nicky couldn't help laughing at the sonorous tone of Travis's misquote. 'Didn't take you for a member of the God squad.'

'Ooh, not me. Mom's the bible-basher. She moved house when Dad died and it was kinda weird, but you get used to it.'

Nicky stared at him, then at Jo. He took a deep breath.

'It's just a shock. I'm still getting my head around the fact that he's gone.' He paused. 'The wuss might have said something to me himself,' he added.

'He probably thought it was up to me,' Jo said, slightly shocked at the way her son referred to his father. The children had always had such respect for Lawrence, and he'd swept it away – years of good parenting – in one impulsive act.

'Whatever, Mum. Only don't defend him. Please.'

'Nicky and I will help out with the painting, won't we?' Travis deftly circumnavigated the family tension.

'Sure,' Nicky muttered.

'You have a play to do,' Jo insisted. 'And anyway, I don't know when I'll get around to it. Or if I will. I'm just going through the motions getting these things down. Actually sanding down the walls and all that bollocks; makes me feel tired just thinking about it.'

Travis smiled at her. It was such a tender smile, her heart contracted. Is that more pity, she wondered. Please, just go away, leave me alone before I make a total fool of myself and do something I'll probably regret and you certainly will, she muttered silently. But she found herself smiling back. And that night, when he got back from an evening out with Nicky and his new girlfriend, she was still up.

Frances Gillard sat next to her in the conference room. The large glass table stretched away from them as they perched at one end on the padded black chairs.

'Thought we ought to touch base about the new outline.'

Frances was intimidatingly elegant. In her forties, with shoulder-length auburn hair always smooth and shining and perfectly cut, she power-dressed in tailored suits and blouses in muted navy, stone, white, accompanied by toe-crushing, spine-damaging heels that elevated her five feet to a passable height. But once you'd got past her appearance, her gutsy laugh and no-bullshit take on life made her surprisingly approachable. Jo felt lucky to have her as her editor, but with her confidence at rock bottom, she'd been dreading this morning's meeting.

In front of them on the table were two printouts of Jo's proposal.

Frances smoothed the paper with her small manicured hand. 'I felt the premise was good, Joanna. I just worry that not enough happens. I think we need a twist or two to really make it zing.'

Jo's heart sank. 'Does it have to be complicated? I wanted to do a book with a single thread, keep it really clear. Surely it's twist enough to have all these relationships with boys and girls turning out to be fantasy . . . all in his mind?'

'Hmm, yes . . . but I thought perhaps we could include an online predator scene? A groomer? Make it really current. What do you think?'

'Not a bad idea,' Jo said. 'But I've just been re-reading a Georgette Heyer – *These Old Shades*. Her stories are so simple. No sudden twists, no reveals, just a good honest narrative well told.'

'Yes, love her. But she was writing, what, eighty, ninety years ago?'

'Her books still sell.'

'They do, because she's a classic, iconic.'

'I reckon it's because she has brilliant characters and tells a great tale.'

Frances's frown said it all. 'It's all changed, though, hasn't it? We're in the grip of Marketing now. A good tale isn't enough any more. There has to be a hook.' She gave Jo a wry smile. 'Gotta keep up.'

Is this a dig at my age? Jo wondered, shocked. 'Of course. Anyway, I like your idea, the groomer one,' she said briskly. 'I'll work it in.'

'Great and if you can think of anything else, you know, to spice it up a bit . . . these are teenagers, they have a very short attention span. We must keep 'em guessing.'

'Do you want to see another outline, or shall I get on with it?'

'Just ping it over when you've got something and I'll cast a quick eye. But I think we know where we're going now.' Frances glanced down at her phone and sighed. 'Sorry, must run. Thanks so much for coming in, Joanna. I'm thrilled we've got an agreement on this. I really like your work, as you know.'

Jo trailed out of the massive glass structure, stalling at the turnstile in the foyer, which was activated by the card she'd been given on arrival. Without her reading glasses – which were buried in the bottom of her bag – she couldn't see where to place it and had to summon the help of the security guard, making her feel exactly like the person Donna had evoked: the bent old bag in a cardie.

She pulled out her phone and dialled Maggie's number.

'It went well I think. She wanted "twists" and "zing" and "spice" as usual, but she seemed to think the outline worked in theory.'

'Good. So we're on track. Well done. And although

the money's rubbish, think of all those lovely royalties.'

Jo wasn't comforted, given that it would take her six months to write and another year to publish and God knows how long to sell and be paid any hard cash. She was looking down the barrel of two years at least earning only a few thousand pounds.

'Now I've got to write it,' she said.

Maggie laughed. 'That's the general idea.'

Jo forced a laugh too, but the thought of the blank white document on her computer waiting for her narrative pearls filled her with dread. She'd done no writing at all since Lawrence left three months ago, beyond the thousand-word outline. And for the first time in her life she had no desire to do so. It had been such a compelling part of her world ever since she could remember. A way to exorcise the demons of her childhood, cathartic and soothing to her psyche – she lost herself for hours while she was writing. But she hadn't written about Lawrence. Not a line.

'Frances thinks I'm too old for the job.'

'What on earth do you mean?'

'She said we've got to "keep up" . . . with the marketing aspect of publishing. Marketing rules the world.'

There was a puzzled silence on the other end of the phone. 'OK. Well, that's not exactly the same thing as saying you're too old for the job, is it? She probably just meant we all have to keep an eye on marketing. Which is true these days.'

'I think she meant my books were old-fashioned.'

'I wasn't there, obviously, but I'm sure she was just talking generally . . . wasn't she?'

Jo thought about the conversation. 'Yeah, maybe.'

'Are you OK, Jo? You sound very down.'

'I'm fine. Just she was definitely pointing out that publishing had changed and I ignored it at my peril.'

'But it's not about age,' Maggie said tartly. 'People of all ages write successful books. And you aren't old anyway, you're barely sixty and no one would guess it to look at you. I tell you what though. If you go on banging on about how ancient you are, people will start to believe you.' She paused, softened her tone. 'I know you've been through a hard time recently, but it won't help to wallow.'

'OK, take your point. I . . . Oh, my God—' Still clutching the phone to her ear, she stopped dead, staring across the road. On the opposite pavement, walking along, laughing together, positively jaunty, were her husband and the Russian professor. Arkadius wore jeans and a v-necked charcoal sweater, a brick-red scarf looped European-style round his neck. He looked chic as usual, but whereas in the past Jo had admired the way he dressed, now she saw it as threatening and manipulative. Her husband was also in jeans, a blue shirt, and his familiar Harris-tweed jacket. She remembered buying it with him years ago in

145

Sayers, an old-fashioned men's outfitters in Ealing. Lawrence had been so pleased with the jacket, twisting and turning in front of the long shop mirror for hours. And it still looked good on him, dammit.

'Jo? Jo, are you all right?' She heard Maggie's voice, urgent in her ear.

'Yes . . . no.' She wanted to turn away, had no desire whatsoever to be seen by them. But she found she was rooted to the spot, unable to tear her eyes from the two men. 'I've just seen Lawrence . . . with *him* . . . the man,' she whispered into the phone, although there was no way they could have heard her from the other side of the road.

'God. What are they doing?'

'Nothing . . . just walking along.'

They were past her now, going at quite a pace, clearly engrossed in their conversation, Arkadius doing most of the talking, Lawrence cocking his head to one side to catch the Russian's gems above the traffic noise.

'Did they see you?'

'Umm . . . no . . . no they didn't.' Jo let out a long, slow breath. 'Sorry. That was a bit of a shock.'

'I'm sure. Poor you.'

'Call you later.' Jo felt dazed as she said goodbye to Maggie and put her phone back into her jacket pocket. They had looked so normal, so at ease with each other, so . . . alive. It made her feel sick. That could have been her. It *had* been her, for years and years, she and Lawrence, striding along the street talking and talking, laughing. A couple. Could I ever have that with someone else, she wondered as she sat in a nearby café, recovering. Would it be possible to have that closeness, that synergy again? Her thoughts turned to Travis.

Nothing had happened between them since last Friday night, but they saw each other every day, and they had fallen into a pattern of sitting together and talking late evening – mostly outside if it was warm enough, but inside if it wasn't – after he got home from rehearsals. She hated that she had begun to look forward to seeing him. It scared her. But he seemed as keen as she was to hang out.

He's got a choice, she told herself. He could stay out, or go straight to his room. There's no obligation to sit up and drink wine with his land-lady if he doesn't want to. And the more they talked and laughed, the closer they got. Travis wasn't afraid of personal stuff, she discovered. She was able to talk to him about anything, including her bizarre childhood. And he talked about his own family – his over-religious mother, his workaholic father – and his relationship with a girl whom he'd nearly married.

'We were together for close on four years when I went home after drama school,' he'd told her. 'But she sorta didn't get the acting thing. I guess she thought I'd grow out of it . . . but I never will.' He'd given Jo a wry smile. 'Even if I never get another part my whole life, even if I end up in a

147

crap job, my heart'll still race at the thought of being up there on the boards, in front of all those people. I just love it.'

'Me, I'd rather walk across Niagara Falls on a tightrope than do what you do.'

He'd laughed. 'Bet you've had your moments . . . nativity? High school dram soc?'

'Nope. I was always the spear-carrier in the school play because I was tall and incapable of saying a line without trembling.'

'It's just practice. Bet I could stop you trembling with not a lot of coaching.'

'Thanks, but I'm not sure *you* could—' her words were spontaneous, but that didn't prevent her cringing with embarrassment when she realized what it might sound like to him. Until that moment she'd been scrupulous not to give Travis the impression that she found him attractive. It wasn't easy. His smile, so engaging, drew her in, his glance frequently sought hers. If it weren't so unlikely that her feelings were reciprocated, she would have been convinced he was flirting.

He'd just looked at her and replied softly, 'Is that so?' And she'd made some excuse and hurried inside.

Now, although it was barely midday, she was already wondering if he would be home tonight – and hoping fervently that he would.

'Nicky was going to come by, but Amber got to him first,' Travis said. It was nearly nine and he'd just got in. 'It's hotting up, only one more rehearsal before the previews. Everyone's on edge.' He stretched his arms to the ceiling, rolling his head around as if his neck were stiff. 'Christ . . . I think I feel a tremble coming on at the thought.' He lowered his head, his eyes full of amusement.

'Don't tease,' she said, turning away but unable to repress a smile.

They were in the kitchen. Jo had made him a fried egg sandwich – he'd offered to make it himself, but she'd insisted – and they'd opened a bottle of Beaujolais.

'I'll look forward to it . . . you trembling. Unmissable,' she said.

'Thanks.' He grinned through a mouth full of sandwich.

She didn't have time to say more as the front door suddenly banged open and Cassie's voice called through, 'Mum!'

Jo got up and a second later her daughter burst into the kitchen, dumping a tatty backpack on the tiled floor and throwing herself at her mother.

'I couldn't stand it any more,' Cassie declared as they embraced. Then she saw Travis and pulled away from her mother, looking disconcerted.

'Oh. Sorry.'

The American got up, wiped his hand on his jeans and held it out to her. 'Travis. The lodger.'

Cassie's face cleared. 'Ah, Nicky's friend. Hi.' She shook his hand across the table. 'Mum said, but I couldn't remember you.'

'No reason you should.' He hesitated. 'Listen, I'll head off upstairs, let you guys catch up.' He grabbed his sandwich and glass of wine and made for the hall.

Cassie raised her eyebrows at her mum. 'Hot lodger, Mum. You didn't mention that part.'

Jo didn't comment. 'What's happened, darling?'

Her daughter let out a long, tired groan. 'I couldn't stand it,' she repeated. 'We had yet another row about something utterly pointless, and he was vile—' She saw her mother's look and added hastily, 'Not violent, Matt'd never hurt me . . . but he's so cruel when I don't agree with him. I can't live like that.'

'You haven't left him, have you?'

Cassie's expression looked immediately hostile at the suggestion. 'So what if I have? He deserves it.'

Jo frowned. 'You're saying you've left Matt?'

Tears sprung to her daughter's huge grey eyes. 'I don't know, Mum. I don't know anything any more. All I know is that I want a comfortable life. I don't give a fuck about the planet at this point. We never laugh, never have sex, we don't even talk like we used to. We just scrunge around, worrying about compost and lettuces and off milk. It's fucking insane.'

'Did you manage to have the conversation, tell him how you feel?'

'I tried. But he wasn't listening, and he's always got a smart answer anyway. He virtually said he'd

150

heard it all before and that I'd got to decide if this was the life I wanted, because it was the life *he* wanted. So I called his bluff and left.'

'And what did he say when you told him you were going?'

'Nothing. He said nothing. He just pulled that stupid beanie over his stupid head and disappeared into his stupid shed. Basically he couldn't give a fuck about me, Mum. I'm nothing but a convenience, his own private skivvy.'

'I'm so sorry, darling.' She reached for Cassie's hand and gave it a squeeze. 'It's lovely to see you, even under the circumstances.'

'I just can't wait to open the fridge and get the milk out.' Her daughter's laugh had the edge of hysteria. 'And sleep in my lovely soft bed. I mean why can't we have a proper mattress? There's nothing environmentally unfriendly about box-springs. Why does it have to be a hairy futon?'

Jo laughed. 'I don't know, why does it?'

'Regular mattresses are hard to recycle properly, Matt says – no one bothers to unpick and separate the insides. Whereas when a futon gets old you just cut it open and put the cotton on the compost or make cushions and benchseats with it. Thrilling, eh? Can't hardly wait.'

'See your point,' Jo said.

'I want some fun. Simple, ordinary fun.'

'Stay here for a few days, have a break. You'll have to talk to him sometime, but let's not think about that when you're tired.'

151

Cassie raised her eyebrows. 'You sound as if you think I've done the wrong thing. Do you? You're the one who said Matt was a nutter, Mum. I hoped you'd be more on my side.'

'I didn't quite say that, nor have I implied that you've done the wrong thing. But you will have to talk to him, darling. You can't just walk out and leave your relationship hanging like this.'

'Great, well thanks.' Cassie got up, her face set and angry. 'Like I don't know that. Maybe I shouldn't have come here. I can always go and stay with Hatty if you disapprove.'

Jo sighed, recognizing the familiar shape of previous arguments, when her daughter would ratchet up the tempo with wild assumptions about what Jo – or whichever family member – was thinking, feeling or saying, without her actually having thought, felt or said any such thing. She gave her daughter a tight hug.

'Don't be like that. You know I'm on your side. If you don't want anything to eat, then why don't you go and snug into your box-springs and have a good long sleep.'

For a moment Cassie's body was tense in her arms, then she felt her relax.

'Sorry, Mum. I didn't mean to get at you.'

'It's OK. Nothing more frustrating than relationship squabbles.'

'This is more than a squabble.'

'Go on, get to bed. We'll talk in the morning.'

Jo was too wired to sleep. She curled up on the

sofa, finishing the remains of her wine that Travis had poured earlier. Concerned about Cassie, she knew nonetheless that the drama-queen in her daughter could be exaggerating the problem with Matt – she'd done it before. She kept trying to push away a more selfish thought: Travis. Cassie's presence would most certainly put a stop to her increasingly intimate and pleasurable evenings with the American.

'Didn't see you there.' Travis spoke softly behind her. She jumped. She hadn't heard him come downstairs. 'Is everything OK with your daughter?'

Jo got up, stretched. 'I think so. Just a marital tiff, although they seem to have quite a bit to work out.'

They both walked through to the kitchen.

'I came down for some water,' Travis said. 'Can I get you some?'

Jo nodded. 'Thanks.' She suddenly felt tired, too tired to think about Cassie's problems. 'They never stop worrying you,' she said.

Travis smiled. 'Yeah, that's what Mom always says.'

CHAPTER 9

14 September 2013

'Please don't come to the previews,' Travis begged Cassie a couple of mornings later.

'But that's the fun of it, seeing it in the early stages before it's been polished up,' Cassie objected. They were sitting opposite each other having breakfast. Cassie had cooked herself bacon and fried eggs, Travis was having granola and yoghurt with diced apple.

Jo sat silently at the end of the table, nursing a cup of coffee. She'd been up since six, unable to sleep and had eaten a slice of toast long before the others were stirring. Donna would be round shortly to take her off to Pilates, although she had absolutely no desire to go.

'Why see it raw when you could wait and see something much better?' Travis was asking.

'Raw is fun. And if I like it, I can always come again and see the better version.' She grinned. 'No good trying to keep me away.'

'Not trying to—'

'Just bricking it?'

He smiled. 'Yeah, could say that.'

The banter between them went on, Jo a silent bystander. She was pleased when the bell rang, even it meant going to the dreaded class.

'Hi darling one,' Donna gave Cassie a big hug. 'This is a surprise.' She glanced at Jo. 'You didn't say my favourite surrogate daughter was coming up.'

'She didn't know. I arrived unannounced,' Cassie replied. 'Great to see you, Donna. How's my boyfriend?'

'Oh, pining for you, of course. Hardly eaten a morsel since you abandoned him,' Donna joked.

'Tell him I'll be over later to give him a cuddle.' Cassie turned to Travis, clutching her hand to her breast in a melodramatic gesture. 'Maybe that's what's wrong with my marriage; my heart still belongs to dear Maxy.'

'Stiff competition,' he said, as they both started to laugh.

'They seem to be getting on well,' Donna observed as they walked towards the gym. 'I suppose they know each other from before.'

There was a chilly wind and Jo wrapped her jacket closer around her body. 'No, they don't. They probably bumped into each other at one of the drama school shows, or round the kitchen table, but neither claims to remember.'

Donna turned to look at her. 'You OK with it?'

'With what?'

Her friend shrugged. 'Don't know, you don't seem in such a great mood this morning. Thought perhaps you weren't too keen on sharing actor boy.'

'Don't be ridiculous! Travis isn't my property, Donna.'

'Hmm . . .' was all Donna replied, her eyes still on Jo, who assumed a nonchalance she was very far from feeling. Typical Donna, she thought, always right on the button.

'OK, Mum, I'm cooking tonight. Travis says he'll bring Nicky back after rehearsals. He thought they'd be here by eight at the latest. I'm going to do a fish pie. Travis loves fish. Suppose it comes from growing up in San Francisco.'

Jo, her muscles already stiffening up from the class, sat down heavily in the kitchen chair.

'I like fish too, and I grew up in Gloucestershire.'

Cassie was squatting on the floor in front of the washing machine, loading a pile of clothes she must have dug out of her drawers from years ago. She rolled her eyes at her mother.

'You know what I mean.'

'I'm glad Nicky's coming. I hardly see him since the advent of Amber.'

'Yeah, well, she'll probably tag along too. But I'm dying to meet her. Travis says she's super-pretty but a bit of a plank.'

Travis hadn't told Jo that. In fact he'd said he thought she was 'OK'.

'He's really sweet, Travis, isn't he?' Her daughter straightened up, brushing her heavy, gold-blonde hair out of her eyes and twisting it behind her head before letting it drop down her back in a glossy coil. 'It's great to have a normal conversation for a change. We had such a laugh about Amber. God, seems like a bloody age since I laughed.'

'It's probably good for Nicky to be in love. He hardly ever is,' Jo said, trying to ignore Cassie's admiration for Travis.

'True. And she's got to be better than the last one . . . the dreaded Loulou.'

Jo laughed. 'Famous last words! I'll ask Donna over as well, shall I?'

Cassie nodded enthusiastically. 'Good idea . . . make it a party.'

The evening was raucous from the start. Donna brought a bottle of gin, one of dry vermouth, her cocktail shaker and a lemon.

'Martinis! Straight up with a twist OK with everyone?' she'd asked, without waiting for an answer. But the ratio of gin to vermouth was about a hundred to one – she barely waved the bottle over the gin. And as a result, they became very drunk, very quickly. All except Amber, that is, who looked like an alarmed child when handed her cocktail glass, sipping the chilled liquid gingerly and pulling a face, her pretty nose turned up, mouth puckered, cornflower-blue eyes wide with horror.

Her starved, doll-like beauty – long, floaty, pale-copper hair halfway down her back, minimum make-up, demure pink T-shirt, everything in miniature – rang serious alarm bells to Jo.

'You don't like it?' Nicky, never more than an inch from his girlfriend's side, offered immediate sympathy. 'It is quite strong.'

Donna snorted. 'A weak martini is a contradiction in terms.'

Jo drank hers quickly. She wanted the hit. Her low mood had persisted all day, and she knew exactly why. I'm such an idiot, she told herself as she watched Cassie blatantly flirting with Travis. And Travis responding with his charming smile and quick banter, obviously finding her daughter irresistible. And why not?

Cassie somehow managed to get the impressive fish pie on the table even under the influence of two of Donna's cocktails, to much praise from the table. The pie was followed by cheese, then fruit salad and ice-cream. It was a lovely supper, but Jo just wanted it to be over.

'I think we'll get going,' Nicky said, in answer to Cassie's question about who wanted tea or coffee. Amber had said not one word, just toyed with her food, sipped her glass of white wine as if it were cough mixture and looked as though she were on another planet. Jo had tried to engage with her a few times during the evening, but Amber had just nodded and smiled and given nothing back.

'Blimey,' Donna said, seconds after the front door closed behind them. And they all knew what she meant.

'Maybe she was intimidated by us,' Jo suggested.

Travis shook his head. 'Nope, she's always like that.'

'Really? You told me you thought she was OK.'

He looked apologetic. 'I didn't want to diss her before you met. Didn't seem fair.'

'It won't last,' Cassie said. 'Once Nicky's got over the fact that she's so pretty, he'll lose interest fast.'

'Hmm, not sure about that. She's not only amazing to look at, but she's vulnerable and child-like too. A lethal combo for any man.' Donna spoke like someone who knew.

There was silence while the table mulled this over.

'Not this one,' Travis said eventually.

'You prefer a girl with a brain?' Cassie gave him an arch smile, her body leaning across the corner of the table towards him, her hair falling seductively across her breasts. Jo knew that she was drunk.

'Doesn't have to be smart. Gotta have a sense of humour, someone who lets me know who she is. Amber's a closed book: all that blue-eyed innocence thing going on. Like a mask. Scares me.' As he spoke he didn't look at Cassie, instead he met Jo's glance, his eyes lingering a split-second longer, as if he wanted to communicate something to her. That was how she chose to interpret it anyway.

'It's unfair to assume she's stupid just because she never speaks.' Jo's tone was brisk as she tried not to blush.

Cassie laughed. 'Don't look so worried, Mum. If Nicks does marry Amber, at least you won't have to talk to her!'

When Donna had tottered back next door and the table was cleared, the dishwasher stacked, Cassie yawned and stretched.

'Nightcap anyone? Don't feel like going up yet.' Her question was not directed at her mother.

Jo held her breath. She heard Travis groan.

'Please can we not mention alcohol right now?' Cassie pouted. 'Lightweight.'

'Yup, that's me. Sniff of the barmaid's apron . . .'

'Go on, just one?' Cassie wheedled. But Travis was not to be persuaded.

As Jo lay in bed she wondered how long she would have to watch her daughter trying to seduce the man she herself was becoming quietly obsessed with.

Jo knocked hesitantly on her daughter's bedroom door the next morning. It was after eleven – Travis had been gone for a couple of hours and there was no sign of Cassie. A muffled 'Mum?' greeted her knock.

'Can I come in?'

Cassie was pulling herself up in bed as Jo opened

the door, rubbing her face, brushing strands of hair out of her eyes as she tried to focus.

'What's the time?'

Jo told her as she put the mug of tea down on the bedside table.

'God, thanks, Mum. I just couldn't sleep. I was still awake at three, and then I must have crashed.'

'Worrying?' Jo perched on the wicker chair heaped with discarded clothes.

'Yeah. Well, thinking, trying to work it out.' Cassie took a sip of tea and sighed.

'Has he been in touch?'

'No. He's stubborn that way.' She gave a small smile. 'We both are.'

Jo didn't reply immediately, keen not to say anything which would make her daughter fly off the handle.

'So what's your plan, darling?'

'I don't have one. I don't know what to do. If I go back, it'll all just stay the same. But if I don't, it's quite possible he'll never talk to me again. He's quite capable of just burying his head in the sand, pretending none of it – *us* – ever happened.'

'Really? I can't believe that. Surely he loves you enough to make the effort.'

Cassie shrugged. 'Maybe. But I can't do anything right now. I'm too angry. If I go home we'll just do what we did before, blame each other.'

'The longer you leave it, the worse it'll get.'

'Yeah, yeah, so you keep saying. And you're right, I know that. But *how* do I do it? Tell me. How do

I sort out a relationship with a man who has only one focus, and that focus isn't me?'

Jo had no idea.

'Maybe you need to talk to him with someone else there to mediate.' Her mind flashed back to Hugh, the Tuesday mediator and she wondered how he was.

'You mean counselling? Matt wouldn't be seen dead with a woman in a flowery skirt asking him personal questions about his sex life.'

Jo laughed. 'They're not all like that.'

'In Devon? Really? I think you'll find they are. Anyway, that's not an option.'

There was silence for a moment.

'I'm just worried that you'll get into something else, something you'll regret . . . if you don't sort it out sooner rather than later.'

'Get into something?' Cassie frowned. 'You mean have an affair?'

'Well, yes, I suppose—'

'Thanks for the vote of confidence, Mum. Anyway, so what if I do? I haven't had sex with Matt since one solitary night in April when we both got drunk. He's so bloody knackered all the time . . . and . . .' Cassie's eyes filled with tears, 'I don't think he finds me attractive any more.'

'Oh, darling. I'm sure he does . . . he's just lost his focus a bit.'

Her daughter sniffed, reached for crumpled tissue on the bedside table.

'You've got to stop worrying about me, Mum.

I'm thirty-two. I'm a grown woman. If I want to have sex with someone else, it's not really any of your business.' Her tone seemed to close down the discussion.

Jo got up. 'OK.'

'I'll sort it, Mum. I will. Soon.'

Jo went into her study, hardly reassured by her conversation with Cassie. Am I trying to get rid of my daughter so that *I* can flirt with Travis? she asked herself. She was dismayed by the thought, but she couldn't deny the twisted knot of jealousy she'd experienced when Cassie and Travis had been laughing together the evening before.

'Don't tell the guys,' Cassie whispered the following day, glancing towards the stairs. 'But I've got a ticket for tonight . . . the first preview.'

'You're just going to turn up?' Jo was envious. She was dying to see the play, see Travis on stage. And her son too, of course.

'If I tell him and Nicks, they'll freak and ban me. This way they won't know I'm there till afterwards, when it'll be too late.'

'Up to you.'

'Promise you won't tell them? I've got to meet Hatty this afternoon, so I won't be back before the show.'

'I promise.'

Cassie had dragged Travis off the night before to a pub in the West End to meet some of her friends. He'd had the evening off before the previews began. Jo had sat at home, bereft. And jealous. All evening, through supper, a glass of wine, a blood-soaked Danish detective drama on Sky, she had wondered what they were talking about. If Travis was flirting with her daughter. If he was fancying her. If he was *kissing* her. It made her feel quite sick. Not just because of the stabs of jealousy, but because it was her *own daughter* of whom she was jealous.

In the end she had gone next door. She knew Donna wouldn't be in bed before midnight. Her friend was in her tracksuit bottoms and a light sweater, an open book by the armchair she'd been sitting in. Jo threw herself on the sofa.

'Sorry to interrupt. I saw your light and I really need to confess something terrible,' she told Donna when they both had cups of mint tea in their hands.

'You've had it off with actor boy? At last!'

'I wish,' Jo muttered. 'No . . . this is far worse.'

'Go on.'

Jo let out a long sigh. 'OK. This goes no further, right?' She watched Donna nod impatiently. 'I think Cassie is going to seduce Travis and I'm green with jealousy.'

Her friend stared at her. 'And that's it? Your grisly secret?' She roared with laughter. 'God, darling, if that's the worst it ever gets, you're one lucky girl.'

'You don't think being jealous of your own daughter is *bad*?'

'Oh, sweetheart, it's normal. All mothers envy their daughters at some time. They're at the height of their youth and beauty as yours starts to wane. What's not to envy?'

'But I never have before. It feels horrible.'

'Not fair, is it? You and actor boy getting all cosied up, then in comes the gorgeous Cassie and scuppers your chances. I'd be distressed too. Can't you call Matt and instruct him to come and fetch his wife back to the eco-prison pronto?'

'Good plan.'

'Or, Plan B, you could just get on and seduce him yourself.'

'Under the beady eye of my daughter? I think not.'

Donna considered this. 'Hmm . . . you may have a point.' She paused, a small frown on her face. 'OK, what about this? You invite Matt to stay, under the guise of helping them sort out their marriage.' She looked pleased with herself. 'And Travis backs off when faced with hubby in situ.'

'One snag with that. Matt'll never leave the farm for more than a day.'

'Then you've got a problem. The only way round it is to pick a really, really bad fight with Cass until she ups and leaves. Then you hope Travis doesn't go with her.'

Jo gave a tired laugh. 'What am I like? Even thinking there was any mileage with Travis, or that he'd prefer a sixty-year-old to a girl of thirty-two. Bloody ridiculous.'

'It's not ridiculous. Does seem a bit fraught, though, when there're lots of muscle-bound forty somethings out there you could have it off with *sans* hassle.'

'I'm not talking about "having it off" with anyone.'

'You're not? Well what's all the fuss about then?'

Jo didn't answer. She knew she liked Travis a lot, but to jump to actually having full-on sex with him was too much to imagine. Any fantasies began and ended with a chaste kiss.

'I've got so much to do. I haven't written a word of the new book.'

'So maybe you should. Immerse yourself in work and stop angsting about what actor boy and Cassie are up to. For all you know, he's still pining for you. He's just got caught up in your daughter's seductive charms and doesn't know how to extricate himself.'

'I don't think so . . . anyway, you're right. I've just got to get on with life and forget about him. He's my lodger, period.'

When she finally got home close to midnight, there was still no sign of Cassie or Travis.

'The play was a bit shit,' Cassie announced in a stage whisper when she came down the next day, her eyes darting upwards to where Travis still slept. 'But Travis and Nicks were brilliant. The perfect double-act.'

'Can't wait to see Nicky onstage.'

'Yeah, he was good.'

'When you say the play was "a bit shit" . . .?'

'Sort of pretentious? Poet-ish? Which is fair since it was written by one. Not sure you'll like it, Mum. But the audience seemed to be lapping it up. And two cute guys in the lead roles always helps.'

'Oh, dear. What did you say to them afterwards?'

'That they were fantastic, which they were. I think they agree that the play's a tad up itself . . . but obviously they can't say it – or even think it. Not yet.'

She took the plate of toast Jo offered. 'We had a drink at the theatre bar, then went for a Chinese. Amber, you'll be staggered to hear, doesn't eat Chinese – or, indeed, anything spicy, for future reference. Or anything at all – so they bailed after one drink. It was just me and Travis.'

'You're not getting too close, are you?' Jo blurted it out without thinking, on a wave of hot, stabbing jealousy. 'I mean, you seem to be seeing each other quite a lot. And with you and Matt . . .' she added lamely. Her daughter looked horrified.

'Christ, Mum! What are you accusing me of?'

'I'm not accusing you of anything. I just think you should be focusing on sorting your marriage out before you leap into another relationship.'

Jo was ashamed of herself, knowing *what* she was saying was fair – this wasn't her picking a fight, as Donna had suggested – but also that her motivation for saying it was definitely not.

167

Cassie continued to stare at her in amazement.

'Mum, I'm not even *thinking* of a relationship with Travis, for God's sake. I think he's incredibly cute, who wouldn't? But you know what? It's *my* life. Even if we did get into something, it's none of your bloody business.'

And with that her daughter stormed out of the kitchen and upstairs.

Jo had no time to make amends. She was going to Oxford to have lunch with a friend of hers, Rosie – they'd worked together at the BBC, way back. She'd put this visit off twice, and didn't feel she could cancel again, but she was not looking forward to telling her friend about Lawrence and seeing the shock on her face. Rosie wasn't judgemental exactly, just pretty conservative.

But in the event she didn't have to. She was halfway there on the Oxford Tube when she got a text from Rosie saying she'd had to take John, her husband, to hospital to get stitches for a gash on his leg. Jo got off at Lewknor Turn and took the next bus back.

When she got home, there was no one about, only the remains of a meal on the kitchen table: two plates, two glasses, a half empty salad bowl and the nub end of a French loaf.

She was at the bottom of the stairs about to call out, when she heard voices coming from Cassie's room – the first one on the landing to the right. Low voices, Travis's nasal American tones, Cassie's giggle. The door was firmly shut.

168

No! She stood stock still, hardly able to believe what she was thinking. Surely not? It went quiet for a minute, then she heard more giggles, a muffled exclamation from Travis.

Jo didn't know what to do. The sounds turned her stomach, unwanted images flashed across her mind. If she called out, the thought of them emerging, red-faced and possibly half-naked from the bedroom was more than she could take. She quickly gathered up her bag from the hall table and opened the front door quietly. She would call her daughter from a café or somewhere and say she was on her way home.

As she hurried sheepishly, head down, away from her own house, towards the Shepherd's Bush Road, jealousy and indignation bubbled in her gut. Was there any rational explanation for the two of them being shut in Cassie's bedroom together? She couldn't think of one. This must be payback for her accusation this morning. But did Matt mean so little to her daughter that she would cheat on him within days of leaving home? And would Travis, knowing Cassie was upset and all over the place about her relationship, really have taken advantage of her? He must be a real operator if he had. By the time she got to Café Rouge on the corner, she was furious. How dare they? Had they no shame?

With shaking hand she dialled her daughter's mobile. Cassie answered it on the third ring.

'Hey, Mum. What's up?'

Jo tried very hard to control her voice.

'Umm . . . John fell down some steps or something and had to go to hospital for stitches . . . so I came back.'

'Bummer.'

'I'll be home in about fifteen minutes.'

'OK, see you then.'

Cassie had sounded perfectly normal, cheerful even, no hint of any embarrassment.

When she got in, Travis was clearing the lunch. Cassie was nowhere to be seen. He turned and smiled at her.

'Hi . . . wasted journey then?'

She nodded.

'Can I get you some tea?'

'Thanks, yes please.' She'd only just finished a cup at the café, but she accepted without thinking. 'Where's Cassie?'

'Taking a shower. She's off out to meet a friend.'

The shower at two o'clock in the afternoon didn't bode well, but Travis seemed completely at ease, Jo could detect no trace of guilt or lingering sexual ambiance. He handed her a mug. They both stood against the side, facing each other, tea in hand.

'So,' she affected a breezy tone, 'what have you two been up to?'

Amusement was clear in his eyes. 'We ate lunch, then I fixed the shelf in Cassie's room. A tad challenging . . . it was listing to starboard, but I couldn't get the damn thing off the wall to straighten it up.'

'Which shelf?'

'Small one – kind of a bookcase – on the wall behind the door. She has a bunch of china things on it.'

'Oh, right. That's been crooked for years.'

'Not any more! Anyway, it fell on us at one point. D.I.Y. is so not my thing.' Travis laughed, then his expression sobered, his voice dropped. 'You know, talking to Cassie, she's still convinced her father'll come to his senses. That he'll be back.'

Jo didn't reply immediately. She felt slightly mad. So Travis and her daughter were not having steamy sex while she was on the Oxford Tube. He was mending her book-case. The relief she felt, on all counts, was tempered by the fact that her life suddenly seemed to be sliding out from under her. Hiding in a café? Not trusting her daughter? Or Travis? Obsessing about them both. It had to stop.

'He won't,' she replied, her heart finally beginning to harden towards Lawrence.

Travis was looking at her, unblinking.

'What?' she asked, almost snappishly. She wasn't in the mood for pity and she was sure Cassie would have discussed her plight with Travis at some length. Said how worried she was about her mother, how old, how lonely she must be. How her father needed to come back to save her.

'Miss our evenings, just you and me on the terrace,' he said quietly.

She caught her breath.

'That guy's a nut-job . . . walking out on you.'

'Maybe it's me who's the "nut-job", as you so delicately put it.'

He grinned. 'You did have a kinda crazy look in your eye when you came in.'

She didn't laugh, just looked discomforted. Travis, seeing it, was puzzled.

'OK . . . was it something—'

'No . . . nothing,' Jo interrupted his question, turning to put her mug in the sink. But she felt happy for the first time in days.

CHAPTER 10

19 September 2013

'Lawrence. What are you doing here?' Jo stood at the front door, taken unawares by her husband there in the flesh. His familiarity, as usual, ambushed her heart.

'Sorry to barge in on you,' he said, making no move to come in, his stance apologetic as he waited on the path, his hands in his faded black chino pockets. 'But Nicky said Cassie was staying, I thought I might catch her.'

Jo stood aside to let him in.

'Did you tell her you were coming?' Cassie hadn't mentioned her father since she'd pitched up nearly a week ago. Whenever Jo tried to talk about him, she just held up her hand to silence her mother.

'She won't answer my calls. I've been calling and texting for weeks . . . months . . . and I get no response.'

'So she doesn't know you're coming.'

Lawrence shook his head. 'I thought if I told

her – or you – she might go out.' He sounded infinitely sad.

Jo pushed him through to the sitting room. Lowering her voice she told him, 'Cassie's not in a good way. She's walked out on Matt and doesn't seem to have any plan to go back.'

'She's actually left him? Nicky seemed to think she was just taking time out.'

'I've really no idea. She won't talk about it. You know how stubborn she is.'

'And what does Matt say about all this?'

'Nothing, as far as I know. She was adamant that he wouldn't bother to contact her, but Travis told me that he's called about ten times and Cassie hasn't responded.'

'Travis?'

'The lodger. Nicky's friend.'

Lawrence nodded acknowledgement. 'So what's your line with her?'

'The obvious one, that she should talk it out with Matt. But she insists he won't listen.'

It felt good to discuss their daughter with the only other person in the world who understood the situation as she did.

'Should I try and persuade her?'

In the past it was always Lawrence who got through to Cassie, the designated peacemaker after one of their daughter's bouts of hysteria. Now Jo gave him an amused look.

'I think you've got enough ground to make up without dragging relationship counselling into it.'

174

Her husband gave her a sideways glance. Then he sighed.

'I suppose I have. Do you think she'll see me?'

'She might, now you're here. But go easy, you know how unpredictable she can be . . .'

'He's a good guy though, Matt. Isn't he?'

'He is. But I think he's been neglecting her in pursuit of this bizarre personal nirvana of his.'

There was silence between them.

'Easy to do,' Lawrence said, and Jo wondered if he intended the remark to have a wider context. 'So how are you getting on?'

'I'm fine,' she said firmly, her tone, she hoped, closing down the conversation. She had no desire for reciprocal disclosures and knew that any talk about her current situation would quickly come round to the house and when she was going to sell it.

'She's in her bedroom.'

'OK. Should I go up?'

Perhaps he was waiting for her to do it for him, to go and prepare her daughter. No chance.

'Your call.'

She moved into the kitchen, trying not to listen to what was going on upstairs. After five minutes she heard footsteps but it was only Travis.

'Lawrence has dropped in to see Cassie.'

The American's eyes widened. 'Right. No idea that was on the agenda.'

'It wasn't. I'm hoping you heard sounds of rapprochement as you passed?'

'Didn't hear squat.'

Jo frowned. 'Not good.'

'I'd say not. Cassie can be wilful I imagine.'

'She wouldn't return his calls. I suppose he had no choice.'

He shrugged. 'I'd have done the same . . . if it was my kid.'

They sat in silence as Jo poured some coffee for Travis, both unable to ignore the muffled voices now coming from upstairs, which rose and fell rhythmically. Initially Cassie's was the dominant one, her tone angry and insistent. But as time passed, it was her husband's deeper, conciliatory voice that came through.

'Maybe I should take off? Don't want to get in the way of family stuff,' Travis suggested.

'No need. Lawrence and I don't have anything to say to each other.'

He must have heard the steeliness in her remark.

'Still . . .' he was about to get up as Lawrence came into the kitchen. He looked exhausted.

'Phew,' he said, rubbing his hands over his face. 'Well, at least we've talked.' He looked at Travis enquiringly, his eyes flitting over the coffee, the two of them sitting together.

Jo introduced the American. Odd, she thought, that Lawrence was now the guest in the house, the outsider, Travis the resident.

Jo breathed a sigh of relief to see the new theatre. She hadn't been to the Bush since it moved from a poky, claustrophobic pub venue on the other side of the green, to this relatively palatial one – a conversion of the old library – round the corner on the Uxbridge Road. The seats were bench and padded, as in all London fringe theatres, but these were still new and comfortable, set in two tiers on opposite sides of the stage space, the bare brick walls lending an unpretentious, contemporary atmosphere. The set for this production was bleak and futuristic: steel cubes and pods, a bank of computer screens, distressed mesh partitions in rust and grey.

Jo secured herself a place on the end of a row, dreading the possibility of being crushed up tight in the middle and unable to breathe. It was hot, but mercifully only two thirds full. She had tried to drag Donna along with her, but her friend was going to a fundraising gala at the Royal Opera House with one of her walkers.

As she waited for *Soft Landings* to begin, she thought about Lawrence's visit. He'd seemed nervy, a bit worn down, the easy charm, the self-assurance he'd shown since the day she'd met him strangely absent. What's going on with Arkadius, she wondered. Wasn't it working out as her husband had hoped?

'She's so angry with me,' Lawrence had told her after Travis tactfully disappeared upstairs.

'Angry with all of us. But you got through?'

'Sort of. She ranted, I tried to calm her down . . . but what can I say?'

Jo didn't reply.

'I asked about Matt. She said she needed some "space", whatever that means. She did insist she still loves him though.'

'I'm sure she does. But it's not always enough.'

Jo's comment was not intentionally loaded, but Lawrence seemed to wince, his expression closing down. That was the problem these days. No exchange between her and her husband was taken at face value, everything – on both sides – was filtered through his betrayal.

'Maybe she's waiting for Matt to make a move.' She talked to fill the silence. 'Prove that she's more important to him than his eco-world.'

Lawrence nodded wearily. 'If she is . . .'

Jo *almost* felt sorry for him . . . almost. Whether he had worked it out and decided sacrificing his children's love was a fair price to pay for Arkadius, or whether he had taken none of the fallout into account in his state of intoxication, she didn't know. His look suggested the latter. But then perhaps it was worth it to him.

As Cassie had suggested, Jo found the play annoying, the dialogue deliberately heightened and obscure, the philosophy laboured. But Nicky and Travis saved the day, both acting from the heart, the spark between them rendering the trite construct at least watchable. And despite any shortcomings, she found she loved every minute. Loved being able, for once, to observe Travis at close quarters, unimpeded by manners and subterfuge. She had permission – indeed she was *required* – to stare at him. And her son of course. She felt a stab of guilt as the cast took a bow that she had spent so little time watching her son.

After the play they met up, as Cassie had, downstairs in the theatre bar. Nicky and Travis were high, loud, laughing and confident. It had been a good audience.

'What did you think, Mum?' Nicky gave her an ebullient hug.

'I thought you were brilliant, both of you,' she said. 'Brought the stage alive. Interesting concept.'

Nicky beamed, but Travis's grin was knowing. 'Think maybe I detect some dissembling? Or am I being paranoid?'

She laughed. 'Totally paranoid.'

'What do you mean?' Nicky asked, catching the glance between her and his friend.

'Play's not quite doing it for your mom,' Travis explained. But Nicky wasn't listening.

'There she is.' He was off towards the double doors of the library-turned-theatre, gathering up his sweetheart in a close embrace. Amber looked as beautiful as ever – many eyes turned at her entrance – and as vacant.

Travis groaned. 'There's a limit to the amount of coo-ing I can handle . . .'

'I'll suggest an Indian. She doesn't do spicy.'

'Yeah . . . do it.'

Nicky and Amber had a short, whispered exchange

and then began making their way through the crowd to join them.

In the event Jo didn't need to manipulate.

'Amber's not feeling so great,' her son announced before they'd even had time to greet the girl – who offered them a wan smile but no further explanation. 'I think we'll head off home.'

Nicky cast a sideways glance at his mother as if he expected her to object. He was in no doubt that she hadn't exactly warmed to his girlfriend. But his loyalties were crystal clear.

'No problem, darling.' Jo could afford to be gracious.

After the two had said goodbye, there was a sudden silence between her and Travis.

'So were you serious about that Indian?' Travis said, biting his lower lip as if he were nervous.

'Absolutely . . . if you're up for it. Or we could get a takeaway and sit outside? It's so warm.' Jo felt her body suddenly alive with nerves, as if someone had thrown a switch on a circuit board.

'Sure, sounds perfect.'

Jo had been hungry earlier, but by the time they were seated at the wrought iron table on the terrace, the cartons of Tandoori chicken, tarka dal, sag aloo, rice and raita between them, each with a glass of wine, she found her stomach was balled so tight she could barely swallow, let alone eat.

They talked for a while with their usual ease, general subjects that avoided her having to be honest about the play. There was a lightness between them tonight, a lot of laughter. Maybe it was the wine, which seemed to have gone straight to her head, but Jo felt heady and reckless.

'You're a nightmare,' she said as the first bottle of wine was set aside for the second.

Travis raised his eyebrows, his brown eyes lit up in the candlelight.

'Moi? I sure hope you're not blaming *me* for your alcohol intake.'

'That . . . and for being so bloody disturbing.' There, she'd said it. Her words stood solid, suspending the moment.

'OK,' the sound was drawn out, soft, almost a caress. 'But hey, you must share *some* responsibility.'

They stared at each other. Jo felt unable to move or speak as Travis got up and came round the table. He put his hand beneath her elbow and pulled her gently to her feet, drawing her into his embrace. His body felt so deliciously warm and strong. She looked up at him. The hesitation in his eyes was only momentary, then his mouth was on hers, a soft, fluttering kiss, then another, testing her response. And when a small moan escaped her, his lips pressed hers more confidently, the kiss suddenly urgent and full of desire.

After a while, Jo, trembling, drew back. 'This is mad. We can't . . .'

He seemed amused. 'Why not? Why can't we? You and me . . . both free agents last I checked.'

Which was true, but she hadn't got around to

thinking of herself as free. She still felt tethered to Lawrence, or at least to his imprint on her life, now his shadow. But Lawrence Meadows had gone. She was, to all intents and purposes, free as a bird. She took a deep breath, sank back against Travis's chest, inhaling the faint scent of nutmeg and lime on his skin, bringing her arms round his body to caress the small of his back, turning her face up to his for another kiss.

It was only the sound of the front door that tore them apart. Jo, brushing her hands across her face as if to erase all evidence of Travis's kisses, shot back to her chair and began picking up the cartons – still mostly uneaten – from the table. Travis snatched up his wine glass and stood with his back to her, looking out on the dark garden.

'Hey guys. Still up?' Cassie sounded tired.

'Yeah . . . had a takeaway after the show,' Travis replied, which was lucky, as Jo wasn't sure she could speak.

'God, I'm knackered,' Cassie said. 'Jason is such an old bore. I don't know why I bother.' She peered at the curry in the candlelight, reaching over for a piece of chicken and dipping it in the raita. 'Mmm . . . and we never actually got to eat. Just sat in the smelly pub with a bag of pork scratchings all evening.'

'Do you want me to heat this up?'

Cassie shook her head. 'Thanks Mum, but I'm not really hungry any more.'

Travis helped Jo collect the plates and glasses, taking them inside.

'Tea, anyone?' she asked. But they both shook their heads.

'I guess I'll go up,' Travis said, smiling at Jo. 'Thanks for the curry, Jo.'

'A pleasure. Thanks for the play.'

He waved his hand at them both and disappeared upstairs.

Jo felt dazed, almost disorientated and was relieved that he was gone. She got a glass from the cupboard and ran the cold water.

'So did you like it?' Cassie asked in a whisper.

'What?'

'Doh . . . the play.'

'Oh yes, the play. No, not really. You were right. But it was fun seeing them act.'

'He's a real talent, Travis. Don't you think?'

Jo nodded. 'Nicky's really good too.'

'Yeah, he is. But it wasn't a big enough part to really stretch him. I think he owed a lot to Travis's performance.'

'That's a bit mean.'

'I didn't say he wasn't good. I just said you couldn't really tell from that role.'

Jo wasn't about to get involved in what sounded like sibling rivalry. She was barely keeping it together; her body was buzzing, her skin burning with the feel of Travis's touch. Surely Cassie could see.

'How did you escape the silent Amber?'

'She said she wasn't well. Nicky took her home.'

'Maybe she should eat occasionally, it helps,' Cassie said waspishly, then gave her mother a broad grin. 'I'm kind of enjoying seeing Nicks so besotted. Mr Cool finally meets his match!'

Jo waited till it went quiet upstairs, then she fetched the rug from the back of the sofa and drew it round her shoulders as she went outside again to sit in the darkness. There was a chill now, the day's warmth giving way to the autumn night, but the blanket was cosy and soft as she hugged it to her body, preserving the intense pleasure she'd experienced with Travis, the darkness a cloak for her arousal. Questions flitted about her mind: what happens next? Now he's kissed me, will he want to kiss me again? What if Cassie finds out? But she chose to ignore them and just savour the moment, remembering the desire in his eyes, the feel of his hand on her breast. It had been decades since anyone had looked at her that way.

There had been years of sensual enjoyment with Lawrence – they had been lucky she felt – but inevitably their physical relationship had been absorbed into the mundane flow of their life, the occasional peaks of intensity taken for granted along with other pleasures, such as the exchange of ideas between them, a good meal in the sunshine, a bike ride by the sea, the children. It was how it should be, she thought now. And had she died in her husband's arms, she wouldn't have felt cheated of another passion. But she would not die in Lawrence Meadows' arms. Not now.

'Coffee?' She waved the cafetière at Travis as he came into the kitchen the following morning.

'Sure, thanks.' He hesitated for a split second, looked around, then came over, planting a soft kiss on her cheek, pausing, then kissing her again, this time on the mouth. He tasted deliciously of toothpaste, his skin smooth and faintly scented with shaving soap. 'Good morning,' he whispered, his face alight with mischief.

Jo found her own expression breaking into a delighted smile.

'Good morning indeed.'

'Did you sleep?' he asked.

She shook her head. 'Not a wink.'

'Me neither.'

He took the cup she offered.

'Travis . . .'

He held up his hand to stop her. 'Please . . . don't say it again. Don't tell me we can't, or we shouldn't, or it's wrong.' He shrugged. 'We're not hurting anyone.'

'Cassie and Nicky . . .'

'What about them?'

'Just . . .'

'If you don't want to, that's different.' His look was cautious, appraising. She felt her heart contract.

'Want to?' Her question was like an echo, it was all she could manage.

He put his mug down, laughed, a soft, musical sound, his hand running up and down her bare arm. 'Well if you don't know what I mean . . .'

For a reply she leaned forward and stroked her fingers gently across his mouth, his breath warm on her skin.

'Oh, I definitely know what you mean.'

She heard a soft gasp. 'God . . . don't do that.' He pulled her fiercely into his arms, but she heard Cassie's door and moved quickly away, trying to control her breathing and still the ferocious pounding of her heart.

Trained actor that he was, Travis greeted Cassie with the utmost normality. Jo, meanwhile, took out the whole-meal loaf she'd made the day before – to pass the time – set it on the board and began vigorously slicing, her back to the room.

'Hi, darling,' she said, without looking round.

Cassie, already dressed, her hair freshly washed and shiny, plonked herself down at the table. Jo set the coffee pot in front of her with a mug.

'I'm making toast.'

'Thanks.' Her daughter hesitated. 'OK, guys . . . progress on the marital front. Matt and I talked last night and he's coming up.' She sounded nervous but Jo could tell she was also pleased. 'He said he'd take an early train, so he should be here by midday.'

'Is he coming here?'

'That was the plan, but if you think it's be awkward, we could meet somewhere else.'

Jo found it hard to focus her thoughts, drag them

away from the man only inches away from her, calmly sipping his black coffee.

'Umm . . . it's up to you, darling. We can make ourselves scarce, can't we?' She glanced at Travis, who nodded.

'Sure, I have to be in town to meet a guy about a job this morning. I'll stay out until I get the all clear.'

Cassie gave him a vague smile, but didn't say anything for a moment. 'I suppose if we're going to argue, it'd be better not to do it in public.'

'Negative thinking. Not good,' Travis said, coming to sit next to her. 'See it as a chance to reconnect, not an opportunity to fight.'

Cassie stared at him. 'You obviously haven't met Matt.'

'He's right, though.'

'Yeah, well, OK for you two to say. Of course I'm going to try and be positive, but he's so bloody stubborn.'

Jo smiled. 'Takes one to know one.'

Her daughter glared at her for a moment, then her face relaxed into a grin. 'Maybe that's the problem.'

'At least he's making the effort to come up and meet you, leave the farm for once. That must mean something.'

'I suppose.' She gave a long, drawn-out sigh.

Matt texted to say he was on his way just after half past eleven. Jo had been in her office, trying unsuccessfully to write and mostly Googling Travis, finding a number of publicity photos of him which she inspected with care. She had no idea what she would do while Matt was here, or if she should even stay to greet him. As she sat there at her computer, staring at a headshot of the American there was a ping from her mobile. A text from the man himself: 'Lunch?'

She barely hesitated, 'Where?'

They agreed to meet at a pub by the river in Chiswick. She'd been there once, years back, with Lawrence. She rushed into her bedroom to change, settling on black jeans, a pretty, dark-green vest top with a lacy edge, pumps and a soft, stone-coloured cardigan.

'Wow, you look nice,' Cassie, still at the kitchen table reading the newspaper, greeted her. 'Where're you off to?'

'I thought I'd go into town and potter about. Do you want me to stay and say hello to Matt?'

'Would you? If you're not here, he might think you're angry with him or something.'

Matt looked tired and out of place. He had made no effort to change out of his jeans, heavy boots and anorak – he looked as if he'd come to do the garden – although mercifully the hat was missing. If he'd arrived in the 'stupid beanie', as Cassie called it, Jo knew it would have been all over.

'Hello.' Jo went to hug him.

'Hi, Jo.' He put his backpack down.

Cassie got up and they gave each other a self-conscious hug.

'Was your trip up OK?' Jo asked.

'Yeah . . . pretty much. Took ages. I left at six-thirty.' He brushed his dark hair off his face, tucked it behind his ear and looked around slightly bemused, as if the environment of a normal house were totally alien to him. Jo was immediately aware that there was no recycling bin – although she did make an effort to recycle bottles and newspapers when she remembered.

'I'll make some tea,' she suggested. Cassie hadn't said a word, and the stubborn look on her face didn't bode well.

'No, Mum. I'll do that. You get off.' She turned to her husband. 'Mum has a meeting in town.'

'OK.'

'I'll be back later,' Jo said, dying to get away from the strained atmosphere. It'll be better when I'm gone, she thought, searching around for her keys as the silence continued behind her. 'Text you when I'm on the way back,' she said to Cassie as she gave her a kiss goodbye. 'Eat anything in the fridge.'

She cringed as she let herself out, hoping Matt wouldn't think the fridge reference was a deliberate dig.

The pub was ancient, the bar room tiny with an open fire. Travis had texted her to say he was outside, one of the few people to be so – it was

189

quite chilly and looked like rain – seated at a table overlooking the river. Busy on his iPad, he leaped up as she approached.

'Hi.'

'Hello.'

'Is outside OK? We can move if . . .'

'It's great.' She sat down next to him.

'You're not cold?'

She smiled. 'Not yet.'

'This place is awesome.' He waved towards the historic building. 'You know Alec Guinness and Hemingway drank here?'

'Really?'

He grinned. 'You're not impressed?'

'No, I am. I just wonder what Hemingway was doing out this way?' Jo almost shook with anticipation beside him. She talked, but she hardly knew what she was saying.

'So how did the audition go?'

'Hard to tell. The guy was super friendly, all over me. But that means nothing.'

'What was it for?'

'Experimental theatre group. They do weird things in warehouses with people wandering about in the dark.'

'Grim. Hate all that. I've never recovered from a trendy audience-participation thing at the Roundhouse in the seventies. A chicken landed in my lap and I nearly died of fright.'

He laughed. She laughed. The formality dropped away.

'Glad you could make it.' He took her hand.

They ordered hamburger and chips, diet Cokes. Travis's choice, but she went along with it – the menu was a step too far for her wandering concentration.

She knew only one thing. She wanted to kiss him, right then and there, in the open air, at the table by the river. Let everyone see them . . . from the passing boats, from the river walk, from the pub behind them. She held her breath.

'You know this is bonkers.'

He nodded. 'Sure.'

'What should we do?'

'Hmm . . . I know what I'd like to do right now.'

His arm went round her, pulling her towards him. The kiss was tender, drawn out. The flood of pleasure from his touch washed away any need to pin down the future. Life was short. She must savour every tiny, perfect moment she was being offered.

'Did you see Matt?' he asked, when the arrival of their lunch drew them apart.

'Briefly. Not very promising.'

'Was he angry?' Travis picked up one of his hot, salty chips and took a tentative bite.

'Not sure. He looked exhausted. And Cassie didn't exactly welcome him with open arms.'

'Oh dear.'

'Surely they'll work it out. They've only been married for ten minutes.'

Travis shrugged. 'Doesn't take long for a marriage to fuck up.'

'Took me decades.'

'Yeah, but *is* your marriage fucked? He's having a moment, maybe you are too. Doesn't have to be over.'

She stared at him. 'I can't think like that, it drives me mad.'

There was silence.

'Hey . . . don't look so sad.'

'Sorry.' She tried to smile.

'You know you have incredibly beautiful eyes.'

Lawrence had said so, many times, but that didn't diminish the intense pleasure she got from Travis's quiet declaration.

'I wish there was somewhere we could go,' she whispered, her body on fire, absolutely bursting with pent-up desire. 'Maybe Matt will whisk Cassie back to Devon . . .'

Travis didn't reply.

It started to rain, just spitting at first, but the wind had got up, the clouds overhead dark and threatening. He held his hand out for hers.

'I guess we oughta get undercover.'

CHAPTER 11

25 September 2013

Travis passed his iPad across the kitchen table to Jo with a grin. The *Independent's* review of the play – the first night had been yesterday – was displayed on the screen. It was respectful of the production over all, but a bit constrained in its praise, saying that the writing lacked 'depth'. However, Travis had been singled out for his 'vibrant' performance.

'Good, hey?'

'Fantastic. I'm so pleased for you. Are there others?'

'Yeah . . . a few so far. One said I was "worth watching", another that mine and Nicky's performances "outshone the dialogue" . . . all good for both of us.'

'I'm glad he got a mention too.'

Travis had been absorbed by the play in the days since their lunch by the river, the first night hanging over his head, obsessing him, making him distracted and tense. Jo had welcomed the time to herself. She found the

193

courtship overwhelming. Part of her wished it would end there, with a few sweet kisses, those magical moments of sexual desire that had woken her out of her lethargy, brought her back to life. But that part of her barely had a foothold. Travis was taking up all her waking thoughts, despite her knowing it could never have a future. Did she honestly have the willpower to stop it before it went any further?

And there was Cassie. It hadn't gone well with Matt, as Jo had predicted. The day he'd visited, Jo had returned from the pub on her own to find her daughter lying sobbing on the sofa.

'I don't know what to do,' she'd gasped out the words as soon as she saw her mother. 'It was horrible.'

'What was horrible? What did he say?'

Cassie had dragged herself upright, blowing her nose and wiping her eyes with a wet, crumpled tissue clasped in her hand.

'It wasn't so much what he said, but he was so cold . . . so judgemental. Basically he expects me to snap out of it, get my priorities straight.'

'Snap out of what?'

'My princess behaviour? Apparently it's the only thing holding me back from my destiny by his side.'

'What did you say to that?'

Cassie let out a long-suffering sigh. 'I said I needed to know he still loves me. But Matt doesn't talk about love very well. He sort of takes it for granted that we love each other. Thinks it's childish that I have to keep asking.'

'That's not fair.'

'Yeah, well, you've met his mother . . . touch of your *Mommie Dearest*. And maybe he's right. Maybe I am a princess, a spoiled brat who's missing out on the real world.' She mumbled something that Jo didn't catch and burst into tears again.

'He wasn't always like this was he?' she asked, when Cassie had calmed down a bit. 'That's one of the things I liked about him, he really seemed to love you.'

Her daughter gave her a wan smile. 'Perhaps the *only* thing you liked about him.'

'No . . . I mean Matt's always been a bit . . . serious . . . but Dad and I never doubted he was a good man.'

'Doesn't mean I can stay married to him.'

'So how did you leave it?'

'It was a bit of an impasse. Neither of us would really admit we were at fault. But we were sort of making a go of pretending things'd work out until he realized I wasn't coming home with him. Then he just stormed out.'

'Oh, dear.' Jo felt sympathy for her daughter, but she was despairing of the outcome. She didn't feel she had the energy right now to deal with Cassie moping about the house all day. And selfishly she wanted the place to herself.

'So what are you going to do next?'

Cassie shrugged. 'Get a job. Have some fun.' She shot a glance at her mother. 'Stay here for a bit . . . if that's OK, Mum?'

'I don't think you can give up on Matt like this, darling. You told me you still love him.'

'I *do*.'

'Well, you can't just throw in the towel after one row. Dad and I had millions of them over the years. You just have to work through it.' Which was true, she and Lawrence had rowed. But the subjects had been petty, mostly the normal flashpoints between couples, such as use of money – Lawrence, the tight-wad, Jo, the spendthrift – childcare and whether one of them should have turned left or right at the last junction. They hadn't even rowed about Arkadius.

Cassie raised her eyebrows. 'But Dad loved you, Mum. It was totally obvious, even if he didn't say it much.'

Jo just nodded. She hated Cassie's use of the past tense.

They both heard the front door open.

'Hi. How's it going?'

Her daughter sat up straighter at the sound of Travis's voice and brushed her rumpled hair back from her face.

'To be honest, darling, I'm sort of over all this prevarication,' Donna commented, not lifting her head from the pot on the wheel. They were once again in her studio hut, early in the

196

morning. Jo had fallen into a pattern of not being able to sleep. She would drop off, then wake around three and just lie there, her mind whirling with thoughts of Travis. This morning she had given up on sleep as soon as she saw the lights on in the hut. Donna's face was already streaked with dried grey-white clay, like a Native American, her hair sticking up at all angles, her apron tied over tartan cotton pyjamas. 'Why can't you and Travis just come clean about your relationship?'

'It's not a relationship,' Jo objected.

Donna rolled her eyes. 'Whatever. Look, neither of you is attached in any way. You're not blood relatives. You don't have an STD . . . as far as I know. So what's the problem?'

'I don't know . . .'

Donna waited for her to continue.

'Don't get annoyed, but his age I suppose. It's embarrassing. I couldn't bear Cassie or Nicky finding out. They'd be disgusted.'

'He's not twelve, for God's sake.'

'I know, but it's so undignified. And hitting on such a gorgeous man – way out of my league.'

'No point in hitting on a man who *isn't* gorgeous, darling. And he's hardly objecting, is he? In fact from what you say, he's the keen bean.'

Jo absentmindedly ran her finger along the wooden table, lifting the edge of the cotton duck cover. It wasn't just Travis's age that bothered her. It was something much more fundamental.

Acknowledging her sexual feelings for the American cruelly reminded her of her own mother. Rampant and sexually indiscriminate throughout her marriage, Betty – Jo found out later in an excoriating denunciation by her father – had hit on anything that moved. As a child, Jo had been unaware of the cause of her parents' continual fights. But as she reached teenage and began to notice the coy, flirtatious behaviour her mother exhibited towards the men who visited the house – from houseguests to Jo's piano teacher to handymen or the gardener – the light dawned. It was the advent of the teenage boys from the correctional facility down the road, employed to help with the garden, which finally proved Betty's undoing. Jo silently shuddered as she remembered that May morning. She'd never told anyone except Lawrence, not even Donna, what she'd found when she went out to take the Labrador, Duke, for a walk.

'Now Cassie's staying . . . there's no chance we'll be able to take it any further.' She sighed, shaking off the past, her thoughts returning to Travis, the feel of his lips touching hers. Her body melted at the thought. 'And maybe that's for the best. Maybe he should hook up with her anyway. It'd be much more suitable.'

'Suitable if he fancied her, which clearly he doesn't.'

'Not so sure. She's such a beautiful girl.'

'Sexual attraction isn't to do with beauty though,

is it? It's to do with something indefinable . . . affinity . . . something.'

Jo didn't reply.

'Can't you get rid of Cassie for a couple of days? Send her off to stay with a friend or something?'

'How? And it'd probably be pointless . . . nothing'd necessarily happen.'

Donna yanked the wheel to a stop and shook her head at Jo, her face breaking into an amused grin. 'Listen darling, if you've already made up your mind that you can't have him, then so be it. Give up. It may be your only chance to have hot sex with a totally stunning guy you clearly fancy the pants off . . . but hey, your choice.'

Jo smiled back. 'OK, get the message.'

'Obviously it's safer to sink into dignified old age. Obviously. But you may never meet someone you're this attracted to again. Think of hens' teeth . . . rare as . . .'

'And the children?'

'Why don't you just bonk him and worry about the consequences later? That's what Lawrence did and they're still speaking to him.'

The Shepherd's Bush house settled into a strange sort of rhythm. Ignoring Donna's advice, Jo avoided Travis as much as possible. And if she did see him, made stalwart efforts to restrain herself from flirting, because she couldn't deal with her own insecurity. He had his play to concentrate on, she reasoned, and she should be working too, making a proper start on the book.

Cassie was all over the place, crying hysterically at times, quietly manic at others as she made too many cupcakes or sanded every inch of rust off the garden table. She might stay out late with friends or sit morosely in front of a weepy rom-com nursing a glass of wine. But whatever she was doing, Jo couldn't get through to her. At every attempt to discuss how Cassie was feeling, to find out what her plan was, she came up against a brick wall:

'I'll sort it, Mum. I will, promise.'

Instead her daughter poured out her heart to Travis whenever she got the chance. Jo would find them together at the kitchen table, heads bent close, Cassie in full flow about Matt and the iniquities of a sustainable life in Devon.

Jo cringed as she watched her daughter's wide grey eyes become translucent with impending tears, Travis's face a mask of concern. With every passing day she steeled herself, forced her feelings for the actor deeper inside, burying them beneath a practised rationality which had saved her in the past: It was over. It had been sweet while it lasted. She was a fool.

One Saturday night, Cassie was out at a concert with some of her old college friends. She knew Travis wouldn't be back until late – Saturday being the night when he and Nicky and other friends who'd come to see the play would go drinking. Jo sat reading on the sofa. She must have dropped off momentarily, because the next thing she was aware of was Travis delivering a light kiss to her mouth. She hadn't heard him come in.

Shaking herself, her heart jerking into a frantic rhythm, she looked up into his face as he leaned across the sofa back, his broad shoulders straining the washed out navy T-shirt. He had an uncertain expression on his face.

'Hey,' he said softly, his eyebrows raised in question. He came round and sat down beside her, gave her a quizzical look.

'So is it over . . . you and me? Kinda got the impression you'd backed off this last week or so.'

Jo found she was tense, having him so close.

'I suppose . . .'

He waited, his brown eyes unwavering. 'It's OK if—'

'No. No, it's true I've backed off. But not because my feelings have changed.' She paused. 'I thought, you've got the play . . . and Cassie being around . . .'

He looked puzzled. 'So you and me are good?'

Didn't he understand? she asked herself. He spoke as if their relationship were completely straightforward: you liked someone. Your feelings were reciprocated. End of.

'I just find it impossible, living on the edge, seeing you every day, not being able to . . . you know . . . be with you . . . be open about what's happening because of Cassie and Nicky.' The words stumbled over each other in her desire to explain. 'We never have time alone and we're not likely to and it's driving me mad. But even if we did, we'd always be looking over our shoulder in case they find out.'

Travis, as soon as she paused to draw breath, began to laugh.

'Awesome . . . you're awesome. All this churning around in your head and you don't say zip to me? What's that about?'

Jo was baffled at his laughter. 'I didn't know how to say it.'

'So it's not an "I'm-just-not-into-a-relationship-right-now" moment?'

She could tell he was teasing and she smiled.

'OK, OK . . . this isn't easy for me, you know,' she said. 'You're all Californian about stuff . . . all "whatever" . . . but me, I'm old-style British with my feelings.'

He didn't answer. He just pulled her into his arms and held her tight against him until she gave in and relaxed in his embrace, her head tucked into the crook of his neck.

'I find you incredibly attractive,' she heard him say. 'And we are sort of alone . . .'

Jo caught her breath, swallowing hard.

'We can't . . . Cassie might come home any minute.'

Travis shrugged, playing with a strand of her hair. 'The gig's at the O2. Finishes around ten thirty, then she'll hang out, have some beers, the journey home'll take for ever. Midnight, earliest . . . which leaves us . . .' he checked his phone, 'An hour and a half.' It was as if he'd worked it all out in advance.

He was already off the sofa, pulling her to her feet, his eyes suddenly shining and full of desire. 'It's now or never.'

The limited time slot drove them on. Without another word, they ran, light-footed, hand-in-hand upstairs. Her room, the bed, so exclusively the domain of her marriage to Lawrence – she still slept on 'her' side – looked different tonight. The coloured quilt, the pure white duvet and pillows appeared almost anonymous to Jo, just the perfect haven for their thwarted desire. And he gave her no chance to worry about her body, whether her breasts were firm enough, her skin soft enough.

'Let me,' Travis said, staying her hands as she began to undress, his fingers fumbling with the buttons on her shirt in his haste. Carried away on a wave of desire, every cell in her body aching for his touch, she let him. Then panic swept in. Revealing her body to him, surely then he would reject her, see her finally for what she was: an old woman.

She pushed his hands away, stood solid and shaking, almost in tears she wanted him so much, but at the same time felt she couldn't possibly deserve him. Travis gave her a quizzical look, then pulled her to him, still clothed, his embrace so tender that the tears did well in her eyes.

'You do want this, don't you?' he whispered. 'Say if you don't.'

She couldn't speak, couldn't move. But, as Travis began to drop urgent kisses on her mouth, his breath ragged, his body wired as it pressed hard against her own, she forgot that she was old, forgot that she was scared. All that existed was her need. And when finally she stood naked before him, she felt no shame at all, just an overwhelming elation, an intoxicating sexual power.

'God . . .' she heard him expel a long, slow breath as he lay on his back, naked beside her. 'That was awesome.'

She wanted to laugh, to sing, the pleasure bubbling up inside her.

'Wasn't it,' she whispered, 'Just perfect.' Although at first their bodies had been awkward together, bumping limbs, eager but clumsy like teenagers in a car. But their desire quickly made the mechanics irrelevant as they found in each other matching heights of sexuality and passion.

'I thought it'd never happen,' he said.

She rolled on to her side to look at him. His body was breathtaking: lean and muscled and golden, a tan line marking out the lower, paler part of his stomach where his swimming costume must have been over the summer. Just looking at him aroused her again, she wanted to caress every inch of his skin, but she was once again self-conscious of her own less than perfect figure, reaching for the duvet and quickly pulling it over herself. He seemed not to notice her discomfort, laying his palm against her cheek so lovingly, smiling into her face. She closed her eyes for a second, revelling in his warm touch.

'I should probably go,' he whispered, glancing over her shoulder at the bedside clock. 'It's almost twelve and we don't want to turn into pumpkins.' He bent down and kissed her lightly on the lips, his expression breaking into a satisfied grin. 'Can't trust a guy to stick around once he's had his evil way.' He leaped out of bed, gathering up his scattered jeans, T-shirt and boxers from the floor as he went.

She lay there after he'd gone, dizzy from their lovemaking. Compared to what had become of her sexual relations with Lawrence over the past year, it had been explosive. But you can't compare, she cautioned herself, remembering lazier but no less sensually satisfying moments with her husband over the years.

Now her body resonated with Travis's caresses. She felt he was still by her side as she snuggled down under the duvet and closed her eyes, the final release of her desire leaving her limbs light and insubstantial, her head giddy.

Minutes later, she heard the front door closing, her daughter's tiptoed step on the stairs and along the corridor to the bathroom. She reached over and clicked off the bedside light, holding her breath in the dark at the close call, anxious not to have to confront her and pretend all was normal. As she did so she heard Cassie whisper outside her door, 'Night, Mum.'

'Night, darling,' Jo replied.

'Penny for 'em . . . you were miles away.' Cassie took the coffee jug from the table and poured herself a cup.

Jo, clutching her own mug, came to guiltily. She'd been replaying the lovemaking as she sat at the kitchen table the next morning – she almost couldn't believe what had happened – and wondering if this was how Lawrence felt about Arkadius. Wondering, if the boot had been on the other foot, would she have left Lawrence for Travis? But however much she yearned to gaze on his face, to touch his cheek, to make love to him right now, she knew she wouldn't even have looked at Travis if she and Lawrence had still been together. Well, she thought, repressing a small smile, I might have looked . . .

Cassie, not waiting for an answer, sat down. 'Matt was on the phone for hours last night. He rang at bloody two in the morning.'

She did look exhausted, her face wan, huge dark patches beneath her eyes. And she'd been crying. Jo took a deep breath and tried to banish Travis from her mind for a moment.

'What did he say?'

'Basically, if I choose not to come home, he'll see it as tantamount to a decision.'

'You mean a decision to break up?'

Her daughter nodded tiredly.

'I suppose he has a point . . . in that you'll probably never sort it out from here.' Cassie didn't look at her, just picked at a bit of candle wax on the table. 'Don't you think?'

'Yeah . . . yeah.'

'If it doesn't work out, then at least you gave it your best shot.' Jo didn't know what else to say. Another discussion about her daughter's marriage – which would inevitably be circular, with almost no chance of resolution – was quite beyond her this morning.

'You think I should go, don't you,' Cassie muttered resentfully.

'I think you should, yes.' Jo took her daughter's hand. 'You're in limbo here. It's not good for you.'

'I suppose I could go for a week . . . I can always leave again if he's being ridiculous.'

'Give it a proper go, though. Don't just issue an ultimatum and then leg it if he doesn't comply.'

Cassie's eyes hardened. 'Like I'd do that, Mum. You don't have much faith.'

'Of course I do.'

'Yeah, but you never thought I should have left him in the first place. OK, so your generation just rolled over and let the man get his way, however it made you feel. But we're not like that. We expect to be happy . . . and what's wrong with that?'

'Nothing. And I didn't "roll over", as you put

it. Dad and I had a pretty equal relationship. I didn't let him get away with things.'

Cassie raised her eyebrows. 'Ha! You reckon?'

'What do you mean?'

'Well . . . just that you always did all the cooking and cleaning and shopping and gardening and maintenance and childcare and he just wandered off to his much more important work whenever it suited him.'

'It wasn't like that.'

'You didn't even make a fuss when he left you, Mum. You just let him go as if it was another one of the perks of being married to you. Sure, darling, if you really fancy him, you'd best get off and do what you have to do.' Cassie's face was set and angry.

Jo just stared at her, fighting back a sudden urge to cry in the face of her daughter's attack.

'I didn't see there was anything else I could do,' she said quietly.

'You could have fought for him! Told him not to be such an idiot, told him that he absolutely COULD NOT leave you.' Cassie paused. 'Told him you loved him, Mum. He was probably just testing the waters . . . most likely he never actually meant to go. But when you just sat there and let him, without a word, he must have thought you didn't care.'

'You have no idea what I said to your father.'

'Haven't I? OK, I wasn't there, but you said on the bus from the station, when you came to stay, that nothing had really changed for you. I mean what sort of a message is that to a man? That his presence is so irrelevant that him leaving you doesn't affect your life in the slightest.'

Jo was stunned. 'I never said that.'

'You did. Honest, Mum.'

She was silent, quickly dismissing the notion that Lawrence didn't know she cared. Of course he did. Anyway, it would be ridiculous to test her in that way. And of course she'd told him that she didn't want him to leave . . . she must have. Then she had a thought.

'Is this really about you and Matt? About him not saying that he needs you? OK, maybe I should have been tougher when Dad told me about Arkadius. But I don't want to be with a man who is in love with someone else . . .' She stopped, looked hard at her daughter. 'You don't think Matt's in love with someone else, do you?'

Cassie shook her head, began to laugh. 'Blimey, not sure how you came to that bizarre conclusion. Christ no! Unless it's Hammy, one of the new pigs . . . he does spend a great deal of time with her.'

Jo didn't laugh. She should be used to her daughter's onslaughts, but they always caught you unawares.

'This thing with you and Dad,' Cassie was saying, 'has made me think, obviously . . . about marriage. If you two can fall apart so quickly, after so long, it makes the whole thing seem a bit pointless. I mean, how can you trust anything in a relationship?'

Jo didn't know how to answer. Cassie's face was suddenly contrite.

'Listen, I didn't mean to badger you like that. I'm not blaming you for Dad being a prat . . . he doesn't need help with that. I just hate to see you giving in like this. As if you didn't care.' She put her arms round her mother as she sat there at the table and squeezed her shoulders, dropped a kiss on her cheek.

'You know I care,' Jo said.

'Course I do. I just wonder if Dad does.'

Jo sighed. 'Well if he doesn't, then he's a bigger numpty than either of us takes him for.'

Cassie laughed. 'Yeah, well.' She turned away. 'I *will* go back . . . just not yet. I don't want him thinking he can click his fingers and I'll come running. I'll go next week.'

CHAPTER 12

13 October 2013

For the next two days, Cassie barely left the house. Travis kept sidling up to Jo whenever they were momentarily alone and putting his arms around her, whispering 'Come to bed' in her ear, making her laugh, driving her mad with lust. Finally Cassie went off to buy a new backpack, some trainers, a pair of jeans, so as to avoid the charity shops on her return to Devon.

Minutes after she had gone, Travis was lounging against the wall, watching Jo as she loaded the washing machine and thrust a pouch of lavender liquid detergent to the back of the drum.

He grinned suggestively. 'Cassie's out. What say you we go upstairs and fool around for a while?'

'Now?' She knew she must have looked shocked.

Travis roared with laughter. 'Never saw the rule says you have to wait for cover of darkness before you make love.'

'You've obviously been very badly brought up then.'

She began to laugh with him, and soon they

were giggling out of control, gasping for breath. When he eventually took her hand and led her upstairs, she was ready for anything.

Later, as they lay next to each other, his arm beneath her head, Jo said softly, 'You don't mind, that there isn't a plan?' Their lovemaking had begun playful, teasing, this time, not like the explosive haste of that first night, but soon became just as intense. Unlike Lawrence – and Jo found it hard not to make the comparison – Travis liked to take his time, bringing her to the brink and back, taking her body to an almost unbearable pitch of sensation where she was beyond thought, unaware of anything but his expert touch. Jo's body still sang from it, her skin almost bruised by the unaccustomed physicality.

'A plan for what?'

'Us.'

'OK . . .'

'I've always had a plan before. Sort of A follows B follows C. Now there isn't one.'

Travis turned to her and kissed her hair. 'What sort of plan did you have in mind?'

'I don't know.' She sighed. 'I mean . . . I know there can't be one . . . but I struggle with that . . . I want to just go with what's happening . . . but . . .'

'Everyone's the same,' he said. 'It isn't normal not to project into the future.'

'So you do too.' She looked up at him.

'Sure I do, but I try not to. I got kinda obsessed with *The Power of Now* a while back. Studied it every night for months, going over and over it, trying to leave my ego behind, stay in the moment. Real hard, but I want to live my life like that if I can. Not forever angsting about the past or projecting into the future.'

He sounded earnest suddenly, and very young.

'Isn't that just an excuse for wandering through life never making any commitments?'

'The future has a habit of sorting itself out if you don't look it in the eye too much.' He sounded almost detached as he spoke. 'Way Mom raised us,' he went on, 'it was all about waiting for Judgement Day. Which basically meant closing your life down, never enjoying any damn thing along the way . . . just in case it was a sin.'

'At least you die good, I suppose.'

'Die of *trying* to be good, more like.'

She smiled. 'No fun in that.'

Neither of them spoke.

'I don't have anything to offer you except now, Jo,' Travis said softly.

And she knew he was right, knew it would have to be enough.

The weather had turned nasty. It was cold, with autumn gales, a lot of rain. The plants in the garden were soggy and bedraggled. But Jo liked this time of year, the drawing in after the summer, the cosiness of a fire and warm jumpers, hot stews and sleeping longer because of the late dawn.

Cassie still hadn't gone back to Matt. There was always an excuse: the dentist; meeting a friend she hadn't seen for ages; a bad cold. So Jo and Travis took their chances when they could: breathless, thrilling, snatched moments, made better by their unpredictability.

It was after one such moment, a Sunday morning, when Cassie had stayed over with her friend Hatty, that Jo's phone rang. She was still lying in bed beside Travis, although it was late. It was the first time they had slept together all night and they were revelling in the fact. Jo saw her husband's name on the phone display and groaned. Classic, she thought, that he'd pick *this* morning to ring. She didn't take the call, just waited and listened to the voicemail. He hadn't rung for weeks now, not even to hassle her about the house, and she wondered what he wanted.

'Umm . . . Jo, it's me,' she heard. 'Will you call me as soon as you get this message. It's important.'

Jo sat up in bed. 'He sounds serious. I'd better call him.'

'Shall I go?' Travis was already half out of bed but she pulled him back.

'Stay. I won't be long.'

Travis sank back against the pillows as she dialled. Lawrence answered on the first ring.

'Jo, hi. Thanks for ringing back. Listen, I just

got a call from Janet . . . your dad's neighbour? It's . . . not good news.'

Jo held her breath, clutching the duvet to her naked body. 'Is he dead?'

'No, but he's in a bad way. A massive stroke. He's in the Queen Elizabeth The Queen Mother in Margate. Janet says they aren't sure he'll make it.'

'Oh.' She didn't know what else to say.

'I'll come with you if you like.'

'No, no. Thanks, but I'm not going.'

There was silence on the other end of the phone.

'Jo . . . it might be best . . . to see him.' His voice was soft, loving in a way it hadn't been, she realized, for a long time.

'Why did Janet ring you and not me?' she found herself asking, irrelevantly.

'You remember, the last time we went . . . I gave her my number as we left?'

Jo didn't remember, but she wasn't surprised she hadn't.

'And I suppose, well, she must have thought we'd be in the same place.'

She wasn't listening to him. Just trying to beat off memories of that horrible day.

'Jo . . .'

'I've got to go,' she interrupted him. 'I'll ring Janet now. Thanks for letting me know.'

She didn't wait to hear if he spoke again, just clicked off her phone, suddenly unable to move.

Travis was looking at her. 'Bad news.'

'My father. He's had a stroke. He's in hospital.'

'Hey . . . sorry about that. Was he sick?'

She shook her head. 'I don't know. I haven't seen him for a long time . . . four years . . . maybe longer.'

'You fell out?' He crawled over to her and sat next to her on the side of the bed, taking her hand.

'You could say that.' She felt the air restricted in her chest and tried to take long, slow breaths. 'I'm not going,' she said, although Travis hadn't spoken.

'I'll come with you.'

She stared at him, pulling her hand away. 'Didn't you hear what I said? I'm not going.'

'Sure I heard. But people say things they don't mean when they're in shock. You should go. He's your dad.'

'Is this some Christian thing? You think I need to forgive him?'

Travis looked puzzled. 'Listen, I don't even know what went on between you guys. But I know it'll mess with your head if you don't see him and he goes ahead and dies.'

'Let it.'

He raised his eyebrows. 'I'll drive you. We shouldn't waste time if he's so sick.' He stood up and began to pull on his black jeans, his shirt, his navy sweater. Jo just sat there silently, watching him.

'I can't.'

Travis pulled her to her feet, hugged her close. 'Come on.'

'You don't know what he said to me the last time I saw him. He hates me.'

'Doesn't matter. He's dying. He'll want you there. And once he's gone, it's over. You won't get a second chance.'

So she did what Travis told her, too stunned to argue. Finding herself, what seemed like moments later, fully dressed, in the car, Travis at the wheel, the Sat Nav burbling on, directing them to the A2 and Margate.

'You didn't have to do this,' she said. 'You'll be late for the theatre.'

'It's Sunday.'

'Of course it is. I forgot.'

She left brief messages for Cassie and Nicky, only telling them that her father was ill, not possibly dying. Neither of them had seen their grandfather since they were small anyway – he'd never been interested – but she knew they would be concerned on her behalf and she didn't want them panicking. She also spoke to Janet.

'Had he been ill?' she asked.

'Oh no. He was always very spry, Mr Hamilton . . . kept busy gardening and the like, tinkering with that old car of his. He never said anything to me about feeling poorly. But then he wouldn't have, would he? Wasn't the sort to complain.'

True, she thought, a stoic to the last. If he'd had

symptoms, he'd never have mentioned them to anyone, least of all bother the doctor.

Gerald Hamilton lay still, his eyes closed, a drip line leading to the back of his veined hand as it rested on the white cover. Jo was shocked at his gaunt appearance, his lack of substance. Her father had never been overweight, but he'd been big, a tall man who held himself in an almost military stance, a presence in any room. Now he lay diminished, almost childlike. She had no desire to wake him, so she sat on the blue hospital armchair beside the bed and waited, feeling suddenly foolish. Why have I come? she asked herself. This was stupid. He doesn't need me. He never did. She tried not to feel angry all over again. Then he opened his eyes.

For a moment the gaze meeting hers was unfocused. Then she saw recognition light in his eyes.

'Joanna?'

'Hello, Daddy.' She found herself taking his hand, despite herself, and he clasped it weakly in response, his hand dry and icy to the touch.

'What are you doing here?' The question wasn't aggressive, just bewildered.

'You've had a stroke.'

He didn't answer.

'You're in the hospital.'

'I know that.' His voice held that old sardonic note – so familiar to her.

'OK . . . well, that's why I'm here.'

'I'm dying, I suppose.'

'They say you're very ill.'

A small smile flitted across his dry lips and Jo saw a flash of the handsome, if cold, man who was her father. 'You never think it'll be you.'

'I suppose not.'

He closed his eyes for a few minutes and Jo thought he'd gone back to sleep. When he opened them he seemed almost surprised she was still there.

'Better say what I should have said a long time ago . . .' he paused, taking short, shallow breaths. 'Your mother . . .'

'There's no need to—' Jo said.

'Let me finish,' he interrupted. His pale eyes were sharp as he held her gaze. Jo was silent, intimidated even now by this frail, dying man, in exactly the way she had been all her life. 'Your mother . . . hurt me very badly. I still don't know why she did . . . what she did.' He took a few more breaths, swallowing with difficulty. 'But it was wrong of me . . . to blame you.' More breaths. 'Very wrong . . . unforgivable . . . for a father.'

'It's all right, Daddy.'

'It's not . . . all right . . .'

Gerald closed his eyes again, clearly exhausted by the exchange, his face falling back into itself. After a few minutes it seemed he had dropped back to sleep, his cheek-bones stark through the papery skin. She waited until the grasp of his hand loosened, then carefully extricated her own and crept from the room. Once outside she took a huge breath, as if she hadn't breathed at all as she sat next to her father.

Travis was waiting, sitting on a moulded plastic chair against the wall in the corridor. He jumped up when he saw her.

'OK?'

She nodded.

'Was he awake?'

'For a bit,' she said. 'Can we get some coffee?'

They sat side by side in silence in the hospital café, two sausage rolls and two mugs of strong tea between them – the coffee had looked suspicious to their spoiled London expectations of lattes and Americanos.

'Funny how you always want to love your parents . . . even if you don't much like them.'

'You never liked him?'

Jo wondered if she had. 'I think I was always scared of him. He was cold, so disapproving. And I got the feeling *he* didn't like *me*. But just now . . . seeing him so vulnerable . . . I don't know . . . it felt a bit like love.'

Travis stroked her hand. 'Must be hard.'

'He said he was sorry. Or at least he said he was wrong to think what he thought. Daddy never did do "sorry".'

He didn't ask what Gerald was sorry for, but now, unwillingly, she found herself telling him, reliving that day four years ago when she and Lawrence had made their annual visit to her father.

220

The visit – arranged always by Jo out of a sense of duty – had gone according to plan. Gerald, as usual, paid scant attention to her, his conversation mostly focused on Lawrence. They sat in the small sitting room of his seaside flat discussing world politics, particularly China, seldom referring to her or her opinions, as if the two men were totally alone. She and Lawrence had learned not to expect anything different; they just went through the motions.

As they were getting up to go, Lawrence asked if Gerald enjoyed living by the sea. His father-in-law had suddenly made the decision the previous year to move from Gloucestershire to Ramsgate. He had not looked at Lawrence, but stared hard at her.

'It's fine here. I know nobody. It suits me.'

The vindictive tone of his remark had puzzled her, made her wince, but she said nothing.

'It was all right for you, Joanna. You got out.'

'Of Gloucestershire?' she asked, not knowing what he was getting at. He'd lived in a village not far from the house she'd grown up in for decades and seemed perfectly content.

Then Gerald's face – normally so shuttered and controlled – had suffused with anger. He'd moved up close to her, his arms tight to his sides.

'How do you live with it? You killed that lad. You and your vile mother.'

Jo found she was shaking, as if he'd physically attacked her. 'Me?'

Gerald snorted, the sound harsh and cruel. 'Oh, Miss Innocent. Yes, you. Acting as your mother's pimp. Seducing him, drawing the poor boy in so that *she* could have him. You thought I was a fool, that I didn't know what you were both up to . . .'

Lawrence had moved between them now. 'Gerald, stop it, for God's sake. That's ludicrous. Jo was a child. She had nothing whatever to do with the boy's death.'

But her father, still strong enough to do so, pushed him roughly aside. 'Stay out of this.'

Jo didn't reply to her father. Her mind was elsewhere, back at that clear spring morning. How she'd got up, desperate to be outside, smell the cool air, feel the early sun on her skin. Duke, the Labrador, had been a willing companion as they left a trail of footprints across the dew-soaked lawn, making for the small gate behind the fruit cage which led to the open fields beyond. The Wellington tree, large and ancient with the oddly spongy bark she loved, sat in front of a wall of rhododendron bushes to the right of them. Something caught her eye as she drew level with the tree, and she turned to look. At first she couldn't process what she was seeing. It looked like a scarecrow dangling there, turning in the breeze, half hidden beneath the branches, dappled by the morning sun. But as she drew closer, she realized it was Bobby, seventeen years old, from the correctional facility down the road, helping with the garden that summer under the watchful eye of Mr Bennett, their full-time gardener.

Yes, she'd met Bobby in passing, around the garden, noticed his slim, dark good looks, his shy smile. She was fourteen, went to an all girls' school, hardly met members of the opposite sex of her own age. But she'd never said more than 'Hello' to him. He'd never said even that back, just shot her a shy grin.

She didn't remember much about the mayhem that followed her discovery. Only Duke barking frantically, jumping up at Bobby's swinging feet, heavy in the black scuffed work boots, half-laced. Then her running, heart bursting from her chest. Her mother screaming and screaming. The police. And her father, his face a mask, quietly patrician and in charge as he dealt with the local constable, but not speaking to, or looking at her or her mother throughout. Not once.

Then watching out of her bedroom window two days later, as he left the house without saying goodbye to her, throwing one small holdall into the boot of his precious ultramarine Alfa Romeo Giulietta. Setting off down the gravel drive at a sedate pace, as he might if he were heading for the golf club for a round with his friends. But never coming home.

'*Did* your mom seduce the boy?' Travis was asking.

Jo was hardly aware that she'd been speaking out loud. 'Who knows. I couldn't ask, but I very much

223

doubt it. He was so shy and so . . . young. Mr Bennett said the police put it down to Bobby being a bit disturbed, the location of our garden just a "convenience" . . . such an odd choice of word. The boys weren't popular in the area, as you can imagine. People attributed all sorts of stuff to them, mostly unfairly I'm sure.'

'But she had before . . . I mean with other men.'

Jo nodded. 'Apparently. My father said so anyway. Made a point of telling me what a dreadful slut Mum was the next time he saw me.' She paused. 'And he was certainly right that she was very flirtatious with men. But whether or not she seduced Bobby . . . and if she did, was it a contributory factor in his death, no one will ever know. She was certainly different after that: tearful, nervy, very needy. I felt I had to look after her.'

'Christ . . . how tragic. But he never accused you of pimping for her till four years ago.'

'No, that was a new one.'

'What did you say when he accused you?'

'He didn't give me a chance to say anything. Just went off on this crazy rant, as if Mum was the Madame of a brothel and I was the chief prostitute. I was just so stunned I couldn't speak. Lawrence had to drag me out. Dad even followed us outside, still yelling. It was appalling.'

'Must have had some kinda brain episode. It happens. They go a bit crazy sometimes, old people: lose their inhibitions. Basically lose their minds.'

'I know. But he seemed so sane until he started shouting at me. And he obviously remembers it, or he wouldn't have said what he did just now.'

'Tough on you whichever. Doesn't go away, shit like that.' Travis laid his arm across her shoulder, pulled him towards her. She closed her eyes, rested her head against him, grateful for the support.

'Jo?' She opened her eyes to see Lawrence standing on the other side of the grey laminate table, his eyes wide with surprise.

She sat up. 'Lawrence! What are you doing here?'

Her husband glanced at Travis, then at her. She knew she ought to feel embarrassed, but she had no energy for it. Travis had withdrawn his arm, but he still sat close, almost protective.

'I thought . . . you said you weren't coming. I just thought someone ought to.'

She nodded, touched that he would bother.

'Is he . . .?' Lawrence pulled out a chair, scraping the legs on the polished linoleum floor, and sat down.

'I spoke to him about an hour ago. He's very weak. But he was talking, knew who I was.'

Lawrence was clearly constrained by Travis's presence and the American got up.

'I'll go get some fresh air. Text me.' He touched her briefly on the arm and walked out through the swing doors. Jo watched him for a moment, then turned to her husband.

'Don't go there,' she warned, as she saw his eyebrows raised in question.

Gerald died that evening. Without a fuss, as he had lived. He waited till Jo, who had been sitting by his bedside all afternoon, holding his hand, slipped out for another cup of tea. He hadn't opened his eyes again, hadn't spoken to her in the interim. To Jo, his earlier apology seemed like the beginning of something, not the end. And although she knew better than to expect him suddenly to gaze into her eyes and say he loved her, she found herself waiting nonetheless; waiting for something more.

Jo sent Lawrence home. At one point he'd tried to hug her, but she held him off. She was anxious not to rely on him, it would have been too easy, because their shared history with her father seemed to supersede what had happened since – Lawrence knew her better than anyone else in the world.

'What do you want to do?' Travis asked, when the preliminary formalities had been dealt with. It seemed to Jo to be pretty straightforward, dying. A few forms to sign, a bag of personal possessions – which she didn't want but Travis insisted she take – numbers exchanged. Now they were making their way to the car park. It was nearly one o'clock in the morning, drizzling and cold. Jo shivered, clutched his arm.

'Don't know.'

'I can drive you home . . . or we can hole up somewhere, get some sleep.'

'I'd rather go home. Unless you're too tired to drive.'

226

'Home it is.'

Cassie must have been listening out for them.

'God, Mum. I'm so sorry.' She came down in her dressing gown, wrapped Jo in a long hug. 'I'd have come, but you made it sound like it wasn't serious.'

'It's OK,' she said. And it was. Travis had warned her she would have a reaction later, when it sunk in that her father was dead, but Travis had loved his father. She knew the only reaction she felt – and would continue to feel – was relief.

The funeral was miserable. Just Jo and the children, Janet from next door, Beth, the girl who'd cleaned for Gerald, huddled in the chilly crematorium in Margate. The vicar – a tough, direct woman in her fifties with the grey pudding-basin haircut so favoured by women priests – had called Jo in advance for background about her father for the eulogy. But Jo found it almost impossible to answer her questions. She put her in touch with Janet, who seemed to know him better.

The three of them sat in silence in the car on the way home.

'Are you sad, Mum?' Cassie asked.

'Sad for him, I suppose. I'm not sure he had such a great life. And selfishly, sad for me . . . that I didn't have a father I could relate to, one I could properly love.'

Neither of her children replied. She wondered if they were thinking about Lawrence, who'd asked if he could come to the funeral, but Jo had said no. He'd sounded upset that she didn't want him there, but pretending they were all still a single unit seemed like a lie. Was she punishing him? In a practical sense it didn't seem much of a punishment to be let off a visit to a dismal crematorium, miles from anywhere, for the funeral of a man he had hardly admired. But still, she knew she was exerting a mild form of retribution, telling him: you can no longer take it for granted that you're part of this family.

CHAPTER 13

1 November 2013

'Y ou'll come to the last-night party?' Jo was
sitting with Travis and Cassie in front of
the fire in the sitting room, each with a
glass of red wine. 'It's after the show Saturday.'

'Won't it just be the actors and play people?'

'I'm coming,' Cassie said, ignoring her mother.

'Reckon it'll be everyone,' Travis said. 'And
Nicky'll want you both there.'

Jo wasn't so sure about that. Nicky had been
strange since the funeral. She'd rung him a few
times, left messages, but he hadn't responded.
When she asked Travis if he was all right, the
American had seemed unaware that there was a
problem, beyond the usual one of the girlfriend,
of course.

'Have you spoken to him?' she asked her
daughter.

'Briefly, this morning.'

'It's just he hasn't returned any of my calls or
texts.'

Cassie shrugged. 'You know Nicks. Not the

229

greatest multitasker on the planet. It's Amber, Amber or the play, the play or Amber. You may get some action when at least the play's off the slate.'

'Maybe. I feel I've hardly seen him for months now.' She knew she was sounding peeved. She had to admit that her son's obsession with his girlfriend had proved surprisingly painful for her – despite always pitying women who couldn't let their children go. But it wasn't that at the moment. She was sensing a different sort of snub from Nicky.

Both Travis and Cassie were looking at her with sympathy, and she quickly made a joke of it. 'Yeah, yeah . . . jealous of another woman. Pathetic, isn't it?'

'Know how you feel,' Travis grinned. 'Hardly seen him myself, except on stage. Those two are so totally full-on.'

'He's pussy-whipped, poor boy,' his sister said, her tone infinitely superior. 'But he'll get bored, watch this space.'

Jo didn't need to worry about who would be welcome at the party at the theatre bar. As Travis had implied, the world and his wife were there, the place packed, the crowd chattering and ebullient, most holding drinks – some sort of sparkling wine, glasses of which were laid out in serried ranks along the length of the bar which ran the entire righthand side of the room.

Dotted around the walls were hanging posters of the play, a blurred image of Travis, his eyes dark and hypnotic, staring out from behind the play's title.

Cassie spotted Nicky and Travis talking with a group of people by a pillar in the centre of the room and they began to push their way towards them. There was no sign of Amber.

Travis saw them first. 'Hey . . . you made it. Great. I'll get you a drink.'

He began to elbow his way in the direction of the bar. Jo turned to Nicky.

'Hi, darling.' She went to hug him, but his face tightened and he stood stiffly, unwelcoming. 'Hi, Mum.' He gave her a perfunctory kiss on each cheek, then turned away almost immediately to talk to Cassie.

Jo was shocked. She wanted to grab him, ask him what the matter was, but she couldn't, not in this crowd of his fellow-actors and associates. She stood, numb, until Travis returned and thrust a glass into her hand.

'Cheers!' she said, putting aside her confusion to raise a glass to him. 'Congratulations!'

He grinned, 'Thanks. Yeah, it's been awesome. But kinda gutting when it's over and you know you'll never do it again. I guess the end of a run always feels like you lost a limb.'

She drew closer to him. 'Nicky's being weird with me . . . do you know why?'

The actor looked puzzled. 'Yeah? He hasn't

said anything to me.' He glanced across at her son, who was studiously ignoring them both. At that moment, a wiry, intense woman in her fifties, faded-blonde hair past her shoulders, dressed in jeans, a gold-coloured camisole and black jacket came up and grabbed Travis by the arm.

'Come with me, dearest, I need you to meet one of your biggest fans.'

'The producer,' Travis whispered to Jo, giving her an apologetic grin. 'Back in a sec.'

Jo didn't know what to do. She stood, clutching her glass, trying not to stare at her son, feeling foolish and very much alone in that crowd of chattering thespians. She tapped Cassie on the shoulder as she was talking to one of the other guests.

'I think I might sneak off.'

'Now?' Her daughter frowned. 'It's only just started.'

'Parties aren't really my thing.'

'OK . . . do you want me to come with you?'

'God no! But will you say goodbye to Nicky for me? Say I wasn't feeling well or something.'

Cassie gave her a puzzled look. 'He's just there, Mum.' She pointed to where Nicky stood, only feet away. 'Can't you tell him yourself?'

'Umm . . . don't want to interrupt . . . it's his night . . .' She kissed Cassie quickly on the cheek and moved off before her daughter could ask any more questions.

She tried to catch Travis's eye, but he was

leaning against the bar engrossed in conversation with a balding man about her age – heavy grey-tweed coat hanging open to reveal an expensive white shirt and jeans – whose florid complexion implied that he hit the bottle rather more than he should.

Jo walked home, hardly aware of the journey. She knew what was wrong with Nicky. Sensed it as soon as he stopped returning her calls. Lawrence. He must have told their son that he'd seen her in Travis's arms in the hospital canteen, the day her father died. And obviously Nicky was blaming *her*, not his friend, because Travis hadn't noticed anything amiss in their relationship.

On an angry impulse, she called Lawrence as she walked, not caring that it was late.

'I just asked him what was going on,' was Lawrence's reply to her accusation. 'I assumed he knew. You weren't talking to me, and I didn't want to bother you when your father was dying. But I think I have a right to know who you're having a relationship with.'

'You don't have a right to one single thing about me or my life, Lawrence.'

'All right . . . take that attitude if you like. But why are you so angry? And why haven't you told the children?'

'Why do you think? I know you don't find it the least bit embarrassing to be having sex with someone young enough to be your son, but I certainly do.'

233

There was silence at the other end of the phone, broken only by a martyrish sigh.

'So you *are* having sex with him. Nicky said that was ridiculous.'

'Well it might be ridiculous to him, and to you too, obviously. But I am. And I'm enjoying it hugely.' Her anger drove her to emphasize the last word with unnecessary relish.

'God, Jo . . .'

'What? Too much information?'

'No . . . no, of course not.' He sounded jumpy. 'I just wish you'd told me, that's all.'

'I don't see why it matters to you. *You've* got what *you* want.'

'It does matter to me. Of course it does.' There was a pause. 'He's living in my house, for starters.'

Jo was so astounded at Lawrence's words that her mobile almost slipped from her hand. She grabbed it and pressed it back to her ear.

She took a deep breath, steadied her tone. 'So basically it's the house – *your* house – you're worried about. Your concern has nothing whatever to do with Cassie and Nicky.'

'That's being childish. But it does make me wonder if he's the reason you're hanging on to it.'

'I'm not even going to answer that,' she said.

'You'll have to deal with the house situation sooner or later you know.' He had adopted his head teacher's tone. 'You can't keep burying your head, Jo, carrying on as if nothing's happened. And there's the children.' He was on a roll now, pompous ass. 'Even if you don't think I have the right to know, they certainly do.'

Jo didn't answer, regretting the impulse to call her husband in the first place. She was not going to admit to him that he was right about the children, although he was; she should have told them weeks ago. But just thinking of what she and Travis did together made her blush. And imagining Cassie and Nicky imagining it made her feel absolutely sick.

'Let's not argue,' she heard him say, his tone infinitely weary.

'No, let's not.'

The silence that followed implied they were unable to find a way to talk without doing so.

'Please don't discuss me and Travis until I've had a chance to talk to them,' she begged, hearing an echo of Lawrence's own words all those months ago, about Arkadius.

'I won't. But I really think we should get going on the house. Otherwise we'll have to wait till after Christmas.'

His words sounded suspiciously like blackmail to Jo: I won't cause trouble with the children over Travis as long as you play ball and put the house on the market. She didn't want to have another fight, so she said, 'I don't want to talk about that right now.' But there was no way on earth that she would even consider his request until after the New Year.

When she got home she was cold and shaken. She ran herself a hot bath and soaked in it for hours, her mind whirring. Thoughts about Cassie knowing – would Nicky have told her yet? – about facing Nicky, about Travis. Travis. The play was over. It wouldn't be long before he was offered another job. And it wouldn't be in London. It was bound not to be in London.

Jo dried herself and got into her pyjamas, but she knew there was no chance she would sleep yet. Maybe I should wait up and talk to Cassie tonight, she thought. So she wrapped herself in the rug and settled down to some late-night TV, channel-hopping back and forth, taking in little of the mainly brash, braying Saturday night chat shows or stand-ups on offer as she waited for the others to come home. When she heard the key in the lock, she sat up quickly, swung her legs off the sofa. Cassie, looking exhausted and hollow-eyed.

'What are you doing up, Mum?'

'Waiting for you.'

'Yeah . . .' Cassie peeled off her coat and scarf and threw herself in the armchair next to the sofa. She gave Jo a steady look, which she found hard to interpret.

'Nicky told you?'

Cassie nodded, let out a long breath. 'And I spoke to Travis. Nicky's furious. He and Travis are having it out as we speak. Nicks said he was only waiting till the play was over to say something.'

'I should have been more honest.' She couldn't meet her daughter's eye.

'You should. But I can see why you weren't.'

Jo was surprised that her daughter didn't appear more upset.

'I do feel a tad foolish . . . you two sneaking about behind my back, all loved up . . . and me not having a clue what was going on.'

'I know. I'm really sorry, darling. I'm ashamed of myself. But I thought you'd be so disgusted with me. Donna said I should come clean ages ago, but I just didn't have the nerve.'

'God . . . like I ever imagined my own parents . . . Go, Dad. Go, Mum. Tied first in the Most Embarrassing Parent competition.'

'I'm so sorry.'

Her daughter was silent for a moment.

'But you know what? Finally it's your life. Dad started it. I honestly don't blame you.'

'You don't? Even though he's so much younger than me?'

Cassie pushed her hair back from her face, gave out a big yawn. 'Our family used to be so normal it was almost worrying. Now look at us.' She started to laugh.

Jo, from sheer relief, joined in. Cassie came over and sat beside her mother, took her hand and gave it a squeeze. 'You're not in love with Travis are you, Mum?'

Jo held her breath. Love. She didn't know how to answer. 'It was so unexpected, finding him attractive like that,' she said eventually. 'And I never thought he'd feel anything for me in a million years.'

'Doesn't answer my question.'

'No . . . well, I'm not sure I can.' Jo took a deep breath. 'Anyway, he'll be off soon. And we both knew he would be. It's just . . . what it is.'

Cassie laughed. 'Right. That's perfectly clear then.'

'Sorry . . .'

They both stopped talking at the sound of Travis opening the front door. He came in without a word and sat down heavily in the chair Cassie had just vacated. He shook his head at them both.

'I guess I had it coming.'

'What happened?' Jo asked.

'We rowed, then I took off before he had a chance to land one on me. Boy was he mad. Said we'd all betrayed him . . . including Cassie. Said you must have known about us this whole time.'

'He's such a baby,' Cassie said. 'And I reckon that Amber girl winds him up. Us-against-the-world sort of stuff. It's how she keeps him onside.'

'Where was Amber by the way?' Jo asked.

'Probably at home starving herself,' Cassie said.

'Cassie . . .' Jo gave her daughter a reproving glance.

'She's been in all week,' Travis said, 'waiting for Nicky at the end of the show.'

'Then it's us she's trying to avoid,' Jo said. 'Can't blame her. I'm so sorry Nicky was such a pain,' she added, apologizing yet again. But she was sorry. Not that she and Travis had got together – she'd never regret that – but sorry it had caused such fallout.

'I'm going to bed,' Cassie declared, dragging herself off the sofa. 'Night guys. Sleep well.' Jo saw the embarrassed look her daughter shot between her and the American before she left.

Travis came and sat beside her as soon as they were alone. His arms went round her and she clung to him.

'Feels good,' she whispered as he bent to kiss her.

'Where have you been all my life?' Donna shrieked, as soon as she saw Jo outside the hut the following morning. 'Come in, come in. I haven't seen you properly in weeks.'

It was still early and the hut was absolutely freezing, despite the blow-heater blasting away in the corner. Donna hadn't started work yet. She was sitting on her bench, cradling a mug in hands encased in fingerless mittens. She was wrapped as if for the Arctic, her small body bulky and misshapen with layers of jumpers and scarves, a brightly coloured, knitted Chullo hat with earflaps pulled down over her dark hair. Jo shivered, clutching her jacket round her body against the cold.

'It'll warm up in a minute.' Donna waved a hand towards the steaming coffee pot. 'Help yourself.'

Jo shook her head. 'Where's Max?'

'Waiting inside till it's hotter. He's no fool.' Her friend watched Jo settle on her favourite stool, then with one eyebrow raised said, 'So? Been too busy bonking actor boy to talk to your old friends?'

Jo laughed. 'Sorry . . . yes, something like that. But it all kicked off last night . . . bloody Lawrence told Nicky about me and Travis.'

'And I take it he was underwhelmed?'

'Could say that.'

'And Cassie?'

'She knows too. But she's been amazing. Doesn't seem angry, just thoroughly disappointed in her parents.'

'I must say . . .'

'Don't.'

'So what did Nicky say?'

'Nothing . . . to me at least. But he had a set-to with Travis after the show. He refuses even to have the conversation with me.'

'Oh dear. What'll you do?'

Jo shook her head. 'You know what? I'm not going to do anything. It's his problem. I've apologized in about five messages to him. There's nothing more I can do if he continues to sulk.'

Donna clapped her gloved hands. 'Good to hear you being so robust about it, darling.'

'I think he's being childish. Fine, be cross with me if he has to. But as you've said a million times, I'm not hurting him. And if Cassie can be OK with it . . .'

'Obviously Lawrence was jealous though.'

'Jealous?' It had never occurred to her. 'I don't think so. What makes you say that?'

'Why else would he have dobbed you in to Nicky behind your back?'

'He didn't dob me in, exactly. He assumed Nicky knew. But it's his precious house he's worried about. Thinks Travis is getting his feet under the table and robbing him of his inheritance.'

Donna laughed. 'LOVE IT. Serves the idiot right. You should do just that.'

'I wish.'

'So it's going well . . .'

Jo's shoulders slumped as she let out a low groan. 'It's great.' She looked up at her friend. 'But he'll be gone soon . . . another job somewhere. This play's been good for his career.'

'Ouch.'

'Can't think about it.' But despite her words, she could think about little else. She and Travis had stayed a long time on the sofa, lying in each other's arms, the night before.

'Don't like to leave you,' he'd said.

'Don't like it either.'

He'd laughed softly. 'This is where the Power of Now is supposed to kick in. To rescue us from the future.'

'Hmm,' she said, after a moment's consideration. 'Not working for me so far.'

'Nor me neither. But hey, I haven't gone yet. It might be a while . . .'

They'd both known that wasn't true. He'd already told her that the man in the tweed coat – one Jack Lebus – was considering him for a part in an HBO mini-series about to start shooting in New York. He was waiting to hear from his agent today.

'This is why,' Jo told Donna now, 'I refuse to waste time on Nicky's hurt pride at the moment. I might only have a few more days with Travis.'

'God, darling. This is worse than *Brief Encounter*. Aren't you heartbroken at the thought of losing him?'

Jo shrugged. Have I ever really had him to lose? she wondered. It was almost as if Travis were a will-o'-the-wisp, a beautiful figment of her imagination.

When she went back home it was still only a quarter to eight, but Cassie was already in the kitchen with a mug of tea and a slice of toast with Marmite.

'Hi, you're up early.'

Her daughter looked resolute. 'I'm going back to sort it out with Matt.'

Jo sat down at the table. 'Today? Is it because of us, me and Travis?'

Cassie shrugged. 'I am kind of over playing gooseberry . . . but it's not just that, Mum. Hearing you talk about him last night, it reminded me what I'm missing . . . having someone who really gets me, thinks I'm the bee's knees.'

'You don't think you have that with Matt?'

'I don't know. Maybe once. Anyway, I'll give it one more go.' She took a sip from her cup. 'But if he won't let up a bit on the farm, I'm not sticking around to be ignored for the next thirty years.'

'Fair enough.'

'I want kids. And yes, it'd be an idyllic place to bring them up, but not if it's going to be the planet over the children. He should have married one of those tough, red-faced farmer's wives. They put up with all kinds of shit. But I'm not like that.' She shrugged. 'So . . . we'll see.'

'He'd be stupid to let you go,' Jo said.

'Yeah, well, he might be stupid. Men are stupid. Look at Dad.'

She'd already packed her stuff into the new backpack she'd bought, put on her new trainers. By nine-thirty she was gone, Jo and Travis waving her off on the doorstep like an old married couple.

The house suddenly seemed very quiet. Just the two of them. Travis looked at her. She looked back at him.

'Did we run her off? I feel bad if we did,' Travis said.

'We may have. But it's probably just as well. She has to sort out her marriage sometime.'

'Sure. I guess I feel guilty that she had to deal with us too.'

Jo nodded. 'Me too. She was so generous, didn't give either of us a hard time. And she really could have.'

They stood in silence in the kitchen. Jo had put the kettle on and it had boiled, turned itself off, but neither of them made any attempt to get the tea.

Then both of them moved simultaneously towards each other. His arms were round her, her cheek pressed against his shoulder.

'We could always try and assuage our guilt by going upstairs . . .' he muttered into her neck.

She laughed. 'It's a very bad idea you know, using sex to medicate.'

'But hey, we are very bad. We're super-bad. It's been confirmed. What have we got to lose?'

There was a freedom, a joy about their love-making that morning. All anxiety, all restraint had vanished. And they knew each other's bodies by now, knew what the other liked. It was pure pleasure.

'I never thought . . .' Jo began later.

Travis looked at her enquiringly when she didn't finish the sentence. He'd run her a bath and she was lying back in the warm water as he sat in his black YSL trunks, crosslegged on the bath mat.

'I never imagined . . . I would have this . . . not with anyone, particularly not with someone like you.'

'Like me?'

'Well, you know . . .' She didn't want to say 'young', didn't want to say 'gorgeous'.

'Because of Lawrence?'

'Yes. But I mean particularly you.' She turned her head to look at him. 'You're just very unlikely.'

This made him laugh. 'I've never been called "unlikely" before.'

'But you are. To me. And extraordinary.'

Travis looked away, embarrassed. 'I'm so not a girl-in-every-port kinda guy, you know.' He paused. 'I . . . just couldn't resist you.'

His simple statement brought tears to her eyes.

'I haven't told you . . .' he began.

She held her breath.

'Bobby rang late last night. I got the part. Leave Friday.'

She didn't ask why he hadn't said something sooner. It didn't matter. The normal sensitivities between two people who were contemplating a life together – such as assessing the other's long-term suitability on all fronts, including sex, money, trust – were irrelevant. But nothing was going to stop her heart contracting at his news. She pulled herself up in the bath.

'You got the job. Fantastic! Congratulations.'

He grinned. 'Yeah, thanks. HBO, a full-on mini-series set in a New York apartment building on the Upper East Side. It's a co-op . . . you know, the ones where the residents' board decides who gets to live there.'

'What's your part?'

'I'm the son of one of the apartment owners, squatting really, and not approved of. Being manipulated by a society hostess on the floor above. All dumb soap stuff, sex, money and politics . . . should be awesome.'

'I'm so pleased for you. Don't let them murder you in the first series.'

Travis laughed, stood up as Jo did and held out the towel as she stepped out of the bath, wrapping her in it and pulling her into his arms again. She felt almost dizzy at what he was telling her.

They didn't say, 'We'll keep in touch'. He didn't say, 'I'll be back soon'. She didn't say, 'Don't leave me'. But the thoughts were there. They constantly pricked the edge of her consciousness, and she saw Travis's in his eyes – that hesitation sometimes, when he would just gaze at her but say nothing.

In the days left to them they closed out the rest of the world, ignored all calls, enjoying the brief time uninhibited. Often they just talked and talked together about life, the universe and each other, with a freedom based in their imminent separation. And they made love, of course, lingering over each other's bodies, savouring every element that gave them pleasure, as if committing the softness of skin, the contour of a muscle, the scent, the line of lips and cheek, to memory.

Early on Friday morning – Travis had to leave for the airport by ten – they lay for the last time together, their bodies tight against each other. Jo had been awake for hours in the night, and she knew Travis had been restless too.

'Will you be OK . . . on your own?' he asked, his tone hesitant as if he didn't want to offend.

'I don't know,' she said honestly.

He looked down at her. 'You know this has been magic for me.'

'And for me.' She swallowed hard, but she was not going to cry.

'Kiss me one more time . . .' he asked.

'You'll be late.'

He laughed. 'It'll be worth it.'

CHAPTER 14

11 November 2013

It was Monday morning, two days after Travis left, and Jo hadn't been outside all weekend, hadn't spoken to anyone since walking with him to Hammersmith Tube station so that he could catch the Piccadilly line train to the airport. Donna was away staying with friends, but Jo was relieved. She wasn't ready to share her loss with anyone, not even her best friend.

And she wasn't bereft. She was still basking in the glow of the powerful attraction they'd been lucky enough to share. Travis seemed to be there with her still. There was no proper realization yet that she might never see him again. So she lay naked in the bed they'd shared, wrapped in the warm duvet, the faint scent of him still on the pillows, the sheets. She wandered about the house, sat for hours just staring into space, opened a book and had no idea what she'd been reading, listened to the radio and had no idea what she'd just listened to, barely aware that Travis was really gone, that it was just her now, her life waiting to be redefined for a second time in less than six months.

It was her agent, Maggie, who broke the spell.

'Just wanted to find out how it's going . . . with the book?'

Jo held the phone to her ear, paralysed, not knowing how to reply.

'Jo?'

'Hi, yes, I'm here . . . sorry.'

'Did I interrupt something?'

'No . . . no, it's just . . . well, I haven't really made much progress.'

'OK. By "not much progress", what do you mean exactly?'

Jo let out a short laugh. 'About fifteen thousand words.' she lied fluently, knowing she should care more, both about the lying and about the fact that she'd actually written barely fifteen hundred. But she found it didn't seem important. Maggie was silent for a moment.

'Are you stuck? Or just unsettled . . . what with all that's been going on for you.'

'Sort of both. But it's still three months till the deadline.'

'Six weeks. End of the year.'

'Oh.'

'Jo . . . are you OK? Should I be worried?'

'Frances won't get to it till the end of January though, will she? She never reads them immediately.'

'But it's still important you deliver on time. We

249

don't want to risk her cancelling it because you've missed the publication slot.'

'I suppose not.'

'Do you need more time?'

'No. No, I don't think so. It's only fifty thousand words. I can do that in six weeks, I have before.'

'Right.' Her agent was trying to sound relieved. 'Well, let me know how it's going, will you?'

'I will. Promise.' Jo took a deep breath. 'I'll get something to you by Christmas, so you can look through it before we send it off.'

After the call was ended, Jo just sat there at the kitchen table, her stomach churning. She had no idea what she was going to write. The existing story outline was somehow foreign to her now, the whole thing about bisexuality, about Lawrence really, seemed like a nasty taste in her mouth. How was she to invent a sympathetic character around a subject she just wanted to forget? But write it she must. I'll start tomorrow, she thought, and slowly made her way upstairs and lay down under the duvet, pulling the covers snug round her head.

When Jo finally sat herself down in front of the computer and read what she'd written, she found the words, few as they were, sounded flat, rote and uninspired. No Young Adult is going to read any further than page one, Jo thought, and deleted the whole lot. She had been true to her word and this Tuesday morning she had forced herself out of bed earlier than usual, stripped the bed, tidied the room, cleaned up in the kitchen, made herself a cup of coffee and retreated to her study and the document that should have been a nearly finished draft of her next book.

Even her young hero's name was wrong: Jake. Won't do, she thought, searching around for the right one, something sensitive without being feminine, strong, definitely not trendy – a likeable name, but class-neutral. She flicked through one of the boys' names sites on Google. The name had to be up to date, no Martins or Mikes or Daves. And it struck her, as she plumbed the Zacs, Oscars and Lukes, that it was pretty insane, a woman of her age thinking she could get inside the head of a modern-day teenage boy. But she'd done it in the recent past, and successfully too. Bobby, she thought. A good name. Then the appealing face of the boy who had killed himself flashed across her mind and she dismissed it quickly. Robbie, maybe?

The cursor winked at her: in out, in out. The page read: 'Chapter 1' in an authoritative way. Nothing. And then she suddenly found herself crying, as if the document had somehow upset her with its blankness. The tears were followed by panic, a sense of unreality, as if her body were collapsing, falling inwards as she sat there in her ergonomic chair. Like a person who has died and not been found for weeks.

And who would find her if she had? None of the men in her life, that's for sure. Her father dead, Lawrence defected, Nicky insulted beyond comprehension – an open wound that she tried not to think about – Travis far away and gone across the sea. Only Cassie and Donna remained to care, and Cassie was busy rebuilding her own life among the pigs and bolting lettuces. For a while Jo didn't move, the dark screen the only witness to her distress. It was a while before the tears gradually began to falter, then stop, as if she had come to the bottom of a deep reservoir, simply run out of tears. Everything went very still, her mind empty, almost peaceful. Just me. The words floated across her brain, testing her. Just me. And the more she heard them, the less they seemed to frighten her. Just me . . .

She had no idea how long she sat there, almost in a trance. But eventually, the breath began to fill her lungs again, her spine straightened. And she found her fingers reaching out for the keyboard, almost with a will of their own. They hovered above the letters, pausing for a moment as if waiting for the off at the beginning of a race, then began moving fast and sure. Letters, words, sentences which became paragraphs began to appear on the previously blank document, her hands apparently channelling words that she herself was unable to hear.

Out came thoughts and feelings she'd skimmed over for a lifetime, things she barely understood: about her mad mother and her cold, unloving father; about the leering men hanging about the house; about Bobby; about her father's sudden absence and a lost teenage looking after her selfishly distraught mother. About Lawrence and his inability to hear her, to take her seriously much of the time. And her denial that he had. About her loss . . . of them all.

But these seemed to be words formed as her fourteen-year-old self. As if her development had not moved beyond that time when she was faced so starkly with the cruel reality of life. The text, which rapidly filled up the pages, sounded youthful, frightened, lost. She was writing from a place beyond her rational mind, ostensibly about her own pain, but the character – who had morphed from a boy called Jake to a girl called Tess without any conscious thought on her part – took on a life of her own, two lives in fact. One was the good, functioning teenager who looked after her younger siblings and her alcoholic mother. The other, angry and wild, who ran rampant with a gang of town boys getting up to all kinds of trouble related to sex, drugs and crime.

And as Jo wrote, the two versions of Tess, at first so separate, gradually began to come together into one more functioning whole under the almost mystical auspices of her online mentor – a woman or a man, Tess never quite knows which – to whom she talks daily and who is her support and only reliable friend.

Three days later, the word count now way beyond the fifteen thousand she'd pretended to

Maggie she'd already reached, the outline firmly in place, she realized she had a book. Not the book she'd been commissioned to write, admittedly, but she pushed on nonetheless, knowing now that she couldn't stop. If it didn't work and Frances didn't like it, she would just have to risk the consequences.

She was sitting having a cup of tea at the kitchen table when her phone rang. She heard Travis's voice with a sudden lurch of her heart. 'Hi, it's me.'

'Hi, you.'

'Thought I'd call and see how you're doing.'

Jo laughed. 'I'm OK. Well . . . if I'm honest, a bit bloody manic.'

'Doing what?'

'I've been on a loony writing jag. How's it going your end?'

'Yeah, pretty good. Met the director and the producers. Think it's going to be OK, but I don't start shooting for another ten days and I'm just hanging about right now.'

'Miss you . . .' Jo said into the silence.

'God, me too.' She heard him sigh. 'Sure made me laugh, though, the way we said goodbye. It was like we were distant friends who'd bumped into each other on the station. Bye, see you around, must hook up, kinda thing.'

She laughed. 'We were so keen to pretend we didn't mind!'

'As if.'

'That's why I've been so focused. "Doing" stops "thinking".'

'Is that so?'

'Not really. Well, sort of. For short periods anyway. But it's not all bad, thinking about you . . . in fact it's positively pleasurable if you take away the fact that you've gone . . . completely gone . . . just upped-sticks and deserted me.' Jo adopted a melodramatic tone, keeping the truth in her words from becoming too real for either of them.

'Yeah, the leaving bit's a bummer.'

They both began to laugh, not because it was at all funny, just enjoying the contact, the sound of each other's voices.

'It's been good talking,' Travis said later, at the end of their long conversation.

'Very.'

'Take care of yourself.'

'And you.'

'Bye now.'

As Jo put her phone down she had a feeling they wouldn't talk soon, or perhaps ever. It was over. Like a mirage in the desert he had come into her life without warning, gone just as suddenly – shimmering, tempting, hardly real. She quickly put her mug in the sink, ran some water into it and hurried upstairs to bury any yearnings for Travis in another page full of text.

'Go away, Lawrence.'

There was a baffled silence on the other end

of the phone. 'What did you say?' her husband asked.

'I said go away. I can't be bothered listening to another bloody whinge about the house right now. Just leave me alone.'

And she put the phone down and got on with her writing, barely giving him another thought. She was pinned to the computer from morning till night, and now, nearly three weeks after Travis had gone, she was nearing the last five thousand words of the book. It was virtually writing itself. It was only in her tea break that she finally got around to reading Lawrence's texts – three separate ones sent over a period of a couple of hours that morning.

First text: 'Are you OK, Jo? I really need to talk to you. L.'

Second text: 'It's not about the house.'

Third text: 'It's v. important. Pls ring. L.'

God, she thought. What does the man want this time? What can be so important if it's not the house or money? She hadn't even asked him for any money, not since she'd borrowed a small amount from Donna a month ago. She wasn't spending much at the moment anyway. With a sigh she dialled his number.

'Hi.' Lawrence's voice was frosty.

'What's up?'

'We need to talk, as soon as possible.'

He still sounded chilly and was obviously waiting for Jo to apologize.

'OK, well, go ahead, I'm listening.'

'Not over the phone.'

'Oh, come on, Lawrence. Cut the cloak-and-dagger stuff. Just get on and tell me what the problem is. I'm busy.'

'I don't know what's come over you, Jo. There's really no need to be so offensive,' he said. And she could picture his mouth pinched in that prudish way he had when he thought he had the moral high ground.

She didn't answer.

'If you must know, it's Nicky.'

'What about him?' Jo was not in the mood to be given another lecture about her behaviour towards her children, not least because she was very upset by her son's continued refusal to contact her. Since Travis's departure she had texted or left messages for him on an almost daily basis, but he'd returned none of them. Cassie said he was being a 'plank', and that she should ignore him. But Jo was finding that hard to do.

Lawrence could be heard taking a long breath.

'Amber's pregnant.'

'Oh, God . . .'

'But it's not as simple as that. I'd rather talk to you face to face . . . if you can tear yourself away from whatever it is you're doing.'

'All right. Where?'

She went to the back of the café, where there were squashy armchairs and ordered a green tea as she sat waiting for her husband, her mind totally taken up with fictional Tess as she worked out the next sentence, the next paragraph.

Lawrence gave her a curt smile as he sank his long body into the chair opposite.

'Glad you could spare the time,' he said.

She ignored his huffiness. 'Tell me about Nicky.' It was only hours since Lawrence's phone call about the baby, and she was having trouble getting her head around the fact that her son, still so young in her eyes, was going to be a father.

He shook his head slightly, clearly bewildered.

'Well . . . Amber's ten weeks. And she's adamant she doesn't want it.'

'And Nicky does?'

Lawrence nodded. 'He's distraught that she's even considering aborting it.'

Jo frowned. 'Didn't she know she was pregnant before this? I mean ten weeks is pretty far gone.'

'Apparently not. She doesn't have periods very regularly, Nicky says.'

'Probably because she doesn't eat enough.'

'Whatever . . . but Nicky wants us to talk to her, persuade her not to get rid of it.'

'Us? As in, you *and* me?' She paused. 'He hasn't spoken to me in weeks, Lawrence. It's been really upsetting. All the messages I've sent and nothing back. Know how you must have felt with Cassie . . . but this is a godsend if it means we can be in touch again.' She paused, hearing how that must sound. 'You know what I mean . . .'

Lawrence nodded. 'He wants your input more than mine seemingly. A woman thing. But he feels awkward ringing you. I think he backed himself into a corner and now feels plain stupid.'

Jo felt a flood of relief that her son needed her. 'Do you think it's a good idea, them having a baby?'

'Well, that's the thing. She's so young – barely twenty – and . . . sort of childlike. I can't imagine how she'll cope with a baby to look after.'

'And what will they live on?'

They both stared at each other.

'But it is our grandchild,' Jo said softly.

'I know.'

'Oh, God. I don't know what I think. I agree Amber just doesn't seem capable of coping with her normal life, let alone motherhood. And if she genuinely doesn't want it . . .'

'You see Nicky thinks she does want it, but she doesn't believe *he* does. And he doesn't want to put pressure on her to keep it because he says it's her body and she's going to have to take most of the responsibility. So he hasn't been totally honest about the fact that he really wants this baby.'

Jo groaned. 'I don't see that we can intervene, can we? It'll have terrible consequences if we take one side or another and then it doesn't work out.'

'But he's desperate for our input. We can't just walk away.'

They fell silent again.

'Maybe we should meet up with them. At least talk it through together?' Lawrence said.

'With Amber too? Would she do that? She's never said a word to me, even on a good day. I get the impression she's a bit intimidated by us.'

'Really?' He raised his eyebrows, a half smile on his face.

'What do you mean? I'll have you know I've bent over backwards to connect with that girl, but she never gives anything back,' Jo retorted.

Lawrence chuckled. 'I'm sure you have. But you've got form, Jo, with Nicky's girlfriends. Admit it.'

'Ha! Loulou, you mean? You couldn't stand her either, but you were such a creep you pretended you totally *lurved* her. Anyway, I was perfectly polite to her.'

'Call that polite?' They were both laughing now. 'Remember the time she came round with Nicky and we pretended we had to go out and went upstairs to "change", thinking they'd leave soon, and they didn't and we had to actually change and go out, despite it being knackeringly cold and having nowhere to go?'

'All she talked about was who she knew and what she'd bought. She hadn't a brain in her head.'

'And that voice!'

Jo didn't respond immediately. She'd been brought up short by the ease with which she and Lawrence had fallen back into their previous intimacy. It felt dangerous suddenly, like a slippery slope down which she couldn't afford to slide.

'So what are we going to do about Nicky and Amber?' she said, anxious to get this meeting over with.

'Shall I suggest we all get together, see what he says?'

Jo sighed. 'I suppose. I hope the thing with Nicky won't get in the way . . . I can't have got many Brownie points with Amber over it all.'

'It's probably time you sorted it out anyway.'

She glared at him. 'I have been trying you know.'

'OK, OK, wasn't criticizing. I know how tricky it can be, remember?'

'Yeah . . . sorry. But it's stupid, especially as Travis is long gone.'

His eyebrows shot up. 'Gone? You've split up?'

She wished everyone wouldn't make assumptions about her and Travis. Words bandied about like 'love', 'relationship', 'split up', implied she and the American had been an item, something solid. But the Away-Day nature of what they had together – in some ways part of the charm – was not easy to explain. And although she feigned nonchalance now, she still missed Travis terribly. Not having him there to hold her sometimes felt like a physical pain.

'We both knew it wasn't an ongoing thing.'

Lawrence looked as if he were waiting for her

to continue. When she didn't, he asked, 'And you're OK with that?'

'Yes.' She wasn't going to discuss it with him, he wouldn't understand even if she did.

They sat in silence.

'Can we meet at home . . . if Nicky agrees?' he asked eventually.

'Of course,' she said, getting up. She found she couldn't sit there opposite Lawrence for one more second. He looked surprised. But there was still so much unsaid between them, which made these meetings like picking her way through a minefield.

'Ring me when you've got a plan. I'm trying to finish my book so I'm around mostly.'

She left him sitting there.

On the bus going home her thoughts returned to her son and his girlfriend.

CHAPTER 15

6 December 2013

Jo heard her daughter groan.

'Bloody predictable if you want my opinion. She's nobbled him, hasn't she. I mean, how do you get pregnant these days by accident? Weren't they using contraceptives? And why has she waited all this time to get rid of it if she really, really doesn't want it?'

'You think she's playing some game?'

'God, I don't know. Wouldn't put it past her. "Oh, Nicky, I can't *possibly* have the baby, I wouldn't do it to you. It'd put sooo much strain on you and your precious career!"' Cassie's childish tone was a cruelly accurate imitation of her brother's girlfriend.

'Now, now, that's a bit unfair,' Jo admonished. 'Maybe she's just being realistic. She knows she can't cope.'

Her daughter harrumphed.

'After all, she didn't need to get pregnant to keep Nicky, did she? He's besotted,' Jo added.

'And if she did do it on purpose, then why is she saying she doesn't want it? Doesn't make sense.'

'I've no idea. I just think she's a bit mental.'

'Nicky wants me and Dad to talk to her.'

'Yeah . . . well, that'll do a lot of good. Like she really respects you both.'

'My point exactly. But Dad seems to think we need to make the effort anyway. For Nicky's sake.'

'So what is your position, Mum? Do you think they should keep it?'

Jo sighed. 'I hate the thought of losing our grandchild . . . but equally I do wonder how those two will manage. Nicky earns so sporadically, and Amber . . .'

She heard Cassie laugh. 'You wait. They'll be asking to move in with you. And you won't be able to say no.'

'Don't want to think about that possibility, thank you.' Jo paused. 'We can't influence them. It'd be wrong. They're both adults, they have to make their own decision on this one.'

'Ha! Neat, Mum.'

Jo laughed. 'I'm not trying to avoid responsibility, honest.'

'No, of course not. Anyway, I agree.'

'How's Matt?' Jo's question was tentative. Cassie had said little in the last month about how it was going down on the farm. Whenever Jo asked, she always deflected the query, as if her husband was in the room with her.

Cassie didn't reply for a minute.

'Yeah . . . OK . . .' her voice had sunk to a whisper. 'I think – fingers crossed – that we're getting a *fridge*.'

'That's brilliant news, darling.'

'It's a recycled one, of course. And I'll barely be allowed to open it – did you know that door openings account for seven per cent of fridge energy? But I don't care.'

'It means he's listening, no?'

'I think. Too complicated to tell you now, Mum.' She was still whispering.

'OK,' Jo found herself whispering back. 'Call me when he's out sometime, if you can.'

'Will do. Love you. Bye.'

Amber looked even paler and thinner than usual, if that were possible. She perched tentatively on the sofa in the sitting room, Nicky pressed to her side, hands firmly entwined. Her cornflower-blue eyes were dewy with incipient tears. Jo thought her son looked tired and strained and imagined sleepless nights when the couple went round and round the same unanswerable questions.

'I'll get the tea,' Jo said. 'Will you give me a hand, Nicky?'

Her son cast an anxious glance at his girlfriend, as if, Jo thought, irritably, Amber might be abducted by aliens if he let go of her hand for a few minutes.

Once they were in the kitchen, Jo laying out the flapjacks she'd bought from the local café and warming the pot for the tea, she spoke to her son, her voice low.

'It's good to see you.'

Nicky's big frame shifted from foot to foot, his eyes constantly flitting back to the sitting room as he fiddled with the pile of teaspoons on the worktop.

'Yeah, and you.'

Jo stopped what she was doing. 'I wish you'd called me.'

Her son gave a long sigh, still wouldn't look at her. 'I . . . sorry, Mum. It's been a difficult time . . . and . . .' he stopped.

'It was horrible, not being in touch with you.'

Now he looked at her, his expression contrite. 'Sorry. I can't . . . all the stuff with Amber . . . I'm so sorry, Mum.' There were tears in his eyes and Jo went at once and put her arms round him. He hugged her back, a fierce, tight embrace, but it was only a second before he let her go, as if he were doing something he shouldn't. Jo wondered what went on between him and Amber behind closed doors. Was the girl deliberately separating Nicky from his family?

'If you take the tray, I'll bring the teapot,' she told him.

When Amber refused the tea she held out to her, Jo replied, 'Sorry . . . I didn't think. Would you prefer herbal?' Her tone was deliberately softened, although she was thoroughly annoyed with the girl's blatant refusal to engage, to be

266

normal – it was only a cup of tea, for God's sake! Lawrence had arrived early, to discuss strategy, but neither of them could come up with a plan. Play it by ear, had been the final consensus.

Amber shook her head.

'So,' Lawrence said, his tone business-like. 'You two are probably sick of the subject, but perhaps you'd like to fill us in on what your thoughts are . . .'

Amber glanced at Nicky. Nicky smiled encouragingly back.

'Amber doesn't feel it's the right time to have a baby . . . what with her being so young, and my career not established, no money . . . lots of reasons.'

'And you want the baby?' Lawrence asked.

Nicky nodded. 'But it's not my body. I don't have to go through pregnancy and childbirth, look after it, and so on.'

Jo turned to Amber. 'You genuinely don't want to keep it?'

The girl looked like a rabbit caught in the headlights at Jo's question.

'I . . . don't see how we can,' she stammered.

'But if you could see a way . . . would you want to?'

She shrugged her delicate shoulders. 'I don't see how . . .'

'I know it wouldn't be easy, but people far worse off than us have children all the time,' Nicky said, as much to her as to his parents. It was clearly not a new argument, because Amber just nodded tiredly.

Lawrence, who was famously impatient with indecision, seemed to be restraining himself when he asked, rather brusquely, Jo thought, 'So let me get this straight. You don't want the baby under any circumstances, Amber? Or you might want it . . . you just can't see a way to make it work?'

Amber stared at him. She was picking at the sleeve of her white T-shirt, driving a hole through the thin fabric near the seam with her thumbnail. Jo wanted to tell her to stop, to point out what she was doing, but she said nothing. And as she studied the girl, tears that had been glistening around her eyes gathered momentum, and Jo watched as big droplets coursed silently down her pale cheek.

'I . . . don't know.'

Lawrence just nodded very slowly. Up and down, up and down went his head, his implied frustration obvious.

'Dad, she's scared, OK? She knows all the arguments. We've been over it hundreds of times.'

There was silence as everyone looked somewhere else. The lamp light fell on the sofa and Jo noticed that the navy linen on the front edge of the arms was beginning to fray, the dull brown of the original cover peeking through. We must have had that sofa for over twenty years, she thought. Nicky was still only a child.

'It's just that a decision has to be made one way

or the other, quite soon.' Jo's tone was gentle. 'If you're already ten weeks—'

'We know that,' Nicky said.

'Have you thought about talking it through with a pregnancy counsellor?' Jo suggested.

Amber shook her head. 'I don't see how anyone can help. We know all the pros and cons.'

Lawrence got up. 'Shall I make more tea? Or something stronger?'

Jo frowned at him, tugged the back of his sweater. 'I think we ought to concentrate.'

Her husband twisted his mouth and sat down again.

'What do *you* think, Mum?' Nicky asked, his eyes boring into her as if he thought her opinion might be the defining one, the solution to all their problems. Jo was touched by his faith in her wisdom, but she had no idea what she should say.

'I think . . . that it must be very frightening to be suddenly pregnant at your age. I think it's a huge responsibility for you both. I think you haven't known each other for very long. And obviously the financial side is going to be difficult.' She paused. 'However. A baby is a baby. Your child, ours too. What should you do? I don't know, and I wouldn't want to influence your decision even if I did. Which isn't very helpful, obviously.'

Nicky sighed, deflated. They both looked so helpless, so exhausted by it all. Jo wanted to hug them, to somehow make it all right.

'I think you should seriously think about booking the abortion . . . if you really don't want the baby. Or it'll be too late.' Lawrence's voice was toneless, neutral.

Jo gave a small gasp. Amber's cornflower eyes widened until they threatened to take over her entire face. Nicky looked stunned.

'Dad!'

Lawrence's eyebrows went up. 'I know, horrible word, "abortion", but if that's what we're talking about, you really don't have much time.'

Nicky got up, pulling his girlfriend to her feet.

'Thanks, Dad. Thanks a fucking bunch.'

They almost ran towards the front door, grabbing their coats, neither looking back. Within seconds they were gone.

Lawrence looked at Jo and grinned at her expression.

'Shock tactics.'

She continued to stare at him.

'I just wasn't sure either of them – particularly Amber – had completely faced the fact that if you don't want a pregnancy, then the only way out is abortion. The baby isn't just going to magically disappear.'

Jo nodded. 'Seemed a bit brutal.'

'I think it worked, though. Did you see their faces when I said it? Nicky was obviously upset – as he would be – but so was Amber. She looked absolutely horrified. I mean she seems quite naïve, but surely she's heard the word before?'

'You're one sneaky bastard,' she said, almost in awe.

'Well, we'll see if it helps to change her mind.' He took a deep breath. 'God, that was knackering. Fancy a drink?'

Jo laughed. 'I'd bloody kill for one. I think there's a bottle of Donna's vodka in the freezer.'

Jo poured a slug of Grey Goose into two Duralex tumblers, adding grapefruit juice in the absence of tonic water, and ice. She handed one to her husband, who chinked her glass as he toasted, 'Perhaps to our grandchild?'

They each took an appreciative sip.

'Mmm . . . needed that,' Jo said. They sat down at the kitchen table. 'But you do realize that this is going to be a whole other drama, if you're right and they keep the baby.'

'Hasn't she got family who'll help out?'

'No idea. I hardly know anything about her. Cassie is convinced they'll want to move in here.'

Jo spoke without thinking, realizing too late the implications for Lawrence regarding the house. She saw him frown and steeled herself for what would inevitably follow.

But he didn't respond, just went silent and brooding.

'How are things with you?' she asked.

He looked up. 'Fine. Everything's fine.'

'Good,' she said, but she'd known him too long and didn't believe a word. Something was up.

'Jo . . .'

She held her hand up. 'Don't say it.'

'What? Don't say what?'

'The house?' she said. 'Weren't you going to start on again about selling the house?'

He took a long breath. 'Umm . . . no, actually.'

She waited while he stared at his glass, swirling it around as the ice jangled in the remains of the vodka – the only sound in the kitchen. He drank that quickly, she thought.

Finally he raised his eyes to hers. 'Arky wants me to move in.'

'OK . . . that's good.'

'Not really.'

'Because?' Jo had spent so many months not mentioning the man's name, trying her best to blank him from her mind, but now she found she was intrigued as to what was going on between them.

Lawrence sighed. 'I'm just not sure.'

'Well, tell him then.'

'Yeah, I have.'

'And?'

'And he doesn't understand why not.' Again he fell silent. 'He's a bit upset about it to be honest.'

She was having trouble imagining them having this domestic, and the incomprehensibility of their relationship hit Jo anew.

'What's the reason you don't want to?'

He gave a tired shrug. 'I just can't see myself . . . living with him . . . sharing it all . . . like a couple.' He threw his hands in the air. 'I just can't see it, Jo.'

No, well, she couldn't either, so she understood where he was coming from. But she said, 'Perhaps you need more time?'

'No, I don't. This isn't something I can see myself getting used to. I never envisaged moving in with Arky.'

'Really? So you'd be happy to go on living in different places for ever?'

'For ever?' Lawrence echoed, as if the concept had never occurred to him.

'Well, yes. I mean, people do and it seems to work. Remember Dom and Sarah. They always had separate places and they were devoted to each other.'

He frowned at her. 'They died.'

She couldn't help smiling, even though their friends' deaths – Dominic from heart disease, Sarah from an embolism after surgery – had been far from amusing at the time.

'Yes, but not as a result of living apart.'

'He says it's a deal-breaker,' Lawrence's voice was heavy with gloom. 'He says if I don't move in, then it must mean I'm not committed to him.'

'Sounds a bit childish.'

She watched her husband's face brighten. 'You think?'

'Well, yes. I mean, if you were both twenty, then perhaps he'd have a point. But at your age . . . do you need to prove anything to him?'

'Arky doesn't see it like that. He's accusing me of having cold feet . . . about being with a man.'

'Right.'

This is too weird, Jo thought. Me giving relationship counselling to my own husband about his boyfriend.

'Top up?'

He nodded enthusiastically.

When the glasses were refilled, she took some crisps out of the cupboard and poured them into a bowl. Lawrence fell on them, munching absent-mindedly, his thoughts clearly with the Russian history professor's tantrums.

'But otherwise your relationship is good?'

'There is no "otherwise". He's become obsessed.'

'Oh, dear.'

'Yeah, well.' He gave her a wan smile. 'Sorry to dump on you like this, Jo. You're the last person who wants to hear. Just all this stuff with Nicky, Arky badgering me, Cassie's marriage teetering by a thread, money . . . it's all very worrying.'

Jo was so familiar with that phrase. Lawrence was a Class A worrier. Things would get inside his head, even quite trivial things, like minor set-tos with colleagues or students, and make him fret for days and weeks, out of all proportion to the initial cause.

'Matt's allowing her to buy a fridge.'

'Really? So things are improving?'

'We haven't had a chance to talk properly, without him in the background. But even that

274

fact says something. In the past she seemed to be on her own most of the time. It's a good sign I think.'

Her husband relaxed back in his chair. 'That's one thing off the list then.'

'And Nicky and Amber will sort something out. They're grown-ups, even if we don't see them as such.'

He gave her a wry smile. 'So that only leaves Arky.'

'Yup.' She sipped her drink, the edges of the day worn quickly away by the alcohol. 'But you still love him?'

It took Lawrence a moment to reply. 'Love him? I . . . yes . . . yes, I suppose I do.'

And Jo found she didn't want to hear that.

The pet shop that Donna had dragged Jo into as they walked along Notting Hill was empty of customers, the girl behind the counter texting on her mobile. Maxy immediately began snuffling around the various carefully placed toys on the floor – rope bones and chewable rabbits and rattling balls – like a kid in a sweet shop.

'Look at all these things . . . it's ridiculous,' Jo whispered to her friend, casting her eye along the shelves and displays.

'Yeah, I know. But I need to get Max a new winter coat. That one he's got has lost its strap. It's stopped being waterproof.'

'He's a Border Terrier, Donna. That means he

comes from the Scottish Borders. He doesn't need a coat in West Eleven.'

'Yes, but he's getting older. And that shed is like a tomb at this time of year.' Donna was examining a quilted Barbour coat. 'Isn't this the cutest thing?' She held it up for Jo to approve.

Jo grinned. 'And check this out. A dog jumper.' She waved a tiny red cable-knit garment with tiny sleeves. 'Angora . . . blimey. And this tweed Sherlock Holmes hat. Oh my God, he's got to have that.'

The girl glanced up at them. 'The tweed's very popular.'

Donna smiled politely. Jo knew there was no way Max would ever be allowed to wear a deer-stalker.

'No! Look. A rawhide cupcake.' Jo bent to stroke the dog, waving the cellophane packet in his face. 'Things don't get much better than this, Maxy.' She turned to Donna. 'I'm definitely getting it for him.' Jo suggested they stop for a coffee on their way back home. It was freezing that December morning, the wind-chill making the air biting and painful. All the people on the pavement were scurrying along, heads bent, hats and scarves pulled close, suffering expressions on their faces.

'Christ.' Donna shivered as they closed the door on the blissfully steamy café. Max was allowed to come in as long as he was kept on his lead, and they settled by the window.

'Maybe he was suggesting coming home,' Donna said, once their lattes were in front of them.

'He most certainly wasn't. He said he still loved the bloody man.'

'You shouldn't have asked.'

'I know, but he was clearly upset about something . . . and I was curious I suppose. I never ask about them, I don't want to know. But I thought—'

'You thought they might be in trouble?'

Jo shot her friend a rueful grin. 'I suppose.'

'You'd really take him back? Even after actor boy?'

'I didn't say that. And Travis has nothing to do with me and Lawrence. Nothing at all.'

'OK . . . but answer the question. Would you take Lawrence back if the Russian were suddenly to default?'

'No. How could I?'

'By the look on your face right now, quite easily.'

Jo blushed. 'That's ridiculous.' Then she sighed, deflated suddenly. 'It was just the two of us, at the kitchen table, talking about stuff and drinking vodka, and yes, I suppose I did have a moment – just a moment – when I remembered what it used to be like.'

Donna's face was full of sympathy. 'And then you hear that Arkadius is playing up . . .'

Jo nodded. 'Stupid, I know.'

'Not really, darling.'

'I know he's gone. I do.'

'Sounds like it's not all a bed of roses back at that particular ranch.'

'Yeah, but what do I care? I should never have let him start. I'm angry with myself. I was definitely moving on. When Travis was here I hardly gave Lawrence a thought. And I've been so absorbed in my book. This was just a lapse, and it mustn't happen again.'

Her friend laughed. 'That's it, girl. You tell yourself.'

'But you don't believe me.'

'I believe you're trying. And that's what counts.'

Jo's book was her obsession, Tess her only companion during the following week. While she was working she thought of nothing else, the problems in her life like a wash behind a vivid landscape. Late on a Sunday in mid-December, she sat on the sofa, a second glass of white wine in her hand, the printout of her book stacked neatly on the cushion beside her. The house was silent, dark except for the lamp on in the sitting room. Jo, worn out from the previous days of relentless work and slightly woozy from the wine, felt a combination of satisfaction that she had finished another book, and a predictable emptiness. She could sense the worries that she had gratefully put on hold in order to finish the book, hovering, waiting to flood back in. And the future seemed to stretch ahead like a vast expanse of desert; huge and empty and unnerving.

CHAPTER 16

21 December 2013

'Not sure what you're saying, Jo,' Maggie said. 'The book is different in what way?'

'Every way. Totally different. I couldn't write the other one. And this one just popped up instead.'

'"Popped up"? OK . . . but it's still Young Adult?'

'Oh, yes. Listen, read it, and then we can talk. I know Frances wanted something else, but I think this works, and I'm sure she hasn't done any pre-publication stuff yet. She wouldn't until she reads it.'

She heard her agent take a long breath.

'Well, it's a bit of a risk . . . but if it works I don't see why she wouldn't go for it. Send it over and I'll have a look.' There was a pause. 'Are you pleased with it?'

'Umm, can't say at this stage. I've written it very quickly and it seems to have energy . . . but whether it works as a book . . .'

'I won't get to it till after Christmas now. In-laws arriving from Dubai tomorrow.' Maggie let out a

279

long groan. 'But as long as we deliver it by the end of the first week in Jan, when everyone's back at their desks . . .'

Jo emailed the manuscript over as soon as she'd said goodbye to Maggie. Nothing more to do at the moment, she thought, the day stretching ahead blankly. Just Christmas looming.

She'd lied to everyone about her plans for the holiday. She'd told Donna she was probably going to Devon. She'd told Nicky she was spending it with Donna. She'd told Cassie she was too tired to travel to Devon. The thought of having to be jolly and festive – never an easy task for Jo – was beyond her this year. It would be the last Christmas in her home anyway. Tina, the estate agent, had been given instructions for mid-January, and she wanted to stay at home while she could, be curmudgeonly, ignore the celebrations for once. She was actually looking forward to the peace and quiet. It was just another day, why did everyone have to make such a fuss?

But it was not to be. Late on Christmas Eve there was a pounding on the front door, a finger pressed continuously to the bell. Jo was already in her pyjamas, a large jumper over the top and furry sock slippers on her feet against the cold. She'd been wrapped in a blanket watching *The Godfather* all evening – a comfort film for the whole family – and it was nearly midnight.

Shocked, she stood still by the sink for a moment, the tap running for her glass of water. Then she heard Nicky's voice, desperate and pleading, 'Mum . . . Mum! Wake up. Please, let me in . . .'

She opened the door to her son, who flew past her into the house, bringing with him a freezing blast of air. He was wrapped in a heavy donkey-jacket, a grey wool hat over his blond hair. It must have started sleeting, because his clothes were layered with a fine mist.

'She's gone! Amber's gone.'

Jo, for a split second thinking her son's girlfriend had died, stared at him, horrified.

'What? What's happened?' She pushed Nicky into a kitchen chair. 'Take your coat off.'

Breathing heavily, he struggled out of his coat, ripped his hat off, slinging both on to the table. Brushing his hands over his hair, clasping his head as if he thought he might lose it, he cast an agonized look at his mother.

'Tell me,' Jo urged.

'She's left me. Just gone.'

'Wait . . . start from the beginning.' Jo sat close to her son.

He took a deep breath. 'We were going out tonight . . . with Rob, you know, my friend from school, and his Japanese girlfriend. Just a drink. I'd gone to the supermarket to get some last-minute stuff to take to Dad's tomorrow. I was only out forty-five minutes, but when I came back she'd vanished. Just disappeared.'

'Was there a note?'

'Nothing.'

'So how do you know she wasn't called away urgently by someone . . . family for instance, and didn't have the chance to explain?'

Nicky looked at her as if she were half-witted. 'She doesn't have any family, Mum. And she's not answering her phone.'

'Maybe she was just panicking about the baby . . . wanted to get away for a few hours. She's probably at home right now.'

'Then why isn't she calling me? I left a million messages.'

'Her phone ran out of juice? Or she might have lost it, had it stolen. It happens.' She took his cold hand. 'Honestly, darling, I think you're overreacting. You didn't have a fight or anything, did you?'

He shook his head.

'And things were good between you . . . with the baby?'

Her son just stared at her, his expression bewildered as he blinked back tears.

'Mum,' he said quietly, 'there is no baby.'

'What?' Jo found she was shivering. 'What do you mean? Did she go ahead with the abortion?'

'She wasn't ever pregnant.' His words sounded heavy and dull.

'She wasn't pregnant? You mean she . . . made it up?'

'No, no, she was just mistaken. She thought she was, and the test said she was . . .'

'Didn't she see a doctor?'

'She was going to but she didn't want to till we'd decided what to do.'

'But, but, her periods . . . other symptoms. She must have wondered why she didn't have other symptoms.' Although as she said it, Jo remembered a number of girls she'd known in the past who hadn't realized they were pregnant till they were four or five months gone.

'Amber's not very worldly. She didn't know what to expect.'

Jo shook her head. 'So how did she find out she wasn't pregnant then?'

'She got a period . . . and she went to the doctor. And he said she wasn't and hadn't been.'

'God. When did she find this out?'

'Two days ago. She wouldn't talk about it. I thought maybe she was just relieved and didn't want to rub it in, knowing how attached I'd got to the idea. Or maybe she just felt a fool.'

'Were you upset?'

Nicky sighed. 'I don't know what I feel. Relieved in a way, I suppose. And just sort of baffled. I can't make the whole thing out. Did she really think she was having a baby, or was it a sort of fantasy?' He threw his hands up in the air. 'But all that's kind of irrelevant if she's left me.'

Jo thought for a minute. 'Should we be worried about her . . . her safety, I mean. She wouldn't do anything, would she?'

'You mean throw herself under a bus or something? Christ, Mum . . . don't wind me up.'

'It's just if she's depressed . . . maybe she invested more in the pregnancy than you realized. She could be in shock.'

Nicky sat up, his bewilderment replaced by an anxious frown.

'Well, what should we do? Call the police?'

'I don't know . . . has she got any friends she might have gone to?'

'A couple of girls. But I don't have their numbers. One, Bea, she works with, but her office will be closed now for days. I have no idea how to get hold of her.'

'The police won't pay any attention till she's been gone more than just a couple of hours.'

'But where can she be? It's freezing out there. All the bars and cafés are closed . . .'

'I'm sure she's with one of her girlfriends. That's the most likely scenario. She probably needed to process what's happened, and you're too close to it all.'

Nicky nodded. 'Perhaps. Yeah . . . yeah, that does make sense.'

'Shall I make some tea?' Jo asked. She was putting forward a best-case scenario to calm her son down. And she genuinely did think it was the most likely explanation. But there was a nagging doubt that maybe Amber was more unstable than Nicky understood. That she was out there somewhere, wandering the streets, freezing and distressed, her mind temporarily unbalanced.

'Thanks, but I think I should get back. She might

be there. I don't want her coming home to an empty flat.'

'OK. Call me if there's news, won't you? Whatever the time.'

Nicky nodded, put on his coat, clutching his hat in his hand. He came over to give her a hug.

'Thanks so much, Mum. So sorry for bursting in in the middle of the night . . . I didn't know what else to do. I tried to phone you but you weren't picking up.'

'I left it charging upstairs in the office. Sorry. Listen, I hope you find her,' she said, kissing him on the cheek. 'Love you.'

After her son had gone, Jo sat up for a while with a cup of chamomile tea. She was wide awake, and worried for Amber. All the meanness and jokes about her seemed so petty now. But she was definitely a strange girl, who clearly had problems, whatever the truth behind the baby fiasco. Yes, Jo knew it was possible, occasionally, to get a false positive on a test, especially if you didn't do it right. But what girl these days doesn't see a doctor when she thinks she's pregnant? And that thing Nicky had said about her not having family? She must have some family, somewhere. Then there was the potential eating disorder . . . all very odd, she decided. When she finally got to bed it was gone three.

The phone woke her. Nicky, she thought, and grabbed her mobile from the bedside table.

'Happy Christmas, Jo,' Lawrence's voice greeted her.

'Thanks . . . Happy Christmas. At least I suppose it is.'

She heard Lawrence laugh. 'Whoa, your best Eeyore voice. Try to sound a bit more enthusiastic. Did I wake you? It's gone ten.'

She pulled herself up against the pillows. 'I got to bed late. Nicky came round. Seems Amber's gone AWOL.' She explained what their son had told her. 'I thought it might be him calling to say she was home.'

'I'm sure she's absolutely fine. Nicky'll have to get used to the dramas if he's going to stay the course.'

'You're probably right.' She paused, unwilling to get into a forced conversation with him, especially as Arkadius might be listening. 'What are you both doing today?'

'Arky's in Russia visiting his parents. He flew out yesterday. Nicky and Amber were supposed to be coming over for lunch.'

'I doubt that'll happen now.'

'Not by the sound of it. You're spending the day with Donna, Nicky said.'

'I lied.'

He laughed. 'Christmas was never your thing. I'd better ring Nicky and find out how it's going, what his plans are.'

'Yes.'

Silence.

'Listen . . . if Amber hasn't pitched up and Nicky's in a state . . . maybe we should all be together today? For Nicky.' He paused. 'Not sure how comfortable you are with that.'

Not at all, was the answer. And yet . . .

'Nicky won't want to come over if she's still missing,' she said, avoiding the issue.

'I think that's exactly when he'll need our support. He'll be going crazy stuck in that grisly basement flat all on his own, worrying about her.'

Jo gave a mental sigh. He was a bulldozer, her husband. Once an idea had fixed in his mind, he was relentless. She knew she could resist, but was there really any harm in spending a day together for the sake of their son? What was she afraid of, exactly?

'I haven't got any food,' she said.

'I have. The lot. Only it's a chicken instead of a turkey . . . but then you hate turkey. I'll give you a call when I've talked to Nicks.'

As soon as she ended the call, she regretted what she'd done. The thought of Lawrence cosily ensconced in her space – as it had become – falling into the comfortable patterns of the past, pouring the wine, eating at the table, chatting with her and Nicky, while all the time in love with someone else, just waiting for him to come back from Russia so they could fall into bed together, was infuriating.

She rang Nicky. If Amber was home, maybe they could still go to Lawrence's as planned, and she could make some excuse.

'Hi, Mum.' His voice was leaden.

'Have you found her?'

'Yeah, she's fine. She texted me this morning.'

'Where was she?'

'At Bea's, where I thought.'

'So is she coming back?'

'No.' There was a pause. 'She's dumped me.'

'Dumped you?' Jo echoed.

'Yup.'

'Oh, darling. I'm so sorry. Why?'

She heard him sigh. 'She said the whole baby thing freaked her out. Thought I was way too serious. Said she was too young to be so full-on in a relationship.'

'Right.'

'Mum . . . I don't know what to do. I love her so much.' At this stage Nicky began to cry and Jo had trouble understanding what he was saying.

'Listen, come over. Your father is threatening to bring a chicken.'

'I can't. God, the last thing I want is a sodding Christmas dinner . . . sorry, Mum, don't mean to be rude or anything.'

'It's OK. But you've got to eat at some stage. Anyway, it'll feel better to talk about it, get some perspective. You shouldn't be alone.'

'I know you mean well, Mum. But I'm too gutted to think straight right now. And whingeing to you won't help.'

But after some cajoling from Jo, he did agree to call her in a couple of hours and see how he felt.

★　　★　　★

In the end it was after five when Nicky slouched in, pale and unshaven, looking as if he'd slept in his clothes, and smelling strongly of alcohol.

Lawrence, however, had been round since early afternoon. He and Jo had started in on the cold Cava soon after his arrival, both awkward at being alone together, both tacitly agreeing to blur the lines.

But as they waited for Nicky, Jo found they had no trouble making conversation. As long as he doesn't mention Arkadius, she thought.

'Are you seeing your mum?' she asked.

Lawrence pulled a face. 'Tomorrow. She won't know it's Christmas anyway . . . probably won't even know it's me.' He grinned at her. 'You can come too if you like.'

'Ha, ha. There's got to be some benefit to being abandoned.' She didn't intend to get at him – the alcohol had loosened her tongue. But he looked thoroughly disconcerted. 'Sorry, you asked for that.'

He gave a weary nod. 'It'd be nice if Rick did his filial share once in a while. He hasn't seen her in over two years.'

'He's in Borneo, Lawrence.' His older brother was an anthropologist and spent most of his time in some rainforest or other, much to Lawrence's annoyance.

'So?'

She couldn't help laughing at his peeved expression.

'I'm going to cook,' he said, unpacking two large supermarket canvas bags and laying out the contents on the work surface. Lawrence was a diligent shopper; he would take literally hours in the supermarket. He said he found it soothing. So everything was there, from the chicken and the stuffing to the chipolatas, bacon, the bread sauce, cranberries, sprouts, a pudding and cream. Jo was surprised. Lawrence had seldom done much in the kitchen – division of family labour was always along gender lines in the Meadows family.

'OK,' Jo said, without hesitation.

But then Nicky still didn't show, so they drank some more. And the second bottle was already breached when he finally put in an appearance. Jo gave him a long hug.

'Do you want to go and have a shower while supper's cooking?' Jo asked, eyeing Nicky's stubble, lank hair, and noting the unmistakable reek of old alcohol.

'That bad, is it?' Their son gave her a half smile. But he seemed disorientated.

She nodded.

'Yeah, OK. Might do that.' He disappeared upstairs.

'Going to be a long night,' Lawrence said. 'We'll have to chivvy him up.'

'I don't think he's ready to be chivvied exactly. *We* both know he's had a lucky escape, but he's not going to see it like that any time soon.'

'Whatever you do, don't slag Amber off.'

Jo frowned at him. 'Like I'd do that.'

He grinned. 'Just checking.'

She sat at the kitchen table and watched her husband as he approached the preparation for dinner methodically, lining everything up in order of execution, perusing the instructions on each and every packet, occasionally referring to Jo for some pan or utensil he couldn't locate. He seemed to be actually enjoying himself.

'Do you think I'm obsessive?' Nicky stared at Jo across the table. He'd come down from his shower looking fresher but still sunk in gloom.

She remembered his rigorous pursuit of various childhood passions, such as collecting Transformers, then Pokémon cards, taking fencing classes, spending hours working out Cassie's Rubik's cube.

'I'd say focused rather than obsessive.'

Lawrence nodded. 'Nothing wrong with that.'

'Amber says I stifled her, that she felt she couldn't move without me watching her. I'll admit I did monitor her food. But she never ate, and that worried me sick. You saw how thin she was. We often had fights about it, but what was I supposed to do? Just sit and watch her starve herself to death?'

Nicky had spent most of lunch delivering a monologue on his relationship with Amber, not seeming to care if they responded or not.

'I haven't seen her much, but is it possible that

291

she's just a picky eater, neurotic about being slim? Lots of women are these days,' Jo said.

'How would I know, Mum? I'm not an expert in eating disorders. And she claimed the throwing up was down to being pregnant.' He closed his eyes, rubbed his hands wearily across his face. 'Except she wasn't.'

'Must have been difficult,' Lawrence put in.

'She made me feel I was the one with the problem and she was perfectly normal.'

'That's part of the illness.'

'So what should I have done?'

Lawrence patted his son on the shoulder. 'There's not a lot you could have done. You can't force someone to get help if they don't want it.'

'Great chicken,' she said, to deflect the conversation away from Amber for a while. 'In fact I'm impressed with the whole thing.'

Lawrence grinned. 'Not quite Heston, but at least I can put together a meal . . . which I certainly couldn't when we were . . .' He looked away. 'Before . . .' he finished lamely.

It was Jo who broke the silence. 'And there's Christmas pud too,' she said, cringing at the forced note of enthusiasm in her voice.

'Yes, but no brandy butter, I'm afraid,' Lawrence said in the same unnatural tone. 'You're the only one who likes it and I didn't think I'd be seeing you.'

'If she sorts out the eating thing, maybe there'd be a chance for us.' Nicky hadn't heard a word they'd said. He was almost talking to himself. 'I mean, apart from that, we had a brilliant relationship. I loved her and she said she loved me.'

'There isn't really an "apart from" though, is there,' Jo said, hearing the echo of her husband's complaint about Arkadius. 'If it is an eating disorder, it'll take precedence over everything for Amber. And you standing in the way, pointing out what's really going on, won't work for her.'

Her words seemed to clear Nicky's gloom.

'But if I could stop getting at her . . . at least try. Maybe it's not as serious as I thought. Maybe, as you say, she's just a picky eater.'

Jo and Lawrence gave each other a worried glance.

'You wouldn't be doing her any favours, Nicky,' Lawrence spoke softly.

He stared at them, then slumped back in his chair. 'OK, OK, I'm just clutching at straws, aren't I? I just can't believe it's over.'

Jo's mobile rang. She looked at the display.

'I'll take this upstairs,' she said.

'Hey,' Travis said softly.

'Hey, yourself. Where are you?'

'California, with Mom. Just a flying visit. Have to be back in the city day after tomorrow. How's it going?'

Jo groaned. 'You honestly don't want to hear.'

She heard his infectious laugh and found herself joining in.

'Try me.'

'Really . . . you don't.'

'Whoa, that bad. But you're good, Jo?'

'Mostly. Today's just a crap day. Hate Christmas.'

'Least you don't get generous helpings of God with the turkey and pumpkin pie. Mom's relentless.'

'Sounds like a walk in the park compared to Christmas lunch with ex-husband and recently dumped son.'

'Ooh, Amber done a runner? Didn't see that coming.'

They talked on, Jo tingling with pleasure at hearing his voice again. It was in these moments, when they seemed so connected, that a tiny, ridiculous part of her wondered if they could have a future, more time together. Had their parting been too hasty, too nonchalant? Maybe she could be his base, the place he came back to. Surely most actors had to live like this. It would suit her; she couldn't imagine living full-time with anyone again. And the frequent absences would keep their passion alive. But then she remembered that Travis didn't want a relationship, nothing tying at least, and she laughed at her pathetic delusion.

After they'd said goodbye, she stayed sitting on her bed for a while, her mind returning to the two men downstairs, both of whom – for different reasons – made her heart heavy. And she was tempted to just curl up on the bed and go to sleep.

Lawrence gave her a wary look when she finally went downstairs, raising his eyebrows in question.

'Cassie?'

Jo shook her head and Lawrence had to be satisfied with that. She'd spoken to Cassie that morning. Her daughter had been cooking lunch.

'What are you making?' Jo had asked.

'Shoulder of pork, apples, roasties, the lot.'

'Pork? Not . . .?'

'Don't go there, Mum,' she'd said, laughing. Jo hadn't told her about Nicky, she didn't want to ruin her daughter's day. Cassie sounded happy for once, a lightness in her voice Jo hadn't heard in a long time.

Lawrence served the pudding in silence, but Nicky looked at his bowl blankly, then pushed it to the side.

'Umm, listen, thanks guys, but I think I'll get off now.' He stood up.

'You can stay over if you like,' Jo suggested. But Nicky shook his head. 'I . . . I just need to be on my own, Mum. But thanks. I really appreciate you both being so supportive. And the meal.'

After he'd left, Jo and Lawrence both let out a long sigh and sat down again at the table, deflated.

'I hate seeing him like that.'

'I know. But he'll get over it. He's young. Everyone needs to have their heart broken at least once.'

'Really?'

Lawrence, oblivious, rattled the empty bottle of

red they seemed to have consumed, along with the two of Cava and pulled a face.

'There's some ancient Sambuca at the back of the cupboard,' Jo said. 'We never opened it.'

For a moment, Jo was transported back to Sardinia. It was cooler, finally, on the café terrace that evening. She and Lawrence – relaxed, freshly showered after a day on the beach – sat at a small table, between them a basket of the signature wafer-thin bread brushed with olive oil and salt, soft green olives, glasses of chilled local white. They ate sea bream and warm summer vegetables in chilli, oil and lemon, then tangy slices of hard Sardinian Pecorino and fresh peaches. Even now, Jo could almost smell the scent of juniper and myrtle on the balmy Mediterranean air, mixed with the pungent wood smoke from the pizza oven at the back of the village café. The tiny glasses of Sambuca they sipped with their coffee seemed like the perfect end to a perfect meal.

'It won't taste the same,' she warned.

Lawrence was silent, perhaps remembering a similar evening. Or more likely, Jo thought with a sudden stab of anger, recalling a meal he'd shared not with her, but with Arkadius during their recent holiday to the same place.

'Actually I'm tired,' she said, abruptly getting up from the table. 'You should think about going.' She saw the surprise on his face. 'It's late, Lawrence.'

He got up too. 'No, you're right. I've got to be in Ipswich in the morning.'

She watched him pull his car keys out of the pocket of his navy cords.

'You're not driving!'

Lawrence looked startled. 'Well, how do you think I'm going to get home on Christmas night? You can't get a cab for love nor money without booking it six months in advance. Anyway, I'm not drunk. I haven't had any wine for at least an hour.'

'You're way over the limit, you idiot. We've been boozing since lunchtime. There's no way on earth I'm letting you drive tonight.' She reached forward to try and snatch his car keys from his hand. But he was quicker and raised his arm. A tussle ensued as she refused to give up.

'Stop it, Jo. For Christ's sake, let go . . . it's my responsibility if I drive. This is childish, *let go!*'

And they found themselves so close, holding each other, entangled, both tired and stressed, drunk. Then Lawrence's arms were round her, his lips on hers. She was paralysed for a split second, then quickly planted her hands on his chest and pushed him roughly away.

'What the hell are you doing?'

Lawrence backed off instantly, his face crimson.

'Sorry . . . sorry. I'm really sorry. I just . . . I wasn't thinking.'

Jo realized she was panting, her heart pumping in her chest. She wanted to tell him to leave that instant. But she knew he would just get straight into his car. She swung round and began clearing the table.

Her husband remained standing there like a statue. Then he turned towards the front door, the car keys still in his hand. Did she care if he lost his licence, killed someone . . . killed himself even? Did she bloody care? She took a deep breath.

'For God's sake . . . let's forget about what just happened. You can't drive. Please. Stay. You can sleep in Nicky's room.'

Jo lay like a tree trunk all night: stiff, cold and still. Even though she was worn out by all the tensions, she didn't sleep a wink. Lawrence's presence, yards away down the corridor, tormented her. She was furious with him for trying to kiss her. Furious with herself for being in a situation where he might. How dare he? she kept on repeating to herself. How bloody dare he, when he claims to be in love with someone else? The kiss had been instantly familiar, while at the same time like being assaulted by a total stranger. Now, lying in the dark, she could only think of Travis and the eager desire with which his mouth had sought hers.

In the early hours she must have slept, because when she surfaced the clock showed nine-thirty-five. She got up quickly and went downstairs, but Lawrence, thank goodness, had gone.

'I can't come to the party tonight. Lawrence tried to kiss me.' Jo still wasn't dressed, she'd just put a coat over her night clothes, pulled on her Uggs and banged on Donna's door.

298

Her friend was in the kitchen, organizing her annual Boxing Day bash – a lunchtime buffet with anything but turkey, crates of champagne, and usually about twenty five people. The girl who had let her in went back to vacuuming the sitting room, and Donna filled the kettle.

'Hold on. I don't follow,' her friend said. 'What's Lawrence kissing you got to do with my party? Sounds like a complete non sequitur to me.'

Jo stared at her. 'Donna, did you hear what I said? He *kissed* me!'

Donna was grinning. 'Yes. Why?'

'*Why?* I don't know.'

'OK . . . when, then?'

'Last night, when I wouldn't let him drive home drunk.'

'When you were supposed to be in Devon?'

Jo looked sheepish. 'Yes, well, I couldn't face going anywhere and I knew you'd try and persuade me.' Donna always had Christmas with an astronomically rich American couple with a walled mansion looking over Holland Park. Jo had been asked to join them this year.

'So instead, you had your *very* ex-husband over for a cosy-up? Good call.'

'It wasn't like that.' Jo explained about Nicky, Amber, the car keys.

Now Donna was really laughing. 'God, darling. Sounds like the Christmas from hell. Poor you.'

'I'm exhausted.'

'So what did you say . . . after he lunged?'

'I told him to forget about it and go to bed.'

Donna pulled a face. 'Very grown-up. I hope he was apologetic.'

'He looked sort of surprised at himself, and really embarrassed. I'm telling you, it was grim.'

'And did you see him this morning?'

'No, and I don't plan to, not for a very long time.'

Her friend frowned. 'Hmm . . . so what does this mean, do you think? Is Arkadius on the wane? Has our Lawrence seen the light at last?'

'God, no. He said he still loves him. Remember? I stupidly asked last time I saw him. That's why the kiss made me so angry.'

'Probably just a drunken fumble, no? Your fault for asking him over.'

'I know. It was dumb.'

'But . . . it shows, doesn't it, that he still has feelings for you.'

'And that's supposed to make me feel better?'

CHAPTER 17

Mid-January 2014

Jo sat gazing at the pictures of her house that Tina Brechin had emailed to her. They made it look like a palace. The estate agent had seemed unconcerned that Jo had never got around to painting the downstairs rooms.

'We'll see how it goes,' she'd told Jo, her neat eyebrows raised a little as she glanced round the kitchen again. 'If we're getting poor feedback, it might be worth a re-think. But I'm pretty sure there won't be a problem. The market is buoyant at the moment. And this is a lovely house.'

Jo was only half listening. This woman seemed to talk a lot without really saying anything. Quite a skill.

'Viewing is by appointment only, of course. And one of us will always accompany the client.' Tina went on. 'But I'd advise you to be as flexible as possible. People move on if they can't get access when they want to.'

'By "flexible", what do you mean?'

Tina waved her manicured hand in the air. 'Oh,

nothing too intrusive. We're talking mostly ten till six. But sometimes those city boys can't get over here much before seven or eight.'

Jo nodded. The house wouldn't suit a 'city boy' anyway.

Where am I going to go? she asked herself now, as she clicked through the photos for the fourth time. It agitated her, thinking of someone seeing them, walking through the door, loving it as she and Lawrence had all that time ago. Tina wouldn't have given the area, let alone the house, a second glance back then, in the years before gentrification. Jo felt a sudden nostalgia for those times, when there was no social pressure outside your front door, no requirement to lay a deck or prune a hedge or replace nets with slatted blinds or have your door painted Lichen or French Grey. And when there was not a latte in sight.

She began to imagine what it would be like to buy her own flat, live there by herself. Be a single woman. An older, single woman. But oddly even the 'older' bit didn't depress her as much as she thought it would. She typed in 'Flat', '2 beds', 'Shepherd's Bush', 'this area only', into the online agency, and wasn't too disappointed by what she saw. Her spirits lifted.

Maggie's call interrupted her property porn.

'I love *Tess's Angel*.'

Jo held her breath.

'It works. Tess is great, a real character. Well done, Jo. Back to your old form.'

'You think so?'

'Now . . . how do we present this to Frances?' Maggie asked. 'I haven't told her yet that it's not the book she commissioned.'

'My instinct is to just send her the book with a note saying it turned out differently,' Jo said. 'Then she'll read it, and if she likes it, we might be OK. If not . . . well, we can cross that bridge when we come to it.'

'If you're happy with that, will you send it off then? And copy me in so I can see what you've said.'

Jo said that she would. She felt quite calm about it. Almost fatalistic. There had been a strange shift in her mind since Christmas Day. Lawrence's kiss seemed to have severed something, pushed her apart from him more completely than all the months of absence had. Now she had the odd sensation of lightness, of freedom from her past. She would find a flat she liked and have her own space for the first time in her life. And maybe love it. She might even find someone else to share it with one day.

'I'm not looking forward to people poking round the house,' Jo told Cassie over the phone, 'saying rude things about the decor.'

Her daughter laughed. 'Don't be there then. Give the keys to Ms Foxton and come and stay with us.'

'Thanks, darling, but I think I should keep an

eye. I trust Tina to do the right thing, but I don't know anything about her co-workers. They might leave the front door open and I'll come back to find hordes of squatters dossing in my bedroom.'

'Good point. You aren't too depressed are you, Mum? It's such a huge thing, you must be dreading it.'

'You know, strangely I'm not. Obviously the thought of packing the place up is a bit challenging, and finding somewhere else to live. But I think I'm sort of OK about it now.'

'Wow.' Cassie was silent. 'And Dad?'

'What about him?'

'Is he pulling his weight with the house stuff? It's his bloody fault you're having to sell up after all.'

'I haven't spoken to him.' She heard the sharpness in her voice.

'Umm . . . has something happened with Dad? You sound pissed off. I thought you two were kind of OK now . . . well, in the context of being not OK, of course.'

'Everything's fine,' Jo said. There was no way she would ever mention the kiss to her daughter. But it still rankled. Yes, as Donna said, from his point of view it was probably just a drunken fumble, something to which he gave little thought. But to Jo it symbolized Lawrence's continued proprietorship. Leave her, take her, she was still his, whatever and whenever he fancied.

'Like I believe that,' Cassie was saying. 'You

two'd always say you were fine, even if the house was burning around your ears.' Jo heard her chuckle. 'Sort of old-school Brit . . . fine, fine, we're all absolutely fine, darling. Bad manners to complain.'

'Do we say that?'

'But hey-ho,' Cassie went on as if Jo hadn't spoken. 'I probably don't want to know about any more prattishness from Dad.'

'He wasn't always a prat,' Jo said.

'No . . . no, he wasn't.'

The tall blonde woman, stick thin and unfairly tanned for January – no doubt Christmasing in Mustique, Jo decided, the current on-trend watering hole – waved her hand at the wall between the sitting room and the kitchen. 'We could knock that down, make it into one big space. That front room is quite poky.'

Here we go, thought Jo, hovering by the door as Tina took her client round the 'property', as she insisted on calling it.

Now Tina was nodding in agreement. 'Most of the properties in the street have done that a while back,' she said, as if Jo's house with its 'poky' front room was stuck in the Dark Ages.

On they went, talking absolute nonsense about room heights and ensuites and potential for loft conversion and Godolphin & Latymer girls' school, not to mention house prices, house prices, house prices, until Jo was ready to smack the pair of them. Tina agreed enthusiastically with everything the blonde said, and they seemed to be actually vying with each other on what vast amounts they knew about selling houses.

When the blonde had been dispatched, Tina came back in.

'Hopeful?' Jo asked.

Tina shook her head. 'Oh no, definitely not. At least I'd be very surprised. She wants Notting Hill, but her budget's Shepherd's Bush. She won't buy here if she can help it.'

Great, Jo thought. 'So all that stuff about loft conversions was just so much hot air?'

'Part of the process, Mrs Meadows. People like to talk through their options. But I can always tell within three minutes if a person is serious about a property.'

'Really? Must make your job really hard, having to pretend for the other seventeen.'

The estate agent's mouth – tastefully defined in matt coral – pursed. 'I'm not pretending exactly. More listening.'

'Of course. I didn't mean . . .' Jo ground to a halt, knowing she would only dig herself deeper.

But give Tina her due, she was certainly getting people through the door. Jo was constantly jumpy during daylight hours, every small laziness, such as not folding a towel properly, not replacing the patchwork counterpane, not washing up a cup or tidying away a newspaper, were banished. She renewed the flowers, polished the furniture, swept the kitchen tiles, bleached the loo, abandoned her occasional afternoon nap in case Ms Brechin-spelled-B-R-E-C-H-I-N caught her – oh, horror! – in bed. It was stressful, and with each passing week she became more and more anxious for it to be over, for the die to be cast.

'So are you going?' Donna asked, waving the invitation card at Jo. She'd dropped round one morning in early February.

'Not sure.'

'Oh, come on. It'll be sensational if Ruthie's in charge. She never does anything by halves.'

'Craig must be really hurting. All that dosh . . . and on something so frivolous.'

Donna laughed. 'She probably threatened to leave him if he didn't. Only the prospect of a crippling divorce would get him to open his purse that wide.'

The party was on Valentine's Day, a fortieth wedding anniversary for a couple who'd lived in the house opposite Jo and Donna until last year, when they'd sold up and moved to Norfolk. It was to be a grand affair, thrown in a smart venue near Euston Station.

'The sixty-four-thousand-dollar question is: what the hell are we going to wear?'

'It says "Dress: Winter Wonderland",' Donna said, checking the heavy cream card which she'd thrown down on Jo's kitchen table, running her finger over the expensively embossed script.

Jo groaned. 'Noo . . . not fancy dress. Didn't notice that bit. I'm definitely not going then.'

'Calm down. It doesn't say fancy dress. It just means we have to dress like the White Witch from Narnia.'

'Ha, ha. Now if I looked like Tilda Swinton . . .'

'We wish. Probably silver would do, or white. Something sparkly. Shouldn't be too difficult.'

'For you, maybe. I don't do sparkly.'

The doorbell rang loudly.

'Oops, better clear off. That'll be another skinny blonde with too much money and a four-by-four.'

'Sorry.' Jo gave her friend an apologetic grin. 'If there was any other way . . .'

Donna sighed. 'I know, darling, I know. Not your fault at all. But I can't say I'm looking forward to the new regime. What if she has brats and parties? It's been so perfect, you and me and Maxy.'

Frances raised her eyebrows at Jo. They were back in the conference room at the publisher, perched at the end of the long glass table. Her editor had emailed her the day before. 'We need to talk. Can you come in tomorrow morning around ten?' it said. But nothing about what Frances had thought of *Tess's Angel*. Maggie decided it wasn't a good sign.

'If she'd really liked it, surely she'd have said.'

Jo sat very still now, her heart fluttering with anxiety. She kept telling herself it wouldn't matter if Frances rejected the book, but she knew it would.

'So where did this come from?' She indicated Jo's novel, printed out and bound with two brown rubber bands crossed in the centre.

'Not sure. I was having trouble with the other story – I just couldn't get a handle on the character. And stuff was happening at home . . . my father died. Then this one sort of appeared from nowhere and I just went with it. Couldn't do anything else.'

Frances nodded but seemed to be waiting for her to continue.

'Look, I know it's not what you commissioned. And I'll quite understand if you don't want to go ahead with it. But the other one we had the treatment for wasn't working.'

'Hmm . . . I wish you'd told me earlier.' The editor shook her head backwards, stroking her auburn hair out of her face. 'I made such a palaver about the other outline with the powers-that-be. Really pushed it. Looks so unprofessional to pitch up with a totally different title, a totally different book.'

'I know. I'm really sorry. I got so absorbed in the writing that I didn't think . . .'

Frances let out a long sigh, her French manicure tapping lightly on the pile of paper.

'Well,' she said, finally smiling at Jo. 'I like it. I like it a lot.'

Jo held her breath.

'It's the best you've done, in my opinion. And that's including *Bumble and Me.*'

'Seriously? You think it's better than *Bumble?*'

Frances nodded. 'It's very powerful. The Tess character is heart rending. It deals so well with teenage alienation. Generally a very modern feel.' She paused. 'But. I'll have to get support.'

'So you'd like to publish it?'

'Definitely. But I can't promise anything, not until I've had a chance to pitch it to Sales and Marketing. Swapping to the new title isn't a problem; we often change those after the event.'

'What might be a problem?'

Frances considered her question.

'Hopefully nothing.' She gave Jo a warm smile. 'Sorry to hear about your father.'

'Thanks.'

'Right, well, I'll set this all in motion and let you know as soon as we have a decision.' She began to gather up her phone, her pen, the manuscript. 'But well done, Joanna. And don't worry, I'll fight for Tess.'

Frances ushered Jo out, giving her a brief hug as they stood waiting for the lift to arrive.

As soon as Jo was outside the building, she called Maggie.

'Woo hoo!' her agent shouted. 'Brilliant news.'

'Steady on. It's not definite yet. The others – whoever they are – might not be as enthusiastic as Frances.'

'Oh, of course they will be. It's a great book. It works. Who wouldn't want to publish it?'

Jo laughed.

'You must be thrilled.'

'I am. And thoroughly relieved.'

'OK, well let me know as soon as,' Maggie said. 'I have a feeling about this one,' she added, making Jo smile to herself. Her agent was the cautious type; she'd rarely heard her so upbeat about her work.

'Jo? Can I come in?' Donna's head poked through the changing room curtains.

Jo was struggling into a silver dress, shiny and skin tight, which looked like something Barbarella, from the seventies film, might have worn. Donna had insisted she try it. She pulled the curtains back to see what her friend had on.

'You like?' Donna twirled in front of her in an ivory, sequined bodycon dress.

'Love it! You look about twelve.'

'Twelve in a good way?' her friend's face clouded with doubt as she smoothed the material over her hips. 'It's short, but that doesn't matter, does it? It didn't say ball-gowns.'

'Look, nobody cares in the end what anyone else wears. And it looks great. You should get it.'

Jo caught sight of the ridiculous dress she had on and laughed. 'So you're OK. What about me?'

Donna frowned as she looked Jo up and down. 'Yeah, that's not doing it. Try the black one.'

'Black's not exactly Winter Wonderland.'

'No, but you could jazz it up with a silver stole or something.'

In the end Jo bought nothing. The black dress had suited her, but it was a hundred and eighty pounds, which she didn't want to spend.

'I've got the navy one with the lacy sleeves. I'll wear that.'

It was a clear, cold February night for the party. Donna and Jo took a taxi to the address in Tavistock Place.

'Lawrence won't be there, will he?' Donna asked.

'The invitation was for both of us, so clearly they don't know we've split up. And I haven't mentioned it to Lawrence, obviously. So, no. He won't be there.'

'That's good. You can relax then.'

Although 'relaxed' nowhere near described Jo's state of mind. Butterflies churned in her stomach, she felt awkward and uncomfortable all dressed up – it was months since she'd worn anything other than jeans – and she was absolutely dreading having to socialize with the people who had known her and Lawrence as a couple for so many decades. Added to which, Jo – never good at parties – had always hidden behind Lawrence, let him make all the running.

The taxi pulled up at the entrance to the courtyard, over which tall, silver branches met, twinkling with tiny white lights.

'Here we go,' Donna said. 'Let's party!'

The elegant, late-Victorian rooms had been transformed by Ruthie's extravagant taste into a fantasy of grottos and ice-mountains and caves, all sparkling silvery and white and lit with thousands of battery candles and loops of Christmas tree lights. Glowing icicles hung from the mesh-swagged ceiling, accompanied by large silver hearts on which were written Ruthie and Craig's names in red glitter – the only colour in the decorations.

Donna and Jo looked around, speechless, sipping the delicious – and obviously expensive – champagne they'd picked off a tray held by a waiter looking decidedly uncomfortable in a sequined white onesie.

'Darlings!' Ruthie was upon them, carefully air-kissing their cheeks, obviously keen not to damage her make-up or hair with smoochy hugs so early in the night.

Jo shook her head in awe. 'This is incredible, Ruthie. Totally magic. God, it must have taken years of planning.'

'I've never seen anything like it. You're a genius,' Donna added.

Their friend, plump and blonde and bouncy, wearing a ridiculous silver Grecian-style dress and a diamond tiara – Jo failed to see the Winter Wonderland connection – roared with delighted laughter.

'Isn't it utter bliss? Craig'll never recover, of

course. But I can divorce him now we've had the party.'

They both laughed as Ruthie rushed off to greet some more guests.

'Shall we check it out?' Donna pointed through to another room, where there were tables set out and a dance area.

Jo nodded, already feeling the beneficial effects of the champagne on her nerves. 'Oops, keep moving, just spotted Robert and Alison at two o'clock.'

'Occupational hazard,' Donna whispered as they speeded up. 'Not sure I really bonded with any of those people we met at their barbecues. I mean, they weren't horrible or anything, just . . . different world.'

'So what are we doing here?'

'Getting drunk, having a laugh. We don't have to talk to anyone if we don't want to.'

'Just don't leave me for one single second.'

It was two glasses of champagne and some caviar and sour cream blinis later that Donna spotted Lawrence. She clutched Jo's arm as they chatted to a very amusing couple Donna had picked up, pointing towards the doorway.

'Noo,' Jo groaned.

'Can't see Arkadius yet,' Donna said after a moment checking the throng of guests.

'Probably doing the coats.'

Her husband looked uncharacteristically

awkward, despite his elegant dinner jacket – bought over twenty years ago, at some expense, but hardly worn – and Jo noticed his only concession to the party theme was a silver bow tie. It surprised her. Lawrence was not averse to fancy dress in the way she was. He had, on one occasion, dressed up as a 94 bus – to much raucous acclaim – for a Scarlet and Black party an old college friend had thrown. But clearly he wasn't in the mood tonight.

'Are you going to speak to him?'

'Don't have much choice.'

He was making his way across the room. Jo watched him go up to Craig and shake his hand, give Ruthie a hug. Then he was on his own again, looking round, seemingly at a loss.

She sighed. 'Back in a mo,' she told her friend. 'Hi, Lawrence.'

'Jo . . .' She held her glass in front of her with both hands, so as to avoid an embrace of any kind.

'I didn't know you were coming,' she said.

'I bumped into Craig getting off the Tube at Oxford Circus last week. He said they'd sent an invitation to the house.'

Jo ignored the implied criticism. 'Did you tell him we were separated?'

'I had to.'

'Ruthie didn't say anything just now.'

'No, well . . .'

'Arkadius not with you?'

'No . . . he couldn't make it.'

There was silence between them in the crowded

315

room, the Schumann played by the string quartet in the corner like a Greek chorus to their private drama.

'Listen, Jo . . . about Christmas . . .'

'Gotta drag Lawrence away I'm afraid, darling, there's someone who's dying to meet him.' Ruthie shot Jo a wide-eyed glance behind his back as she took her husband's arm and walked him firmly away. Rescuing me, Jo thought, embarrassed.

The evening was lively and drunken. No formal sit-down for dinner, Jo was relieved to see, just a buffet of smoked salmon, baked ham on the bone, sirloin of beef, cold sea trout delicately layered with sliced cucumber, huge dishes of dauphinoise potatoes, French beans and salads.

'God, I'm ravenous,' Donna announced as she sat down next to Jo at one of the tables dotted about the room, her plate laden with enough food to last them both a fortnight.

Jo laughed. 'You'll never get through even a quarter of that.' Donna ate like a bird.

'I know, but buffets confuse me. I take something, then further along I see something else I want more, but I can't really take the first thing off, so I just keep on piling it up.' She inspected her plate. 'But it does look delicious, doesn't it.'

'OK if I sit here?' Lawrence put his plate down next to Donna and sank gratefully into the chair before either of them had time to speak.

'Good party, eh?' Donna said.

He nodded. 'Fantastic.'

The conversation became general round the table as two other couples joined them, both of whom were old friends of the Carpenters and had been at the summer barbecue most years.

Jo said almost nothing. The initial high from the champagne had dipped to a slightly out of control intoxication where she wasn't sure she was walking straight or talking sense.

Lawrence's presence constrained her still further and maybe constrained him too, as he said surprisingly little, allowing Donna – in her element at any social event – to do all the work.

When the band set up on the podium and the speeches were over, Jo breathed a sigh of relief. No one would need to talk now.

The band struck up the first song, Stevie Wonder's 'You Are the Sunshine of My Life', and the anniversary couple took to the floor alone, Craig taking charge for once and shuffling his wife expertly round the floor to much laughter and applause.

'Dance?' Lawrence asked Donna when the band went on to Elton's 'Crocodile Rock', his glance avoiding Jo and a possible rejection.

'Love to,' Donna leaped to her feet with alacrity and they were gone.

Jo was envious of her friend. She and Lawrence had always been enthusiastic dance partners when they got the chance. Dreading one of the other men at the table asking her, she got up and trod a careful path to the Ladies, miles away down a flight of polished wooden stairs, where she took a long time doing not much to her hair and face. But when she got back they were still dancing. In fact everyone seemed to be dancing except her, alone at the table and feeling idiotic, until Craig came up behind her and pulled her to her feet.

'We can't leave the gorgeous Joanna alone on a night like this,' he said, in an awkward attempt at gallantry. Craig, a hugely successful accountant, was a decent man, a wonderful husband to the flighty Ruthie, but he had virtually no conversation skills. Jo had dreaded being put next to him at dinner parties in the past. She didn't know the right questions to ask about accountancy, and he never asked about her life. They usually ended up in the safe zone of The Government.

Tonight his bald head was shining with exertion as he pressed his plump belly, tightly swathed in a vintage maroon cummerbund, against Jo, his feet – surprisingly neat in patent leather lace-up evening shoes – guiding her about the floor in the semblance of a waltz. He was about four inches shorter than Jo in her heels, but this didn't seem to bother him.

'Fabulous party,' she shouted.

Craig beamed and nodded.

'We miss you, in the street,' she said.

'Sorry?'

'We miss you. In the street,' she repeated, closer to his ear.

He beamed and nodded again.

Jo gave up, deciding just to enjoy the dance. Donna and Lawrence had gone back to the table and were deep in conversation, their heads pressed closely together, presumably in order to hear the other's words. Jo wondered what Donna was saying to her husband. She could be quite brutal when she chose.

A couple of songs later, Craig carefully escorted her back to the table. Donna and Lawrence stopped talking as soon as she sat down, both their expressions tense and preoccupied. It obviously hadn't been party chit-chat.

'Hi . . . good dance?' Donna asked.

'Great. You?'

'Can't go wrong with the old favourites.'

She saw Lawrence gazing at her and looked away.

Geoff, one of the other guests at the table, asked Donna to dance, and Jo was left alone with her husband. He moved over into Donna's seat so that he was next to her. For a while they just sat there, as they had on so many other similar occasions in the past, facing the dance floor, watching the couples, tapping the rhythm out on the white table cloth.

'Jo . . .' He leaned closer. 'Listen, I know you've been avoiding me since Christmas Day, and I understand why. I was totally out of order hitting on you like that. I'd had too much to drink – you said so yourself – and . . . well, it just happened. But let's not fall out about it. It's stupid us not being able to talk to each other.'

'You just don't get it, do you Lawrence?'

He was staring at her intently. 'Get what?'

'That kiss . . . like you owned me. Pick me up, put me down, whatever turns you on . . .'

'That's really not fair.' His eyes were wide with indignation. 'It wasn't even remotely like that—'

'Your boyfriend's away in Russia – and anyway, things are a bit tricky at the moment – so you think you'll just pop round and get your leg over the ex?'

'Jo, come on. That's ridiculous. You know I'd never behave like that in a million years.'

'I have absolutely no idea how you'll behave, Lawrence. Not anymore.'

Rebuked, he dropped his gaze. When he raised his head again, his eyes were imploring.

'Please . . . please, Jo. You know I respect you more than anyone else on earth. I'd never intentionally take advantage of you, make you feel used. Never.'

Jo suddenly felt very tired. 'Respect'? Wasn't that the word people used to distance themselves? She didn't want to be respected by Lawrence as if she were some aged aunt or senior work colleague. She wanted to be loved. She seemed to be losing the thread, her head spinning with that last glass of white she'd drunk.

'God, I hate this. I hate it so much.' She swallowed back tears, turning her head away, reaching for the jug of water in the centre of the table and pouring herself a glass. She didn't want him to feel sorry for her.

'I hate it too.' His voice was soft and low, but she still heard him above the strains of another Stevie Wonder song.

They stared at each other, and Jo saw the anguish in her husband's eye.

'Why?' she whispered, feeling the tears gathering despite herself.

For an answer, Lawrence placed his hand gently over hers.

'God, way too much exercise.' Donna breezed back from the dance floor, flopping one arm across both Jo's and Lawrence's shoulders, dipping her head to their level. 'What's going on here?' She giggled drunkenly, turning from one to the other, her eyebrows raised.

Jo pulled back as Lawrence shifted quickly over to his own chair so that Donna could sit down.

'Tell me,' Donna plumped down between them, letting out a sigh of relief, checking each of their faces in turn. 'Go on. What have I missed?'

'A heated debate about climate change?' Lawrence said, straight-faced.

Donna looked at him in disbelief. 'Ha, ha.'

The music had slid into a slower tempo as the evening began to wind down. Jo was suddenly aware of the opening bars of Roberta Flack's 'Killing Me Softly'. This was *their* song, hers and Lawrence's. The first time she'd heard it was the very first time they kissed, at a drunken birthday bash for his university mate, Jono Lacy, held in his father's grand Mayfair flat. Lawrence told her later that he thought she'd be impressed he knew such people, although in fact she didn't give a fig about Jono, his father's money or anyone else there. Even though she and Lawrence had only met up once before for a hasty coffee before she caught a train to see her mother, she had already decided she was in love with him. And Roberta had seemed to confirm this. For a moment she was lost in the long-distant past.

Now Lawrence heard it too and raised his eyebrows at her. She didn't reply, but he got up and came round to where she was sitting, holding out his hand.

Jo only hesitated for a moment. Then she too got to her feet and walked in front of him towards the floor. They danced. And it felt so good, to be in his arms again. He held her close, as if he were relishing it as much as she. Neither of them said a word. And when the song ended they quickly pulled apart and went back to the table, almost sheepish that they had allowed such intimacy to happen.

Donna was chatting to Geoff's wife, Hannah, but Jo, shaken by the yearning the dance had evoked, interrupted them.

'I think I'm going to make a move,' she said. She was aware of Lawrence hovering, but she was desperate not to get into a situation where they left alone together again. 'You coming?' she asked her friend, carefully not looking his way.

Donna groaned. 'God, yes. Take me home, darling. If I don't go soon, you'll have to carry me.'

The three of them said their goodbyes, collected their coats and made their way into the freezing night. Once on the pavement, Lawrence turned to Jo, rubbing his hands together in the chilly air.

'Shall I find you a taxi?'

'Thanks, we'll be fine.'

'Sure? I'm just the other side of Senate House, so I'll walk.'

He kissed Donna goodbye on both cheeks, but Jo made a pretence of fumbling in her bag when he turned to her.

'Night, then,' he said, thrusting his hands in the pockets of his overcoat.

'Bye.'

Jo watched him stride off into the night.

Donna slumped in the back of the taxi, eyes shut, head lolling on the seat. Jo thought she'd passed out, until she heard her friend murmur, 'All is not well with the Russian.'

CHAPTER 18

15 February 2014

'We've had an offer.' Tina sounded cautious on the phone.

'OK . . .' Jo sighed inwardly. She was tired and hungover from Ruthie's party and didn't feel like having to deal with anything serious this morning.

'I'm afraid it's a bit cheeky. Twenty thousand below the asking price, so I'd advise you to reject it.'

'Who is it?' Jo asked, although she was certain she knew. The two men – Derek, forty-ish and immaculately dressed in a charcoal designer suit, buttoned black polo shirt and chunky steel wristwatch, and Gary, slightly older, plump, kitted out from head to toe in Hackett – had been round three times in the previous week, and spent hours muttering to each other at various points in the house.

Tina confirmed her suspicions.

'You think they'll come up?'

'Almost certainly. They're just testing the waters.

They want the place, and they definitely have the money.'

'How do you know?' They looked well-off, but Jo had long been aware that you could never tell a book by its cover.

'They've just sold a penthouse in Sussex Gardens. Must have gone for at least three mill., conservative estimate.'

'And they're downsizing to Shepherd's Bush?'

'Gary's mother lives in Brook Green apparently. Plus they've got their eye on a weekend place in Somerset. Anyway, I think we can assume they're good for at least another ten on your place. Perhaps even the whole twenty. I've already told them you're not in a hurry to sell.'

'Well, do your best, Tina.'

The agent was silent for a moment.

'Derek implied he'd want to complete as quickly as possible if it all goes ahead. How do you feel about that, Mrs Meadows?'

'What does "as quickly as possible" mean, exactly?'

'Well, depending on their solicitors . . . they're cash buyers . . . it could be as soon as a month, six weeks?'

'Wow.' Jo felt her pulse begin to race.

'How would that fit in with your plans?'

'I haven't found anywhere yet. But I can rent until I do.'

'I could push them up to two months, if that'd help. But we don't want to lose a good sale.'

As she put the phone down, Jo took a long breath, trying to stem the panic. She should be focusing on a place to live, but all she could think about was what Donna had told her about Lawrence and Arkadius. Her friend had perked up by the time the taxi dropped them at home after the party and they'd settled on Donna's sofa with a much-needed cup of mint tea.

'He said Arkadius had given him an ultimatum,' Donna told her. 'If he's not prepared to properly commit and move in, then it's hasta la vista.'

'Arkadius would actually be prepared to split up over it?'

Donna had nodded. 'Sounds like it. He's taken it badly . . . maybe invested a whole lot more in the relationship than Lawrence realized. Won't hardly speak to him at the moment, apparently. And if he does, it's just one long row.'

'So what did Lawrence feel about that?'

'Obviously he hates being blackmailed.' Donna had paused to sip her tea. 'From what he said, I gather it's making him really reassess their relationship.'

'But he's still in love with him.'

'He didn't say one way or another. I assume he still has feelings for Arkadius, or the decision would be easy, wouldn't it?'

'So what's he going to do?'

Her friend had shrugged. 'He didn't seem to know.'

Now, Jo sat at her desk and wondered. What had Lawrence meant when he'd said 'I hate this too', when he'd put his hand over hers, when he'd asked her to dance with him? Just that he was sorry? It had felt like more than that.

She shook herself. It was stupid to even think like that, she knew, especially as she couldn't envisage them being together again in any real-life way. What had happened last night was just nostalgia, nothing more. Remembering what it had been like to love each other.

'We've got a buyer.'

Lawrence took a moment to reply. 'Really? Oh . . .'

'And at the asking price. Isn't that great news? I'll be sending over stuff for you to sign in the next week or so, when I get the contracts from Mark. I'll answer all the questions myself and give them the info they need, so you'll just need to countersign and send it back to him.'

'OK . . . well, thanks for doing all that, Jo.'

He didn't sound as happy as she'd thought he might, as she filled him in about the details, told him about Derek and Gary.

'Well, I'm glad they like the house so much. When's completion?'

'Six weeks, if it all goes according to plan and the searches don't throw up anything dodgy.'

'Six weeks? That's quick. So have you got something lined up?'

'Nope. I'm going to rent. I can't get my head around buying anywhere yet.'

Her tone, she knew, was unnecessarily brusque. But they hadn't talked since the party five days ago and Jo found herself unwilling to give Lawrence the impression that she'd taken the events of that night at more than face value. She didn't want him to think she still cared.

'You must be thrilled,' she added tartly, when he didn't reply.

'Yes . . . yes, I suppose I feel relieved, on the money side . . . but the thought of the house no longer being there—'

'The house isn't going anywhere, Lawrence.'

'You know what I mean.'

'Donna's delighted it's not a thin blonde with a four by four.'

Lawrence gave a short laugh. 'Yes, I suppose she's been dreading you leaving as much as you have.' He paused. 'You'll miss not having her next door.'

I'll miss more than that, she thought, but held her tongue. There was no point in being angry with him any longer.

'I'll come and help pack, obviously,' he was saying. 'Just let me know when.'

'There's lots we'll need to get rid of, so I think we should go through the house as soon as possible, and decide what's going where. There's a local housing association that collects furniture and household stuff. We can tag it, then I can arrange for them to take it all away before the removal men come.'

'God . . . it's going to be quite a number. The accumulation of thirty-odd years . . .'

There was silence.

'Anyway, I'd better get on,' she said.

'Muuum . . . I can't believe it,' Cassie wailed down the phone. 'It's actually sold? Our lovely house?'

'You knew it was on the cards.'

'Yeah, but it was still ours. I don't think I really believed someone else would ever actually live there.'

Jo wasn't really in the mood to indulge her daughter's angst.

'Anyway, we've got to get on with sorting stuff out. I've only got six weeks. Any chance you could come up for a couple of days and help out? I've no idea what you want to keep from your room.'

'Sure. Of course I'll help. When shall I come?'

'The sooner the better. Dad and I are going through the house at the weekend.'

'OK, I'll talk to Matt.'

'How are things with you?'

'Yeah, good, actually. Really good.' Cassie paused. 'Listen Mum, you've got to nail somewhere to live. What'll you do if you can't find anything?'

'I'm looking.' Jo wished everyone wouldn't sound so worried about her. Nicky had been similarly anxious when she said she hadn't found a flat yet. But you could only look for rentals six weeks before you wanted one apparently. And she wasn't worried. She felt almost carefree about it. The burden of clinching the sale, dealing with all the service companies, getting rid of decades of mess, packing up the house – which meant spending a lot of time with Lawrence – organizing removals men and storage, was so stressful that she'd virtually stopped sleeping altogether. What happened afterwards she was sure would feel like freedom. A nice, clean, anonymous flat, with no responsibilities for the roof, the boiler, random leaks, the garden? It sounded like heaven.

'Let me help. We could do a blitz, check out Rightmove and Primelocation and then spend the day seeing a load of flats. It'd be fun. And one of them's bound to be OK for a few months until you buy a proper place.'

'Thanks, darling. I'll see how it goes. Donna's said I can stay with her for as long as I want if I can't find somewhere. Please, don't worry about me.'

'I *am* worried, and so is Nicks. He says you seem almost blasé about the whole thing.'

Jo laughed. 'You'd rather I was sobbing into my coffee?'

'No . . . it's just you do need a place to live, Mum.'

'Yes, darling. I get it. I'm not an idiot. I appreciate your concern, but honestly, I've got it under control.'

'OK . . . I'll call you later about when I can come up. Love you.'

Jo said goodbye and went back to her lists.

'So . . . where shall we start?' Lawrence looked positively enthusiastic about the day ahead. And Jo was grateful for his presence. She'd been going quietly insane the last couple of days. Every room she went into, every cupboard and drawer she opened, she saw the piles of possessions as a threat of vast, tsunami-like proportions.

'Coffee first?' she suggested.

They sat at the table to drink it.

'So, D-Day then.'

'Yup.' Jo's response was abrupt, her thoughts too distracted to focus on anything.

'Are the children coming to help?'

Jo nodded. 'But not till next week. So if we can get the bulk of it done today and tomorrow, then they can do their rooms, I'll get everything collected, then it's just packing the rest, you taking yours, me taking mine or putting it in storage, them taking what they want . . .' she stopped her manic listing, blowing her cheeks out in a long sigh.

'You look exhausted,' he said, eyeing her with concern.

'I feel it.

'It'll be better once we make a start.'

'You reckon? You've forgotten how much rubbish there is. I walk into a room and think, Oh, nothing much here, then I open a wardrobe or look in a drawer . . . it's massive, Lawrence.'

He laughed. 'Well, we can only do what we can do. In the end it's only stuff, and if it goes to the wrong place, or gets chucked when it shouldn't, it won't be the end of the world.'

'No . . . no, I suppose not. You're right, it is only stuff.'

'So we're starting with the attic, then?' he said.

Dusty, dark, up a rickety pull-down aluminium ladder, the bare floorboards hurt her knees as she bent over one box after another under the eaves.

Lawrence, hunkered down in the far corner, sat back on his heels.

'Can't imagine why we kept most of this,' he said, holding up a battered wooden tricycle with a wheel missing.

Jo smiled. 'You remember Nicky on that, out on the terrace? He was like a demon.'

'He used to do it for hours on end, back and forth.' He put it aside and picked out something else. 'Hey, come and see.'

Jo crawled over to his side. In the dim light from the bulb swinging from the ceiling, Lawrence was peeling open a small plastic photograph album, with a collection of wonky, discoloured Polaroid snaps of the family on a beach.

'That was Cassie's. I remember her doing it.'

'Look at you,' Lawrence said, pointing to a shot of Jo lying full length in a bikini. 'What a figure.'

'You don't look so hot,' she laughed, pointing to

332

a blurred one of Lawrence's broad back view, hunched over a sandwich, hair – still a golden-blond then – damp from the sea. It was a Scottish beach, the West Coast, during an improbably warm summer. They had even swum in the sea, which was just about bearable if you kept to the top two feet of surface water, but numbingly cold if you dropped any lower. Jo remembered hugging Nicky's little body – icy, blue, teeth chattering, tight-wrapped in a towel – in her arms. She could almost feel him still. And taste the chicken-and-ham paste baps and hot tea they'd brought for the picnic.

'God, we were so young,' Lawrence was saying, his voice wistful. 'You forget, looking at Nicky and Cass, that when we were their ages we had two children, jobs, a mortgage . . . this generation is so immature.'

'That's a bit harsh. Anyway, if they are, it's probably our fault.'

He nodded, giving her a wry smile. 'Bin it?' he waved the album over the black bin bag.

'We ought to keep it, till Cassie's had a look.' Jo turned her attention back to an ancient purple-velvet Biba jacket.

The day wore on and all they seemed to achieve was looking at things and putting them back in the same place. But Jo and Lawrence had settled into a rhythm with each other. The initial unease Jo had felt at having to confront the past with him had gradually faded as they both became completely absorbed by items they'd forgotten they had, unearthing memories only they shared, memories which, at least for that moment, erased the present, the delicate situation they found themselves in now.

'God . . . my knees are killing me. Time to break for lunch?' Lawrence asked after a while.

Jo made them both a tuna-and-lettuce sandwich and a cup of tea. They didn't speak as they ate, Jo, certainly, still caught in the web of family memories.

'What will you do with the money?' she asked eventually.

He shrugged, let out a sigh. 'Umm . . . I suppose I'll buy somewhere.'

'But not with Arkadius, I hear.'

Lawrence didn't answer. He seemed miles away. She watched his face go tense, his eyelids flutter.

'Jo,' he stopped, swallowed. 'Jo, I need to tell you something.'

She waited, remembering the last time he'd said those very words and the devastating consequences. Nothing, she thought, could ever be that bad again.

'Arkadius and I have split up.' He looked pained as he said the words.

'Split up? Oh.'

Lawrence was staring at her, and she wondered what he expected from her.

'And how do you feel?'

'Honestly? I'm gutted.'

'You still love him, then.'

Lawrence took a moment before he responded, then he gave a light shrug. 'Things change . . . you can't sustain that crazy, In-Love thing for long . . . you wouldn't want to.'

She didn't reply. What could she tell him he didn't already know about love?

'I don't even know if love is the right word, but however you define it, the thing is I'm not gay, Jo. Not in the way Arkadius is. He's always known, since he was eight, he says, and he's never wavered. It's so different from me. I can't do that share-a-home, couple thing with him. It would be a lie. It's just not me.'

'You can't blame him for thinking it is,' she said.

He glanced at her, his eyes sharp as if he thought she might be criticizing him, then his gaze softened.

'No, no, you can't. But I told him right from the start that whatever I felt for him, I couldn't see myself fitting into his world.'

Jo thought about what he was saying.

'Explain,' she said, trying to understand.

'Surely you, of all people, can see?'

'I get that he's a man surrounded by men and you're used to relating to a woman . . . women,' she said. 'But if that's not you, how did you find him so attractive in the first place?' He was looking uncomfortable, but she ploughed on. 'Unless you're telling me it really was purely about sex.'

'It wasn't just sex,' he said. 'It was more than

that . . . I've said it before . . . a sort of madness. I can't explain it better, Jo, really I can't. He's an extraordinary man, Arky. And I really care for him. But . . . but he's gay.'

Jo raised her eyebrows at the obviousness of Lawrence's remark.

'And I'm not. I'm ninety-nine per cent attracted to women. Only the other one per cent to men. And only to the extent that I've occasionally – very occasionally – found a man attractive . . . in the way we're all sometimes drawn to someone else . . . without doing anything about it. Or even considering it might be possible. Or wanting it to be.' He paused in his speech, which gave the sense of thoughts trying to find a path through the jumble in his mind. Thoughts held back for lack of an audience. 'But then with Arkadius it was just overwhelming, and I gave in to him. Personally. Not to his lifestyle. It's not a lifestyle thing. I liked my life with you. It's who I am.'

Jo didn't reply.

'And when we were . . . me and Arky . . . before you found out . . . it was great . . . intoxicating.' He stopped, dropped his eyes. 'Look, I know how selfish that sounds. And I'm fully aware I'm digging myself a huge hole. But I really want you to understand, Jo.'

'Why?'

'Why what?'

'Why do I have to understand? Especially at this stage.'

Lawrence buried his head in his hands, his elbows on the table, his sandwich barely touched.

'God!' When he looked up, his eyes were full of pain. 'It seems so stupid, selling this house. Why on earth are we doing it?'

Jo was stunned. 'For Christ's sake!'

He didn't respond, just got up, his balled fists pushed to the bottom of his jean pockets, and went over to the window. As he stared out on to the garden, Jo watched his back, the flick of his thick white hair just above the collar, the set of his shoulders beneath the black sweater, the way his long legs always appeared to bend in the wrong way. Her Lawrence, supremely confident, successful in his work, at home very much the head of the family, a loved husband and father, seemed to have been shaken into a very different mode. These days he was quieter, more insecure, less bullish – a changed person. Although now he was clearly making a determined effort to get a grip as he turned to her, the expression in his blue eyes steadier, his voice calmer.

'Listen, I haven't been totally honest with you, Jo. I didn't think it was fair on you, not after the way I've behaved. But part of what's going on with Arky is not just about him wanting me to move in, or him belonging to a different world. Or even how I feel about him. The problem is I miss you, Jo. I really, really miss you and the life we had together. I was mad, totally insane to do what I did.'

She stared at him. 'What are you saying?' Her voice was hardly above a whisper.

Lawrence walked slowly back to the table and sat down. He leaned forward, his hands clasped in front of him.

'I don't know . . . I don't know what I'm saying. I'm so sorry. But this morning, looking over all those things in the attic, remembering what we had. You, me, the kids. It's been our whole life. You won't believe me, but all these weeks since I exiled myself from you . . . I never stopped loving you, not for a moment. And now the house, our home, is gone and it feels so desperately sad . . . I can't bear it, Jo. I feel like I've cut off my right hand on a whim. How could I have done that . . .'

It was Jo's turn to get up, move away from those tormented eyes. 'Stop. Please. I can't hear any more, Lawrence. You're making no sense. With one breath you say you still love Arkadius, that you're "gutted" he won't see you. The next you're almost sobbing at my feet saying you've made a terrible mistake.'

She realized she was cold, feeling almost sick. All these months past when she would have given her eye-teeth to hear his words. Yet now they seemed like so much melodrama . . . and indulgence.

'Sorry.' He looked away. 'I knew it was a mistake coming here today. Every time I see you now . . . like on Christmas Day or at Ruthie's party . . . I find I just want to forget that there was ever a problem between us.'

Jo felt a surge of anger at his words. As if what he'd done could ever be *forgotten*.

'Christ! I don't know how you *dare* talk about forgetting, after everything you put us through.' She could hardly breathe. 'Coming here with your self-indulgent whining. I love him, or at least I *sort of* love him. But I love you too . . . oops, sorry . . . such a mistake. Expecting me to just fall at your feet and forgive you when basically you don't have a clue what you're even saying. *Or* what you want. Please . . . just go, will you. Go away and leave me alone.'

'But . . .'

She held her hand up.

'OK . . . OK.' He got to his feet and she noticed how tired he looked.

While he gathered his coat, wound his tartan scarf round his neck and made his way slowly towards the door, Jo held her breath. It was only with the sharp click of the latch behind him that she finally let it out and burst into tears, the violent sobs tearing at her chest as if they were trying to break her in two.

'He wants to come back. I told you he would.' Donna and Jo were in the car, heading to a series of rental viewings. The first one was on the other side of Hammersmith Broadway, in one of the mansion blocks near the river.

'He doesn't know what the hell he wants,' Jo said.

'This thing with Arkadius . . . do you think it's really over?'

'No, I'm sure it's not. Arkadius is just putting the thumbscrews on to get Lawrence to commit. If Lawrence holds out, Arkadius is bound to relent and take him back . . . if he really cares for him.'

'Yeah, but it sounds like it's Lawrence who's wavering.'

'Only because he's on his own. Which he loathes. So he gets all sentimental and nostalgic about his family. Then we have a rummage through the past and he finally understands we've actually sold our lifelong home and that it isn't just about money after all . . . and has a moment. But if push came to shove and I said, OK, Lawrence, come back, all is forgiven, he'd probably run a mile.'

'You think? From what you say he said, he's never really moved past you. Arkadius is just a bit of an aberration.'

Jo backed into a parking space just past the flats and turned to her friend. 'A *bit*? Understatement of the decade. But honestly, it doesn't matter if he's over him or not. I'm furious. How dare he walk in and give me this cheesy spiel about love? About caring and missing me and all that rubbish, when he's still in bed with his toy boy?'

'Hmm . . .' Donna looked doubtful. 'But is he?'

'If he's not, it's a technicality. He certainly has been till about two weeks ago.' She yanked the handbrake on and opened the car door. 'Anyway, the point is, he's in complete emotional meltdown. I can't take anything he says seriously.'

'So here we have the kitchen . . . stunning original tiles,' Sean, the man from Winkworth, pointed at the drab, seagreen Victorian tiles that covered every inch of wall and gave the room a dismal, subterranean feel. 'The cupboards and work surfaces are all new.' He droned on, clearly just going through the motions, his eyes constantly flicking back and forth to his smart phone, held discreetly by his side. As they progressed further down the labyrinthine corridor to the bedrooms it got darker and gloomier with every step.

'Blimey,' Donna whispered, 'you'd need a ball of string to find your way out of here.'

Sean gave her friend a sharp look. 'You don't have to keep the furniture. It's furnished or unfurnished, the owner's flexible,' he said.

The next one, a modern conversion near Ravenscourt Park, was the opposite: light, white plasterboard, no fireplace, no bath and the size of a crisp packet.

The third one, off Hammersmith Grove, was high-ceilinged, smelly, peeling and cluttered with the current occupant's tatty second-hand furniture, dirty nets at the window and freezing cold.

'Gross,' Jo said, as they made their way back to the car. 'Those photos online are such a con.' She sat back in her seat. 'I'll never find anywhere that isn't a million dollars.'

Donna laughed. 'You've looked at three.'

'Five, I saw two yesterday.'

'OK, but hardly time to slit your throat. Anyway, I've said, you can camp at mine if necessary.'

The sixth for that day, for which Jo almost cancelled the viewing because she was so tired and jaded, had definite promise. A garden maisonette three streets away from her house, towards the green, with a small paved garden, two bedrooms, a free-standing bath with claw feet – which Donna adored – and a large sitting room.

'I think I could live here,' Jo told her friend. 'It's more than I want to pay, but if it's only for a year.'

'You've seen the cheaper ones, darling.'

'The owners are working in Australia for a while,' Agnieszka, the quiet Polish girl from Douglas and Gordon said. 'It's their family home.'

'It's close to me, that's all I care about,' Donna said.

Jo took the flat.

CHAPTER 19

2 April 2014

Jo awoke in her new home, mildly disorientated even after five nights there. But as she lay snug beneath the duvet, gazing up at the strange ceiling – freshly painted in a pale duck-egg blue instead of the faded white of her old bedroom – noting the sun coming through the slatted blind, checking the dial of the familiar alarm clock, she was aware of a quiet freedom. I've done it, she thought.

The previous weeks had passed in a blur. Nicky had been brilliant, a constant presence by her side, methodically making lists to counter her lists, packing boxes where she merely rummaged, chucking things she couldn't chuck, creating zones for the different destinations of the boxes, replacing panic with diligence. She couldn't have done it without him.

'So cheers to the end of one amazing era, and the beginning of the next one.' Donna had raised her glass to Jo and Nicky on the evening before the removals men were due. Nicky had ordered in pizza and red wine and they were sitting at the kitchen table surrounded by towers of brown cardboard. The boxes were all taped, sealed, labelled, the furniture tagged, all except Jo's bedsheets, a towel and some crockery.

Everyone clinked glasses. Max, sitting hopefully by Jo's chair and clearly identifying her as the most likely person to pass him a tit-bit, wagged his tail, his bright eyes looking up at her as if he approved of what she was doing too. Jo reached down to stroke him.

'How are you feeling about it, Mum?'

Jo considered her son's question.

'You know what? I'm excited. Once tomorrow's over, I can relax, get on with my life.' She paused. 'It'll probably take months for it to sink in that I don't live here any more, and obviously I shall miss it . . . but honestly, I'm looking forward to it.'

Donna laughed. 'So glad you feel that way, darling.'

'Yeah, me too,' Nicky agreed. 'You've been great.' He reached across and gave his mum's hand a squeeze.

'You must be sad about the house too?' she asked him.

'Sort of . . . nah, not really, not any more. It was a shock at first, but you get used to it. Packing helps . . . makes the place more anonymous. And we're taking everything that matters with us.'

When Cassie had arrived, she and Nicky had

kept up a constant banter about the things they were unearthing from their childhood, teasing each other about items of sentimental value to one or the other, such as Nicky's box of battered Transformers and Cassie's collection of snow globes from foreign cities.

Nicky pulled another triangle of pizza out of the box, folded it and took a huge bite. 'Wish Dad was as happy as you are,' he added through his mouthful.

'How do you mean?' Donna asked.

'He's really down at the moment.'

'I'm sure all that money will cheer him up.' Donna had raised her eyebrows, given Jo a look. But Jo had just shrugged. She'd had no desire to dwell on Lawrence's state of mind. He had rung the day after his outburst and said he thought it best he stay out of the way and she hadn't argued. He sounded almost angry when he told her to chuck anything that was his. She hadn't, of course. She'd boxed up the things she thought he would miss and directed them to the storage place near Brent Cross.

'You'd think.' Nicky said. 'That flat he's in is horrible. It's one of those modern student blocks behind Tottenham Court Road and it's noisy and stinks of rubbish all the time. I'd shoot myself if I lived there.'

'Sounds like an odd choice,' Donna said.

'He wanted to be near Arkadius,' Jo finally put in.

Her son raised his eyebrows. 'Yeah, well that may not be such a big deal any more. When I asked how it was going, Dad just looked me in the eye and said, "It's over, Nicky." Like, no argument, seriously end of.'

Jo got slowly out of bed and pulled up the wooden blind. The back of the flat looked over a primary school, and even in the short time she'd been there, she'd begun to know what time of day it was by the sounds from the playground. But now, early, it was quiet, the spring sun slanting through the translucent leaf-shoots, lighting up the buds on the magnolia next door. For a moment, Jo wished she could see the Yoshino cherry in her old back garden – the pale pink blossom always made her think of innocence and hope.

She brewed coffee and watched a robin sitting on the fuchsia bush outside the window, feeling lazy and unwilling to start the day. She felt much more independent here than she had in her old house, having cut herself loose from all that was familiar. The house had been her protection, her sanctuary when Lawrence left. And there had been Donna and Max over the wall. And Travis. But this flat was hers and hers alone.

She and Travis hadn't spoken since Christmas Day. Neither had made any attempt to call the other. Jo had often been on the verge of dialling his number, but finally there didn't seem any point. It would just remind her that sometimes she still longed to have his arms around her, to watch his dark eyes light up at something she said. But four months on, their time together still seemed like a fleeting illusion, a brief burst of sunlight on a cloudy day. So she was stepping into her new life alone and this morning she was surprised to find that it didn't seem at all scary.

Her messages, when she finally got to her computer, contained an email from the copyeditor, sending her the manuscript of *Tess* marked up in Track Changes. The publisher's enthusiasm for the new book was a massive relief to Jo – Frances, as promised, had got them all onside at Century – but seeing the document now, she groaned. Although she completely appreciated the advantages of the software, she dreaded the sight of the endless columns of balloons at the side of every page, with deletions and comments and formatting changes – some of them tiny – all of which she had to check and make decisions about. It made her go cross-eyed, peering at the type.

So she worked. And she pottered. Her routine over the weeks that followed included a walk in the morning to Holland Park, then a café and newspaper, then home to work – an idea for her next book was already shaping up – then evenings with a glass of wine, the radio, TV or a book. Spring was well advanced and the weather was beautiful, so she would sit out late on the patio, or drop round to Donna's, see a film, have Nicky over for supper. She was waiting to be bored, waiting to be frightened of her solitude, but in fact she just felt healthy and calm and motivated to write.

'I'm not saying it'll last,' she told Donna as they meandered back from the Shepherd's Bush Odeon one hot May night.

'Why not? It's how I live.'

'No you don't. You're out three or four nights a week partying and flirting with lecherous ambassadors.'

'I am so not! I haven't been out for . . . well, this is the first night this week I've been anywhere.'

'It's Tuesday, Donna.'

They both began to laugh.

'But seriously, I'm the exception, darling. It's novel for you at the moment, but being alone does pall for most people. Do you really not miss having someone around?'

'You mean a man? No, not at all. In fact, quite the reverse.'

Donna turned to peer at her. 'Really? Not even Lawrence?'

'Particularly not Lawrence. I haven't spoken to him in yonks and it's such a relief.'

'So you don't even know if he got back together with Arkadius?'

'No idea. The children say he's gone quiet, won't speak about it, which could mean anything. Whatever he's doing, I don't want to know.'

Donna said nothing.

'It's just so peaceful, not having to think about anything or anyone but myself,' Jo added.

'Oh, I get the selfish part. But I worry that you're shutting yourself off, spending too much time alone. When you were next door we had coffee almost every day . . . now I barely see you.'

'I'm just getting on with my life, Donna. Stop worrying. Honest, I'm really fine. And don't suggest I buy a cat. Or go to a party.'

'Ha, ha. OK . . . well, if you change your mind, you know where I am.'

They walked along in silence for a while, the light sinking to a deep royal blue over the West London rooftops.

'In fact Swedish Brian is coming over in a couple of weeks. Are you up for a supper together?'

Jo didn't answer immediately.

'Nothing sinister, just supper. I promise, from now on I won't set you up with anyone . . . unless you ask me to, of course. But we had fun the last time, remember?'

'I remember the hangover, for sure,' Jo said.

Jo lay awake later, mulling over what her friend had said. She hated the thought that anyone might see her as lonely and sad just because she didn't have a man: the maiden-aunt syndrome.

She was just dropping off when her mobile rang.

'Jo? It's me.'

'Lawrence? What is it? What's the matter?' His voice sounded so dull, so desperate that she was catapulted into a sitting position.

'Umm . . . I've had a bit of an accident . . . I'm OK . . . well, not OK actually . . . and I didn't know who else to ring . . .'

'What do you mean, an accident? What sort of an accident?'

She heard him clear his throat. 'I came off my bike yesterday. This girl stepped off the pavement right in front of me. French tourist, didn't realize which way the traffic was going down Tottenham Court Road.'

'Is she OK?'

'*She's* OK . . . but I went over the handlebars. I've broken my right wrist, cracked three ribs and buggered my knee.'

'Oh, God. What a nightmare. Are you in hospital?'

'No . . . they straightened the wrist out and put a plaster on in A&E, but then I went back this morning and they said it wasn't right, so they took the plaster off again. Now there's what looks like a couple of meat skewers poking out from the new plaster.'

'So how are you coping?'

There was a short silence. 'I'm all right . . . well, I'm not really. I can't do anything properly, and just now . . . I . . . God, this is so embarrassing . . . I peed my trousers because I couldn't get them off with one hand . . . and now . . .'

She heard him swallow and knew he was about to cry.

'I'm coming over. I'll be there in twenty minutes.'

'Can you? Oh, thank you . . . thank you so much.'

'I'll ring when I'm close.'

Nicky had been right about the flats smelling of rubbish. The stench was nauseating, especially on a hot night like this. Jo held her breath as she made her way up to the sixth floor. The flat door was ajar when she arrived and she pushed it open. Lawrence was sitting on the two-seater navy sofa in his underpants, an aluminium crutch by his side. His trousers lay in a heap on the floor. He was unshaven, pale as a ghost, his right arm in plaster up to the elbow, held up by a blue nylon arm sling, his right knee covered by a black elastic support bandage. A bruise spread down his right cheek from a black eye, below a nasty graze on his forehead.

He seemed bewildered, his eyelids blinking rapidly. 'Sorry.'

She glanced around, shocked. There was mess everywhere. Cups, glasses, plates and crumbs littered the cheap brown-wood coffee table along-side a half-open Styrofoam carton and an oily pizza box. An empty bottle of wine sat on the floor, there were papers and books piled on every surface in the boxy, featureless space. It looked like a student squat on a bad day. And her husband was always so careful, so tidy, so obses-sively clean.

'Pretty grim, eh?' he said, noticing the way her

gaze took it all in. 'I'm so sorry, Jo. This isn't fair.'

'Let's just sort it out.' She picked up his trousers and boxers and located the washing machine under the worktop in the galley kitchen. Pouring some hot water into a bowl she found under the sink, she helped him wash himself down with a flannel, found some old jogging bottoms he could pull down and up himself, made him a cup of tea and gave him two paracetamol. Then she put all the crockery into the dishwasher, vacuumed the stained carpet, wiped the surfaces and put out the rubbish.

'God, Jo, you're a saint. I'm so sorry.'

She smiled down at him as he sat on the sofa. 'You must have said "sorry" fifty times in the last hour. Enough already!'

'Sorry,' he said, and laughed. 'But it was gross in here. It's just with only one hand, and the left one at that, I can't do a damn thing. I can't butter toast, or shave without cutting myself, or carry a mug of coffee. If it wasn't for my knee, I could probably manage, but I feel so weak and I have to use the crutch with my left hand, so I can't take anything from A to B. And the button on my trousers got stuck so I couldn't get them down in time.'

She rotated the leather chair that faced his desk in the corner and sat down.

'How did you get the bottle of wine open then?'

He looked sheepish. 'That was from the day

352

before the accident . . . in fact a lot of the mess was. I've sort of let things slide recently I'm afraid.'

'Why didn't you call Nicky? He'd have helped you.'

'He's up in Manchester doing this TV thing. I didn't want to worry him. And anyway . . . I hate the thought of the children seeing me like this.'

'OK . . . well, will you be all right for tonight?'

Lawrence nodded. 'I'll be fine. I'm so sorry, dragging you out in the middle of the night, Jo. I can't thank you enough.'

'Yeah, yeah,' she said. 'I'll come back in the morning and see how you are. Bring you some food.'

'No, no, please, you don't have to do that.'

'You can get to the shops, can you? Carry a bag of stuff home? Don't be silly, Lawrence.'

He looked miserable. 'I can order in . . .'

Jo raised her eyebrows and gave him a reproving smile. 'Right. Pizza's such a nice healthy option to get your strength back.'

She got up. 'I'll call you before I come, but give me a key so you don't have to let me in.'

His nod was reluctant.

'Sleep well,' she said softly, as she closed the flat door behind her.

On the way home in the car she realized it was nearly three o'clock in the morning. The streets, even in the West End, were relatively clear, and it had rained, freshening the air and washing the grimy pavements.

How hard was that, she thought as she drove. Not only seeing him so broken and . . . well, *old*. But not knowing how to relate to him, except as a bossy carer.

'He shouldn't be alone,' Cassie said, when Jo rang her the next morning and told her about her father. 'He sounds in a terrible state.'

'It was pretty depressing. I've never seen him like this.'

'Why doesn't he come and stay here? I know the country's not Dad's thing, but he needs looking after till he can walk properly.'

'That could be weeks, darling.'

'Whatever. Only you might have to bring him down, Mum, us not having a car and all.'

'No problem. Why don't you call him and see what he says. He seemed pretty resistant to being helped, especially as far as you and Nicky are concerned, which I can understand. But it's worth a try. I'm going over there in a minute anyway, so I'll let you know how he is this morning.'

Lawrence had clearly made an effort. He looked as if he had managed to wash and shave, and his cup and plate were in the sink. Jo had brought him a number of ready meals he could microwave, cartons of soup, some softer butter spread, bags of salad to just tip on to the plate, fruit.

'You're brilliant,' he said, when she'd handed him a fresh cup of coffee and a croissant.

'Did Cassie ring you?'

Lawrence nodded as he munched. 'She was adorable, said I should come and stay with her till I was better.'

'And?'

He raised his eyebrows at her. 'Look, I really appreciate her offer, but I don't want to go anywhere, least of all there. Much as I'd love to hang out with Cass, that house is a bloody nightmare. I'd tip off that wobbly loo, for a start. And I'd never be able to get up off the futon.'

Jo laughed. 'True.'

'Anyway, I'd be a pain. I was miserable before the accident . . . why should I inflict myself on my poor daughter?'

'Yes, but that's when you need people around, Lawrence. You'll just sink further if you stay in this place on your own.'

'Yeah, I know. It is a bit of a dump,' he said, seeing the slightly disdainful expression on Jo's face.

'OK, listen,' she took a deep breath. 'Why don't you come and stay with me, then. Just for a week or so, till your knee's better and you don't have to use the crutch?'

Lawrence looked taken aback. 'No. No, definitely not.' He swallowed. 'Don't get me wrong, it's an incredibly kind offer, Jo. But I couldn't.'

'Well, I'm not going to leave you here on your own. I'm only being selfish, I don't want to spend every day trekking back and forth to Totty Court Road to check on you.'

He was still shaking his head. 'No way, Jo. You don't have to do this . . . come every day. I've told you, I can manage. And Nicky's back at the weekend, I'm sure he'll do the shopping for me until I can carry a bag.'

'It's not just the shopping. You look like shit,' she said.

'Thanks.'

'You know what I mean. How long have you been like this?'

He shrugged, wouldn't look at her.

'It's Arkadius, I presume.'

'That . . . and . . . well, everything. I've made such a mess of my life, Jo.' He looked as if he were about to cry. 'I had it all. And now . . . now I feel I've got nothing.'

Unwilling to witness him collapsing in tears, Jo's voice took on a brisk note. 'That's ridiculous. You're going through a tricky time, that's all.'

'You think? Seems a bit more than "tricky" to me.'

'Well, it will, if you're depressed. Please, Lawrence, let me take you home now. Just for a few days till you're back on your feet.' She spoke from the heart, at the same time hearing the small voice in her head that violently resisted her offer. But it would only be for a week, and she didn't feel she had a choice.

'No.' The word was almost a bark. 'I won't do that to you, Jo. Thank you, but no.'

She shrugged. 'Well, up to you. But the offer

still stands if you change your mind.' The day was hot again and the flat stuffy. Jo got up and opened the window, letting in the noise of traffic from below.

'Do you want me to come out with you, get some fresh air before I go?'

She could see he hesitated. 'It's OK . . . I think I'll just rest up today.'

On the way home from the Tube she dropped in on Donna in her studio.

'You *what*? Darling, you're insane.'

'Why?'

'Letting your crippled, depressed, whingeing *ex* come and live with you so you can nurse him back to health? What are you thinking?'

Jo couldn't help laughing. 'Just for a few days.'

'How do you know? It could be weeks before his knee's better. Knees are a nightmare.'

The door was open to the garden, a soft breeze making the wooden hut pleasantly cool. Max kept trotting in and out as if he were checking how the conversation was going.

'You should have seen him, Donna. He looked about a hundred.'

'At least he had the sense not to take you up on your offer.'

'But I'm worried about him. He really wasn't coping.'

Donna wiped her hands on her apron and stood up from her stool. She came over to Jo and placed her hands on her friend's arms, clasping her firmly as she looked up into her face.

'Look, you're either with him or you're not. You don't seem to have quite made up your mind. This shilly-shallying isn't good. I mean, why did he ring you? Why didn't he ring the children? Or Arkadius. They split up much more recently than you two did.'

Jo thought about this.

'True. I suppose . . . I suppose he thought I'd help.'

'Exactly. He thought he'd take advantage of your kindly nature. And I don't blame him. But honestly, he doesn't have that privilege any more.'

'No . . . OK, I hear what you're saying. But surely nearly forty years of marriage means we can stay friends. And I was only being friendly.'

Donna raised her eyebrows. 'Maybe. But I'm just saying. He doesn't deserve your help.'

'He's not a monster, Donna.'

'I never said he was.'

'You'd have done the same thing if you'd seen him.'

'I seriously doubt it. I'm not the caring type.'

Jo laughed. 'You're a hard, hard woman, Donna Freeman. He's not trying to worm his way back into my life, if that's what you're implying. He's just in a bad way, that's all.'

'Fine, well, I hope he gets better really super-soon,' Donna said, her mouth pursed.

* * *

Jo went back the following day, and the one after. Lawrence appeared not to have moved, except for the accumulation of dishes in the sink. The only difference was that each time she saw him he looked paler. The fourth day she had the car because she'd gone early to the storage unit to pick up some books and a lamp.

'It's me,' she announced as she breezed in around ten-thirty, only to find him still asleep, his long body, fully dressed, curled up like a child on the sofa, his plastered arm crossed over his chest. He was covered with a thin blanket, the crutch on the floor by his side. He opened his eyes but just stared at her and shut them again.

'Lawrence, come on. Wake up.' It looked from his sleptin clothes as if he hadn't been up yet today.

He finally dragged his head higher against the arm of the sofa.

'It's not good for you to sleep all scrunched up like that,' she said.

'I was just too tired to move,' he muttered, rubbing his eyes with his left hand.

For a moment she stood looking down on him. 'OK . . . enough of this. I'm taking you to mine. You need fresh air and sunlight. You can sit in the garden, it's a beautiful day.'

He shook his head. 'I'm fine.'

'So you keep saying. But you're not, Lawrence. You're a mess.'

She leaned down and helped him into a sitting

position. 'Come on, get up. I've got the car down-stairs and it's on a meter.'

Jo could tell he no longer had the energy to protest, and slowly he began to do as she said. It was a long time before he was ready to go, shaved and dressed in clean clothes, a cup of coffee inside him.

'You don't have to—'

'I know I don't.'

By the time Jo got him home, Lawrence was exhausted. She made up the sofa bed in her study for him and he sank gratefully into the clean sheets and slept until she went in to wake him around two.

'This is nice,' he said, waving his fork to take in the lunch on the wooden patio table – ham, potato salad, lettuce, beetroot and brown bread – the garden, the flat behind them.

'Better than your dump,' she joked. 'What possessed you?'

He grinned, the first smile she'd seen in days. 'You know me, cheap.'

She nodded. 'You could afford to do better now, though.'

'I know. Just don't have the energy.'

After lunch she gave him the paper and a cup of coffee and went upstairs to her computer. During the course of the lunch he had definitely perked up, seemed more interested in things and was making an effort in conversation. But Jo felt she hardly knew him. It was like passing the time of day with a virtual stranger.

Round about five, she went outside again. Lawrence was just sitting there, the paper open in front of him, but clearly he was not reading it.

'I should get home,' he said. 'Thanks so much for today, it's been lovely. You were right, I needed a bit of light and air.'

'Why don't you stay the night? I'll drop you home in the morning. The traffic will be murder for the next few hours.'

She saw him hesitate.

'Could I?'

Jo felt her heart contract. His pale eyes looked so tired, so sad.

'Of course you can.'

Nicky, his blond curls cut unnaturally short – a legacy of the sports coach he'd been playing in a TV drama – stared at his father through the kitchen window of Jo's flat.

'How long's he going to stay, Mum?' He spoke in a whisper.

'His knee's much better . . .'

Her son frowned. 'But?'

'He's still quite depressed.'

'Really? He seemed perfectly normal just now.'

'Yes, well . . . I worry when he goes home he'll just sink again. It's such a horrible place . . . you've seen it.'

Nicky nodded. 'Vile. I wouldn't spend a single

night there.' He shook his head. 'But that's not your problem, Mum, is it?'

'No. No, it's not.'

'Do you *like* having him here then?'

Jo didn't answer at once. Lawrence had been staying for nearly two weeks now. Every evening during the first week, he'd said he should go home. And every evening she had said he could stay if he liked. Gradually it had begun to feel normal. They had settled into a sort of routine together. Not as they had been before, but a new, quiet sort of companionship, his previously quick, slightly cutting intelligence blunted by his circumstances. He seemed kinder, less self-absorbed to Jo and they'd had some good discussions, talked about things not pertaining to their current life with their old vigour. She realized Nicky was waiting for a reply.

'Umm . . . it's OK. He's not himself.'

Nicky gave her a quizzical look. 'Is that good or bad?'

She laughed. 'Just different.'

'Well, as long as you don't feel you *have* to have him here.'

Jo assured him she didn't, but this wasn't quite true. Lawrence's stay in her flat had reminded her that the love she felt for her husband, built over a lifetime, had not been completely dismantled. Seeing him brought so low had allowed that affection to resurface, unimpeded by other considerations, such as the Russian history professor, and she did feel a certain responsibility to make sure he was all right. No more than that, she told herself. But when she asked herself if she was happy having him there, her answer seemed to be that she was not *un*happy.

CHAPTER 20

Mid-May

'I think I'll go back tomorrow,' Lawrence said that evening, after their son had left.

'Did Nicky say something?'

He frowned. 'Say something? About what?'

'No . . . nothing.'

'I can't stay here for ever and I need to work . . . the book . . .'

They were outside, another warm evening, and Jo was cutting chives growing in a terracotta pot on the terrace, alongside some mint and thyme. Lawrence was sitting in his now-favourite wooden garden chair in his faded blue cargo shorts, his bad leg stretched out in front of him – the support bandage still around his knee – resting on the step that led up to the main paved area of the small garden.

'How's it going?'

He hadn't mentioned work once since he'd been there, and Jo hadn't liked to ask.

'Yeah, OK . . .'

'Have you settled on an outline yet?'

She noticed a pained look flit across his face. He shook his head.

'To be honest, I've barely started. I . . . just can't seem to concentrate. I've done a lot of reading, but that's as far as I've got. Not having the discipline of turning up to college every day has thrown me for six. It's hard to find the motivation on my own.'

'What's the deadline?'

Lawrence had been talking about writing an accessible history of the Ming Dynasty – with aspirations for a TV series in mind – for years now. The era of Chinese rule was his passion. He had two academic publications on the subject under his belt, but one of the reasons he'd given Jo for retiring early was to nail a more popular history and establish himself as one of the go-to brains for explaining things Chinese. Of course now Jo knew the real reason had been Arkadius.

'Don't have one. A couple of publishers have said they'd like to look at a pitch and some material . . .'

Jo knew what that meant. Not a lot.

She stood up, clutching a handful of herbs in one hand, the kitchen scissors in the other. Lawrence had fallen silent.

'I'll get on with supper,' she said.

It was getting dark but they still sat on at the garden table. There was no candle, just the light from the kitchen.

'Jo . . .'

Neither of them had spoken for a few minutes, and Jo immediately heard the changed tone of her husband's voice.

'Jo . . . I don't want you to think I'm taking advantage of your incredible kindness to me – which I fully appreciate I don't deserve – but . . . well, I thought I'd say it anyway, before I go.'

He stopped, bit his lip. 'I . . . we seem to have got along pretty well together these last two weeks. And . . . I just wondered if you'd consider the possibility . . . of us making another go of it.'

Jo felt her breath go very still in her body, her heart small and constricted. It was as if it had gone solid, immobilized by his request, which, although out of the blue in the actual sense, had been hovering unspoken between them for days. Jo had tried to prepare herself, but now, faced with the reality, she didn't know what to say. She watched Lawrence take a deep breath.

'I know I've hurt you, Jo. What I did was unforgivable. And I'm not stupid enough to think we can go back to how it was. But it seems to me that we still have such a strong bond. This time together has shown me that. Couldn't we make something new . . . sort of phoenix from the ashes?'

Jo's mind was in turmoil. She saw his expectant face, his expression infinitely nervous.

'I don't know,' was all she could manage.

'Don't know if it's a possibility? Or don't know

if you want to try?' His voice was soft, controlled, as if he didn't want to frighten the horses.

'Both I suppose,' she said after a long moment of silence.

'If you're worried about Arky,' He held her gaze in a determined way. 'Jo, it really is *over* between us. Totally, completely *over*. For ever.'

She nodded, believing him.

'About us. I don't mean that we move in together or anything. Nothing like that. Just . . . well, see each other. Go out.'

'Like a date, you mean?'

His grin was sheepish. 'I suppose. Yeah, why not like a date?'

She raised her eyebrows, let out a long breath.

He reached his un-plastered hand across the table, then apparently changed his mind and put it firmly in his lap again.

'I still love you.'

Jo heard the words as if from far away. She knew they were entirely genuine, but they didn't seem to mean a thing. She looked off into the London darkness, heard a shout from the street behind her. This was her place, her life. She felt a surge of irritation that he had interrupted that.

'Will you at least think about it?' he asked, when she didn't respond.

And she agreed that she would.

The following day, after Lawrence had left and she'd folded the sofa bed away, put the sheets in the washing machine, the duvet in the cupboard, cleared away the book he'd borrowed and the glass he hadn't taken to the kitchen, returned the room to her own space, she found herself trying to analyse her feelings for Lawrence in the light of his request.

Did she trust Lawrence not to do it again with someone else? Perhaps if they'd been twenty she couldn't have been sure. But after thirty-seven years of fidelity and one lapse – however big – was it something she'd worry about? She thought not. Lawrence had been entirely trustworthy in every other aspect. She knew he had always been there for her – until, of course, he wasn't.

Forgiveness. Tricky one, this. Jo had never been quite sure what it meant. Was it just a decision? Sort of, I've decided to forgive you. Or was there some process that had to be gone through? If she hadn't met Travis, maybe she would have been unable to understand Lawrence's defection. But she knew first-hand how powerful desire was. Anyway, there wouldn't be any point in making a go of it with Lawrence if she were perpetually blaming him for what he'd done.

And love. She remembered Lawrence telling her that he loved her still. And how empty the words had sounded, despite her believing what he said. She felt she loved him. But maybe it was now just a powerful echo.

The most difficult question was *Do I like him?* This caused Jo to hesitate. Because 'liking' seemed more important than anything else at this juncture. And whereas you could be In Love with someone and not particularly like them, she was sure you couldn't truly love a person without also liking and respecting what they represented. He had broken that respect when he left her.

Lawrence pushed open the double doors to the cinema ahead of her.

'Are we sure about this?' Jo asked, gazing up at a poster for the film they'd finally decided on, showing a spaceman floating loose at the edge of the world. 'Space movies aren't exactly our thing.'

'It's had brilliant reviews,' Lawrence insisted. 'Martin says there's an incredible first shot that lasts fourteen minutes or something.'

Jo laughed as they approached the counter to buy their tickets. 'Not sure if that's encouraging or not.'

'We can see something else if you like,' Lawrence said, his gaze suddenly anxious as if he were worried he might have overstepped the mark.

In fact she was looking forward to it. Pure fantasy escapism was exactly what she needed. This was the third time she had gone out with Lawrence in as many weeks – first, supper at a Thai place in Charlotte Street. Second, the Tate and tea. And it had been very odd, a bit awkward so far. They'd nominally set the parameters of a 'date', yet there was no hand-holding, no kissing, no prospect of anything sexual. Their encounters were formal, unnaturally polite as they carefully avoided the past and the future and anything at all emotional. Instead sticking to safe subjects such as the children, the news, books they'd read, films they'd seen, their work.

Jo was surprised when she found the film breathtaking, literally.

'Oh . . . my . . . God.' Jo clasped her hand to her chest as they staggered out of the cinema into the spring evening. 'That was terrifying. I feel as if I'm suffocating!'

Lawrence laughed. 'Wasn't it brilliantly shot? How on earth did they do it, all that weightlessness . . . the sequence where she swims through the capsule was incredible, no? Must have been a ton of CGI.'

'Bit of a thin story though. Girl lost in space, has a few personal revelations, gets back to earth, end of.'

'Yes, but tense and classily done, don't you think?'

'They shouldn't have cut George loose so early.'

In the past they might have linked arms as they made their way down the road beside the green. But tonight they just walked primly side by side.

'Do you fancy a drink?' she heard Lawrence's tentative enquiry.

Jo had eaten before the film and, as she was close to home and they were passing the Tube where Lawrence would catch the Central Line into town, the evening could end right here. Neither of them really knew how to play it.

'Umm . . . OK. Maybe I need just one, to debrief,' she said.

They went to a Mexican place along the Westfield stretch and sat at a table outside with a beer each.

'I really enjoyed that,' Lawrence said.

'Me too.'

For a while they talked about the film, then about other films. Safe stuff.

'Have you seen Nicky recently?'

'He came round for a cup of tea on Sunday.'

'Is he OK?'

'Hmm . . .' Jo paused. 'Slightly concerned that Amber is making a comeback.'

'Really?'

'Maybe I'm wrong . . . it's just he said he'd seen her a couple of times. He stressed just as friends, but it's clear he's still got feelings for her.'

'Bit like us?' Lawrence smiled at her.

Jo just looked at him. 'Have you got feelings for me, Lawrence?'

He looked almost indignant. 'Of course I have. You know I have.'

'But what sort of feelings?'

'I . . .' He let out a long breath. 'Oh, Jo. I don't know how to define what I feel for you. It's so confusing. I love being with you, but it's weird, unnatural, us going out like this. Being together and yet not together. I find it almost painful.'

She nodded. 'Know what you mean.'

'What should we do about it?'

'Not sure there is anything.'

Into the silence, Lawrence said, 'I don't think it's going to get any easier unless we bite the bullet and try living with each other again.'

'No!'

'That bad, is it?' He gave her a wry smile.

'No . . . no, it isn't. Sorry, I didn't mean that . . . like it sounded. It just seems way too soon.'

'So we go on having these stupid dates and not touching or kissing and being ridiculously polite like we're barely even friends?'

'Do you want to touch and kiss me?' She felt her heart flutter at the thought. Not from desire so much as nervousness.

'Of course I do,' he said, but there was a fatal second of hesitation before he spoke.

They lapsed into an awkward silence.

In that moment, all she could think of was Travis: his passionate caresses, the eager hardness of his body against her own. Was Lawrence, similarly, thinking of Arkadius?

'Perhaps I'd better get going,' he was saying, his face set, as if he could intuit her thoughts.

'Yeah, it's late.'

'Not well,' Jo said, in answer to Donna's query.

They were lying in a darkened room on padded loungers, wrapped in fluffy white towelling robes. Whale music was warbling gently, and candles wafted soothing scents of lavender and ylang-ylang – according to Donna, who knew, having been to the spa before with her friend, the Mexican ambassador's wife, Camila. Donna had co-opted Jo when Camila cancelled at the last minute. So far they'd been brushed and oiled and massaged and cleansed and wrapped with what was trailed as 'Lime and Ginger Salt Glow Treatment'. They were now lying in a state of soporific bliss.

'I mean, we enjoy certain things about being with each other – at least I assume Lawrence enjoys them. But it's so . . . awkward . . . formal.'

'And what happens when you kiss?'

'We don't.'

'Darling! Why ever not?'

'We haven't got that far.' Jo turned her head on the lounger to look at Donna. 'To be honest I'm not sure there's the will. He says he wants to, but he doesn't seem very enthusiastic . . . probably because he's still got Arkadius in his head. And I can't help remembering Travis.'

'Yeah, well that'll happen until you replace Travis with Lawrence. And he replaces Arkadius with you.'

'But how?'

Donna rolled her eyes. 'Do I have to spell it out?'

'We can't just have sex on demand, without really wanting to.'

'So you don't want to?'

Jo sighed. 'I suppose I'm nervous. It'll be so weird after what's happened.'

'Hmm . . . OK. But you do still fancy him.'

'Yes. Well, I suppose I would. I certainly used to. But I don't feel any sort of excitement when I'm with him. He says we should just move in together and thrash it out. But that sounds even worse.'

They both contemplated the problem, whale song filling the silence.

Donna finally said, 'Just get drunk and leap on him. Can't think of any other way.'

'Grey Goose to the rescue.'

'I mean, how bad can it be? He was your husband for decades, after all. And if it really is a complete disaster, you can call it quits. Or sink into a dreary slippers-by-the-fire companionship with separate beds and a Teasmade.'

Jo laughed. 'God, Teasmade. Do they still have them?'

'Probably. But to get back to your dilemma. It is worth it, isn't it? Pushing the envelope a little. Better than suffering prim little dates till you both lose the will to live.'

'I suppose . . . it just seems so false.'

'Give it a go at least. Can't see the harm.'

The door opened and the pretty Malaysian girl who had massaged Jo earlier came in carrying a tray with ginger tea in two small china cups.

'I'll cook supper,' Jo said.

'Oh, great. Are you sure?'

'I'd like to. It's a beautiful day, we can sit outside. About eight?'

'Great, thanks. See you then.'

Jo said goodbye to Lawrence and put the phone down. She pulled a face, stared at the phone for a moment. The Grand Seduction, as Donna called it, had begun. Jo was to 'lighten up', 'relax', 'stop analysing', 'have some fun'. But she drew the line at a bustier and stockings – Donna's most radical suggestion.

Lawrence arrived on time. He looked scrubbed and buffed, elegant in a light blue shirt and jeans. Jo thought he seemed more like his old self as he snapped the ice out of the tray and loaded two glasses ready for the vodka Jo had retrieved from the freezer.

'No plaster!' she said, noticing the blue wrist support.

'Had it off yesterday. Such a relief.'

'Does it still hurt?'

'Not really. It's stiff and I can't put weight on it or rotate it properly yet . . . but we're getting there.'

She had poached salmon, made a green salad and couscous, but first they sat outside, a dish of olives and some Parma ham on the table between them, breathing in the warm evening air, the light gentle and shadowy as the sun dipped behind the houses to the west.

'This is lovely,' Lawrence spoke softly, raising his glass to Jo. 'You found such a peaceful spot.'

She smiled. 'Your flat must be hellish in this weather.'

'Worse than hellish. Stinky and stuffy and pretty unbearable.'

'You should get out of there.'

'Yes . . .'

The sudden silence was typical of recent meetings.

'How's the book coming along?' she asked.

'Yeah . . . not bad at the moment. Still in the early stages of research, but it's beginning to take shape. Yours?'

'I've started on the next one, but I'm waiting for them to offer me another deal. Maggie says they will, but you can't be sure.'

'Sounds like good news though. I'd like to read your latest.'

'I'll send it to you.'

Silence. Jo stood up and cleared away the olives. 'Top up?' She indicated his empty glass. Lawrence got to his feet.

'Jo,' he took the bowl from her hand and put it back on the table, gently taking hold of her arm and pulling her towards him.

'Come here . . .'

She went to him, her heart beating faster as he bent to kiss her. 'Can we?' he asked after a moment, his head nodding towards the kitchen door. And she led him inside, up the stairs, into her bedroom. The room was dim, but she didn't turn the lights on. Lawrence held her, kissed her again, then began to help her take off her T-shirt, his right hand still clumsy from the accident. She found she was almost embarrassed to be naked in front of him again. But Lawrence – never one for much foreplay in the past – seemed to be on a mission to give her as much pleasure as she could handle. She heard Donna's words in her head, 'lighten up', 'relax', and she made a conscious effort as he stroked her breast, played with her nipple. But she found she was holding her breath, not able, completely, to let go, especially when his lovemaking became increasingly frantic, almost desperate, as if he needed to finish because he had a train to catch.

'Slow down . . .' she whispered.

Then a moment later his erection abruptly subsided and he rolled off her on to his back.

'Sorry . . . sorry, Jo.'

'What happened? Did you come?'

'No . . . no, it just . . . don't know . . .'

She raised herself on her elbow to look at him. 'It's OK. Doesn't matter.'

Lawrence wouldn't look at her. 'Sorry.'

She flopped back on the pillow and they lay in mortified silence for a minute or two.

'That was a bit of a disaster,' he said.

She gave a half-hearted laugh. 'Were we trying too hard?'

She wanted it to be that, not what she most feared; that they no longer found each other attractive.

'I wanted it to be perfect,' he muttered, laying his bent arm across his face. 'I thought if it was . . . if we could get back to being together . . .'

'Sex isn't the only thing,' she said.

'No . . . no, I know that. But isn't it symbolic?'

She didn't answer. Like Lawrence, she thought it probably was – symbolic of their closeness, their ability to connect. And tonight's lovemaking had been anything but close, except by the real skin-on-skin definition.

He turned on his side to face her, his mouth pinched, his eyes troubled. 'I bet you didn't have this problem with Travis. You said the sex was brilliant with him.'

'I didn't say that.'

'Yes, you did. You said you were enjoying it "hugely".'

So he had been jealous, even back then, as Donna had insisted.

'I don't think it'll help if we discuss the sort of sex we had with our other partners, do you?' Her voice was taut as she brushed away images of what he himself might have been doing with Arkadius.

Lawrence sat up, rubbing his hands across his face, wincing at what must have been a twinge in his newly healed wrist.

'God . . . I'm sorry. I had no right to ask you that.'

Jo held out her hand for his, which, after a second's hesitation, he gave her.

'Perhaps we're not really over stuff,' she suggested. 'Maybe we need more time.'

He lay down again, drawing her into his side, her head on his chest. 'Do you think there's a chance for us, though? Do you want there to be?'

She didn't answer immediately.

'Were you thinking of Arkadius . . . tonight?'

It was Lawrence's turn to be silent.

'Not sexually, no, I wasn't. I promise I wasn't.'

She wasn't sure she believed him. 'But I suppose he is still there, between us . . . somewhere,' he went on. 'It was more . . . I felt so much was resting on us getting on physically, like we used to.'

'But that wasn't enough for you, was it? Before. That's why you ran off with someone else.'

'It wasn't that. I've always loved our lovemaking. I wasn't dissatisfied if that's what you think.'

'Bored, then.'

'Not even that.' She heard him sigh. 'I mean, in a long marriage it can't be thrilling all the time. But we were good together, Jo. The thing with Arkadius was totally separate. I'm not making excuses, but I suppose I was vulnerable . . . feeling old, losing my potency, the dreaded retirement looming. Then along comes this person who makes me feel so young again . . . and desired. I just went for it.'

Jo felt a stab of annoyance that he'd been such a pushover, so eager to defect. Then she remembered Travis, the overwhelming desire she'd felt for the actor still fresh in her mind. She could have easily made a fool of herself with him.

'Tonight hasn't ruined it, has it?'

'No, no, of course not,' she said.

'You're not still angry with me, are you? I'd understand if you were.'

She got out of bed, began to retrieve her clothes from the floor. Was she angry with him? She tried to pinpoint precisely what she felt about her husband in that moment. In a way she wished she did feel angrier. It would have been more concrete, more comprehensible than this wishy-washy doubt, this lack of much feeling at all, except a residual sadness.

Neither of them said much after that. Lawrence didn't stay for supper. He dressed and was on his way, leaving Jo to contemplate the untouched plate of salmon, the dish of couscous, the wooden bowl of salad.

'I don't understand why you're in such a state, darling. The first time was bound to be tricky . . . after all you two have been through.'

'It's not the sex. The bloody sex has nothing to do with it. He thought it did, but it doesn't. We're older, Donna, what does it matter if we don't bonk like teenagers any longer? We should be able to get past that.' She paused. 'No, it's the lack of . . . I don't know the right word, but connection, spark, that thing that holds two people together,'

'Love?'

Jo sighed. 'Love . . . do you think that's it? That I don't love him any more?'

Donna, who had been woken by her friend's

phone call, then dragged out of bed by Jo's prompt arrival at her house on one of the few days she'd chosen to lie in, was slumped in an armchair in a man's navy dressing-gown, four sizes too big – legacy of Walter – balancing a cup of tea-gone-cold on the chair arm, Max curled up on her knee.

'I'm not sure what I think. But maybe you don't.'

Jo lay back against the sofa cushions. She'd poured herself another vodka after he'd gone, and sat outside, miserably trying to understand what had just happened. She realized she'd invested much more in the possibility that it could work out with Lawrence than she'd intended. When it began to get chilly, she'd gone inside and stretched cling film over the bowls, put away the food in the fridge; she wasn't remotely hungry. Then lain awake most of the night. Now she felt achy and exhausted, her eyes scratchy, her mouth dry from the alcohol.

'How did you leave it?'

'We were polite . . . we're always polite these days. He said sorry he wasn't hungry. I said it didn't matter. He said talk soon. I said yes. We said goodbye.'

'Right. And will you "talk soon"?'

'I don't know if there's any point.'

Donna frowned. 'I think you're tired, darling. And overreacting. It was going OK till last night, wasn't it? You seemed keen to see him.'

'He used to make me laugh, Donna. We used to talk all the time. There was never a moment when we were lost for words. Now we just seem to go through the motions. Take last night. We should have been able to laugh about it, not take it all so bloody seriously.'

Donna pushed Max off her knee and got up.

'Come on, I'll make us a decent cup of coffee.'

'Sorry to wake you up,' Jo said, as she followed her friend into the kitchen. 'I thought you'd be in the shed by now . . . I used to know when you were up because of the light.' The thought of not knowing when her friend got up seemed over-whelmingly sad to Jo, and she burst into tears.

'Maybe you just have to accept it's over,' Donna said later, after she'd plied her friend with two cups of throat-searing espresso.

'What's annoying is that I *had* started to accept that . . . months ago. I was getting on fine on my own in the new flat. I told you at the time and you didn't believe me. But I was. Then he got ill. I wish I'd never taken him in. I didn't need to. It was stupid – you were so right – and now I'm back to square one, wanting something that doesn't exist any more.'

'Hey, don't beat yourself up for helping him out. Or giving it a second try. You'd always have wondered if you hadn't.'

'Better to wonder than feel like this all over again.'

When Jo left Donna's, she saw she had missed a call. And a voicemail. From Travis. She stared at her phone as if she'd seen a ghost, her heart suddenly clicking into a faster rhythm.

Listening to the message, she heard his voice, with the familiar touch of laughter, say:

'Hey, Jo. It's me, Travis. Long time no talk.' There was a pause. 'I'm coming through Thursday, for a couple'a days, en route to Bucharest. Are you around? Hope so. Give me a call. Bye now.'

She listened again. Thursday. This Thursday. Travis. No.

CHAPTER 21

7 June 2014

The next time her mobile buzzed she grabbed it, staring at the screen. But it was Lawrence, not Travis. Jo hesitated before answering. Already she felt guilty, just for the message she'd left for the American, which said simply, 'Sorry I missed you. Call me if you have a chance.' Although she wasn't sure what she'd say to him if she did speak to him. Now she took a slow breath.

'Hi, Lawrence.'

'Hi, Jo. Umm . . . just wanted to say thank you for last night.'

'It's OK.'

'Sorry it didn't work out.'

'Yeah . . . listen, Lawrence, maybe we shouldn't see each other for a while. Maybe we're taking things too quickly and trying to push a round peg into a square hole, if you know what I mean.'

Lawrence didn't reply at once.

'I was just having an off day. I was tired from the hospital in the morning and—'

'It's really not about the sex. I just feel we don't . . . we aren't really enjoying it much . . . being together.'

'I am. I love seeing you.'

'Do you?'

'Yes. Obviously it's a bit strange, but it's early days . . . we've got to give it a chance, haven't we? Please. Don't walk away now, Jo. I know I don't deserve a second chance with you.' He stopped. 'But I love you. I really do love you.'

This time Lawrence's words pierced her heart.

'And we're supposed to be going to Jono's on Friday. We can't cancel that.'

Jonathan, Lawrence's friend at whose party they had first kissed, had, like Lawrence, also studied history at UCL. But after college he'd gone into one business venture after another, mostly disastrous, until he'd hit upon a successful formula for importing Italian olive oil into the UK back in the nineties, later expanding to include Italian hams, buffalo mozzarella, truffles, torrone.

'The house is amazing, Jo. Queen Anne, stunning, hardly touched. Remember, I told you I spent a few weekends there when we were at college and his parents were still alive. It's worth going just to see the house. And you love Jono. We haven't seen him in ages.' His voice took on an almost beseeching note.

Which was true. Jono was charming and loud and funny and flirtatious and drank too much, but Jo liked him enormously. Less so his second wife, the frosty Alana, who always seemed cross that Jonathan had a past with friends in it before they met and had slowly begun to slough off all his college mates, delete them from her party lists.

'Have you told him what's happened with us?'

Lawrence hesitated. 'Umm . . . no . . . didn't see the point, now it's over. It isn't anyone else's business, Jo.'

'So he thinks we're together . . . normally together.'

'I suppose, yes.'

'Right.'

'His father died two years ago at ninety something. He says he hasn't done anything to update the place yet – probably dreading the outlay. Alana will have plans, no doubt. Thank God it's Grade II listed, or she'd turn it into a gin-palace or theme park or something equally tasteless. We should see it while we can.'

'I'm sure the house is lovely, Lawrence, but it'll be grim. Probably freezing and uncomfortable, especially if it hasn't been modernized. There'll be no heating and lino in the bathrooms; eighteenth-century horsehair mattresses; kidneys for breakfast . . . not to mention the grisly people. Remember that last Chelsea dinner? Anyway, I wouldn't know what to wear.'

'Don't be silly. You always look beautiful. You don't have to eat the kidneys and it's June. How cold can it be?' He paused. 'We have said we're going.'

Said they were going in a moment of nostalgic enthusiasm about Jono, after Lawrence had bumped into him in Soho a few weeks ago. Jo had thought it might be fun back then, when she was still hopeful about her and Lawrence. But now . . .

'We can cancel. Or you can go without me. Jono won't mind. You can say I was ill.'

She heard Lawrence sigh. 'I don't want to go without you. Please. Come.' His voice was quietly insistent. 'Just this weekend, Jo . . . then if it's all a disaster . . .'

Jo took a deep breath. She would like to see Jonathan again and was definitely curious about the house. Maybe being a couple in public again, with our friends, she thought, will be telling, help point up whether we have a future together or not. 'Oh, OK.'

'Great. That's so great. A summer weekend with an old mate in a beautiful house . . . especially if this weather holds. How bad can it be?'

'Oh, thrilling,' Donna squealed when Jo told her about Travis passing through town.

'It's not. I mean he hasn't rung again, and he might not. But if he does . . . I don't know what to do.'

'Uh . . . well, you bonk him, don't you?'

'Donna! I can't. I'm supposed to be getting back with Lawrence.'

'Yes, but you haven't. And you're not sure you want to. So, *technically*, you're still allowed to bonk someone else.'

'Technically, not morally.'

Her friend gave an amused shrug.

Jo dragged her spoon around the edge of her cup, gathering up the foam from her latte, suddenly conscious of the young guy on his computer at the table next to them. But she realized he had his headphones on and probably couldn't hear a thing.

'OK. You've got three options as I see it,' Donna went on, when Jo didn't say any more. 'Bonk him. See him but don't bonk him. Don't see him, don't talk to him, definitely don't bonk him. Basically don't pass go.'

Jo nodded, waited for further enlightenment.

'Think about it. Which can you imagine doing?'

'I definitely can't see him and not bonk him, or want to bonk him.'

'OK, that leaves bonking, or not seeing him at all.'

'I can't have sex like that . . . just once . . . just because he's here. It would be sort of . . . disturbing. I don't want to miss him again when he goes.'

Donna looked pleased. 'Right, this is going better than I hoped. We seem to have narrowed it down to Option 3: Not communicating with him at all.'

Jo gave a stricken look and her friend laughed. 'Clearly not a popular option.'

'No . . . but you're probably right. If I'm serious about Lawrence.'

'Hmm . . . maybe this is telling you something, darling. If you're truly as pessimistic as you sound about your dear ex, then you wouldn't be asking me about Travis. You'd just leap into bed the first opportunity you get.'

Jo thought about this. 'It would feel like a bit of a betrayal.'

'So there's your answer. Drop your phone down the loo till Travis is safely in Budapest.'

'Bucharest.'

'Wherever.'

'I hope he doesn't call when I'm away with Lawrence.'

'If you're not answering, it won't matter,' Donna pointed out, eyebrows raised.

'It would be great to talk to him again, though.'

'JO!'

'OK, OK . . . I hear you.'

In the end, she couldn't resist trying his number again.

'Where are you?' she asked, after they'd said hello.

'San Francisco International, waiting for the New York flight, deciding on nuts with raisins, or nuts without . . . for the plane.'

She laughed. 'No contest. Always without.'

'Yeah? No, I love raisins, me. But this packet has coconut bits and dried cranberries as well. May be a step too far.' He paused. 'Will I see you next week?'

'Umm . . . I think . . . no, probably not.' She hadn't known exactly what she would say if he asked, until she said it. And although the words seemed to have been dragged out of her, it felt like the right thing.

She heard him give a soft chuckle. 'I guess that means there's stuff going on your end? Good, that's good, Jo. Although I can't pretend I'm not gutted.'

'I'm gutted too,' she said, meaning it and just a hair's breadth from changing her mind. But she knew deep down that it wouldn't work for her, seeing him again, even if Lawrence had been nowhere in sight. Nothing had changed, and a casual night of sex whenever Travis was passing through would never work for her.

'I left you alone too long,' he was saying. 'Beautiful woman like you.'

'Teach you a lesson.'

'Not even a coffee?' he asked, wheedling. 'Just one itty bitty latte?'

She laughed. 'Better not.'

He gave a melodramatic sigh. 'Yeah . . . OK. Well, I sure hope he's worth it, whoever he is. Worth you.'

'I hope so too.'

'Listen, take care of yourself, Jo. Give my best to Nicky and Cassie.'

'I will. Bye Travis.'

There was a pause.

'Bye . . . bye now . . .'

She sat on the sofa, clutching her phone, her palm sweaty from tension. But she knew she was relieved, imagining the turmoil she would have been going through if she had made a plan to see him. A plan that would have ended in tears, probably hers. Shame, though, she thought, a faraway look in her eye.

The weather held. Friday was still very warm and Jo was thankful. She packed linen trousers, a grey-and-white jersey dress with a crossover front, black pedal-pushers, a pile of T-shirts, trainers, sandals and some smarter pumps. Then there was the hair dryer, shampoo, moisturizer, sun tan lotion, make-up, a thin cardigan just in case, swimming costume . . . did they have a pool?

'Blimey.' Lawrence, who had driven over to pick her up, eyed her large holdall with amusement. 'We're only going for two nights, aren't we?'

'Very funny. You can't tell with peoples' homes . . . if they'll have shampoo and a hair dryer and stuff. You should stop mocking and be glad you aren't a woman.'

The Friday traffic took forever, but finally they turned into the long drive which led to Jonathan Lacy's Suffolk house. The ancient red brick glowed a soft pink in the evening sun, two rows of long, white-painted sash windows – four on either side of the carved stone front door-case – sat elegantly below a smaller row of dormer windows peeping out from the pitched roof. Sandstone quoins lined the corners of the house, rising to a phalanx of tall brick chimneys. The house was graceful and stylish; dignified rather than grandiose.

'Isn't it wonderful?' Lawrence said softly, staring up at the façade.

'Wow. Stunning. You were right.'

Jo had been quiet on the journey down, unable to stop thinking of Travis. Since Thursday she'd been wired, knowing he was in London, somewhere round the corner, so close. But Lawrence hadn't noticed. He also seemed preoccupied.

No one was about, but the heavy wooden front door stood wide open. Lawrence shouted Jonathan's name, but there was no response, so they walked in. A teenage girl – long blonde hair flying behind her, barefoot, in denim shorts and a skimpy T-shirt – rushed down the sweeping stone staircase which faced them in the large hallway. She totally ignored them, didn't even hesitate, just kept on running towards the back of the house as if they were invisible.

Lawrence raised his eyebrows. 'Was that Beth?'

Jo frowned. 'More likely Connie. Beth must be closer to nineteen by now.'

They put their bags by the wall and wandered after the girl. The French windows in the drawing room were open on to the terrace and the sound of laughter. A small group of people were sitting around – some on garden loungers, some perched on the low stone balustrade which bordered the terrace – all with glasses of what looked like Pimm's in their hands. The lawn stretched for miles in the waning light, bordered by ranks of azalea and rhododendron bushes, oaks and mature shrubs, and bisected by a flagged stone path lined with rose bushes (sporting pink and gold blooms) leading from the terrace to a circular stone fountain. A group of six languorous teenagers – two girls, four boys – lay entangled on the grass near the terrace. Jo took a deep breath as she eyed the peaceful landscape. What am I doing here, she thought, pretending to be Lawrence's wife, pretending that everything is as it was, pretending Arkadius never happened.

Jono – dressed in a faded pink polo shirt, collar up, baggy navy shorts and deck shoes – leapt to his feet when he saw them. 'At last!' He wrapped Jo in a bear hug. 'Welcome! So good to see you . . . it's been far too long.' He clapped Lawrence on the shoulder and shook his hand, drawing back when Lawrence winced, noticing the wrist support for the first time.

'Hey, sorry, Meadows. Whacked someone, did you?' Jonathan was Lawrence's height, but about twice his width, with broad shoulders, a bull neck, ruddy cheeks and tight dark curls now tinged with grey.

'Nothing so dramatic. Came off my bike.'

Jonathan pulled a sympathetic face, then introduced them to the other house guests – two couples Jo hadn't met before. Nervous as she always was in social situations, she decided at once they were horrible, although all four smiled and shook her hand with warmth.

'Is Alana here?'

Jonathan laughed. 'Good question. Last saw her at lunch. She's probably . . .' He didn't bother to finish the sentence, as if it were too tedious even to contemplate where his wife might have gone. 'Now. A drink. Pimm's on the table, or there's anything you like indoors.' He turned to Jo. 'What'll it be?'

'Pimm's would be great, thanks.'

Their room was large, high-ceilinged and chilly, despite the warmth outside, the dusty floorboards partially covered in a threadbare Persian rug, the bedstead a heavy, polished mahogany with barley twist posts, the bathroom a mile down the corridor and shared, obviously, with unknown others.

'I forgot my pyjamas,' Jo wailed, as they began to change for dinner. 'How am I going to get to the loo in the night? And I bet all the floorboards creak. This is a nightmare. I hate staying with people. I don't know why I let you persuade me into it.'

Lawrence laughed. 'Whoa, steady on. You're conflating about five problems in one. How am I to know which to address first?'

'Don't be clever,' she said, realizing with alarm

that they would be sharing a bed that night for the first time in a year.

Both of them sat down. She on a wobbly Louis IV-style chair with tattered maroon upholstery, Lawrence on the bed, which creaked and sagged alarmingly under his weight.

'What's the matter?' Jo asked, after a few moments of silence. He seemed distant, detached and hadn't been his usual robust self when countering Jono's teasing.

He gave her a steady look. 'Nothing really.'

'Come on . . . tell me.'

A pause, then, 'OK . . . well . . . if you must know, it's us.'

She didn't reply, just watched his face go tense, his mouth working as he fashioned his next sentence.

'It's over, isn't it? The love . . . no longer there.'

Jo was taken aback by the bleakness in his voice. Her instinct was to gush that everything was fine, that they should immediately sail off into the sunset together. But she knew that wasn't the truth.

'I do love you, Lawrence.'

He gazed at her, his expression sardonic. 'Yeah.'

'What do you mean?'

'Well . . . I don't know . . . every time we meet, it's as if you're holding back. Tolerating me, no more.' Another pause. 'I think you're still in love with that American.'

'I'm not,' she said quickly, knowing she looked guilty, that her eyes still contained some vestige of her phone call to 'that American'.

But Lawrence was warming to his theme without listening to her.

'The other night, when we were making love, you asked me what'd happened, what was wrong? Well, the truth is, *you* were what was wrong, Jo. You.' He shook his head as if he were bewildered. 'I mean, why did you let me do it if you weren't ready, if you didn't want me? I wasn't exactly begging.'

'If you weren't "exactly begging", then why did *you* do it?' Jo retorted, suddenly furious.

'Because I thought it was vital to get over the hump. I didn't see how we could move past what's happened without finding each other sexy again.' His eyes were narrow and hurt. 'But you made me feel totally rejected, like I was old and useless and undesirable. It was quite horrible.'

'I wasn't making you feel like that. You were feeling that all by yourself.'

'Really?'

She sighed. 'Look, I'll admit I wasn't as engaged as I should have been. I really tried; I wanted to make it work as much as you did. But it didn't feel right. We didn't seem able to connect with each other properly.'

'That's exactly what I was trying to do. Connect.' There was a note of exasperation in his voice.

'OK, OK. I'm sorry. But don't come the

wounded lover with me, Lawrence. You're the one who ran off, remember. And now you expect me to open my arms at the first opportunity? As if nothing's happened? Now that it suits you. *Trust* you again? You had passionate sex with a man, behind my back, for nearly a year before you even told me. And now I'm supposed to just roll over and forget?'

'Keep your voice down for God's sake.'

'Oh, yes, of course. Because Jono doesn't know anything about it, does he. You forgot to mention Arkadius in your reply to his "What's been happening to you, Meadows?" question. No, it's over for you, so it has to be over for everyone else too. Instantly. Never happened. Airbrushed out of all our lives.' She took a shaky breath. 'I'm actually beginning to feel sorry for Arkadius.'

Lawrence didn't reply.

'You asked if I was still angry with you the other night,' she said, lowering her voice and trying to sound reasonable. 'Well, there's your answer. Of course I'm still angry. I'm fucking furious.'

His look, surprisingly, seemed composed, almost as if he welcomed her anger.

'I let you go without a bloody murmur,' she said, in a softer tone. 'You must have been amazed I didn't make more of a fuss. Cassie and Donna both said I should have fought for you. And maybe I should. But you can only do what you do in the moment. I didn't see the point of fighting for someone who was in love with someone else.

Would it have made any difference? If I'd made it hard for you to leave?'

Lawrence shrugged. 'No . . . probably not. I wasn't thinking straight at the time.'

'Do you regret it?' She didn't know why she asked. It was the dumbest question on earth. 'Don't answer that,' she added quickly. She watched his face go quiet, knowing that no one ever regrets falling in love. Only the fallout afterwards.

He glanced at his watch. 'We should get ready for dinner . . . it's nearly eight o'clock.'

Jo groaned. 'Wish we could just leave.'

'Me too.'

He got up off the bed and came over to her. 'Jo . . . can I hug you?'

For a while they stood there together in the dusty summer light. She felt his arms close around her body, and as she leaned against his shoulder, she knew she wanted so much to love him again, in the way she always had, simply and with all her heart.

Alana was standing by the impressive sandstone fireplace in the drawing room, whispering with one of the other women who had been on the terrace earlier, when Lawrence and Jo came down. As soon as she saw them, she seemed to stiffen, don her hostess persona.

'Joanna, Lawrence, how wonderful to see you.' She offered Jo a mwah, mwah on each cheek. 'You've met Caro?'

They said that they had, but Alana wasn't listening as she bustled over to the butler's table by the window, laid out with whisky, gin and vodka in a polished wood and silver tantalus, bottles of white and red wine, various mixes, bitters, a lidded stainless steel ice bucket and tongs, slices of lemon and tidy ranks of cut-glass tumblers and wine glasses. She was restless, always on the move, Alana, never stopping to listen or think.

'What can I get you, Jo?'

'Vodka and tonic, please.'

Her hostess set to, her slim figure elegant in a white sheath dress with black panels on the shoulders which showed off her tanned, shapely legs. With one hand she patted her dark hair, held back by a tortoiseshell clip at the nape of her neck, with the other she handed Jo her glass.

Lawrence asked for the same, both of them subdued, tired from their row. Jo's drink was gratifyingly strong.

Dinner was hours late – apparently due to the vagaries of the ancient oven. Even Maria, the Portuguese house-keeper and cook, couldn't seem to control it.

'This place is worse than Fawlty Towers,' Jono complained good-naturedly as they waited for the meal, everyone now drunk from the relentless flow of alcohol. 'Da hadn't replaced so much as a brick in thirty years, and wouldn't let me touch the place while he was alive. Worried I might do something "modern" – for which read "nasty". But now I don't know where to start.'

Jo was sitting on Jonathan's right, opposite Caro and next to her husband, Edward – a property millionaire whom Jo found virtually impossible to talk to. Four more couples – all local – had arrived, so the long table was full, despite the teenagers having been dispatched to a pizza restaurant in town.

'This is all very jolly.' Jono raised his glass to her in the gap between the guinea fowl and the cheese. It was nearly eleven by now, and Jo was wilting with the effort. 'Glad you and old Meadows have sorted things out. Always thought you two were solid.' He cast his eye down the table at his wife. 'Unlike some I could mention.'

Jo raised her eyebrows at him in question.

'The Russian?' Jono went on, drunk enough to be oblivious to her discomfort. 'These things happen, not a thing you can do about it. But you want to avoid being silly. No point in spoiling the ship for a ha'porth of tar.'

'Lawrence said he hadn't told you.'

'Oh, he didn't. Don't blame him either. Bit of a dark secret, eh? No, Alana has a chum who's married to a Russian. They all know each other, of course.'

'Of course . . .' she wanted to just get up and walk out, drive away as she imagined most of the faces currently around the table wide-eyed and gripped by the salacious gossip about her husband. It made her feel like one of those sad wives photographed at the garden gate for a media moment, holding hands and smiling through gritted teeth at their perfidious spouse. But in the wake of this feeling was a sudden fierce desire to defend Lawrence against all those gossiping mouths.

'Been a bit tricky, has it?' Jono, for all his bluster, was actually a kind man. He reached over and gave her hand a quick squeeze.

'Could say that.' She smiled at him and they both began to laugh.

By the time they got to bed it was nearly two. The weather had changed, a fierce wind blowing up that rattled the sash windows and blew cold air through the cracks. Jo flopped, exhausted, on to the bed.

'Thank God that's over.'

'At least you had Jono. I had some tedious woman who banged on for hours about a drugs scandal at her child's boarding school. And chilly Alana on the other side, who obviously loathes the house and can't wait for Jono to sell it.'

Jo sat up. 'He won't do that.' Her head was spinning and she felt slightly sick, which brought worry about the distant bathroom into focus again.

'Not sure I can take a whole weekend of this,' Lawrence said. 'I was mad to agree to it in the first place.'

'Can we do a runner?'

'They might think it a bit odd.'

'Shouldn't worry about that. They think we're super-odd anyway. They know all about Arkadius – the Russian connection, apparently.'

Lawrence looked stricken. 'God.'

'It was never going to stay a secret, Lawrence. You may not have told anyone, but why wouldn't Arkadius?' She closed her eyes, suddenly sick and tired of the subject. 'But don't worry, Jono referred to it as a "ha'porth of tar", so maybe it's not considered so unusual in their circle.'

'Can we not talk about it?' he asked.

They got into bed, Jo on her side, Lawrence on his, deliberately keeping space between them. Jo shivered.

'These sheets feel damp . . . almost wet.'

After a moment's quiet, Lawrence said, 'Come over here, otherwise we'll both die of pneumonia.'

Jo wriggled to his side, grateful for Lawrence's warmth. The wind continued to howl and soon, as they lay huddled together under the cold sheets and stiff, pre-war blankets, they heard the rain begin to hurl itself against the panes.

'This is more like Baskerville Hall than Fawlty Towers,' Jo whispered, as a sudden bolt of lightning illuminated the room with a silver-blue flash. 'Any minute now we'll hear The Hound.'

Lawrence chuckled, but all they actually heard was a terrifying clap of thunder directly overhead, which seemed to shake the very foundations of the old house. In response he drew her closer and began to rub her back, first quickly to warm her up, then slower, moving his hand in circles, the rubbing now a gentle caress as his fingers wandered over her back, then down over the rest of her body. Jo felt herself begin to relax, allowing first the warmth, then the beginnings of desire to flow through her, all resistance, all thought, driven out by alcohol and tiredness. It was just her and Lawrence, in their own dark, sensual cocoon as the tempest raged outside, responding with heightened pleasure to each kiss, each caress as if it were for the first time.

Jo woke with a start. It took her a moment to realize that cold water was dripping on her face. She sat up, dazed. Another drop, and another. The ceiling was leaking, not just drops now, but a thin stream of water, directly on to the pillow. She gave Lawrence a sharp nudge as she jumped out of bed.

'Bloody hell.' He stared up at the ceiling. 'Where's it coming from? We're not under the eaves.'

'Maybe a blocked gutter or something? The water's travelled across the ceiling till it found a weak spot. No wonder the bed felt wet. It was wet! This probably isn't the first time.'

The light coming in through the window told them it was dawn, but still very early. Lawrence pulled back the curtains, the brocade drapes releasing a cloud of dust over his head. The storm had passed and the day was perfect, washed clean and fresh by the rain, everything sparkling in the morning sun. He checked his watch. 'Ten to five.'

'What are we like?' Jo said, as they looked at each other across the room: naked, bedraggled, hungover, at a loss. Jo felt a bubble of hysteria as she tried to stifle her giggles in the silent house. But the more she tried, the harder she laughed. Lawrence joined her now, bent over, breathless, clutching his side, pointing to the water still dripping from the ceiling.

'Gives a whole new meaning to "ensuite shower".'

'Shh . . .' she managed, between gulps of strangled laughter.

'They can't hear us.'

'I'll never complain about the bathroom being miles away again. We need a bowl or something to put under it. Or we could move the bed,' she said, when she got her breath.

Lawrence waved his damaged wrist in the air. 'Weighs a ton,' he said. 'And then we really will wake the whole house.'

In the end Jo laid the two bath towels put out for them by Maria, doubled over, on the sheet beneath the drip – although the damage was already done.

'What shall we do?' Jo asked, shivering as she went in search of her clothes. 'We can't go back to bed and the others won't be up for at least six hours.'

Lawrence was pulling on his shirt, still grinning.

'Leave,' he said, decisively. 'We're going to pack up, write a note and drive off. If they think we're rude, then they think we're rude.'

Jo laughed. 'Right . . . OK. Good plan, Stan.'

For the next few minutes they tiptoed around the room, hurriedly stuffing belongings into bags, while the water still drip, dripped on to the towels. Jo had no time to think about what had happened last night. But underneath the tiredness and hangover she felt a quiet knot of pleasure.

They crept along the corridor – horribly aware of all the sleeping bodies behind the closed doors – down the stairs, each creak making them stop, pull a face, tiptoe on. The last thing they wanted was to be caught red-handed in their dawn flit by Jono or Alana. They left a note on the hall table, the paper torn from the Moleskine diary that Lawrence always carried, explaining that he was ill – of unspecified origin – and that they felt it better to go home than be a burden on their hosts.

The gravel of the circular drive crunched alarmingly beneath their feet. The doors closing sounded like a bomb going off, the car like a traction engine in the dawn stillness.

Lawrence let out a whoop as they reached the road. Jo realized she had been almost holding her breath for the last ten minutes. They grinned at each other.

'I feel a bit bad about Jono,' Lawrence said as they drove away. 'I didn't get a chance to talk to him properly. But I can't be doing with all this posh-boy stuff. He never used to be like that, before Alana. I mean, he's always been confident, a bit loud, but not in that upper-class braying way he seems to have adopted.'

'No, he's definitely changed. Or maybe reverted. But I wouldn't feel bad. He'll understand. He knows we're going through strange times.'

Lawrence turned his head to look at her. 'Was last night so "strange"? Not the word I'd have used,' he said, a mischievous glint in his eye. And Jo gave a quiet smile, as much to herself as to him.

It was still not yet eight when Lawrence pulled the car to a stop in front of Jo's flat. As the engine died they both sat there in silence, staring ahead through the dusty windscreen. She felt a flutter in her stomach.

'You could come in,' she said. Last night still hung around her like a soft glow. She had always thought that if she and Lawrence ever did make a go of it again, that it would be more of a relief, a comforting return to familiarity. But their love-making had been so intense, surprisingly new. And mixed with the powerful desire was a sadness, a desperate yearning that felt almost painful, and seemed to come from the depths of her soul, and his, as they came together so passionately in that cold, damp bed. She knew there were no guarantees, that they still had a long way to go if they were ever to make it work between them. But last night at least felt like a start, a breath of promise on something she had feared was dead.

'Yes?' The look he gave her was hesitant.

'I'll make some coffee.'

He smiled. 'I'd like that . . . very much.'